Don't miss these other spellbinding novels by
DONNA GRANT

From St. Martin's Paperbacks

SMOKE AND FIRE

DONNA GRANT

St. Martin's Paperbacks

This is a work of fiction. All of the characters, organizations, and events portrayed in this novel are either products of the author's imagination or are used fictitiously.

SMOKE AND FIRE

For information address St. Martin's Press, 175 Fifth Avenue, New York, NY 10010.

ISBN: 978-1-250-07196-5

Printed in the United States of America

St. Martin's Paperbacks edition / April 2016

St. Martin's Paperbacks are published by St. Martin's Press, 175 Fifth Avenue, New York, NY 10010.

10 9 8 7 6 5 4 3

To Kelly Mueller—
You helped save my sanity.
I owe you. So pick your Dragon King!

ACKNOWLEDGMENTS

To my editor, Monique Patterson, miracle extraordinaire. Sums you up perfectly!

To my agent, Natanya Wheeler, for always being ready with an answer no matter what my question might be. And for our mutual love of wine, pasta, hunky guys, and the written word.

To everyone at SMP who was involved in getting this book ready, including Alex, Erin, Amy, the truly amazing art department, and marketing. Y'all are astounding. Thank you!

A special thanks to my friends and family for the endless support and love.

PROLOGUE

Glasgow, Scotland
December

A loud sigh escaped Kinsey as she read the e-mail a second time. Rain splashed on the window of her cottage, but she didn't hear it. Her mind wasn't focusing on her new job assignment, which would take her to Dreagan Industries.

She should be ecstatic to get such a client. Normally she would be. If she could concentrate.

No, all she could think of was one thing—Ryder.

She set aside her laptop and stared at the wall. Kinsey was by turns numb, angry, and afraid. Though she wasn't sure if those feelings were directed at Ryder . . . or herself.

The first time she'd met him, she instinctively knew he was going to change her life. And he had. Drastically. For those precious months were the happiest of her life.

Then he'd left Glasgow with a confusing—and brief—letter telling her it was over. It took her years to get over him.

Just when she thought she'd put Ryder in her past for good, she saw him again.

Kinsey squeezed her eyes closed at the memory. She

couldn't think of that night. It was too horrific, too shocking. Her world had been turned on its side in a split second.

Others didn't seem to notice, or didn't care. But she still struggled to catch her footing at what happened.

She gave herself a mental shake as she opened her eyes. No amount of thinking about Ryder was going to solve the issues at hand. They would never get resolved, because she planned to never see him again.

With a push off the cushion, Kinsey rose and walked to her room. She pulled out her overnight bag and began to pack. She was due at Dreagan by noon tomorrow.

Normally, she'd be thrilled at being personally requested to do a job with such a big corporation, but Kinsey's head hadn't been in her work since that awful night a month ago when her city burned and crazies with red eyes and black and silver hair raced through the streets of Glasgow.

She zipped up her bag and began to gather her makeup and toiletries. The job at Dreagan was pretty big. Then again, she'd proven herself time and again by being the best hacker at Kyvor.

With as large a corporation as Dreagan was, Kinsey suspected it would take her a few days to get through everything, which was why she was packing. But she would get it done—because that's what she always did.

Her personal life might be down the drain, but her professional life was on the way to the top.

CHAPTER ONE

Dreagan

Ryder reached for another strawberry jelly–filled donut from the box and sank his teeth into the pastry. He moaned in ecstasy at his favorite snack.

"You've got powder on your lips," said Dmitri from the doorway.

Ryder grinned and kept chewing as he winked at his fellow Dragon King from over the four rows of monitors that ran in a large semicircle around him.

Dmitri chuckled as he came around the screens and grabbed one of the chairs pushed against the table where Ryder worked. Dmitri pulled the chair toward him and sat, his bright blue eyes directed at Ryder. "Anything new?"

"Nay," Ryder said and took another bite. He didn't need to ask what Dmitri was referring to with the war going on between the Dark Fae.

Dmitri blew out a breath and ran a hand through his short brown hair. "The Dark are suddenly no' interested in Dreagan? Tell me you doona find that odd."

"I find it exceedingly peculiar. But at the same time,

I'm glad we doona have to worry about them right now with MI5 crawling around the estate."

Again, thanks to the Dark Fae releasing the video they shot of the Dragon Kings shifting into their true forms and fighting the Dark.

No sooner had the words left Ryder's mouth than the camera near the gift shop of the distillery picked up two MI5 agents patrolling the area. As if they would find clues of dragons while looking among the flora and fauna.

Ryder shook his head at them. MI5 were so intent on making a discovery that there really were dragons that they were acting like idiots in order to do it.

It'd been almost two months with the mortals on the sixty-thousand-acre property, and Ryder hated it. Every time he saw them it was a reminder of what the Dark Fae had done to the Dragon Kings' world.

Every day Ryder spent hours taking down the videos that kept popping up, showing them in their true form as dragons. Now the entire world was obsessed with dragons. And not necessarily all in a good way—MI5 was a prime example of that.

How ironic, since it was because of the humans that the Dragon Kings sent all the dragons to another realm thousands of years ago.

"This willna end anytime soon," Dmitri said in a voice laced with anger as he watched the MI5 agents on the monitor.

Ryder made a sound at the back of his throat. "With every video of us fighting the Dark that night that I take down off the Internet, a hundred more pop up."

"Ulrik is behind this."

"Or the Dark."

"Or both," Dmitri said.

Ryder nodded in agreement. "Someone sure wants to

keep it out there for the mortals to keep seeing and discussing. I can no' keep it off YouTube, documentaries are all over the place, and the news channels continue to talk about whether dragons are real."

"We are."

Ryder cut him a hard look. "No' to the humans."

"What about all the dragon experts out there?" Dmitri asked sarcastically.

Ryder finished off the donut before he said, "Dragon experts my arse. They doona know what they're talking about."

"Which is what makes things interesting. Right up until they unearthed that dragon skeleton."

Ryder gave a shake of his head. "Doona remind me of that. I thought we'd gathered all of them. How the hell did we miss it? More importantly, how many more did we miss?"

"There were a lot of dragons killed in the war with the mortals. I'm no' surprised we missed one. Need I remind you we didna have a lot of time, either. We went into hiding here from the mortals."

"Aye. Just something else for the humans to have on us. It has to stop sometime."

Dmitri folded his arms across his chest. "I'm going crazy no' being able to take to the skies at night. First we were sentenced to only fly at night, and now no' at all. We're dragons, Ryder. We're supposed to be able to fly, but with the world watching us, we can no' even do that."

Ryder couldn't respond because his eyes were glued to a screen to his left. That camera was pointed to the parking lot of the distillery.

Since they were closed to tourists for the winter, the red Fiat had caught his attention for two reasons. One—because the car made him think of Kinsey. And two—because it wasn't one of the government cars the agents of MI5 drove.

Then he could only stare in shock when the car door opened and he spotted long dark hair pulled into a high ponytail. Kinsey. Even with her back to him, he knew it was her.

His heart missed a beat. What was she doing at Dreagan? Had she pieced it together? The last time he saw her, she'd been running from him. Ryder could've caught her, but he'd remained behind and killed the Dark Fae ravaging Glasgow.

Since he left her three years earlier, he'd watched her from afar, making sure she was safe. Weeks ago, he was the closest he'd been in years. Now . . . now she was at Dreagan.

His palms began to sweat and breathing became difficult. Kinsey was at Dreagan. Ryder didn't know whether to be excited or furious—but he was leaning to the side of thrilled.

"Ryder?" Dmitri said his name.

He held up his hand to Dmitri, not bothering to look at him. As if Ryder could. His gaze was riveted on the woman he'd been in love with for four years.

Even as he began to think of all he would say to her, there was a niggle of worry. What if she was working with Ulrik or the Dark? What if they sent her there to use him for information?

Ryder's enthusiasm dimmed. He didn't want to believe Kinsey would do that, but a gut feeling wasn't enough. The world of the Dragon Kings was in chaos. There was no room for mistakes—of any kind.

Kinsey looked around the parking lot, her eyes searching.

He stared at her heart-shaped face, his heart clutching

at having her so close again. How many times had he caressed her cheek or stared into her large violet eyes? How many times had he kissed those plump lips or simply held her as they watched a movie? Each time he saw her, she got more and more beautiful.

After a moment, she closed the car door and started toward the distillery. Ryder's gaze immediately lowered to her amazing ass and the denim that only showed it off more. The black blazer was casual over the white tee, but like always, she looked amazing.

Dmitri whistled. "Who's that?"

Ryder's gaze moved to the next screen and saw Tristan near the gift shop. He opened the mental link between all Dragon Kings and said his name.

Tristan responded immediately. *"Aye?"*

"There's a woman coming toward you. Her name is Kinsey Burns. Doona let her leave."

"All right."

Tristan left the link open as he smiled and greeted Kinsey after he turned the corner and saw her. Ryder could only watch the monitor and try to decipher what it was Kinsey wanted.

"She said she's here for the job we ordered with the new monitors," Tristan said. *"What do I tell her?"*

"I already installed those monitors weeks ago." Ryder hesitated. Kinsey was terrified of seeing him in dragon form. If she knew he was here, she'd never have come. Not after the way she'd looked at him. *"Kinsey wouldna come here on her own. We need to know who sent her."*

"You know her?" Tristan asked in surprise.

"Aye." It was something Ryder had kept from all those at Dreagan—especially Con. *"Bring her to me."*

Tristan agreed and severed the link.

Ryder sat back and blew out a breath, feeling a flutter of nerves. He laced his fingers behind his head and only realized then that Dmitri was still in the room. He slid his gaze to Dmitri.

"What are you up to?" Dmitri asked. "You know that lass. I could see it on your face. If you have Tristan bring her up here, you'll feel Con's wrath."

Ryder dropped his hands to the arms of his chair. "That occurs all the time, and I do know Kinsey. I'm no' yet sure why she's here. But I aim to find out."

"Meaning?" Dmitri urged.

"We were lovers three years ago. Until I realized that I'd fallen in love with her. I didna want anyone to know that our spell preventing us from feeling deeply for humans no longer worked with me."

Dmitri leaned forward, his brow furrowed deeply. "That was around the time Hal fell in love with Cassie."

"Cassie arrived at Dreagan right after I returned from Glasgow."

"All right," Dmitri said as he rubbed his jaw. "So you fell in love before Hal. No' a big deal."

Ryder lifted one shoulder in a shrug. "I suppose no'. No' compared to her seeing me in dragon form a few weeks ago when I was in Glasgow to protect the city from the Dark invasion."

"Oh, fuck."

Anger crackled through him every time he thought about how close Kinsey came to dying that night. If Ryder hadn't been there, she would've been taken by the Dark, her soul drained. "There was a Dark after her. I shifted into human form to help her. Unfortunately, she saw it all."

"And?" Dmitri pressed with a brown brow raised.

Ryder looked at the screens, following Kinsey from one to the other as Tristan walked her to the manor. "I've never seen anyone so terrified before."

"Of the Dark?"

Ryder wished. That night still haunted him. No matter how many times he thought over what happened, there hadn't been another way to save her. "Of me. I can still hear her scream before she ran away."

"So she doesna know you're here?"

"I doona believe so. She'd rather walk through the fires of Hell than be anywhere near me."

Dmitri sat there for a moment before he gave a slow shake of his head. "You're having Tristan bring her to you, are you no'?"

"I am."

"That . . . could be a bad move."

"It probably is." In more ways than one.

But he wasn't going to pass up the chance to talk to Kinsey one more time. Perhaps he could explain everything. It was a long shot, but he was hoping to have that chance. He knew he'd never have her in his life as he wanted, but the thought of her fearing him cut him deeply.

His only hope was that Con didn't discover she was here until after Ryder had spoken with her. Because once Con found out about Kinsey, it wouldn't be long before Con learned she'd seen Ryder shift. That would lead to Con wanting to have Guy wipe her memories.

Ryder's thoughts halted when he heard Kinsey's voice with Tristan's as they approached. He wiped his mouth to make sure there was no more powder on it. Then he looked to Dmitri for confirmation that he had gotten it all.

Panic struck as he looked down at his clothes. He was in an old Def Leppard concert tee and his favorite pair of faded jeans. Not exactly how he'd have dressed had he known he might see Kinsey. But there wasn't time to change now.

"Here it is," Tristan said as he came to the doorway.

A second later Kinsey emerged. "Wow," she said as she looked at all the monitors. "I should've expected to see so many screens. I gather the security system here is state of the art?"

Then her gaze landed on Ryder.

He couldn't move as he stared into her violet eyes, remembering what it was like to hold her in his arms each night, to feel her lush body beneath his. The hours of conversations they'd had about the future and her dreams.

He'd missed her more than he thought was possible. It physically hurt for him to be so close to her and not go to her.

"What are you doing here?" she asked in a voice filled with shock—and worse—alarm.

CHAPTER TWO

Kinsey felt as if she'd been run over by a train. Her heart began to knock against her ribs. There was a rushing in her ears, and she was sure her knees were going to buckle at any second.

How was it even possible that she was staring into Ryder's hazel eyes, that were a beautiful mixture of green and gold? His blond hair was cropped short on the sides with a little more length on the top. It didn't matter if his hair was long as it used to be or short, he still took her breath away.

Was it his chiseled jaw or penetrating gaze? It could be his mouth and the wonderful things those lips could do to her. She knew there was a possibility it was his body, honed to perfection without an ounce of fat anywhere.

But he wasn't human.

She needed to remember that.

"What are you doing here?" she demanded.

For a moment, he didn't move as he looked at her. Then he sat back in his chair and swept his hand from one side of the room to the other. "This is my domain."

She was damn good at her job, but Ryder exceeded her talent by miles and miles. "You asked for me specifically. Why? Because you had to talk? You could've just called instead of going to such lengths."

"I didna send for you."

There were few times in her life where Kinsey experienced full-on, please-let-the-floor-open-up-and-swallow-me embarrassment. Today, right at that moment, was the worst she'd ever suffered—to a degree that nothing would ever compare.

She wanted to shrink away and disappear, to stop looking into his hazel eyes and trying to figure out what was going on. What did Ryder mean he didn't send for her? Someone had. She didn't just show up on a whim.

The room began to tilt. Kinsey blinked rapidly. She wouldn't faint. She'd never fainted in her life, and she certainly wasn't going to do it in front of Ryder. Hadn't she experienced her embarrassment quota for the next forty years?

Beside her, Tristan cleared his throat. "Kinsey, I think there might've been a wee bit of a mistake."

"There's not," she said and glanced over her shoulder into Tristan's dark gaze. "And I can prove it."

Kinsey pulled out her mobile phone and unlocked it before she went to her e-mails. She was scrolling through looking for the assignment she'd received last night when a chair squeaked.

Her gaze snapped to the man sitting near Ryder. How hadn't she seen him? Just like Ryder and Tristan, she could tell he was tall by the way he dwarfed the chair.

He gave a nod to her with the corners of his bright blue eyes crinkling slightly, as if he found the entire situation a tad amusing. Which didn't put him in her favor at all.

The man was handsome, same as Tristan, but not devastatingly so like Ryder. Which was a good thing because Kinsey could barely think with Ryder near. She didn't need two more disturbing her.

"That's Dmitri," Ryder said.

Dmitri's dark head bowed again. "Hello."

"Hello," she responded automatically. Kinsey suddenly felt like she was being caged in despite the fact that Ryder and Dmitri were sitting. All eyes were on her, waiting to hear what she had to say.

She shifted uncomfortably as a sudden thought struck her. Ryder was a dragon. Were the others?

Her heart missed a beat as fear shot through her. What the bloody hell had she walked into?

"Kinsey?" Tristan urged.

She found herself looking at Ryder. In his hazel depths she could see that he knew where her thoughts had taken her and why she was scared, yet he said nothing. As if he were giving her time to take it all in and calm down.

Calm down. She nearly snorted aloud. Like that was going to happen.

After finding the e-mail and pulling it up, her hand trembled when she handed the mobile to Ryder over the monitors. Their fingers brushed, and she sucked in air at the sizzle that raced along her skin.

Her nipples hardened instantly. She hastily looked away, but she found both Tristan and Dmitri watching her carefully. All she could hope for was that they didn't see how much Ryder affected her.

Hell, for that matter, she hoped Ryder didn't know how he shook her.

She was scared of him now, but that was getting mixed in with the desire he always brought out in her. It jumbled up inside her, making her unsure of which one she felt more.

Fear. It had to be fear.

Ryder set aside her mobile on the table and tapped the black metal tabletop. Instantly, a keyboard appeared. It was integrated into the table, the keys emitting a bluish glow to highlight them.

She almost rushed around the screens to take a look at such technology, but she managed to stop herself. Those keyboards were in the works, but as far as she knew they were years from being ready for the public.

Then again, Dreagan wasn't the public.

Kinsey managed to remain where she was, but she watched Ryder like a hawk. His fingers flew over the keys while his gaze was riveted to a screen. A few more punches of the keys, and he stopped to read.

Dmitri's brow rose as he looked at the screen. Kinsey watched Ryder's lips flatten. He keyed in something else in quick succession.

Whatever popped up had him frowning. He stared at the computer for a long time before his gaze slid to her. There was doubt in his eyes—and a healthy dose of anger.

"The e-mail sent is from Kyvor, the technology giant," Ryder said. "However, there is a work order in place. It has my name on it."

Kinsey shrugged and looked at each of the men. "See? I'm not making this up."

"The work order was placed by you."

Her mouth fell open in shock. "That's not possible. I don't place work orders. We have a division for that. Well," she said, then paused. "There are a few of us who visit a company and will take a work order for future use while we're there. But I've never been here before."

"Tell me, Kinsey. Who wanted to talk to who?" Ryder asked.

Her eyes widened and the words locked in her throat

from her disbelief and anger. It took her a full minute to get herself under control just so she could talk.

She was furious, but she reminded herself she was dealing with dragons. Kinsey wasn't sure how far she could go without them burning her to a crisp.

But she also couldn't hold back the irritation and sarcasm that were a part of her nature.

"You think I did this?" she asked with a laugh and rolled her eyes. "I never wanted to see you again. I ran, remember?"

"I remember," Ryder murmured.

Kinsey threw up her hands. "Then why would I come here?"

"There are numerous reasons," Dmitri said.

Tristan nodded. "Aye, lass."

Her head swung back to Ryder. "I didn't put in the work order. I didn't even know you worked for Dreagan."

Dreagan.

It hit her then like a wrecking ball. Dreagan was Gaelic for dragon. OMG! How could she have been such an idiot not to put two and two together?

Ryder hid the keyboard with a tap and rested his arms on the table. "You're intelligent, Kinsey. It wouldna have taken you long to piece it all together."

"I wanted to forget that I saw you shift. I was petrified. I ran. From you."

She had the thought after she spoke that perhaps she should've waited until she was alone with Ryder to say such things. But it was too late. The words were already out.

"I know exactly what you did," he said in a clipped voice.

So she had hurt him? All because she ran? What had he expected her to do? Run *toward* him?

Then his words penetrated her mind. "What do you mean I would've pieced it together?"

Dmitri made a sound at the back of his throat as he got to his feet. "Nice try."

"What the hell?" she asked in frustration. "I want to know what you're referring to."

"The videos of dragons on the Internet," Tristan said.

Kinsey closed her mouth and took a couple of steps back until she ran into the wall. "Of course I saw the video."

Ryder's gaze narrowed on her, but he didn't say a word.

"That doesn't mean anything," Kinsey argued. "Millions of people have seen that video."

Tristan glanced in the hallway and pushed the door. He looked at Ryder and said, "It willna take Con long to learn she's here. Get this sorted quickly."

"Aye," Ryder replied.

"It's obvious she's seen Ryder," Dmitri murmured.

Kinsey swallowed nervously. Silent looks passed between the three men as if they were communicating. Then Tristan left, closing the door softly behind him.

Dmitri walked to the window and looked out over the rolling hills and the sheep that dotted the countryside. He kept his back to them, but he wasn't going anywhere.

Kinsey returned her gaze to Ryder. "What's going on?"

"Whether on purpose or no', you've walked right into the middle of a war."

She gave a shake of her head. "No. I don't want to be here. I want to leave. Right now."

"You're no' going anywhere," Ryder stated.

Kinsey cut him a look and snorted. "Good luck trying to keep me. My company knows I'm here."

She walked to the door and tried to open it, but the

knob wouldn't budge. No matter how hard she turned, pushed, and pulled, the door wasn't moving.

Breathing hard, she whirled around to the men. "You can't hold me here."

"Your company sent you," Dmitri said. "They obviously want you here."

"That's insane," she argued.

Ryder lifted a blond brow. "Is it?"

Kinsey dropped her purse and bag and put her hands to her head. "Stop."

"That willna change the facts."

"I can't hear this. I can't see any more or learn any more," she said, closing her eyes. As if that would stop all of it.

"I never harmed you." Ryder's voice was a whisper, said in her ear.

Her eyes snapped open. How had he moved so quickly without her hearing him? Kinsey dropped her hands to her sides and shook her head.

Having him so close was a reminder of how she used to feel safe and loved with him. That was before she saw the real him. "Tell me this isn't really happening. Tell me it's all fake."

"It's real," Ryder said. He lifted his hand to touch her cheek, but stopped at the last moment. "This is my life, Kinsey. This is where I live and work. These people are my family."

"Dragons?" she whispered.

"Dragons."

Kinsey didn't know what to say. She'd seen Ryder, the real Ryder. A massive, flying, fire-breathing monster that dove from the sky with scales the color of smoke, and blending in with the night.

"You were never supposed to know that was me," he said. "Then I saw one of the Dark go after you. I couldna attack him without hurting you unless I was in this form."

She wanted to touch him. There had always been something about being in his arms that made her feel as if she could tackle anything and the world wouldn't dare get in her way.

"How long have you been a . . . dragon?" she asked.

His eyes looked away for a second. "The exact time doesna matter. Just know it's been for a verra long time."

"How long?" she pressed. There had been something in his words, something that told her he hadn't told her everything.

Ryder studied her for a long time. Then he said, "Millions of years."

Kinsey gave a dry laugh. "Nice one. The truth, please."

"That is the truth," Dmitri said with his back still to them.

She looked from Ryder to Dmitri and then back to Ryder. "Millions?"

"We can no' die."

"Immortal?" she whispered in awe.

"Aye."

Kinsey put her hand to her throat as it all came into focus. "You were never going to tell me about who and what you are, were you?"

Ryder gave a single shake of his head.

She wanted to cry. All the old feelings welled up just like when he'd left her. "I thought we had something special. I thought you were The One. I saw my life with you by my side. You let me think that. You let me fall in love with you."

"Kinsey," he began.

"Then you left. You left me standing on the sidewalk,

waiting for you to show for our lunch date." She sniffed back her tears, anger beginning to bubble. "You canceled your mobile and your e-mail account. You made sure I couldn't get in touch with you in any way. I thought I did something to push you away."

Ryder grasped her arms. "Never," he said adamantly.

She shoved him away with all her might. He couldn't touch her, because when he did, she forgot all the bad and focused on how he'd once made her feel. "Now I know it wasn't me. It was you. Is this what your kind does? They get involved with us mere humans and make us fall in love, then you leave? Do you laugh at how we have to scrape ourselves off the pavement and try to live again?"

"It killed me to leave you!" Ryder yelled.

"I doubt it."

Kinsey grabbed her purse and bag and walked to the door. If she had to tear it down with her bare hands, she was going to walk out.

But the door opened when she turned the knob.

It was time for her to blow this joint and put Ryder in her rearview mirror for good.

CHAPTER THREE

Ryder intentionally let her leave the computer room. He followed her into the corridor and toward the stairs. Kinsey's black boots made little sound on the thick rug over the hardwood.

She looked back at him as she descended the stairs. "I can find my way out."

Ryder didn't bother to comment. He wasn't following her because he worried she would get lost. He was following her to make sure she didn't run into Con. Her leaving wasn't an option, not after learning the work order had her name on it.

He lengthened his strides and came even with her in the foyer. Ryder opened the front door. She met his gaze as she walked past him, and then came to a dead stop when she saw the sleet.

It was no freak storm. No, this was all the work of Arian. No doubt Tristan or Dmitri had told him to keep Kinsey on the estate.

When Kinsey started to walk from the shelter of the overhang, Ryder stopped her. At her cold look, he released her and held up his hands. "Easy. I doona think getting wet in this cold is wise."

"Because I'm human and can die?" she asked saucily.

"Aye. That's exactly why."

Some of the fire went out of her. Kinsey adjusted the bag on her shoulder. "I can't be near you."

"Because I frighten you," he said with a nod. "I understand, but you also need to realize that what you've seen is no' something we want repeated."

"Who would I tell?"

"Anyone. We've lived in secret for thousands of years. It needs to remain that way."

She wrapped her blazer tighter around herself to ward off the cold. Kinsey looked out at the sleet that was turning into snow. "You still think I wrote that work order to get myself here."

"Nay, I doona." The shock on her face had been too real. "I contemplated it for a wee bit, but I realized it wasna you."

"Damn right it wasn't me," she said with a lift of her chin.

Ryder fought back a smile. He'd always loved her fire, her spirit.

Her lips pursed briefly. "The question then is who sent me?"

"That's what I need to determine. We've a lot of enemies."

She turned to face him then, her arms crossed over her chest as her nose was beginning to turn red. "Someone knew about us."

"That's what I've concluded. Why else would they send you?"

"I don't like this," she muttered.

Neither did he. If she was innocent, Kinsey was a pawn

in this vicious war. "I could use your help finding out who it is."

Kinsey gave a quick bark of laughter. "No, you don't. You're the best I've ever seen with computers."

"I'd like your help then," he tried again. "The Kinsey I knew wouldna have passed up a chance to clear her own name."

She looked away and remained silent for several long minutes. "Look, I don't think it's—"

The sound of Shara's laughter as Kiril chased her through the snow from around the side of the manor interrupted Kinsey. Shara was quickly caught in Kiril's arms, where they shared a passionate kiss.

Before the kiss could get heated, Rhys came around the house. Kiril released Shara right before Rhys tackled Kiril to the ground while Lily came to stand by Shara as they laughed.

"War!" Kiril shouted. "Some help."

Warrick and Darcy walked arm in arm from around the manor. Warrick shook his head with a smile. "I'd rather stay right where I am. Dry."

"Scared of me, huh?" Rhys said as he and Kiril tried to get the upper hand on each other in the snow.

Lily clapped her hands together and smiled at Rhys. "Come on, honey. Kick some ass!"

"Kiril, you can take him," Shara cheered.

Ryder studied Kinsey as she watched the group. He was glad she'd been interrupted, because she had been about to leave. And that was something he couldn't allow. He wanted her to think staying was her idea. Forcing her would only hurt his cause, not help it.

"You were saying?" Ryder prompted after a moment.

Kinsey cleared her throat and turned back to him. "I was saying that I don't think it's wise for you to look for these people on your own. They put me in the middle of it. I want to find out who it was."

Ryder let her lie because it benefited him. He opened the door for her to return inside, sending a wave to the others as he followed her.

They managed to make it up to the third floor and back into the computer room without anyone seeing them. Dmitri was gone, but that's how Ryder wanted it. Though he wasn't sure how he would be able to remain near Kinsey and not pull her against him for a kiss.

Her kisses were breathtaking. Just as she was. He could kiss her for hours, and sometimes they'd done just that. The woman could seriously kiss.

"You can take this seat," Ryder said, indicating the chair Dmitri had abandoned.

Kinsey set her bags against the wall and pulled the chair up to the metal table. Her gaze looked over the monitors. Ryder took a few minutes to point out the location of the cameras and the layout of Dreagan.

"It's bigger than I imagined," she said.

"Dreagan consists of sixty thousand acres. Up until a few weeks ago there was a no-fly zone over the entire estate."

"Until the video was released," she guessed.

Ryder sighed and sat back in his chair. "Everything changed then. MI5 patrols our land for the moment," he said, pointing to several cameras that showed the agents.

"They're looking for dragons."

Ryder shrugged and tapped the table near Kinsey so that a keyboard appeared. He did the same in front of himself. "Hopefully they'll be gone soon."

"The video showed the dragon changing into a human. Didn't they see that?"

"They did," Ryder said. "They've asked us repeatedly

to change into a dragon. We laugh and go about our business. They can no' prove anything."

"Unless you're caught again."

That was exactly what he'd been thinking for weeks now. "Aye," he replied in a low tone.

"How were you caught to begin with?"

Ryder hesitated. Kinsey might know of him, and she had already seen the Dark, but why get her involved more? Though she was already fully involved if someone—and he hated to think it was Ulrik—had sent her to Dreagan.

"I need to know," Kinsey said. "How else can I help you? You said you have enemies. Tell me."

"You doona need to know more than you already do."

"Why?" she pressed.

Ryder ran a hand through his hair. "Because it's no' safe."

"Am I safe if I return home?"

He met her gaze for a long stretch of silence before he grudgingly said, "Nay."

"And I'm not safe here." She said it flippantly and turned to the monitor.

He grabbed her chair and swung it around to face him. "I'll die before I allow anyone to hurt you."

Her face softened. Her unusual, beautiful violet eyes regarded him before she nodded. "That I do believe."

"Good." He released her and allowed her to turn the chair back to the screens.

"Tell me," she insisted. "Those people with red eyes in Glasgow. What were they? I thought they wore contacts and colored their hair. You called them dark."

Ryder grunted. If only that were the case. "They're Dark Fae."

"Excuse me?" she asked and turned her face to him.

Her eyes were wide, disbelieving. This was why he hadn't wanted to tell her anything. It was going to be a lot for her to understand and accept. Considering how violently she'd reacted to seeing him shift, he wasn't expecting things to go smoothly.

"Dark Fae," Ryder said. "There are two kinds of Fae. Light and Dark. Both are so beautiful that it's almost like they're no' real, and both have magic."

Kinsey nodded solemnly. "All right."

"The Light have silver eyes and coal black hair. The Dark are the ones with red eyes and black and silver hair. Their eyes turn red the first time they do evil. The more silver in their hair, the more evil they've done."

"Oh. Okay," she said. "Why were the Dark killing humans?"

"They feed off your souls while having sex with you."

She rolled her eyes. "Like I'm going to let that happen now that I know."

"First, the Fae can use glamour to disguise themselves. Second, you willna be able to resist them. They're a drug to humans. I've seen women strip in the middle of the street to allow a group of them to have her."

"One came after me. I remember that."

Ryder did as well. He relived it in his dreams every time he closed his eyes. It was one reason he didn't sleep often. "I wasna going to allow that to happen."

"So you showed yourself to me."

"Aye." And what had he gotten for those efforts? Kinsey running screaming in terror from him. But at least she hadn't been attacked by a Dark.

In Ryder's opinion, that was more than a good trade.

"Why are you and the Fae fighting?"

He rocked back in his chair and laced his hands behind his head. "Once, a verra long time ago, there were the Fae

Wars. It was us against the Fae—both Light and Dark. Eventually, the Light helped us defeat the Dark. The Dark are our enemy, but the Light have aided us. You've already seen one Light Fae today."

"Who?" she asked with her head cocked.

"Shara. She and Kiril were the first to come running from around the side of the manor. The second couple was Rhys and Lily, and the third was Warrick and Darcy."

She scrunched up her nose. "You know I'll never remember their names."

"I know," he said with a grin.

She shook her head, but there was a ghost of a smile on her lips. "Shara was beautiful. Then again so were Lily and Darcy."

"Shara is the only Fae mated to a Dragon King. The other women you see are mortals."

"Excuse me?" Kinsey interrupted him with wide eyes. "Did you just say 'Dragon King'?"

That was one thing Ryder planned to ease into. He could talk forever about their enemies. It was his hope that he could keep her occupied with those stories and not get into who he was. But he slipped up.

Kinsey always did that to him.

He was so at ease with her that he forgot to be cautious and consider his words. It had been that way from the moment they first spoke to the other.

"I did," he confessed.

She raised both brows as she held out her hands. "And you're just going to leave it there? I don't think so. Spill."

"It's a long story."

"I'm a good listener."

Of that he knew for sure. They could talk about anything and everything, but there had been times they were content to just sit quietly in each other's company.

Ryder blew out a breath. "You know I'm millions of years old and immortal. What you doona know is that the dragons were the first inhabitants of this realm from the beginning of time."

"How many dragons?"

"Millions. Billions. I doona know for sure."

"Do they all look like you?"

He was happy she was asking questions. That was a good sign. At least he hoped it was. "Nay. Imagine the colors of a rainbow. That's how many hues of dragons there were. As for sizes, there was a wide range of sizes. I'm one of the largest."

"And the king part?"

"Each dragon group, or color, had a leader. The strongest and the one with the most magic. I was such a dragon."

CHAPTER FOUR

"That doesn't surprise me," Kinsey said.

He frowned slightly. "Why does that no' surprise you?"

"Because you have that look about you."

"A look?" he asked with a slight grin.

Kinsey shrugged. "That look that says, 'I'm in control. Don't fuck with me.'"

He laughed, and she found herself smiling. Kinsey had always loved to hear him laugh. He did have that look of a man that others knew not to mess with, but she had also seen the boyish part of him who liked to chuckle at the silly things and have a donut in his hand at all times.

His smile died though as his gaze grew unfocused, as if he had gone deep into his memories. "The Kings of each faction held absolute law. But even we answered to someone—the King of Kings. The fiercest and most powerful of the Kings reigned over us. Constantine."

Con. The name Tristan had mentioned earlier. Kinsey wasn't keen on meeting this man. She had a feeling that no matter what, he would see her as a threat, just as Ryder had done at the beginning.

"As strong as each of us Kings were, there was only one who could've challenged Con for the title King of Kings."

Ryder's voice trailed off. For several seconds Kinsey waited for him to continue. When he didn't, she prodded him. "Who?"

He blinked and focused on her. "Ulrik. He and Con were inseparable."

"Did he challenge Con?"

"Nay," Ryder said with a twist of his lips. "Ulrik was happy as a King. He didna want to fight his friend or have that kind of responsibility."

Kinsey tucked a leg under her. "But something happened?"

"Con didna believe Ulrik. I doona know everything that happened, but their once solid friendship was cracked. Ulrik never wavered in his faith in Con as King of Kings. He was always the first to follow Con in whatever he asked of us."

"Was that enough for Con?"

"It seemed to be," Ryder said with a shrug. "Things slowly returned to normal. The mortals appeared then. Before any of us could figure out where they came from, we were transformed into humans. We learned we could shift at will, which made it easier to converse with the mortals."

Kinsey wondered what the humans thought of all the dragons around. Had they been as frightened as she?

Ryder continued his story. "Each King made a vow to protect the mortals since they had no magic. We set them up in territories and ordered the dragons to leave them alone. For a time, it actually worked."

"What changed?"

"The humans. They populated at a rapid rate. We had

to continue to move dragons out of lands they'd always inhabited to make room for the mortals. Every once in a while, a human would go missing, and everyone blamed the dragons. After one of those occurrences, a small dragon would be found dead with nothing but bones and wings left."

Kinsey winced at the brutality. "That's . . . awful."

"We Kings managed to work around those difficult times to keep the peace. Some females had been taken by Kings as lovers by this time. Ulrik was one of those. He loved a mortal deeply, and didn't just bring her, but her entire family into his home. He protected them, giving them anything they could want or need."

"But?" Kinsey asked when a muscle ticked in Ryder's jaw.

He glanced at the monitors, his face darkening when he spotted more MI5 agents. "Just days before Ulrik was to take the female as his mate, Con discovered she was going to betray Ulrik and attempt to kill him."

"Because you can only be killed by another Dragon King," Kinsey said with a nod. "She would've failed. Why not let her fail then?"

"Her intention was to start a war. Con wanted to prevent one," Ryder explained. "In an effort to protect Ulrik, Con sent him away on some mission."

She scrunched up her face. "That was a very bad idea."

"Aye. As we found out. Every King chased her down and cornered her, and we killed her. We did it for Ulrik and to protect the unsteady peace between our two races. Ulrik, however, didna see it that way."

"I wouldn't have either. I'd have been furious with you."

Sadness came over Ryder's face then. "He was angry at us. He'd loved the female, and her betrayal cut acutely. His rage was so deep that it consumed him. Ulrik gathered his Silvers, and they began attacking any human they found, killing them."

"Oh, no," Kinsey said with a frown.

"Aye. Many Kings joined Ulrik in his effort to rid the realm of all mortals for good. The other Kings remained with Con, trying to stop Ulrik."

"Which side were you on?"

"Con's."

Somehow Kinsey wasn't surprised by his answer. She nodded, telling him to continue his story.

"It didna take the humans long to fight back. They began attacking the smallest of the dragons first, wiping entire factions out in a day."

Kinsey couldn't imagine what that felt like to Ryder and the others. Especially after they'd made a promise to protect humans and then been betrayed. "Surely not all of my ancestors knew of the betrayal to Ulrik."

"Of course no'," Ryder assured her. "By the time Ulrik swept across the country killing humans, it no longer mattered. It was war. Us versus them. So many dragons were killed. And a wedge came between us Kings. Those who sided with Ulrik fought those who sided with Con. We lost many Kings."

Kinsey felt sadness for the Dragon Kings when she didn't want to. Especially not when Ulrik was killing humans, and yet she couldn't stop herself.

"Con knew drastic action had to be taken." Ryder cleared his throat and slid deeper into his chair. "We created a dragon bridge, linking our realm to another, and we sent every dragon across it. It was their only chance at survival. Though it killed us to see them go."

"You sent them away?" she asked in outrage. "Ryder, that's horrific. Those were your people. Why would you do that just for the mortals?"

He met her gaze solemnly. "We made a vow to the mortals. And we hoped that we could return the dragons one day. Had we known what would happen, I doona believe we would've sent the dragons away. But the simple fact is, our two races couldna live together."

"We came after you. Yet you sacrificed your way of life for us." Kinsey felt ashamed for the actions of her ancestors.

Ryder's lips softened a fraction. "Sending our dragons away wasna enough. It took Con longer than he wanted, but he eventually got all the Kings back on his side except for Ulrik. We still had Ulrik and four of the largest of his Silvers to contend with. We trapped the Silvers and used our magic to make them sleep."

"Did you send them with the others?"

He hesitated a bit too long. "Nay. They're here."

"Here?" she asked in disbelief. "As in, here?"

"They're in the mountain behind the manor in a cage bound with magic."

That didn't make her feel any better. How could a cage hold dragons? And large ones at that? She decided to move past that for now. "What happened to Ulrik?"

"We united our magic to bind his. He would be unable to communicate with his Silvers. We also made sure he could never shift."

"So he's in dragon form?"

Ryder looked at the floor. "He's in human form."

"Damn," she murmured. "That was cruel."

"We also banished him from Dreagan."

She shook her head at Ryder when he looked up at her. "Why? Didn't any of you realize he was hurt? Why take such drastic measures?"

"He started a war, Kinsey. Because of that we lost

thousands of dragons and hundreds of Kings. And let's no' forget we had to send our dragons away."

Kinsey crossed her arms over her chest. "No, you didn't. You could've stopped all of that from happening by doing several things. First, Ulrik should've been told what his woman was doing. He should've been allowed to do what he wanted with her. Second, vow or no', you could've stopped all the dragon killings by using your magic on humans. Whether to kill them or stop them, something could've been done."

"We were no' thinking that way."

"You reacted almost as harshly as Ulrik. I applaud your race for wanting to look after humans, but in the end, you sacrificed your own kind for us. Look where you are now."

"Doona remind me," he murmured. "Would you rather we had killed mortals and wiped their existence?"

"I'm not saying that. What I'm saying is that Ulrik was punished for a quick reaction, and yet Con and the rest of you reacted just as quickly, but in another way. Both of you are to blame."

Ryder stared at her a long while before he said, "You're the second human to tell us that."

"It's because I'm awesome that way." Then she got curious. "Who was the other?"

"Darcy. She's mated to Warrick."

Kinsey grinned. "Then she's a smart woman. How did she come to my conclusion?"

"She saw Ulrik's memories."

"What?" Kinsey nearly fell out of her chair she was so surprised. "I think you might've skipped some parts."

Ryder leaned up and typed in something on the virtual keyboard before he turned to her. "With Ulrik and his Silvers contained, the rest of the Kings retreated to Dreagan. We bound our border with magic to keep all humans out, and we took to our mountains to sleep. Hundreds of years passed as we waited for mortals to forget and the stories to turn into legends and myth."

"That certainly explains all the dragon myths around the world. In every friggin' culture, I might add."

He grinned. "That's right. We remained hidden while Ulrik had to walk the earth as a mortal. Slowly we re-emerged and began to live again. We began distilling whisky to support Dreagan and our lifestyles. All the while we hid our true selves. We only shifted at night or during thunderstorms. More years elapsed and then the leap in technology made even that more difficult, but we always managed to take to the skies as often as we could."

"Except for now." She felt sorry for him and the others. The kind of sorrow that hurt her all the way to her bones, because there was nothing that could be done about it. It was past decisions and actions that led all of them—dragons, Fae, and humans—to where they were now.

"Except for now," he repeated. "During all this time we kept a close eye on Ulrik. He was often seen in the company of Druids."

Kinsey was going to stop him and ask him to explain, but then she realized that it was no surprise Druids were real. The history books mentioned them often enough.

"Dragon magic is the strongest in the realm," Ryder said. "Every Druid who tried to help Ulrik was killed. Then he met Darcy. Her magic was so powerful that she was able to touch our magic binding his. In the process, she saw into his mind and his memories. She also unbound his magic."

Kinsey was leaning forward in her seat now. "That can't be good."

"In the process, Darcy lost her magic. Ulrik has been relentless in trying to take his revenge against us. He's teamed up with the Dark to help him in that quest."

She drew in a deep breath. "I don't know that I blame him."

"He tried to kill Darcy."

"Well, shit."

Ryder looked down at his hands for a second. "But he saved Lily."

"I think there might be more going on than any of you realize," Kinsey told him.

CHAPTER FIVE

Ryder agreed with her. Even with his vast skills, there was less out there about Ulrik than there was about Con, which was nearly nothing. So finding something that could connect Ulrik to an individual or company was proving harder than Ryder wanted to admit.

He hadn't been able to discern more than a handful of aliases Ulrik used, and they didn't garner anything useful. Ulrik had been very careful about hiding anything about himself.

Ryder placed his fingers over the virtual keyboard and began to search through the top brass that worked for Kyvor to see if there were any connections to Ulrik.

"The problem," he explained, "is that Ulrik is extremely careful and very cunning. He's planned this out to the last detail, making it all but impossible for me to find anything."

"You can't find information? That's hard to believe."

Her astonishment was evident in her tone, and it made him puff out his chest. "Ulrik is that good."

"What are you looking for?" Kinsey asked.

Ryder glanced at her. "Someone has to be connected to Ulrik. I'm going to find them."

"You do that. I'm going to see who placed the work order. They might have used my employee number, but the form didn't originate on my computer. If I can find out what computer was used, I'll know who set me up."

Ryder reached for a jelly donut and smiled. He had no doubt Kinsey would find what she was looking for. Because she was that good.

It's not like he'd gone looking for someone with the same skill sets as him, but it made being with Kinsey that much better because they had that in common.

They spent several minutes in silence, each searching their respective items and watching the information pop up on the monitors. Ryder also kept an eye on the MI5 agents. More and more came each day.

How much longer would it be before they demanded to enter the manor? But the Kings were prepared for that. They would turn to their magic and use it to hide the entrance to the mountain.

There was no use hiding the various dragon relics, paintings, and such. Dreagan meant dragon. It was the first thing Con told MI5 when they arrived. To try and say they didn't know anything about dragons would only make them look guilty.

So Con had told them the video was an elaborate prank by some competitor that wanted to knock Dreagan whisky off as the top-selling Scotch in the world. For the time being, MI5 was buying that lie.

"So the Dark factor in because of Ulrik?" Kinsey asked, her gaze on her screen as her mind worked not just on her search, but on everything he'd told her about the Dragon Kings.

Ryder sat back and let his gaze run over the rows of monitors that surrounded him. It felt right to have Kinsey near him again, but he knew it couldn't last. She might have listened to his story with interest, and even felt something for the dragons. But there was still fear in her violet eyes.

"Nay," he finally answered. "The Fae came to this realm a verra long time ago hoping they could force us to leave in order to have the mortals to themselves. That was the Fae Wars. The Dark have been our enemy since. The Light vary, but most times they side with us."

Kinsey turned her head to him. "And Glasgow?"

"It wasna just Glasgow," he said. "It was Edinburgh, Inverness, Oban, and countless other cities throughout the U.K. The Dark wanted to take over. Dragon Kings were assigned to each city to protect as many mortals as we could from the Dark."

She turned back to the monitor. In a tight voice she said, "I see."

Was it his imagination, or did she sound upset at his response? "Doona travel to Ireland. That's where the Fae live."

"Well, that's good to know," she commented as she typed something.

Ryder focused on his search. One by one, he went through the top executives at Kyvor. When nothing came up, he widened his search and found the smaller companies Kyvor was parent to and repeated the process.

He was running searches on three computers simultaneously. Every so often he looked at Kinsey. She was so absorbed in what she was doing that the outside world fell away. It was how she had always worked, and Ryder found it endearing.

Minutes turned into hours. The longer he went without discovering anything on Ulrik, the more frustrated Ryder became. If there was anything out there, he'd find it. Which just proved there was nothing.

That, however, wasn't possible.

Not with today's smart phones with cameras for pictures and videos. Then there was social media where even the most skilled people sometimes got caught out at a restaurant or crossing the street.

Facial recognition software had been searching for Ulrik's face for the past three hours, and had come up with absolutely zero from all social media outlets.

Ryder pushed back from the table and rolled his head from side to side. Kinsey hadn't moved other than her fingers over the keyboard.

Suddenly, the door opened and Dmitri filled the doorway. He met Ryder's gaze and shrugged before he stepped aside. Ryder then found himself looking into black eyes.

Con.

"I hear we have a visitor," Con said as he walked closer to the monitors and looked over them to Kinsey. She was too intent on her work to notice Con.

Ryder said, "This is how she works. She doesna even hear you."

"Perhaps you should get her attention."

"No' yet," Ryder said.

Con stared at him for a stretch of silence. "Dmitri filled me in on Kinsey Burns. I'd like to hear it from you now."

"There isna much to tell," Ryder said. He hadn't wanted Con to know of the time he and Kinsey had been together in Glasgow, but it was inevitable.

"I knew you were seeing someone during your stay in Glasgow. I gather the woman was Kinsey."

Ryder nodded. There was no such thing as privacy in the world of the Dragon Kings.

Con's gaze moved to Kinsey where he studied her for several minutes. "We'll talk more about that later. Catch me up on what the two of you've found."

"I have nothing," Ryder said and motioned to the screens. "There is nothing that I can find to link Ulrik to Kyvor. Yet."

"Then he's hiding it," Dmitri stated.

Con glanced at Dmitri and said, "I agree. Ulrik is too smart to leave a trail leading back to him. That is, if you believe Kinsey."

"She didna put in the work order," Ryder said.

Dmitri crossed his arms over his chest as he leaned back against the wall. "She'd have to be a good actress to fool us. The shock was genuine. She was sent here."

"To Ryder," Con said with a small frown. "Why?"

"Aha," Kinsey said with a bright smile as she pushed the rolling chair back from the table and threw up her arms. Then she saw Con and Dmitri. She lowered her arms and turned to Ryder. "I found out who put in the work order."

Ryder scooted his chair next to her. "Who?"

She grabbed the table and pulled her chair forward. Kinsey then pointed to the screen. "The name is Clarice Steinhold. She's a new employee hired at the start of October."

"So?" Con said.

Kinsey spared him a brief look. "The work order is dated December fourth. After a little checking I ascertained that Clarice called in sick on the fourth."

Ryder smiled and nodded. "Nice catch."

"Someone used her computer so it wouldna trace back to themselves," Dmitri said. "Can you find out who?"

Kinsey bit her lip. "No."

"I'll see what I can find," Ryder said.

"You learned something new?" Kinsey asked excitedly.

Ryder had kept a lot of his skills from her before. He paused, unsure of what to say.

Kinsey then rolled her eyes. "Ah. I see. You've always been able to do that. You just failed to mention that part three years ago."

"Three years," Con murmured with a raised brow.

Ryder inwardly winced. Con was going to piece it all together. So much for Ryder keeping what had occurred a secret. Then again, nothing stayed private at Dreagan.

He ignored Con's penetrating gaze as well as Kinsey's censoring stare and focused on his task. It took him but a few minutes to hack into Kyvor's private server. He then went back to the date in question.

From there he was able to discover Clarice's employee number that led him straight to her computer. Then he looked back through the camera to a week earlier, hoping that Kyvor was like most companies and recorded their employees.

"Shite," Ryder said as he glared at the screen.

Con walked around the side of the monitors to stand beside Ryder. "What is it?"

"Someone was smart enough to cover the camera on Clarice's computer screen while they were there. Once they finished . . ." Ryder punched a button to show them. "The surrounding area was visible once more."

Dmitri grunted. "Then someone knew you would be able to hack into the system."

"Or they just didn't want to take a chance of being discovered," Kinsey said.

Ryder stared at his monitor. "It has to be someone who works there. I'd wager it's someone higher up in the corporation."

"No' necessarily," Con said. "Ulrik could easily get to someone much lower on the corporate ladder."

Kinsey wrinkled her nose. "That's true. It could be anyone. There are tens of thousands of people working for the company. We can't go through each one."

"We can, but it willna do any good," Ryder said.

Kinsey's head tilted to the side. "Why do you say that?"

"They went to great lengths to conceal their identity. There willna be anything to find."

"So how do I find out who set me up? And why?" Kinsey asked. "I don't like this, Ryder. Someone intentionally sent me here because they knew about us."

Con turned the gold dragon-head cuff link at his left wrist. "How much do they know? That's what we need to determine," he said, looking at Ryder.

"Obviously they know enough," Ryder muttered.

Con shook his head. "No' especially. The wanted us to think Kinsey wrote the work order, but they also had to know her skills—and yours, for that matter. It's why they hid themselves at Clarice's computer."

"Then knew we'd clear Kinsey," Dmitri said, his gaze riveted on her.

Ryder frowned. He didn't like the direction the conversation was turning. "Nay," he stated.

"That would be a hell no from me," Kinsey said. "I didn't willingly come here. Had I known this was where Ryder was, I'd have gone the opposite direction."

Ryder grimaced. It was the wrong thing to say to Con. And Con's icy demeanor confirmed Ryder's suspicions.

"Is that right?" Con asked in a smooth, even tone.

Kinsey gave a firm nod. "Yes."

"Because you saw him in his true form."

It wasn't a question. Ryder closed his eyes, seeing the train wreck that was about to happen.

There was a beat of silence before Kinsey said, "Yes. And before you ask, of course I was scared. I'd never seen a dragon before. How else was I supposed to react upon witnessing something that large flying through the sky breathing fire?"

Ryder opened his eyes, hiding his smile. He had to give it to Kinsey for turning the question back on Con. She had a point.

"Did the dragon come after you?" Con asked.

Ryder watched Kinsey. He knew the answer, but he wasn't sure if Kinsey thought he *had* gone after her.

She briefly met his gaze before she swung her eyes to Con. "The city was burning. People were screaming and running for their lives. There were red-eyed men and women everywhere with droves of people around them. Then there was something in the sky. I didn't stop to ask the dragon if it was going to kill me. I simply ran. As any sane person would do."

Ryder smiled, because she had a very good point. She hadn't known it was him. Not at first. Now, once she had . . . well, that was an entirely different matter.

"That's a good explanation," Con said. "How did you discover it was Ryder?"

Kinsey swallowed and said, "I was being chased by one of those men with red eyes, the Dark. I just wanted to get away. The next thing I knew, there was a dragon flying right toward me. Then it was gone, and Ryder stood there. He killed the Dark Fae."

"And you ran away," Con concluded.

Kinsey's gaze skated to Ryder for a heartbeat. "Yes. I ran."

CHAPTER SIX

Kinsey held Con's gaze. There was no way he was going to make her feel bad for doing what 99 percent of humans would've done in her shoes.

However, she knew that had hurt Ryder. The look on his face that night, and even now while he watched her with hope, told her she had wounded him severely.

"Con," Ryder said, his voice holding a warning.

Kinsey wondered what it was Ryder didn't want Con to say to her. There was no emotion on Con's face. Even his black eyes seemed to see right through her.

It was contradictory to the golden waves of his hair that gave the impression of a relaxed and cheerful man, which was also in direct contrast to the sharp black suit he wore that looked as if it cost more than her entire wardrobe.

"Let him say whatever he needs to," Kinsey told Ryder. "He is King of Kings, after all."

Con's eyes narrowed for a fraction of a second, but it was enough that Kinsey saw it. She felt she'd gained a small victory over him. She should've known that no one got anything on Con for long.

"You shared Ryder's bed, knew him intimately, and yet when he saves you from the Dark, you run away. And you doona believe you have anything to be contrite for?"

"I was scared."

One side of Con's lips lifted in a smile. "You. It's always about you, is it no'? What about Ryder?"

"Enough, dammit," Ryder said as he got to his feet. "I can handle this."

But Con's words filtered into her brain regardless of the fact that Ryder tried to stop it. Was Con right? Was she making it all about her?

Con slowly turned his head to Ryder. "Do you remember what I told you long, long ago on that dark night that changed our lives implicitly?"

Kinsey watched as the two of them stared each other down. Ryder's anger was palpable, and though Con didn't show his fury as Ryder did, Kinsey still felt it. There were no words between them, but once again she felt as if Ryder was communicating with Con in another way.

Con returned his black eyes to her. "Someone went to great extremes to get you here. I want to know why."

"As do I," Kinsey said.

Con tugged on the wrist of his shirt, pulling it from his suit jacket so that his cuff links showed. "Check everything she has. I'll no' have another incident like Iona's."

Kinsey waited until Con and Dmitri strode out before she asked, "What happened with Iona?"

"She was used by her company to gather intel on us. Her phone was bugged, as was her computer."

"Who did she work for?"

"The Commune."

Kinsey drummed her fingers on the table. "I've heard of them. So they were connected to Ulrik?"

Ryder mumbled something that sounded like an affirmation. Kinsey leaned over and tugged her purse and bag to her. Then she swung them around and set them between her and Ryder.

"Look through everything," she told him. "I want to know that my things are clean. They've not been out of my sight for days, but I suspect if someone really wanted to get to them, they could."

Ryder set her large black bag in his lap. "They used an e-mail loaded with a virus to get into Iona's mobile and laptop."

Of course they did. Kinsey knew that was definitely an option, because she'd helped people do that before. It wasn't a service her company announced, but the people with the right amount of money and clout always got whatever they wanted.

She turned back to the monitor as Ryder sorted through her bag. Yet she couldn't concentrate. She kept running Con's words over in her head.

Perhaps she shouldn't have run. Maybe she should've stayed. And did what? Talked to Ryder? People were dying all around her, buildings were on fire, and Ryder was a dragon.

An effing big dragon at that!

She hadn't meant to hurt him. Or maybe subconsciously she had after what he'd done to her. Regardless, her fear ruled her that night. Though that explained her reaction then, it didn't explain it now.

Weeks had gone by where she'd been able to sort through all she had witnessed and experienced. Why then would she still be so fearful?

That's what she believed Con wanted to know. He

hadn't come right out and asked, but there hadn't been a need. She was sure that Tristan and/or Dmitri had told Con what transpired when she saw Ryder.

Kinsey was ashamed of herself. Yes, she was still completely freaked out at the idea that Ryder was a dragon—and that she was surrounded by dragons.

But she'd trusted Ryder implicitly at one time. He was the other half of her soul, the man she had always known would be who she spent her life with.

Should it matter that he was a dragon?

He certainly hadn't cared that she was a vegetarian. In fact, he had gone out of his way to make sure whenever he cooked that she had all she needed for a filling meal, even if he was eating meat.

Now she knew why he always laughed when she attempted to get him to stop eating meat. He was a *dragon*. Dragons weren't herbivores.

Kinsey snorted as she hid a laugh. How was she to know what a dragon was or wasn't? They didn't exactly teach dragon basics in school.

Out of the corner of her eye, she saw Ryder look up at her before he went back to her things. The smile faded from her lips. She knew one big reason she'd treated Ryder the way she had since she walked into the computer room.

When she hadn't been able to get in touch with Ryder after he walked out on her three years ago, she had fallen apart. Weeks later, when she was finally able to pull herself together, she used her skills to look for him. But he had disappeared quite effectively.

She wanted to hurt him for leaving her. How silly for her to think that she was over him as she'd told herself for so long. It was obvious from the way she couldn't stop looking at him, listening to his voice, and yearning for his touch that she'd been lying to herself.

But she wanted him to suffer as she'd suffered. The pain had been so unbearable at times that she honestly thought she might die from it.

At times she'd wanted to die, begged for it. But each day she woke to see the sun.

Kinsey tightened her ponytail, wincing as her head began to ache. She decided to forgo the pain and took her hair down. With a shake of her head, she sighed as her headache began to dissipate almost immediately.

She rubbed the spot where the band had held her hair against her head and closed her eyes. One of these days she was going to learn how to put her hair in a ponytail without it hurting.

After a minute or two, Kinsey opened her eyes and sat back. Only to find Ryder watching her with his hazel eyes darkened. She knew that look all too well.

He wanted her. The desire was tangible, physical.

Her heart skipped a beat and her stomach felt as if an entire flock of hummingbirds was trying to get out. The urge to get up and go to him, straddle his lap was strong.

Then she thought about the last three years where he hadn't bothered to contact her. Saving her life or not, Ryder had been a dick in the way he'd left. She'd be an utter and complete fool to give in to her need for him only to have him push her away again.

She was stronger now. She was the one in charge of her life and her destiny. Even if he was the other half of her soul, that didn't mean she should allow herself to be treated so harshly. She deserved better.

Kinsey pulled her gaze from Ryder and focused on the computer screen before her. She pretended as if she had something important to do.

And she did. If only she could remember what it was.

Oh. Right. Trying to determine who would want her at Dreagan and why.

Kinsey pulled up the list of employees at Kyvor, starting with the highest ranking. Of the thirty executives, she had met two of them. Her boss, Cecil Beltz, a sixty-year-old who had worked his way up through the company for forty years.

And Cecil's supervisor, Harriet Smythe. She was pretty, and one of the youngest executives at just thirty-three. Though she seemingly came out of nowhere, no one could fault her work.

Two of the thirty in top management. That wasn't much to go on.

"What did you find?" Ryder asked.

She glanced at him before frowning back at the screen. "I decided to try and see who all I know at Kyvor. There are thirty in the top brass. I've personally met two of them." She pointed to the first picture. "Cecil, my boss." Then she pointed to the next picture of a young woman with bleach-blond hair and a bright white smile. "And Harriet, who Cecil answers to."

Ryder studied the two for a moment before he began to tap the virtual keyboard. Kinsey was shocked when he pulled up her employee folder and began to look through it.

"You've had four promotions in three years," he said with a nod of approval.

Kinsey sat a little straighter. "That's right."

"You made some major moves through the company, Kins, which means you caught the attention of more than Cecil and Harriet."

She always loved when he shortened her name. Other people did it and she lost her mind, but not with Ryder. It was the way he said it, as if it were an endearment.

"Did you hear me?" he asked as he turned his face to her.

Kinsey could've kicked herself. "Yeah. Of course, I heard you."

"You didna say anything."

She shrugged. "What is there to say? You're stating facts."

"What I'm doing is pointing out that every one of those top executives knows you."

Kinsey dropped her head back against the chair and blew out a breath. If she could stop thinking of Ryder as a lover, and think of him as a co-worker, she might actually get her brain to function properly.

"Right," she said and lifted her head. "I need to see which one has it out for me."

"*We*," Ryder corrected.

Kinsey felt herself softening to him. Dammit. This isn't what she wanted. She couldn't. But it was so-damn-hard not to. She gave a nod, refusing to look into Ryder's hazel eyes again. "A simple search of me wouldn't bring up my love life."

"They didna do a simple search."

At those words she had no choice but to look at him. Kinsey began to worry as she saw the frown deepening Ryder's forehead. "What do you mean?"

"Knowing about us, about our connection, means that someone has probably been following you."

Kinsey shook her head. "No. That can't be right. I'm a nobody."

"You were with me," he said in a voice filled with sadness.

She dropped her head into her hands and then used her fingers to rake her hair out of her face as she squared her shoulders and sat up. "Then they weren't following me. They were following you."

"Most likely. My being with you brought you under scrutiny."

"I still don't understand how anyone at Kyvor could get ahold of such information."

"Ulrik." Ryder said the name as if it were poison on his tongue.

Kinsey shivered, because she had a feeling the more they dug into this, the more she was going to learn about how intricately she and Ryder were joined.

She wasn't sure how that made her feel. Part of her was pleased Ryder was with her, because she knew if anyone could help her through this it was him.

But another part dreaded and feared being part of a world she wasn't ready to accept.

Ready or not, she was planted right in the middle of things.

CHAPTER SEVEN

Ireland
Dark Fae Palace

Taraeth knew he was walking a fine line, but as king of the Dark, it was something he did with style. After all, no Dark had ever ruled as long as he.

And he remained in control because he had a way of putting the right people around him. As well as choosing sides.

It wasn't as if the Dark had a lot of people wanting to be allies. But only a fool would turn down an offer that could gain the Dark dominion over the humans.

"Did you hear me?"

Taraeth hated the British accent Mikkel used when he was attempting to pretend he was better than everyone else. The only time Mikkel's Scots brogue came out was when he was angry.

And the only one who managed to get him angry was his nephew—Ulrik.

"I heard," Taraeth said.

He raised a hand to quiet Mikkel as the Irish folk song continued to play. Didn't Mikkel know not to interrupt such wondrous music?

When the last strings of the song played, Taraeth then turned to his guest. Mikkel sat upon the black velvet half-moon-shaped sofa with one arm draped along the back. He wore a custom-made navy suit with a cream dress shirt beneath and a navy and gold tie. Mikkel's black hair was neither long nor short, but somewhere in between.

Though he wasn't as beautiful as a Fae, Taraeth recognized the appeal Mikkel had on the fairer sex with his height, gold eyes, and his fortune.

That wasn't enough for Mikkel though. He'd had a taste—albeit a brief one—of being a Dragon King. Now, he coveted the highest position within those ranks—King of Kings.

Mikkel had gone to great lengths over many centuries to put himself where he was now. Though Taraeth would never admit it aloud, Mikkel had managed to do quite a lot to the Kings.

However, the credit didn't belong to just Mikkel.

Ulrik had done his fair share against the Kings. All before he even knew his uncle was alive.

Taraeth smiled when he realized how impatient Mikkel had become. "What was your question again?" he asked, just to irritate further.

"I want to know everything you have on Ulrik."

The song, and then asking Mikkel to repeat the question, had bought Taraeth a little more time. Ulrik knew Taraeth was helping Mikkel, but Mikkel had no idea that Taraeth and Ulrik had struck their own bargain.

"And he never will," Taraeth mumbled beneath his breath. In a louder tone he said, "Ulrik is still being . . . entertained . . . by Muriel."

Just as Sinny, her sister, was "entertaining" Mikkel.

"I already know that much." Mikkel's lips thinned. His gold eyes grew hard. "I want to know the rest."

Taraeth rose from the black sofa that mirrored the one Mikkel occupied across the space. He ran a hand down his black silk shirt as he walked to the liquor. There he poured a glass for Mikkel and handed it to him.

As he turned back to the alcohol, he glanced down at his missing left arm. His hatred for Denae hadn't lessened. If anything, he despised her more every day.

Taraeth poured whisky—Irish, of course—into a glass and took a sip. Then he faced Mikkel. "I'm not Ulrik's keeper. I don't follow him around. I thought that was your job."

"I've people watching him," Mikkel admitted. "But he continues to slip past them."

"Perhaps your people aren't as good as you think."

Mikkel tossed back the whisky and lowered the glass. "If they fail, they pay with their lives."

Taraeth shrugged, uncaring. After all, he did the same thing. But he was leading an entire race. Mikkel would never be able to lead the Dragon Kings that way. The other Kings would kill him.

"I also have a few of my people working for him."

Taraeth returned to his sofa and chuckled. "That may not be wise, my friend. If Ulrik finds out . . ."

"He'll never find out," Mikkel said with confidence. "That lad knows I'm in charge. He does what I say without question. And he'll continue to do so."

Taraeth wasn't so sure, but he wouldn't be the one to point that out to Mikkel. Ulrik would do that soon enough. Because though Taraeth hadn't admitted it to his right-hand man, Balladyn, he agreed that Ulrik was the stronger of the two.

Yet there was a slight chance Mikkel would win. Taraeth was still hedging his bets for the moment. That could change tomorrow. Until then, he would placate Mikkel in whatever way was needed.

Mikkel raised his empty glass. Taraeth motioned to the liquor with his head. With a smirk, Mikkel rose and poured himself another drink.

"You had the Dragon Kings," Mikkel said. "Edinburgh, London, Glasgow, Inverness, and all the other cities were burning. Your Dark were feeding on the souls of the useless humans. Why did you pull back?"

Taraeth's good mood evaporated like smoke. He didn't enjoy being questioned by anyone, but most especially someone who wasn't a Fae—like Mikkel.

"We got what we needed with the video. We've dealt the Kings a major blow and focused the world's attention on them," Taraeth answered.

Mikkel brought the glass to his lips and hesitated. "Did you? Deal the Kings a blow, that is?" he asked before he took a drink.

Taraeth wanted to kill Mikkel right then. It was only by sheer force of will that he held himself back. But he would wipe that fucking sneer off his face. "We did more damage in a few hours than your spy working among those at Dreagan."

"Touché," Mikkel said as his gold gaze narrowed.

Taraeth watched Mikkel slowly walk back to the sofa and sit. Tense silence descended over the room Taraeth used for private meetings. Right outside the two sets of doors were Dark Fae ready to kill with just a word from him.

Though Taraeth could take care of Mikkel on his own, if need be. It might one day come to that, but if he ever did, Taraeth would then have to face Ulrik.

And that was one former Dragon King he'd rather not mess with.

There was too much loathing, vengeance, and animosity within Ulrik. It consumed him, devoured him.

That kind of hatred spawned an animal that could never be tamed, an animal that would never stop until it got exactly what it wanted—retribution.

"Ulrik and Con fought," Mikkel said.

Taraeth had discovered that after it happened. He lifted one shoulder. "Isn't that exactly what you wanted him to do?"

"Not until I give the order. I decide when they fight."

"My men tell me there were other Kings there."

Mikkel's lips flattened in anger as he sat back. "Rhys, Kiril, and Darius. All to protect some stupid mortal."

"Darius's mate."

Mikkel rolled his eyes and snorted. "Mates. That's the biggest load of shite I've heard in eons. Ulrik learned his lesson quick enough with that bitch he took to his bed professing to love her."

"You won't take a mate?"

"Me?" Mikkel laughed. "Once I'm King of Kings and you and the Dark rid this planet of every last fucking human, then I'll be the savior of my race and return the dragons. I'll find a beautiful Silver to be mine."

"Because the humans can't carry a Dragon King's seed to term?" Taraeth questioned.

Mikkel lifted his glass in a salute. "Precisely."

"That sounds like a nice plan." It went unsaid that it hinged on Ulrik challenging and winning against Con, and then Mikkel betraying Ulrik.

"That day is closer than you think."

Taraeth finished off his whisky and turned the glass in his hand. "I still remember when I stumbled upon this realm. All those mortals throwing themselves at me, begging me to take their bodies. How were we to stay away? Now there are billions of them out there. They would feed every Fae—Light and Dark—for years to come."

"It's a wise bargain we struck."

Taraeth smiled at Mikkel, wondering if Mikkel was plotting against him as he was scheming against Mikkel. "That we did, my friend."

"Will you help me keep track of Ulrik?"

"That I can't do."

Mikkel's smile was gone. "Can't? Or won't?"

"Can't," Taraeth said again. "Your race may not have to answer to anyone but Con, but the Fae do."

"Who?"

"Death." Taraeth didn't even like saying the name aloud.

Mikkel chuckled and crossed one leg over the other. "You live thousands of years and die. Why would you fear death?"

"No. Death. Death is our judge. For millions of years there has been no sign of Death's associates. Until recently. Now all the Fae whisper about is the Reapers."

"Who are they?"

Taraeth couldn't quite hide his shiver of apprehension. "The Reapers are the hands of Death. Death might be the judge, but the Reapers are the executioners. They police all Fae."

"So kill the bastards."

Taraeth glanced at his glass. "No one knows who the Reapers are. No one has even seen Death. We can't fight what we don't see or know."

"So you're afraid of some whispers?"

"What do you think has been hunting the Fae besides the Kings? The Reapers."

Mikkel made a sound at the back of his throat. "Has anyone ever seen one of these Reapers?"

"You see one, you die."

"Of course you do," Mikkel scoffed.

"Mock all you want. The Reapers aren't just a legend. They're real."

Mikkel gave a shake of his head, as if to say that Taraeth had lost what little sense he had. "Superstitious is what you are. All of you were told that nonsense to keep you in line. Why would only your race have such beings as judge, jury, and executioner? Wouldn't the Kings have had it as well?"

"The Fae are different, Mikkel."

"That's a pile of shite, and you know it."

Taraeth held the glass in his hand but set it on the sofa beside him. "You dare to ridicule my people and our beliefs?"

"I'd ask that you not be so narrow minded."

"You dragons think you're so much better than everyone else. You came to me for an alliance, but even now you look down your nose at me."

"Because this Reaper stuff is nonsense," Mikkel stated in a cold voice.

Taraeth wondered what Ulrik would say if he were sitting across from him instead of Mikkel. Ulrik wouldn't give a royal fuck, that's what he would say. His attention was on one thing—bringing down Con.

"It's like the humans believing fairies are small, winged creatures with pointy ears," Mikkel said.

Taraeth merely smiled aloofly. "But we're not mortals. We've lived for billions of years. We travel from realm to realm, and our magic is feared by many. The Fae aren't some mindless cattle to be swayed by a myth or two."

"But you've never seen a Reaper."

"And I hope I never do. That doesn't, however, mean I don't believe they're here. My people all over the U.K. claimed to see Dark fall dead for no apparent reason. That's one of the modes of the Reapers. Then there was mention of a white-haired Fae with red-rimmed white eyes."

Mikkel sat forward, suddenly interested. "White eyes?"

"The Reapers are Fae who are given greater power, speed, and whatever else Death wishes. They're not to be messed with."

"But I'm a Dragon King," Mikkel said. He set his glass on the sofa, then rose and walked from the room.

Taraeth watched him, waiting until the doors closed behind Mikkel before he said, "You're not a Dragon King."

CHAPTER EIGHT

Through the countless decades, there had been numerous conversations between Ryder and Con about Ulrik. Ryder hated spying on Ulrik. No matter what Ryder suggested, Con wouldn't allow Ulrik to just live his life.

Over the last few months Ryder was focused on Ulrik in a way he'd never been before—and even more so now because the thought of Ulrik pulling Kinsey into this war sent Ryder into a frenzy.

Ryder had every camera in Perth looking for Ulrik's face or his car. Anything to prove that the banished Dragon King was there.

Ulrik proved time and again that he'd do whatever it took to hurt the Dragon Kings. That usually meant he targeted their lovers.

Ryder's blood went cold at the thought of something happening to Kinsey. She had been on her own for three years, and nothing had happened. But that didn't mean nothing would happen either.

The fact she'd been sent to Dreagan was like cannon

fire over the estate. Someone was making a point. No, Ryder corrected himself. *Ulrik* was making a point.

The question was what?

Ulrik could've gotten to her and killed Kinsey easily. Why hadn't he? Why had he brought her to Dreagan?

None of her tech held any signs of a virus or being tampered with. Ryder checked them all three times just to be sure. Her bag, her purse, and even her car had been thoroughly examined. Still, they found nothing.

Unless . . . Kinsey was the Trojan horse.

Ryder swung his head toward her. She far surpassed most individuals who worked with computers doing the intricate things she did. She was kind and sweet, willing to help anyone who needed it. But she wasn't a good actress.

He'd always been able to tell when she lied about anything. Since she walked through the door, she'd been telling the truth.

Yet others had been fooled. Darcy, for one. Ulrik and his old Druid had gone to tremendous lengths to make Darcy think her magic remained, when in fact it had left her the moment she helped Ulrik.

Then there was Iona. Her father was murdered just to get her back to Scotland so Ulrik and the Dark Fae could access Dreagan.

"What is it?" Kinsey asked when she caught him staring.

Ryder shrugged, not wanting to tell her his thoughts just yet. "I'm thinking."

"Apparently hard by the way your forehead is creased. It's about what's going on, isn't it?"

He gave a slow nod. His gaze landed on the box of donuts, and for the first time, he didn't want one.

"Just tell me," Kinsey urged as she swiveled her chair to face him.

"No' yet."

"Why?" she pressed, her voice edged with a hint of aggravation. She suspected he was hiding something.

Ryder shoved a lock of hair off his forehead. "I need to get it all sorted in my head first."

"You look worried. Talking it out helps."

He paused his fingers as he typed and briefly closed his eyes. This he wouldn't lie to her about. "I am worried. Ulrik has a habit of targeting anyone a Dragon King has shown interest in."

"If he wanted to target me, why wait three years?"

"Who says he did?"

Kinsey's violet eyes widened. She blinked, her long black lashes briefly closing. "What does he look like?"

Ryder sent a picture of Ulrik in a suit to the monitor above her. Kinsey stared at it a long while without uttering a sound. Ryder then sent several more pictures of Ulrik getting out of his car, in jeans and a sweater, with his hair pulled back, and with it down.

Finally, Kinsey said, "He's good-looking, and certainly knows how to wear clothes that make him look amazing. A woman doesn't forget a man like that."

Jealousy simmered through Ryder. Kinsey thought Ulrik handsome. And unforgettable. It cut through Ryder, sinking deep into his soul.

He'd never forgotten about Kinsey or the love he felt for her. Even though he'd seen a spark of desire in her eyes earlier, he was beginning to suspect she had moved on.

Not that he blamed her. Ryder had walked out of her life without an explanation. Even if he had been able to tell her who he was, he wouldn't have. Because of exactly what she had done when he saved her a few weeks ago.

He always feared she wouldn't be able to accept him. Ryder had wanted her as his desperately, but it wasn't just that he couldn't tell her who he really was. There was the spell put in place to stop the Dragon Kings from feeling anything for mortals.

It was only recently that they discovered when the Silvers moved in their mountain, it was because Ulrik had gotten back part of his magic.

That's all it had taken to break Con's spell. That's when Ryder realized he loved Kinsey. He returned to Dreagan to see if he could understand what had happened. Then Cassie arrived and Hal fell in love with her.

After that, all Hell seemed to break loose. At every turn, someone or something was trying to get onto Dreagan. The Dark were relentless in their attempts to discover where the Kings hid a weapon that could kill them—so far unsuccessfully.

Ryder was still adjusting to the knowledge that Con and Kellan—the Keeper of History—were the only two Kings who knew where the weapon was. And *what* it was.

Everyone targeting Dreagan could be traced back to Ulrik. It took Ryder time, but he discovered that Ulrik's network of spies, mercenaries, corporations, and everyday people was extensive. That wasn't even counting Ulrik's affiliation with the Dark Fae.

Kinsey's head twisted toward him. "I've never seen Ulrik."

"You didna have to." Ryder hated that his words came out harsher than he'd intended. He knew it wasn't Kinsey's fault that he'd left her. That had been his decision. Now he was paying the consequences. "Ulrik has many people working for him. Any one of them could've gotten to you."

She gave a bark of laughter. "Do you really think I'm

that naïve that I wouldn't know when someone was trying to scam me?"

"No' at all. But these people are good, Kins. Verra good."

"All right," she conceded. "Let's say that one of them did get to me. How? When? Why? You and I haven't spoken in three years."

"Until a few weeks ago. Someone must've seen me shift, and then watched you run away."

Her lips pressed together for an instant. "Those who weren't throwing themselves at the Dark Fae were running away."

"That's true. But they weren't you. As to the how and when? It could've been anywhere, anytime. You visit individuals and corporations as part of your job. You could've been approached at any one of them."

She raised a dark brow. "I see your point. And I suppose you'll say the 'why' is because we were once together."

"Precisely."

"Have any of the other Kings been contacted by past lovers? What about any of your other lovers? With as long as you've been around, you must've had plenty."

Was that jealousy he heard in her voice? That made Ryder want to smile. Perhaps she still felt something for him after all.

"No, to answer both your questions. No past lovers of anyone—including mine—have shown up besides you."

"I'm the lucky one, huh?" she mumbled and returned to face the screen and Ulrik's pictures. "Do you have any photos of his associates?"

"There are literally thousands, by my guess. He's never seen with any of them."

"So that's a no," she said. "You're right. It could be anyone, but the fact is, had anyone mentioned your name, I would've been suspicious."

"They probably wouldna have. What about Dreagan?"

She shook her head. "Not that I can remember."

Ryder could see that she was becoming agitated by not having any answers. He was as well, but when it came to Ulrik, Ryder was used to this.

"Let's start with something we already know is fact. Someone used your name to write up the work order to send you here," he said.

Kinsey turned the chair to face him, leaning an elbow on the arm. "Right. We don't know who that is though."

"No' yet. Truthfully, we may never know. It might be pointless, because it could be just some lackey that Ulrik used to get something done."

She nodded as she listened. "That's a good point. What else do we know?"

"That you are innocent of putting in the work order."

Kinsey chuckled and shoved her hair over her shoulder. "Yes, I am. That's all we know, isn't it?"

Pretty much, but Ryder had gone on less before. "I know Ulrik is involved. I'm going to need time to piece it all together."

"*We're* going to need time," she corrected.

Ryder smiled. He hadn't realized how much he missed being near Kinsey until she had walked into his office.

The problem was, there was too much suspicion still in regards to her. Con would want her isolated from Ryder and the access she had with the computers.

However, Ryder already had an argument in response to what he knew was coming from Con.

"Does it bother you that I'm here?" she asked.

Ryder was so surprised by her question that it took him

a minute to respond. "No. I understand that you'd rather no' be here."

"That was true at first."

"Which means you do now?" Hope sprung in his chest. Ryder held his breath as he waited for her to answer.

Kinsey motioned to the room. "Look at this place. I've never seen a room set up the way you have it. All the latest and greatest technological marvels at your fingertips. You have access to everything you want, and the money to back you if you need it."

Disappointment quickly replaced the hope within Ryder. He should've known she would be completely geeked out by all that surrounded her. It was her passion, just as it was his.

And yet, he yearned for something more.

It could've been his. It had been his.

Until he walked away.

If only Ryder could reverse time and do it all over again. Perhaps if he'd spoken to Kinsey and told her who he really was she wouldn't have been so scared.

That night she saw him shift had been horrendous. It scarred her from within in ways that few would ever understand. But he did.

"Besides," she said with a smile. "I'm going to find whoever set me up and learn why."

"You may no' like what you uncover," he cautioned her.

Kinsey used her foot to swing her chair from one side to the other. "I'd rather know what I'm dealing with instead of walking with my head in the clouds as I have for years. How you must have laughed at me."

There was no heat to her words, but Ryder still heard the pain she couldn't quite manage to conceal. All kinds of responses sprung in his mind at once.

"I never laughed at you," he said. "I marveled at your

enthusiasm for the world. I admired your dedication to your career and your family. I was amazed at your compassion to those in need, including the animals who crossed your path.

"I was astonished by your ability to laugh at adversity and no' allow anything to get you down. And I was in awe at the way you showed me the world through your eyes."

"Those are beautiful words. Too bad they don't mean as much if you hadn't walked out on me."

CHAPTER NINE

Con held the Montblanc pen by the fingers of both hands as he stared at the report on his desk. He didn't like what had been found, and it was number one thousand and seventy-six on the list of things to do that day.

As troubling as the report was in regards to the distilling of the whisky, it paled in comparison to the new visitor at the manor.

Kinsey Burns.

Tristan and Dmitri had told him everything, from her arrival to the interaction with Ryder. Con had also watched the tapes of her arrival at Dreagan and meeting Tristan to get visuals of her face.

What he wished he'd been able to see was when she came face-to-face with Ryder.

Con had become an expert when it came to discovering which of his Kings was in danger of finding a mate. What vexed him was that Ryder had hidden his feelings so well that Con never knew until the arrival of Kinsey.

Oh, Con understood that there had been someone in Glasgow, but at the time, Con still thought the spell was in place. If he had known it wasn't, he might have questioned Ryder more.

After Cassie and Hal fell in love and mated, Con had taken a close look at all the Kings who spent time out in the world away from Dreagan.

He had even paid special attention to Ryder. But not once had Ryder asked to return to Glasgow, nor shown any interest in the city or its occupants. Though with his access to the computers, Con realized that Ryder could have been keeping an eye on Kinsey all these years.

Ryder couldn't deny anything now. Con had only to look to see Ryder was completely in love with Kinsey. Kinsey, for her part, was harder to decipher. Which surprised Con. Mortals rarely did that to him.

Kinsey wasn't thrilled at being held at Dreagan, nor did she appreciate being used by someone at Kyvor to get her there. Yet she was more than willing to help them learn who was behind it.

She reminded him of Elena and Denae. Both situations had turned out to the benefit of Dreagan and the Kings, but Con had a bad feeling about this time. There were too many variables that were unknown, and there were also too many players now.

The most troubling bit was that he and the other Kings couldn't defend Dreagan as they normally would with MI5 patrolling twenty-four hours a day, seven days a week.

Con's thoughts went back to Kinsey. Ryder had notified him through their mental link that none of Kinsey's tech had been corrupted in any way.

Everything was clean from her purse, the bag with all her tech, and even her car. The only thing Con hadn't checked out was Kinsey herself.

Ryder assured him that she wasn't an actress, but

humans could pick up all kinds of skills quickly when it suited them. Who was to say that Kinsey wasn't using Ryder?

Con set down his favorite pen before he broke it. The Kings had been fortunate so far in that all of their mates accepted who they were and what it meant to be a Dragon King's woman.

Had their luck finally run out? Had Kinsey been sent there to betray Ryder much like what had almost happened to Ulrik?

The thought froze Con's heart. His Dragon Kings had all experienced war in its many aspects. They had all suffered loss—though some more than others. And they had all been devastated when their dragons were sent away.

Not to mention having to keep hidden from the world when they should be flying wherever they wished.

The Kings had been through too much already. There couldn't be another betrayal.

Con checked his watch and adjusted his cuff links, fingering the dragon-head design. Any moment now, he expected a visit from Ryder. Not because Con sent for him, but because Ryder would've already figured out what Con would want to do.

With Ryder's visit would come an argument in favor of Kinsey.

Con didn't intentionally set out to piss off his Kings, but they were each so caught up in what they were feeling at the moment that they didn't think ahead.

That's what he was for, and his decisions were rarely accepted eagerly. In most cases, there was a debate. It was imperative that the Kings stay banded together. They had been split once before, and it nearly destroyed them.

On that day, long ago, Con had put his pride away and

thought of their race. It won him back all the Kings but one—Ulrik. The weight of the entire dragon world rested on Con's shoulders.

There were times he strained under the burden. No one would ever know of those times. It would be used against him. It wasn't because he was afraid to show weakness. That he had revealed plenty of times.

No, this was about his strength to rule the Kings and keep everyone together. Every time a mortal joined the ranks, Con's job grew more difficult. At the rate the Kings were finding mates, they were going to have to take turns eating supper because not everyone would fit at the table.

A knock on his door broke into his thoughts. Con closed the file on his desk and set the bone-handled magnifying glass atop it. "Enter," he bade.

The door opened and Ryder with his blond hair and hazel eyes stepped into the office. He gave a nod to Con and closed the door behind him. "I'd like a word."

"I've been expecting you."

Ryder gave him a sly look. "So you think you know what I'll say?"

"I doona profess to know what you're thinking. Why no' just tell me. But first, who is with Kinsey?"

"Dmitri," Ryder answered.

Con laced his fingers over his stomach and jutted his chin to one of the leather chairs before his desk. "Sit down. Then tell me what it is you came to say."

"You're no' happy that she's here."

Con shrugged in response. "Of course no'. Someone sent her because of your involvement with her. And no' just because the two of you were lovers three years ago. This is because you shifted in Glasgow and she saw you."

"I know. I'm no' exactly thrilled with that," Ryder stated crossly.

"Someone was watching her, because they had a suspicion you would return. That means whoever saw the two of you together before you left knew it was something deep between both of you."

Ryder held his gaze. "You want to know if I'm in love with her?"

"I know you are." Con inhaled deeply. "You didna volunteer to go to Glasgow. I sent you there. Had I sent someone else, would you've asked to go instead?"

There was a long pause before Ryder said, "No."

"Why? You love her."

"I feared that I would see her. Then I feared that I might no'. I was terrified I'd find her dead body with Dark all around her."

Con studied Ryder as he spoke. He should've realized Ryder's affections were given to someone. Ryder was one of the few Kings who didn't actively go looking for a woman to warm their beds.

Ryder talked a big game, but he never carried through with any of the women.

"But you went, and you saved her," Con said. "Tell me why you left her."

Ryder's hazel eyes went hard. "No' for the reasons you think."

"You doona know what I'm thinking. I'd rather you just tell me."

"I left because I'd fallen in love, but as far as I knew, the spell you cast was still in place. I worried what you might do to her."

Con was appalled. Did his men think so little of him? "Because you fell in love? I vowed to protect the humans, Ryder. I sent our dragons away for them. Did you really think I'd harm her?"

"I wasna exactly thinking clearly."

So he came home. Con inwardly groaned, because that was around the time Cassie arrived, and Con had worked hard to put the spell back in place so Hal wouldn't love her. No wonder Ryder never said anything.

"Kinsey is here now. For good or bad, she's at Dreagan learning everything MI5 is searching for," Con said.

Ryder leaned forward in his chair and clasped his hands together as he rested his forearms on his knees. "I know her, Con."

"You knew her. Three years is a long time in a human's life. Anything could've happened."

"I watched her."

Just as Con suspected. "Every moment of every day?"

"No."

"Did you see who she spent time with?"

Ryder swallowed. "Sometimes."

"What about the men she dates? She's a beautiful woman who is smart and gifted in her field. Women like her doona stay single long."

Ryder grew very still, his anger obvious. "You know I saw the men she dated."

"I'd wager no' all of them. Did you see what she did on the dates?"

"No," Ryder stated in a hard voice.

"Which means you can no' attest to her character now. You knew her better than anyone at one time, but that doesna translate to the here and now."

Ryder blew out a breath and leaned back in the chair. "I could use her help searching for Ulrik and anyone else involved."

"She's that good?"

"Aye," Ryder affirmed.

Con had been considering this since he'd learned of her arrival. If he separated Ryder and Kinsey, Ryder would get little work done because he'd be checking on Kinsey.

At least with them together, Ryder would watch over her. Hopefully his emotions wouldn't get in the way if he discovered her doing something she shouldn't.

"Nothing she brought in has been tampered with," Ryder said. "It's all clean."

"I find it interesting you didna say she was clean."

Ryder's face fell. "I can no' be sure that she's no'. She's no' even sure if she is. I willna know until I spend more time with her."

Con could see this taking a very bad turn. He leaned forward to rest his arms on his desk. "Do you know what you're agreeing to?"

"I do. I'll be the one held solely responsible if Kinsey does anything while under my watch."

Con shook his head. "I'd no' have that on your shoulders. What if there is magic used, and the only way to stop her is death?"

"Then I'll do it."

Con wasn't so sure Ryder could. However, he knew Ryder would do everything in his control to stop Kinsey. That alone was enough for him.

"Then I'll leave her in your care," Con relented.

Ryder's faced eased into relief. "You willna regret it."

Con prayed he didn't. It was bad enough that Kinsey had run from Ryder after seeing him shift. Ryder was a tough individual—all the Kings were. But they had their breaking points as well.

"Do you think you can earn her trust again?" Con asked.

Ryder gave a brief nod. "I believe so."

"Does she still care for you?"

"That I can no' say."

"Find out," Con ordered. "If she's afraid of you—us—then she may be using you to get close and attempt something."

Ryder lifted his chin. "No' Kinsey."

"Give me proof. I want to accept your word for it, Ryder, but with MI5 here, and Ulrik out doing God-knows-what, I have to be sure."

"Then you'll have your proof."

As Ryder walked out, Con prayed he didn't have to kill another mortal. The first one nearly did him in and lost him a best friend.

This one would lose him everything.

CHAPTER TEN

It usually took a lot for Kinsey to get as frustrated as she was at the moment. It had nothing to do with the equipment—because it was state of the art and gorgeous—and everything to do with not being about to find jack squat on Ulrik or his people.

"Ryder warned you."

"I beg your pardon?" Dmitri asked.

Kinsey threw him a quick smile. "Sorry. I tend to talk to myself sometimes."

"You're looking up Ulrik. Ryder does that daily and rarely finds anything."

Daily? Holy shit. And here Kinsey thought she had some new moves that would show her more and impress Ryder. She was out of luck this time. "Oh."

"Doona be alarmed, lass. We've been doing this sort of thing for years. At least now we doona have to physically watch him. I like the cameras for that reason alone."

Kinsey stretched her arms over her head and rotated her neck from side to side. She had been sitting for so long that she needed to move around and get the blood flowing.

She stood and walked to the window. The snow was falling heavily now, covering the slopes of the mountains in white. It looked magical, as if she were in a different world. And in some aspects, she was.

After a few more stretches, Kinsey remained at the window simply taking in the majestic, wild beauty that was Dreagan. If she peered far to the left she could see the pasture where the cattle were. There were sheep seemingly everywhere.

No one would ever know this splendor was behind all the buildings housing the distillery. Even the manor was hidden, keeping another wall up between the Dragon Kings and the humans.

"What do you see?" Ryder asked as he walked up next to her.

She smiled as she folded her arms over her chest. "I see land that's been sustained and preserved as beautifully as it must have been thousands of years ago."

"And?" he pushed.

He'd always been able to tell when there was more she wanted to say. Kinsey looked at the mountains all around them. "I see a land that shouldn't be sullied by humans. I see a home."

"It is a home," Ryder said. "It's our home. It's the only place left on this realm that we claim as ours."

Her people had taken the rest. Kinsey couldn't imagine how that felt, and she didn't pretend to. "You have every right to protect it." She faced him then, realizing that Dmitri had exited the room without a word. "Even if it's from me."

His dark blond brows rose high in his forehead. "What does that mean?"

"You know exactly what it means. Ryder, if somehow your enemies are using me, then I want to know in what capacity, and I want it stopped. If we can't stop it, then you must."

He held her gaze for long moments. "It willna come to that."

She really hoped it didn't. "What did Con have to say?"

"Did Dmitri tell you where I was?" he asked with a sigh.

"I figured it out."

Ryder clasped his hands behind his back. "Con is thinking of all of us Dragon Kings and the mates and Dreagan when he makes a decision. That doesna always mean the decisions are good."

"Meaning?"

"I knew he'd want to isolate you in case Ulrik has somehow manipulated you to help him. I convinced Con to allow you to remain with me."

"Is that wise?" she asked. "I mean, if Ulrik or his people somehow did get to me. Wouldn't that put you in a difficult position?"

Ryder walked around her to his chair. He flipped the lid on the box and grabbed a donut. Before taking a bite, he said, "Working side by side, I can monitor you closely."

Too damn closely for her peace of mind. She'd managed to keep her hands to herself so far, but how much longer could she do that with Ryder so temptingly close?

And that boyish smile? She had missed that so much. With as slow as it was gaining any information on Ulrik, she could be there for days. Weeks. Months, even.

There's no way she could keep her indifference together that long. She didn't want Ryder to know that she still pined for him. That would be disastrous. Especially since he'd so easily left her the first time.

Somehow she would have to hold it together. After all, she'd spent the last three years without him. It had been a little easier because he wasn't in the same room with her just feet away talking to her, smiling at her . . . looking at her.

There had been a few opportunities for her to move on with her life. She'd met a couple of men who would've been good for her, but none of them compared to Ryder.

Now she knew why.

No mortal man could compete with a Dragon King.

Kinsey returned to her chair and sat. Then she grabbed the table and pulled the chair forward. She had to talk, to take her mind off wanting Ryder. "I don't think Ulrik is in Perth. None of the CCTV cameras have spotted him."

Ryder pointed to the screen to his far left. All the cameras were pointed at different angles, front and back, to a business called The Silver Dragon. "That's Ulrik's business. People have been visiting it all day. He's there."

"How do you know?"

"Because that's where he spends most of his time. Though he has been known to slip out on occasion."

Kinsey looked at the antiques store. "When was the last time you spoke to Ulrik?"

"Before he was stripped of his magic and banished from Dreagan."

"Oh. So just a couple million years or so, right?"

Ryder chuckled. "Right."

"Have none of you tried talking to him?"

"Aye. A few of us, but it doesna do any good. Ulrik willna be dissuaded from his path."

Kinsey looked at one of the pictures of Ulrik. He was in a black suit and pale gray shirt. He didn't wear a tie, preferring to leave the dress shirt unbuttoned at the top.

His black hair was pulled back in a queue, and his gold gaze was directed off to the left.

The people on the sidewalk gave him a wide berth, as if they sensed the lethal, caged animal within. He didn't have what she would call a cruel expression, just one that let others know he wasn't to be trifled with for any reason.

She couldn't imagine how it felt to have the one place she had always called home forbidden to her. How that must sting. But it couldn't be as bad as having those she considered her family turn their backs on her.

"I wonder if I'd feel differently in his place," Kinsey said. "We're talking millions of years walking around as a human. The very beings he blames for everything. That was beyond cruel."

Ryder made a sound at the back of his throat. "We couldna allow him to shift, Kins. He'd kill humans."

"But to take away the one thing he was?" she asked as she slid her gaze to Ryder. "How would you feel if you were unable to shift?"

"All Dragon Kings are essentially grounded right now with MI5 on the property. We know exactly how Ulrik feels."

"So you don't shift at all?"

He looked away briefly. "We go into the mountain when we need to be in our true forms."

It's what she'd thought. "I'm not trying to take Ulrik's side. I'm only attempting to sort through all of this."

"There's nothing to sort through," he stated tersely. "You were no' there. You didna see the slaughter of our dragons or watch them leave this realm, possibly forever. If Ulrik had only stopped killing mortals it might no' have come to that."

Kinsey turned back to her screen. She hadn't meant to upset Ryder, and he was right. She hadn't been there.

However, that didn't mean she couldn't see when something was wrong.

Had the Kings been wrong to banish Ulrik?

Possibly.

Had they been erroneous in binding his magic?

Not at the time, no.

Had they been mistaken in keeping him away from Dreagan and all those who could possibly help mend the hate within him?

Definitely.

But she couldn't tell Ryder that. He wouldn't wish to hear it. None of the Dragon Kings would. Not to mention Kinsey wasn't all fired up to piss off men who could shift into massive beasts who breathed fire. So, she would keep her thoughts to herself.

She decided to pretend Ryder wasn't there. It was easier than thinking of how she missed the way he used to move her hair off one shoulder and kiss the spot toward the back of her neck.

Kinsey found a file labeled ULRIK_SCOTLAND. She opened it to find a map of Scotland. There were red dots, like little pins, that showed all the places Ulrik had been seen. Edinburgh was a favorite destination, as evidenced by the large red dot.

With it being in close proximity to Perth, it was no wonder why. Kinsey then used the code Ryder had written to hack into the CCTV throughout Edinburgh. While a scan began to run looking for Ulrik, she dug deeper into the file folder labeled ULRIK.

Inside, she found a spreadsheet titled EDINBURGH. Kinsey opened it and gaped at the places Ulrik had visited. For all the eyes watching him, the man—or Dragon—was good at hiding. There were only a handful of listings in Edinburgh, and most of them were restaurants.

With a stroke of a key, Kinsey moved to another monitor and began to go down the list of known places Ulrik favorited. Another hack into the cameras of the restaurants and cafes, and she was able to look for Ulrik. Even though Ryder was sure Ulrik was at his business, Kinsey would rather have definitive proof of that, and since they didn't, she opted to search.

One by one, she ticked off the list with no sign of Ulrik. The CCTV scan of Edinburgh would take hours yet with the size of the city and the numerous cameras.

The world and room faded away while Kinsey focused on one city to the next in Scotland. She at first kept her focus on the largest cities, even if there was no record from the Kings that Ulrik had been there.

When she exhausted all those searches, Kinsey sat back and waited for the CCTV search in Edinburgh to complete. A glance at her watch showed it was nearly seven in the evening. It had been well over eight hours since she'd eaten.

Now that she noticed the time, she realized how hungry she was. And she went from starving to nauseous in a split second from not eating. How Kinsey hated her body sometimes.

She swallowed, wishing she had something to drink. Her mouth was dry, and it might help to calm her rioting stomach. With Ryder engrossed in his own search, she was loath to disturb him.

So she closed her eyes to try and fight her rumbling stomach. Every few minutes she would crack open her eyes to check the progress of the search. And each time grew more and more difficult.

"Kins?"

How wonderful it sounded to have Ryder's voice in her ear again. It made Kinsey think back to the days before he'd left her. How they would wake up in each other's arms in the mornings before one of them would start cooking breakfast while the other made tea.

It had felt like a marriage. It *had* been a marriage, of sorts. And she missed it so much it left a hole within her.

"Kins," he said again.

"Five more minutes," she said and turned her head the other way.

There was a soft chuckle, and then it felt as if she were being lifted. Kinsey woke up enough to realize that she was no longer in her chair.

She was in Ryder's arms.

The joy was quickly swept aside as the pain set in. She couldn't allow herself to get close to him again.

She pushed against him as he was walking down the corridor. Kinsey managed to get out of his arms and stumble until she righted herself. "What are you doing?"

"Taking you to bed."

The images those words conjured were a hazard to her health. Kinsey lifted her chin. "Just point me in the right direction."

"You should've told me you were sleepy," Ryder said as he began walking.

Kinsey followed him since she didn't have another choice. He took her past the stairs, and then to the right along another hallway, this one narrower.

Ryder finally stopped at a door and opened it. Then he stepped aside and motioned for her to enter with his arm. Kinsey walked past him into the room and sighed with pleasure at the sight of the bed.

She walked over and climbed onto it, falling on her

stomach with one arm hanging off the side. Her eyes closed. She briefly thought about telling Ryder to leave, but it took too much effort.

Tomorrow she would do a better job of erecting a barrier around her heart. Though she feared it might already be too late for her.

Again.

CHAPTER ELEVEN

A Tropical Island
Location Unknown

Rhi lay on her back beneath the stars with the water lapping at her feet. Beside her was Balladyn. Her best friend from long ago—and her enemy.

And apparently, now her lover.

It had been so long since she'd given herself to another that she'd feared she might forget how. But Balladyn hadn't let her.

He slept with his face turned toward her. In sleep, he was relaxed, the concerns and lines of worry were gone. Leaving nothing but the visage of the man she used to follow with her brother.

Rhi softly touched his cheek and smoothed a finger over one black brow. Her heart caught as she recalled looking into his eyes—eyes that had been silver. Not the red she was used to seeing after he'd turned Dark, but silver.

There was no denying it. At first she'd thought it was her own passion playing tricks on her, but each time she looked at him, Balladyn stared back with the silver eyes of a Light Fae.

Rhi sat up and brought her legs to her chest. She

wrapped her arms around them and rested her chin on her knees while she stared out over the moon-drenched water.

After years of pining for her Dragon King lover who had so easily—and cruelly—tossed her aside, Rhi felt a piece of herself mend.

It was a tiny piece, infinitesimal to the multitude of pieces that was her heart. But it was still a piece.

To be loved so thoroughly made her sigh. There was no doubt Balladyn was an excellent lover. It made Rhi smile as she recalled how completely and utterly he'd loved her.

She'd almost forgotten how it felt to be wanted so desperately, to be desired so fiercely. Now that she remembered, she was going to make certain to never forget again.

All those thousands of years longing for a Dragon King infuriated her. He'd made her look like a fool, but it was her own fault for believing his words of love and forever.

But lies came easily to him.

Rhi refused to dwell any more on him. He'd nearly ruined her chances of finding happiness, and the sad part was that she'd almost let him. But not anymore.

It brought to mind her watcher. He stood behind and to the right. He'd become such a constant that she found herself relying on him—a dangerous thing. Especially since she didn't know why he was following her, or even how he was able to follow her as he did. Nor did she know his name.

He was Fae. Of that she was sure. Light or Dark though, that was the question. If he worked for Balladyn, then her watcher would've left when Balladyn arrived. But he'd remained.

She turned her head to look in his direction. He was constantly veiled, which took an incredible amount of power. Rhi knew because she was able to do the same. The only other Fae who could hold a veil that long was Usaeil, Queen of the Light.

As a previous member of the Queen's Guard, Rhi knew none of them could remain veiled for more than a couple of minutes at a time. Unless they hid the ability, much as she had.

Balladyn's hand touched her lower back right before his Irish accent filled her ears. "What's on your mind, pet?"

"Nothing," she said and once more looked at the ocean.

"Liar." There was no heat in his words as he sat up beside her. "Tell me you don't regret this."

Rhi looked at him and smiled, even as sadness filled her when she saw his red eyes once more. "I don't regret this."

"But you're not happy about it either."

"That's not true," she said and turned toward him.

Balladyn touched a strand of her black hair near her face. "I've wanted you for so long. I told myself I'd wait for you to come to me, but I couldn't."

"If I didn't want what happened between us, I would've stopped it," she assured him.

"Aye," he said with a nod. "But was it really me you wanted?"

Rhi gawked at him. Was he serious? Yes, he most certainly was. "Yes, Balladyn. It was you I wanted."

"Then why are you so sad?"

She swallowed and looked down as his hand took hers, their fingers lacing together. "For a long time I fooled everyone into thinking I had my life under control. It's all been a lie. When you captured me and tortured me—"

"I'm sorry," he interrupted her.

Rhi paused. The depth of sadness in his words touched her deeply. "Something snapped inside me. Suddenly there was this darkness that felt like it was swallowing my light."

"That's my fault," Balladyn said and looked away, desolation lining his face.

Rhi didn't deny the statement.

"I wish I could undo it all."

She put her other hand atop their joined ones. "I don't. Because of that time I discovered new power within me. Perhaps it was always there and just needed a reason to break loose."

Balladyn's gaze swung back to her. "You would've found that power eventually. I don't like knowing I hurt you."

"My life is more out of control now than ever before. I don't know which way is up anymore. I feel like I'm falling, and I'm desperately trying to grab ahold of something."

"Then hold onto me," Balladyn said.

She looked into his red eyes, his plea reflected there. Rhi didn't know what the future held, nor did she try and find out. What she did know was that having Balladyn by her side was what she wanted. "I won't turn Dark."

"I know."

"But you want to rule the Dark. This will never work between us."

"Why not give it a try and see?" he asked. "We'll never know if we don't try."

Rhi lowered her gaze to the white sand. "If anyone ever discovers us, it won't be good."

"Are you frightened of what the Dragon Kings might say?" he asked in a hard voice.

Her eyes jerked to him. "No. But some of them are my friends, and if they need me, I'll be there for them."

"And your King?"

Rhi was thankful Balladyn didn't say his name. "He hasn't been mine in eons. He's already moved on."

Balladyn searched her eyes. "Have you?"

"Yes."

He leaned forward and gently placed his lips on hers. Then he rested his forehead against hers and sighed. "I've loved you for so long that I feared this would never come to pass. Now that I've had you and tasted you, I'll never get enough."

Rhi closed her eyes and smiled, even though her heart was heavy. She didn't understand the feeling, nor could she discern what was causing it.

"You're all mine now," Balladyn whispered.

Rhi's smile grew. "Yes, I am. And you're mine."

"Nothing will ever tear us apart."

She lifted her head to look into his eyes. There, just around the edges, the red was fading to a brilliant silver. Rhi didn't mention it. Whatever it was that pulled Balladyn back to the light was enough for her.

Balladyn went to kiss her again, when he turned his head to the side and let out a string of curses.

"What is it?" Rhi asked worriedly.

He blew out a breath. "Taraeth is calling for me."

"Then go," she urged. "You're his right hand, Balladyn. Remain that way."

"Just until I take over as King."

She gripped his hand when he got to his feet. As she looked up at him, she hated the fear that suddenly enveloped her. "Be careful."

"Always."

"You don't have to be king of the Dark."

He squatted in front of her, a half grin in place. "I most certainly do, my love."

With a wink, he was gone.

Rhi dropped her hand to the sand. She'd known something was developing between her and Balladyn. He'd professed his love earlier, and she had kissed him a few times.

It was how she found herself thinking of him more and more that pushed her to consider letting go of the past and her Dragon King lover. Before her stood a Fae who was willing to do whatever it took to have her.

Why should she pine for a King who would never give her the time of day again? She'd wasted thousands of years on him. She deserved happiness, to be loved and worshipped, and to have a future.

Rhi stood. Behind her, she felt her watcher's eyes on her. She didn't bother to put clothes on. He'd seen all there was to see of her.

For far too long she'd felt the need to hide herself—her feelings, her wants and desires, dreams and wishes. No longer. She was done pretending. Whether anyone liked it or not, this was who she was.

Daire couldn't take his eyes from Rhi. She was stunning, standing glorious in the moonlight. The breeze lifted her long hair so that it billowed out behind her, as if reaching for him. She stood straight and tall at the foot of the ocean.

Her bronze skin glowed a soft blue from the light of the moon. The only sound was the waves crashing onto shore and the palm trees swaying.

Rhi hadn't spoken since Balladyn's departure. Though Daire smiled when she turned to look his way. She knew he was still there, and she didn't seem to mind.

"Are you judging me?" she asked softly.

Daire knew the question was directed at him. He didn't like that she'd chosen Balladyn, but he understood why. Rhi was like any woman. She needed love and attention. She needed to know that someone wanted and desired her, that someone yearned for her and loved her.

She hadn't gotten it from her Dragon King. It was time she received that attention from someone. Daire wished it had been him, though it was forbidden.

None of the Reapers could have relationships. Well . . . that was the rule since Death created them—until recently.

He wasn't jealous of Baylon and Jordyn's happiness. In fact, he was glad that one of the Reapers had found some. Jordyn, a half-Fae, was now a Reaper herself, which allowed her and Baylon to be together.

Daire was fine desiring Rhi from afar. She was someone he could never have, and not even Baylon's coupling could give him hope that he might get the same.

Never, he answered Rhi in his mind. It wasn't his right to judge her—not after all he'd done.

He couldn't talk to her, wouldn't talk to her. Nor was he allowed to show himself. His orders were to follow her wherever she went and determine who she was allied with.

Death saw Rhi as someone important in the upcoming battle, and Daire had to agree. The more he was around Rhi, the more he saw the powerful magic within her.

She might not always make the right decisions, but who did? No one was perfect. What kept Rhi off kilter was the love she had held onto for ages. However, it appeared she was letting go once and for all of whatever hope she had of a life with a Dragon King.

It was the right move, of that Daire was positive. What

that would mean for everyone else though, remained to be seen. He didn't think Rhi knew her potential. Yet.

Once she did, it would change the entire landscape of the current war.

Daire walked to stand beside her. He was close enough to touch, but he kept his hands to himself. His gaze slid to the side and looked at her pink-tipped nipples and taut breasts.

He'd seen her being goofy. He'd seen her focused as she shopped for shoes. He'd witnessed her mellow as she got her nails done.

He'd seen her joy, her pain . . . and her sorrow.

He had witnessed her bravery in battle, and her skill with a sword. He'd watched, mesmerized, as she put herself in harm's way just to help a friend.

It wasn't surprising she was the only female in Fae history to join the Queen's Guard. And she had been one of the very few who walked away from such an honor.

No wonder Death took an interest in Rhi.

CHAPTER TWELVE

Ryder stood and watched Kinsey. The minutes ticked by as she slept the sleep of the dead. She'd always had the ability to be able to sleep anywhere, anytime. And once asleep, she was hard to wake.

He briefly thought about taking off her boots, but her reaction when she found him carrying her kept him at the door.

When he lifted her in his arms in the computer room, it had felt as if he finally had what was missing from his life. He'd simply held her as she rested her head on his shoulder, savoring the moment.

It had felt like heaven. Ryder even contemplated lying next to her in bed. Then she had lifted her head and jumped out of his arms as if he were some monster.

Except to her, he was.

And that's what hurt the most.

Ryder looked to the side when he felt someone approach. Dmitri said nothing as he peered inside the room. Ryder knew he should shut the door and back away, but he couldn't make his feet move.

"If you want her, fight for her," Dmitri said.

Ryder wished it were that simple. "She's terrified of me."

"She didna look too scared earlier when the two of you were talking."

"That is until she remembers what I am."

"Then show her she has nothing to be afraid of," Dmitri said, as if the solution was so simple even an idiot could figure it out.

Ryder glanced at the ceiling in frustration. Then he said, "I left her."

"That makes you a proper bastard then."

Leave it to Dmitri to state it so succinctly. "Aye," Ryder said. "It does."

"The two of you had something special. Find it again."

"She's moved on with her life."

Dmitri snorted loudly and glared at Ryder. "She doesna have a man. That tells me you still have a chance."

Did he? Ryder wasn't so sure. "You didna see the way she looked at me when I shifted. Or hear her scream."

"Give her some slack. She was in a war zone, Ryder."

"Just now she practically flew out of my arms when she woke to find me carrying her."

At that, Dmitri twisted his lips. "You might have more work than I expected. But answer me this, do you want her?"

"Aye."

"Do you love her?"

Ryder nodded. "Verra much so."

"Is she worth fighting for?"

"In every way."

Dmitri slapped him on the back. "Then that is what you need to do. Now. Get your ugly arse in there and remove her boots while I get some food for her."

"Food?" Had Ryder forgotten to feed her?

Dmitri rolled his eyes. "I knew you'd forget. You become focused on those damn computers, and you ignore everything else."

"No' everything," Ryder mumbled as Dmitri walked away.

Ryder slowly moved into his room. He hadn't known where else to take Kinsey. As he walked around the four-poster bed stained so dark it was nearly black, he imagined crawling into his bed and having Kinsey curl up next to him like they used to sleep.

It was a fantasy of his from the first time they'd made love. Once he returned to Dreagan and took a look at his bed, it had been impossible to sleep there and not think of her. Which is why he hadn't used his bed in three years.

One of her feet was hanging off the side of the bed. He tenderly grasped one leg and unzipped the boot before tugging it off. He repeated the process on her second foot before placing the boots beside the chair.

Next, he gently gave her a nudge at her side. Kinsey immediately rolled over, allowing him to tug down the comforter.

When he saw her blazer, he knew he had to remove it. Ryder grasped the hem at her wrist and pulled upward at the same time he got her to turn back onto her stomach. One arm fell out of the jacket.

It took some doing to get her other arm from beneath her so he could tug it free. Ryder then folded the blazer and laid it over the back of the chair.

He turned back to her and had the urge to sink his fingers into her wealth of dark hair. It was so silky smooth that he'd never tired of touching it.

It wasn't just her hair he longed to touch. It was her.

All of her. To have held her, and had her all to himself for a year had been the most amazing time.

If only he could reverse time and remain with her. If only he had known Ulrik broke the spell binding their feelings. If only he had returned to her after Hal and Cassie fell in love.

If only he'd had the courage to embrace the love he felt.

But love—the soul-deep, life-altering emotion—was new for him. It had terrified Ryder, especially since he was the one always in control.

Computers—or any electronics—were easy to manipulate and get to do what you wanted. Ryder was at ease around them. Mostly because they did whatever he wanted.

His feelings for Kinsey, however, were completely out of his control. He couldn't get a handle on them. Even now, years later, he felt as if he was just learning to walk again.

Kinsey was unpredictable and stubborn. She was wildly seductive without even trying. She twisted his insides until he wasn't sure which way was up. All Ryder knew was that with her beside him, the future didn't look so bleak.

"Kinsey," he whispered and touched her hair.

He shouldn't have dared even that, because now he couldn't walk away. Ryder rubbed his jaw as he contemplated an idea. With as hard as Kinsey slept, she'd never know if he climbed into bed with her.

And he'd be gone long before she woke.

Dmitri walked in at that moment with a tray. There was a covered plate and a bottle of water. He set it on the table near the fireplace and straightened. Then Dmitri looked from Ryder to Kinsey before he turned on his heel and left the room without a word.

Ryder closed the door after him so no one else would disturb them. Then he returned to the bed and rolled Kinsey into his arms so he could lay her head on the pillow.

She sighed contentedly, making his balls tighten.

He should leave. It was the right thing to do. Kinsey was frightened of him, of who he was. She didn't want him touching her or even being too close. It didn't seem right to secretly sleep next to her.

Why then was he walking to the other side of the bed?

Ryder sat down on the mattress and kicked off his boots. He lay back on the bed to stare at the ceiling. This might be the closest he'd ever come to being in his bed with Kinsey.

That thought made his chest ache so badly he rubbed it with his hand. How could he have screwed this up so royally with Kinsey? If only she hadn't seen him shift there might still be a chance between them.

To his surprise, Kinsey suddenly rolled over and snuggled against him. Ryder pulled her closer before he tugged the blankets over her.

He closed his eyes and put every detail to memory. The sound of her even breathing, the feel of her hand on his chest, the warmth of her body.

He wished he had gotten beneath the covers with her, but this was all he dared. Nothing was going to happen. No matter how much he might want it.

Kinsey was a kindhearted person. She didn't hold a grudge long, but then again, he had left her. As well as not mentioning what he really was.

Yet there had been something profound and deep between them. Looking back, he thought she might have been falling in love with him.

If she cared for him once, she could again. It just depended on how far Ryder was willing to go for her.

Besides, Dmitri was right. She was worth fighting for.

Ryder tucked his free arm behind his head and smiled.

Kinsey woke famished. She rolled onto her back and rubbed her eyes. Her stomach was rumbling fiercely. She wondered if she could get to the kitchen without running into anyone when she turned her head and spotted the tray.

She jerked upright and yanked the covers off before jumping out of bed. Kinsey opened the bottle of water and downed half of it. Then she took the lid off the plate and gazed at the array of bread, crackers, and cheese. Without hesitation she began to eat.

After the entire plate was cleaned, she realized her boots were carefully placed beside the chair she was sitting on. Since she couldn't remember taking them off, she wondered who did.

Was it Ryder?

A shiver raced over her as she imagined him touching her without her knowing it. If he was going to place his hands on her, she wanted to be awake so she could remember it.

She looked down at her white T-shirt. Where was her blazer? Kinsey rose and turned around, looking for it. She spied it on the back of the chair.

Someone had obviously undressed her that far. She might not toss them on the floor, but she certainly didn't take that kind of care with her clothes.

Ryder.

She recalled how meticulous he could be with his things. He must have removed her blazer and boots. And she slept through it all.

Kinsey hurried back to the bed and looked to see if there was evidence that he'd stayed with her, but the other pillow had no indentation on it.

She should be thrilled about that. Why then was she disappointed?

You don't want him, remember, she told herself. *He's bad for me.*

Ryder made her forget everything but him. All she cared about was being with him, sharing her life with him. It had taken her forever to remember the person she had been before him, and she didn't want to go down that path again.

A knock at the door startled her. She took a deep breath before she padded across the wood floor and the thick rug to the door. She cracked it open and stared into hazel eyes.

"Good morning," Ryder said with a warm smile. "Did you sleep well?"

She stepped back to open the door wider and quickly smoothed down her hair. "Yeah. Oh, and good morning."

"I see you found the tray. I apologize for no' getting you food yesterday."

Kinsey crossed her arms over her chest and put some distance between them. "I should've said something."

"Next time, please do."

"I will," she promised.

They stared at each other in silence. She liked the shadow of a beard on his face. It made him look even more devilishly handsome.

Damn him. Couldn't he look horrible, just once?

But she knew for a fact he always looked this good.

"There's a bathroom behind you," Ryder said as he pointed over her shoulder. "You should find everything you need there."

She nodded. "My bag?"

"In the room as well."

He started to leave, then hesitated. Ryder turned his

head to her. "I doona want you to be scared of me, Kins. I'm the man you knew before. I'm just . . . something more as well."

"But I didn't know you before. You kept this from me."

"It was our rule. We told no one. You'd still be ignorant of it if that Dark hadna attacked you."

She licked her lips. "I told you everything about me. I held nothing back. You held everything."

"I told you all that I could."

"Which was very little. Was anything you told me the truth? What about your parents? Did they really live in the mountains?"

"What I told you about my family was the truth. I merely left out that they were dragons."

That still didn't make up for the other secrets he'd kept. And Kinsey didn't even know why they were discussing it. There wasn't going to be anything between them again. If all Ryder wanted was for her to say she wasn't afraid, then she could do that.

"I'm not scared of you."

Sadness flashed in his eyes before he turned away. "I'll be in the computer room when you're finished here."

She watched him walk out, wondering why he was so upset. He'd asked for something, and she gave it. That should be enough. But she knew it wasn't.

Kinsey dropped her arms and turned around. She found the bathroom and locked the door behind her. As she was turning the water on for a shower, it hit her that she really was in a bad situation.

At least she knew Ryder. How much more awful would it be if she didn't know anyone? It was because of her affiliation with Ryder that she was even in this situation. That should infuriate her.

Instead, it just made her miserable.

It was another reminder that she was alone. The one man who had been her everything turned out to be something else completely.

She removed her clothes. Just before she stepped into the shower, she saw herself in the mirror and the tears that were falling down her cheeks.

It had been well over a year since she cried for what she'd had with Ryder. Being with him brought it all back, shoving it in her face as if it had just happened yesterday.

How in the world would she ever be able to get through it? She wasn't that strong. When it came to Ryder she was as weak as a newborn kitten.

She stepped into the shower, putting her face to the water. The first thing she had to do was wipe away the tears as if they never existed.

CHAPTER THIRTEEN

Ryder stared at the computer screen without seeing it. Kinsey's unexpected—and entirely too quick—assurance that she wasn't frightened of him told him that she was still very much afraid.

He leaned forward, rubbing his eyes with his thumb and forefinger. With a shift of his feet, he rolled his chair to the left and focused on a monitor that was running more extensive searches for Ulrik.

"You look like hell," Dmitri said as he handed a mug of coffee to Ryder.

Ryder merely shrugged and gratefully accepted the drink. He hastily took a sip.

"Where is Kinsey?"

"Showering, I assume," Ryder replied.

Dmitri sat in the chair Kinsey had used the day before. "Did you tell her where the kitchen was so she could eat?"

Ryder shoved back his chair and stalked from the room, furious that he'd forgotten something so important.

He was so wrapped up in his feelings for Kinsey that he repeatedly forgot basic things that she needed—like food.

He made his way to his room and lifted his hand to knock. Then he hesitated. The only way for her to stop fearing him was by being with him more, and seeing that he was just the same as he once was.

Ryder rapped his knuckles on the door. A moment later it opened to reveal Kinsey. She wore a pair of black jeans and a V-neck burgundy sweater that hugged her breasts. She walked to the chair and sat to put on her boots.

"I'm here to bring you to the kitchen," Ryder said. "I figured you might still be hungry."

She zipped her shoes and stood. "I'm famished."

"Follow me," he said and turned on his heel.

They walked side by side to the stairs. Her hair was down and she wore no makeup, just as he liked it. Kinsey pushed up the sleeves of her sweater to her elbows and kept her face straight ahead, though he could see her gaze darting about at all the dragons decorating the manor.

"There's always plenty of food in the kitchen," Ryder said, hoping to make her feel welcome. "The mates make sure of it."

"Mates?" Kinsey repeated.

"Some of the Dragon Kings have found wives. We doona have wedding ceremonies exactly. The women and the Kings are mated for eternity."

Kinsey descended the last stair. "How many mates are here?"

Ryder kept walking as he said, "Let's see. There's Cassie, Elena, Jane, Denae, Sammi, Shara, Iona, Lily, Darcy, Grace, Lexi, and Sophie."

"Twelve," Kinsey said with a nod. "And Con allowed all of them to be mated?"

"Con might be King of Kings, but he can no' stop a King from falling in love."

"Really?" she asked acridly.

Ryder could've kicked himself. He stopped at the doorway of the kitchen and motioned Kinsey inside. "I think Lexi and Elena have been cooking all morning."

Kinsey took a deep breath before licking her lips as if she couldn't decide where she wanted to start first.

"About time you brought her to us," Lexi said as she closed the refrigerator and set the orange juice on the table. "Hi, Kinsey. I'm Lexi. One of the newest women at Dreagan."

The two shook hands. Kinsey's smile was open and welcoming. "Hello. Are you from America?"

"South Carolina. It's my Southern accent that tipped you off, huh?" Lexi asked with a grin and got a couple of glasses down. A moment later and the smile was gone. "One of my best friends was killed by a Dark Fae in Edinburgh. Idiot that I was, I thought I could track him down myself. Thorn saved my hide several times. I, of course, was too much of a temptation and he fell in love with me," Lexi finished with a wink.

Kinsey chuckled. "You're making light of what sounds like a dangerous situation."

Lexi's demeanor became serious. "I tease and joke because it helps. We're at war. But yes, it was a harrowing adventure, and I thank God every day that Thorn came into my life."

Ryder watched the exchange with interest. He hadn't thought about Kinsey interacting with the mates as a means to help change her mind about him, which was stupid on his part.

Who better to convince Kinsey he wasn't a bad guy than the other mates who'd gone through something similar?

"I heard my name," Thorn said as he walked into the kitchen and immediately went to Lexi. They kissed and shared private words before Thorn turned to Kinsey. "You're the talk of Dreagan."

"Am I?" Kinsey asked, glancing at Ryder.

Ryder handed a plate to Kinsey and urged her to choose from the selection of eggs, bacon, sausage, pancakes, and donuts. He shot a glance at Thorn, hoping he would take the hint and talk about something else.

"That's right," Thorn said as he took a chair at the table. "We're all verra curious, lass. It's no' every day we get to meet someone Ryder knows."

Ryder looked at the ceiling and prayed for patience. When he lowered his gaze he saw a look pass between Thorn and Lexi. Ryder didn't even want to know what that was about.

"So he doesn't get out much?" Kinsey asked nonchalantly.

Ryder found his focus on her—as it always seemed to be. He watched the way she piled a little of everything onto her plate before walking to the table and taking the seat across from Thorn.

"You can say that," Thorn said with a smile as he rested his arms on the table.

Ryder looked to Lexi for help, but she threw up her hands, telling him he was on his own as she turned away to get coffee for Thorn.

"Hmm." Kinsey poured some OJ into her glass before reaching for the syrup and drowning her pancake in it.

Ryder rolled his eyes and leaned back against the wall. "I suppose you all are having fun?"

"You know, he's a right genius when it comes to those computers," Thorn stated, as if Ryder hadn't spoken. "We all have our talents, but I doona know how he does what he does."

Kinsey chewed a bit and swallowed as she regarded Thorn. "A genius, huh?"

"Doona tell him I said that."

She gave a little snort. "You don't have to worry about that. I think he already believes it."

Ryder pushed away from the wall. "Right here. Right. Bloody. Here."

Lexi laughed as she came to stand beside him. She leaned close and whispered, "It's not worth it. Thorn has an objective. You know how he gets when he sets his mind to something."

"Aye." Ryder grimaced when he saw Thorn's smile. Thorn could be at it awhile, and though Ryder could take whatever was dished, he thought Kinsey might like some time alone with Lexi and Thorn. "I'll be in my office."

Kinsey didn't so much as look up as he walked out. Ryder tried not to feel the hurt that caused. It was as if he mattered less than a flea.

What did he expect after the way he'd left her? Then showing up during the Fae attack and shifting? He'd always thought he was intelligent, but every time he was around Kinsey he felt like a fool.

He was constantly saying or doing the wrong thing, even when he tried to do something right. Why was it so difficult? It wasn't that he was uncomfortable around her. Quite the opposite, actually.

No, his problem was that he was trying so hard to impress her and make her look at him as she used to that he looked like a wanker.

Ryder made his way back to the third floor and the computer room. But as he sat in front of the monitors, for the first time in a very long time, he didn't care what they showed him.

All that mattered was the woman in the kitchen and the love within his heart.

He squeezed his eyes closed and concentrated once more on finding a hint of where Ulrik was. So far, none of the scans across the entire United Kingdom had shown anything.

Ulrik could be out of the country. Knowing that—as well as Ulrik's affinity for the Dark Fae—Ryder focused on Ireland, which the Fae had proclaimed as their own.

While those scans ran, Ryder looked back through the last day they'd caught Ulrik on camera near his shop in Perth. It ran on fast-forward. As usual, there were the normal visitors who came to the antiques shop.

Ryder paused the recording and rewound it when he spotted a young woman in jeans, wearing a sweatshirt from the University of St. Andrews. With a backpack slung over one shoulder, she looked like any other student.

But there was something about the girl that caught Ryder's attention. The way she moved, the way she covertly took in everything.

He played the tape three times as she walked from the bus stop to the door of The Silver Dragon. It was the way the young woman looked around that troubled Ryder. He'd seen someone do that quite recently. And that someone was Henry North.

MI5 was known to recruit spooks at a very young age. Not to mention Ulrik's past connection to MI5 was also a sign.

Ryder fast-forwarded the recording to see how long the girl was in the store. Fifteen minutes later she emerged with the same backpack, but there was something different about it.

Now focused entirely, Ryder split the screen in half. On one side was the girl when she arrived at the store, and the other when she left.

Ryder rotated the image of her arriving and was able to take dimensions of the backpack. That's when he realized it was sitting higher on her shoulders because it was no longer weighted down by something.

He needed to find out who the girl was. While he ran facial recognition software on her, Ryder also sent her picture to Henry, their one ally within MI5.

Henry had long been a friend of Banan's, and during one harrowing battle with Ulrik, he had helped Banan rescue Jane in the middle of London.

From there, it hadn't taken long for Henry to learn who those at Dreagan really were. Henry helped them on multiple occasions after that. It was just a few months ago that he began living at the manor to help the Kings track the Dark Fae's movements all over the world.

Ryder set down his phone, thinking it would take Henry awhile to learn who the girl was, when Ryder's phone dinged.

He read the message twice he was so shocked.

HER NAME IS ESTHER. SHE'S MY SISTER.

CHAPTER FOURTEEN

Kinsey knew the moment Ryder left the kitchen. She no longer felt his presence, which made her feel . . . unprotected.

That couldn't be right. She feared him. Didn't she? Her feelings and her mind were all jumbled into a huge tangle that grew more convoluted as the minutes and hours passed. That's what made it all the more difficult to keep her distance from him.

"Do you hate him?"

Thorn's teasing words were gone. Kinsey lifted her eyes from her plate and met Thorn's dark ones. His deep brown hair was long and loose about his shoulders. There was no compassion in his gaze, only an intensity that told Kinsey to speak the truth at all costs.

"That's not easy to answer," she replied.

The chair between her and Thorn was pulled out as Lexi took a seat. Her slate gray eyes were filled with sympathy. She then tucked a strand of pale brown hair behind her ear. "It might seem like a difficult answer, but it's really not."

"You know what's going on," Thorn said as he sat back. "You saw it yourself in Glasgow. We willna have someone in our midst who is here to harm one of us."

Kinsey set down her fork, her appetite gone at his words. She gawked at him in wonder and stupidity. "That's a joke, right? You're dragons. You can shift. Who can harm who?"

"Kinsey," Lexi said and rested her hand atop hers. "What my husband is trying—badly—to say, is that though they're immortal Dragon Kings who can shift, their hearts are as delicate as ours."

"Now, sweetheart, I'm no' sure I'd use *delicate*," Thorn admonished.

Lexi raised a hand to quiet him without even looking his way. Kinsey watched in amusement as Thorn looked like a scolded toddler.

The silence in the kitchen extended. Kinsey felt like she was on trial of sorts. Which she had been since she first stepped foot onto Dreagan.

But this was different. This was focused on her feelings, feelings she herself hadn't dared to look too deep into because she was afraid of what she might find.

The truth was, even when she wanted to hate Ryder after he'd left her, she couldn't. She told herself she did in an effort to stop wondering about him. But it didn't work.

"I see," Thorn said in a low voice.

Kinsey jerked her gaze to him. "Excuse me?"

Thorn's look wasn't so fierce. "There's no hate in your heart for Ryder. You care for him."

"I *cared* for him. Past tense. He walked out on me."

"And he told you why."

Kinsey shrugged, annoyed that something so private was being discussed with strangers. "That's supposed to make it all better? That makes it worse, because he could've come back. He didn't."

"He was there to protect you recently."

At this, Kinsey had to laugh. "Me? He was there because Con ordered him to Glasgow. He was there to protect a city, much like you were in Edinburgh protecting it."

"I wasna there to protect buildings. I was there to protect lives—human lives."

Lexi sat back in her chair with a sigh. "Not even coffee is strong enough for this conversation."

"I appreciate you trying to take some of the tension from the room," Kinsey told her. "The fact is, this is my private life we're discussing. Something I don't even do with my sister."

"Sister?" Thorn asked in surprise, his brow furrowed deeply.

Kinsey wasn't sure what the problem was. "Yep. My sister."

"How many other siblings do you have? Are your parents still alive? Where do they live?"

"Thorn," Lexi chided. "One question at a time."

Kinsey looked between the two. Thorn was visibly upset. "Ryder knows I have a sister. She's much younger than I am. My father died when I was four. At eight Mum remarried and they had my sister. My mother and stepfather live in Hong Kong because of his job. My sister is finishing up her last year at university."

"Shite," Thorn said and pushed his chair back as he got to his feet.

Kinsey looked helplessly at Lexi.

"Your family is going to want to know where you are at some point," Lexi explained. "They're going to have questions about Dreagan."

"Everyone has questions about Dreagan from what I hear," Kinsey said.

Thorn paced the kitchen mumbling to himself. Kinsey tried to hear what he was saying, but she couldn't pick up any words.

Lexi shifted in her chair. "There are only five women here who have family or close friends outside of Dreagan. Jane has a half-sister, Sammi, who happens to be mated to a King as well. Darcy has family on the Isle of Skye. Shara is a Fae, so she doesn't have to keep secret who she's married to. Then there's me. My parents have passed away, but my friends who came with me to Scotland have been asking a lot of questions. Oh, I keep forgetting about Cassie, but she and her brother don't talk. I guess that's why I leave her out when I think about this."

Now Kinsey understood. "You have to lie to your family?"

"Yes. They can't know anything. I'll be able to see them for the next five years or so, but after that they'll begin to see I'm not aging as they are."

"It's not like I'll be staying. As soon as my name is cleared and we catch who is behind sending me here, I'm gone."

Thorn made some sound that wasn't close to a word. It sent warning bells off in Kinsey's head that it wouldn't be anything close to that easy.

As if they would allow her to leave, knowing what she knew. She had been working side by side with Ryder seeing into a vast majority of their secrets and getting to know them.

MI5 was prowling the estate. Helicopters and planes continued to fly over the land. Cameras from news stations from around the world were at the entrance of

Dreagan. The only reason the distillery wasn't crawling with visitors was because it was closed for the winter.

Someone would pay dearly to learn a fraction of what she now knew.

Perhaps it was a good thing they knew she had family. It would make it more difficult for them to kill her.

As soon as the thought went through her mind she almost laughed. She knew for a fact Ryder could kill because she'd witnessed him doing it to the Dark in Glasgow. But her? He wouldn't kill her, nor did she think he would allow anyone else to hurt her.

But there were dozens of other ways for them to ensure she never spoke a word of what she knew.

"It doesn't matter that I have a family," Kinsey said. "I'm not remaining here and neither are Ryder and I a couple anymore. Con can be happy in the knowledge that he won't have another King mated."

Thorn stopped pacing and stared at her for a long, silent minute. Then he walked to the table and sat next to his wife, lacing his fingers with hers.

It made Kinsey's chest ache to see them so comfortable together. They reached for each other blindly, and the other was always there. She'd had that once—with Ryder.

And she missed it terribly.

Not just the intimacy, but the quiet times, the laughter, the sharing of everything. That kind of relationship was truly glorious.

"Are you telling me that you'd walk away from Ryder today and no' look back?" Thorn asked.

Kinsey took a deep breath and slowly released it. "I had a past with Ryder. I thought it was something special. I bet my life on it actually. Then he left. For three years I didn't see him until a few weeks ago when Glasgow was under attack."

She pushed away her plate and laid one arm over the other on the table. "The idea of dragons and shifting is common for you because it's your life, but let me assure you that the idea of Fae and dragons haunt my nightmares. I saw so much death and blood that night. Wars are supposed to be fought elsewhere or on the telly. They're not supposed to happen right in front of me."

"Ryder saved your life," Lexi said.

"He did." Kinsey rose to her feet. "I'll owe him a debt that will never be able to be repaid. But whatever was between us is gone."

Thorn raised a dark brow. "Are you sure of that?"

"Positive. I've had years to get over him." Another lie in an effort to make herself believe something she was more confused about than ever.

Lexi got to her feet then. "What if Ryder still has feelings?"

"Then perhaps he should've acted on them instead of allowing years to pass." Kinsey gave them a nod and strode out of the kitchen.

She wasn't yet ready to go to the computer room, but no longer could she stand the questions Thorn posed to her.

It wasn't until she reached the third floor that she realized she had breakfast with a Dragon King and hadn't thought twice about it. She was even curt with him, not worrying about him shifting or attacking her.

That could be because she'd seen him and Lexi together beforehand. Regardless, it made her breathe easier.

If only she could relax when she was with Ryder.

* * *

Con turned the corner into the kitchen and watched Kinsey walk away.

"How much did you hear?" Lexi asked him.

"All of it. I was about to come in for food when I spotted Ryder on the stairs. I decided to wait."

Thorn leaned back in his chair and crossed his arms over his chest as he stared at the doorway where Kinsey had departed. "I think she might still care for Ryder."

"I know she does." Con saw Lexi's eyes widen while Thorn's head swiveled to him.

It was Lexi who asked, "How do you know that?"

"Just watch the two of them together. It's obvious."

Thorn nodded slowly. "It's true she went out of her way to stay away from him so they didna accidentally touch."

"While Ryder remains near her," Con said.

Lexi picked up Kinsey's plate and brought it to the sink. "Are you going to try and keep them apart?"

It wasn't in Con's nature to share such things. He was going to refuse to answer, but changed his mind at the last minute. "Kinsey's fear of Ryder's true nature will no' allow her to accept him."

"She could get over her trepidation," Lexi said, but Thorn was already shaking his head.

"I agree with Con," Thorn said. "Kinsey wasna just in the middle of a war with the Dark Fae, who she didna even know existed until recently, but she saw the man she cared for shift from a dragon. Her mind willna be able to acknowledge such things easily. I believe Kinsey when she said that whatever might've been between them is gone."

Con saw the argument on Lexi's lips, but she kept it to

herself. This was another case of how different the Kings were from mortals.

Humans were tenacious in their need to hold onto hope. Whereas a Dragon King realized the futility and let it go.

Kinsey was a complication Dreagan didn't need. The sooner she was gone, the better. It was why a handful of Kings were scattered throughout England, Scotland, and Ireland looking for Ulrik or anyone connected to him.

Con heard Ryder's voice in his head, heard the anxiety. He raced up the stairs with Thorn right behind him. They rushed past Kinsey before she reached the computer room.

Dmitri and Henry were in the room as well. Con looked at each of them as Kinsey walked around them, a curious frown puckering her brow.

"This can't be happening," Henry said, his English accent thick. His plain brown hair was sticking up at odd angles. His clothes were rumpled, and he had a full beard from not shaving. Lines of strain bracketed his mouth. Dark circles were under his eyes, but it was the stunned and shaken look in his eyes that caught Con's attention.

Even the normally cool Dmitri seemed dismayed by whatever was on the monitor.

"Ryder," Con said.

Ryder lifted his eyes to Con and used his hand to swipe across the screen. The pictures went onto the wall behind Con.

Con turned to the pictures. The first one showed Henry with a much younger girl as he walked her to school. They were both smiling. They had the same nondescript brown hair and hazel eyes, the same plain features that allowed them to blend in anywhere.

Next to that picture was one of the girl several years older walking into The Silver Dragon.

"She told me she declined MI5's offer," Henry said.

Ryder's chair squeaked as he leaned back. "Perhaps she did."

"MI5 or Ulrik? Both are bad," Henry said, his voice rising.

Con felt the weight of more troubles settle on his shoulders. After all Henry had done for Dreagan—was still doing for them—Con wasn't going to sit back and not help. "We'll get to the bottom of this," he promised.

"I've hacked into MI5 files before," Kinsey said. "I can do it again. We'll be able to determine if she really is working for them."

Henry tried to smile as he looked at her. "I don't know who you are, but thank you. I tried using my clearance, but I didn't find anything."

Ryder nodded to Con as Dmitri vacated the chair and Kinsey sat. "While Kinsey is doing that, I'm doing a search in Ireland."

"Oh," Henry said to Ryder and rubbed his eyes. "I almost forgot. I was on my way to see Con when I got your text. There's been massive movement of the Dark in Ireland."

Dmitri shook his head, mumbling, "Bloody hell."

"Come." Con motioned to Henry. "Let's leave Ryder and Kinsey to their work."

As they left the computer room and Henry began to talk, Con felt the strain of everything teetering precariously. One wrong move and all they'd worked for and built could be destroyed.

He didn't worry about dying. The Dragon Kings would

live through anything the humans tried to kill them with. But his men had already lost so much. Their homes, their way of life, their families, and their dragons.

If this new world they'd lived in for millions of years was yanked from them, Con wasn't sure what would happen. They could all turn on the mortals.

And Con wasn't so certain he wouldn't join them.

CHAPTER FIFTEEN

Kinsey waited until it was just her and Ryder before she pulled her chair forward and asked, "Who was that man with the English accent?"

"Henry North. He's a friend who also happens to work for MI5."

She was so shocked that she stopped typing and turned her head to Ryder. "What? Are you serious? You trust him?"

"He's been our friend for many years, and he's proven himself on many occasions when we've needed help. Aye, we trust him." Ryder rubbed his temple, something he did when he was worried.

Kinsey looked back to the virtual keyboard. "It'll take me a few minutes to hack in. Though I'm sure you could do it quicker."

"You're verra capable of hacking MI5."

She couldn't help but think he was just giving her work to do. Kinsey knew all too well that Ryder could have six projects going at once and not be deterred at all.

Still, she felt pride from his words. She timed herself,

and did a little mental jig when she got into MI5's computers in less than two minutes.

"Who am I looking for?" she asked.

"Esther North." Ryder leaned over to look at her monitor as she keyed in the name.

Though Kinsey didn't know Henry, she was hoping that his sister wasn't part of MI5. But within seconds her picture popped up on the screen with red letters across it reading DECOMMISSIONED.

"Dammit," Ryder said and raked a hand through his hair.

Kinsey scrolled through the file. "I'm sorry. I was hoping we wouldn't find her, but from what I'm reading, she was very good. Almost as good as Henry, from what her reports state."

"Henry is one of the best."

"How do you know he's not spying on you?"

Ryder rolled his chair next to hers. "We don't allow just anyone into our home. Do you know when Esther was decommissioned?"

"She was with MI5 since she was eighteen. It seems they recruited her right beneath Henry's nose."

"He's no' going to like that."

Kinsey wouldn't appreciate it either if it were her sister. She'd be furious enough to want to take physical action against such people. "They practically put her in the field immediately. She had less than a few months' training before she was working as an undercover agent."

She scrolled through some more while she and Ryder read. Most of it was about her missions and how well she did. Her superiors all raved about her ability, comparing her to Henry on multiple occasions.

"She just stopped working," Ryder said when they came toward the end of the file.

"There's nothing more." Kinsey checked to make sure nothing was hidden. "Just her last mission, and then she was decommissioned."

Ryder's frown deepened. "What was her last assignment?"

A sick feeling came over Kinsey when she read, "Ireland."

"Henry doesna need this." Ryder shoved his chair back to his station and pressed the heels of his palms into his eyes. "He's barely holding it together now."

"What's wrong with him? He looks sick."

Ryder dropped his hands to his thighs and slid his gaze to her. "I guess you could say he is sick, in a way. He made the mistake of falling in love with a Light Fae. Her name is Rhi, and she's a friend. We warned him to keep his distance, but humans can no' help themselves."

"Did she take part of his soul?"

"They didn't have sex. They kissed, but that's all it took for Henry to fall in love."

Kinsey felt her stomach grow queasy from all the grease from the bacon. "Gotcha."

"Henry has been searching for Rhi for months. He willna give up, and it's only going to cause him more heartache in the end."

Kinsey knew all about heartache. She'd spent months—years!—pining after Ryder. She understood all too well what he was feeling.

Kinsey had even tried to use her skills to find Ryder, just as Henry was searching the world over for Rhi. Oh yes, she could sympathize with him on everything.

"We can't keep this from him," Kinsey said. "He knows we're looking into his sister. He'll be here soon wanting an update."

"It'll likely do him in. I'd rather no' do that to a friend."

"And he'd rather have the truth," she argued. "A lie will only prolong the pain. The truth is always better. Even if it's difficult to say."

Ryder released a long breath, his gaze going to the ground for a heartbeat. "I wanted to tell you who I was, Kins. I'm sure you doona believe me, but I did. I wanted you to know everything."

"Then you should've told me."

Regret filled his eyes. "I couldna."

"You knew me, Ryder. You knew I'd never have shared such information."

"It doesna matter. We have a code for a reason. It might seem senseless or trivial, but had you endured the war with the humans as we did, you'd understand."

She leaned back in her chair as she stared at the picture of Esther North. Would they bring her to Dreagan if she was in danger? Henry was their friend, so they might very well do just that.

It made Kinsey think about her talk with Lexi and Thorn that morning. There were other women at the manor. Several, in fact.

"Tell me, did every Dragon King wait until they were mated to their women before they showed them who they really were?" she asked.

The silence lengthened between them. Kinsey didn't look away from the monitor. She didn't want to see Ryder's face or any emotions that he might try to hide.

Her heart thumped in her chest, and her blood iced with nervousness. Because she knew the answer. She only wanted Ryder to admit it to her as well as himself.

Tears stung her eyes. She hastily blinked them away. Hadn't she been good enough for him? Wasn't their closeness enough?

The night she came home to find the note on the table

she had been going to tell him she loved him. Kinsey could still feel the hollow ache in her chest from discovering he'd left her.

She had fallen to her knees, the paper crushed to her chest as she cried. Desolation, despair. Anguish. She'd been bombarded with those emotions, battering her until she was no longer strong enough to stand against them.

Her world turned gray and bleak. When, days later, she managed to pick herself up and try to find Ryder, she found no trace of him.

Ryder hadn't been the first man to end a relationship with her, and Kinsey had ended her fair share as well. But it was the sheer depth of her love for him that affected her so deeply.

It wasn't until that moment when she finished the letter and comprehended that he was gone that she realized how fragile a heart could be, how profoundly she could love.

How acutely she could hurt.

Three years later, that pain remained. It became a part of her, closing around her heart, blending with her muscle, sinking into bone.

It molded her, shaped her.

Changed her.

And yet it teased her from time to time in her dreams with memories of Ryder. Or worse—hints of what her future could have been with him.

How callous a heart that once loved could be. It hardened to keep anyone out, then cruelly opened the door in dreams to remind her how vulnerable she truly was.

Deep within her frozen heart was a tiny kernel of hope that continued to live. It was dying a slow, agonizing death though. When it was gone, Kinsey would finally be free of the heartache that lingered.

"No."

She blinked and frowned when Ryder's word reached her. It took her a moment to remember she'd asked him a question. So he finally admitted that the other Kings hadn't waited to tell their women who they were.

It was a victory for her. Why then did it feel like the worst defeat?

"I doona want to lie to you anymore," Ryder said.

Kinsey sat up in her chair and placed her fingers on the virtual keyboard. "That's reassuring."

"I've hurt you again."

She snorted and shot him a flat look. "I knew the answer before I asked the question."

"You wanted me to admit it."

"Of course." With a punch of a key, she moved her search to another monitor. There she began to dig into Kyvor's servers. She might get lucky and find something in an e-mail, because people were just that stupid sometimes.

Ryder turned to face her. "You've changed."

"Time changes everything."

"I did this to you."

Kinsey stopped typing. She then slowly turned her head to him. "Yes, you hurt me, leaving the way you did. But I'm not some broken thing you can claim and fix."

His brow furrowed. "That's no' what I meant."

"It certainly is. As you've said, you've lived for millions of years. You want to be the hero to the damsel in distress, but let me be the one to burst your bubble. I'm not a damsel, and if I were in distress, I could save myself."

His hazel gaze stared at her a long time. "I've always known that. It was your strength of character and soul that drew me."

"Then you needn't worry about me."

"It's my nature."

She shrugged, hating that she liked that he might actually feel concern for her. Responsibility? Definitely. But to have him troubled over her was something she hadn't expected.

And greatly enjoyed.

That flare of hope within her heart brightened briefly. Kinsey refused to acknowledge it. Ryder wouldn't get close enough to hurt her again. Ever.

"You didn't tell your friends I had family," she said.

Ryder mumbled something beneath his breath. "Who asked?"

"Thorn." She lifted her chin then. Though she didn't stand a chance against Dragon Kings or the might of Dreagan, she still said, "Let me be perfectly clear. No one here, not you or Con or anyone else, is going to threaten my family."

Ryder gave a nod of his head. "You have my word."

How much was that worth now? At one time, Kinsey would've believed anything he said. Now, she knew his focus was Dreagan and all those who lived there.

Everyone else was on their own.

CHAPTER SIXTEEN

Dark Fae Palace
Ireland

For every hour that Balladyn was away from Rhi, he felt as if a millennia passed. Taraeth kept Balladyn by his side, as if the king of the Dark knew Balladyn wanted to leave.

"You've had something on your mind," Taraeth said as they walked side by side down the wide corridor from the king's throne room to Taraeth's private sanctuary.

They turned the corner and Balladyn saw into one of the many vast rooms where the Dark congregated. He spied Mikkel and the female Dark sent by Taraeth to spy on him. "I've told you my thoughts on your alliance with both Mikkel and Ulrik."

"You don't think I can handle the situation?"

Balladyn clenched his jaw when he heard Taraeth's voice dip deep in aggravation. It was time for Balladyn to do damage control. "Never, sire. We're dealing with two Dragon Kings, both of who want Con's position."

Taraeth halted, the guards following instantly fanning out to give him room. He took a step closer to Balladyn. "Mikkel was a Dragon King for only a few minutes."

"With Ulrik's magic bound, hasn't he been the King of the Silvers the entire time though?"

"Mikkel sure thought so," Taraeth said with a smile. "But I've recently come across some information."

Balladyn wasn't fooled. He knew exactly who that information came from. "Ulrik actually shared such knowledge with you?"

"I can be very charming." Taraeth's red eyes crinkled in the corners as he smiled. "Truth be told, I think Ulrik has about had enough of the leash Mikkel keeps tightening."

"Ulrik would've never told you anything he didn't want to get back to his uncle."

Taraeth absently rubbed the nub of his left arm. "What Ulrik told me anyone could figure out if they but took a moment. Mikkel is too power hungry to even contemplate the fact that he might be in over his head."

Balladyn studied his king. "So you're going to side with Ulrik?"

"I didn't say that. Now, if Ulrik had all of his magic back, perhaps."

What if he did? Balladyn thought about how easily Ulrik had snuck up on him. No Fae could do that. The Dragon Kings had been able to do that on a few occasions.

Which meant that in order for Ulrik to perform such a feat, he had all his magic back. Taraeth and Mikkel didn't know. Ulrik was keeping his secrets close, which was the only way he would come out ahead in the end.

But why lie? Why not tell—or better yet, show—Mikkel that he was back in charge? Because if Ulrik had his magic returned, he could speak to his Silvers locked on Dreagan. And if he could wake his Silvers, then he could start the war with the mortals once more.

Balladyn was more curious than ever as to what Ulrik's plans were. Though Taraeth might not be willing to pick a side, Balladyn already had. Ulrik's.

He gave a shrug to Taraeth. "You've still not told me what Ulrik shared."

"Hungry for information to use against our enemies?" Taraeth asked with a laugh.

"The more knowledge we have, the better."

Taraeth looked him up and down before he began walking again. Balladyn fell into step beside him as the guards surrounded them. He waited for Taraeth to speak, but they continued in silence.

It wasn't until they were in Taraeth's private chambers with guards posted outside that he sat on the red velvet sofa and motioned for Balladyn to take the other.

"I wish we would've been here when the Kings were at war with the humans," Taraeth began. "We would've been able to see firsthand what happened with Ulrik."

Balladyn rested both arms on the back of the sofa and stretched out his legs, his ankles crossed. "We know what happened."

"We know the story. Mikkel doesn't even know all of it. He wasn't there to witness everything. He saw Con and the other Kings bind Ulrik's magic. That's how Mikkel became a Dragon King. The power of the King reverted to the next strongest Silver."

Balladyn nodded. "The Kings already had four of the largest and most loyal of Ulrik's Silvers put into sleep and caged on Dreagan."

"Exactly," Taraeth said with a smile.

Balladyn chuckled then. "Con made sure that even if the Silvers woke, none of them would be able to become a Dragon King."

"Which is why Mikkel was only a King for a short

time. He desired to be King long before Ulrik took over from his father. Mikkel thought it should've been him from the beginning. He's always hated Ulrik for being stronger and more powerful. Mikkel believes he has Ulrik at a disadvantage, and as long as that's in place, Mikkel will use it to his advantage."

"What happens when Ulrik gets all of his magic back?"

Taraeth shrugged. "Mikkel says he has a plan in place. Once Ulrik kills Con, then Mikkel will kill him. As soon as Ulrik has all of his magic unbound, he'll once more be King of the Silvers. Nothing will be able to stop that. Nor will Con be able to bind Ulrik's magic again."

Balladyn inwardly smiled at Ulrik's cunning to make everyone believe his magic wasn't fully unbound.

Balladyn wanted to test his theory. Taraeth could hide a lot of things, but if he had a secret he believed no one else was aware of, he liked to gloat about it.

"What if Ulrik's magic is unbound? What if he's faking it?"

Taraeth laughed loudly. "Look at Ulrik, Balladyn. He was King of the Silvers for thousands of years. Do you really believe he'd sit by and continue to allow Mikkel to use him if he had his magic? More than that, do you really believe Ulrik wouldn't attack Con right away?"

"He's waited thousands of years for his retribution. I think he's planned it down to the last detail."

"Without a doubt. It's going to be a glorious war, and we have front row seats."

It was Taraeth's certainty that he would remain king of the Dark, as well as his conviction that he didn't have to choose between Ulrik and Mikkel that told Balladyn it was nearly his time to take over.

An image of Rhi flashed in his mind.

His hands clenched as he recalled how he'd held her body against his, caressing and stroking. Her cries of pleasure still echoed in his mind. Just as he would never forget how it felt to slide inside her.

He wanted her as his queen. Rhi would be an amazing queen. But she would never turn Dark.

And he was Dark.

Balladyn blinked, focusing on Taraeth's face that was inches from his as he snapped his fingers next to Balladyn's ear. He held back his natural reflex to knock Taraeth away.

"What's wrong with you?" Taraeth asked with a sneer. "I've been talking to you, but you wouldn't answer."

Balladyn held himself still until Taraeth straightened and returned to the opposite sofa. Only then did he respond. "I was thinking about the upcoming battle with Ulrik and Con."

"Oh, yes. I know how much you hate the Dragon Kings."

Apparently not all of them. Balladyn was beginning to like Ulrik. "I want to be there to watch it unfold."

"You will be," Taraeth assured him.

By that time, Balladyn fully intended to be king of the Darks. The entire force of Dark Fae would be at the disposal of one entity—him.

It would be at his leisure to choose if they aided Ulrik or not. And knowing Ulrik, the Dragon King wouldn't need anyone's help.

As for Mikkel . . . that was another matter entirely.

"You still have Sinny spying on Mikkel?"

Taraeth nodded absently as he eyed a mortal who was being carried into the chamber. Her red hair was long and bright, just as Taraeth liked it.

She was young, her body lithe and supple as she lay

naked in the arms of one of Taraeth's guards. He motioned to the guard to take the human to his bed in the next room.

"Sinny will continue to spy on Mikkel just as her sister, Muriel, is spying on Ulrik." Taraeth stood with an excited smile as he faced his bedroom. "We'll finish this later. It's time for my snack."

Balladyn rose to his feet and walked out with the loud moans of the female following him. He strode down the hallway thinking of all the mortals he'd taken after he became Dark. There were so many he couldn't recall all of them.

Rhi wouldn't approve.

He made his way to a doorway and immediately went to Rhi's island. He needed to have her arms around him, to know that she was his.

But the island was deserted.

Balladyn stood in the sun with the water a few feet away. It was the spot where he had made love to Rhi. He removed his clothes and walked into the water.

The sun, the bright flowers, the beautiful water, they were all things a Light Fae needed. He didn't need them anymore, but yet there he was.

Balladyn dove under the water trying to imagine what Rhi saw as she swam with the brightly colored fish and coral. He could imagine her smiling as the fish darted around her.

It wasn't until he walked out of the water an hour later that Balladyn realized how long he'd remained at the island. He halted at the shore, his chest tightening.

He enjoyed it. All of it. The sand, the water, the fish. The sun.

His gaze landed on the hammock, and for just a moment, he contemplated remaining. Then he remembered his plans. He had a throne to claim and a king to kill.

Balladyn scrunched his toes, the wet sand sinking between them, clinging to his skin as the water rolled in and out. The wind glided across his damp skin and caused the palm trees to sway, their fronds rubbing against each other.

It was so peaceful. No wonder Rhi had chosen it. It was secluded as well, which suited her. More and more she was pulling away from everyone.

It seemed both of them were in the midst of change. Though Balladyn now knew that Rhi would fight the darkness inside her with everything that she was.

She didn't even know that yet. It made him smile, because it proved how strong she was. Not just her magic, but her character, her spirit.

Her essence.

She feared the darkness was taking over when in fact her light was drowning the darkness. The darkness clung to her, trying to sway Rhi and tempt her. A few times it even came close.

But each time her light killed it.

How could he have ever imagined that he could turn her Dark? Even in the thrall of rage and revenge, he should've seen the sheer might of her.

Instead, he'd been blinded by the darkness within him. The one person in all the realms he'd never wanted to hurt, he had done just that. And she forgave him.

She was the very best of the Fae. How did no one else see that?

Balladyn snapped his fingers as he walked out of the water. His clothes and shoes were back on, and all traces of his time in the water were gone.

He teleported to Cork and *an Doras*. As soon as he walked into the pub, a hush fell over the crowd of Fae. It was a Dark Fae holding, but the occasional Light would make an appearance.

Balladyn walked to an empty stool and sat at the bar. The barkeep walked up with a glass of whisky in hand. As soon as he set the glass down, Balladyn's hand wrapped around his wrist.

Wide red eyes looked at Balladyn. "I've paid my rent and taxes."

"I don't take care of such things." The male began to tremble in Balladyn's hold. "I want information."

"Wh-what kind?" the Dark stuttered.

"Tell me all you've heard of the Reapers recently."

CHAPTER SEVENTEEN

Ryder was attuned to every sound, every movement that Kinsey made. He found it nearly impossible to focus on anything except her.

With his mind constantly bombarded with questions from the other Dragon Kings, he found himself ignoring their verbal calls on occasion.

The hours crawled by until lunch. Kinsey didn't so much as look his way again as she went about her work. Ryder attempted to come up with reasons to ask her questions, but it didn't take long for her to realize what he was doing.

As soon as Dmitri walked into the computer room, Ryder jumped up from his chair. "I'll be back," he told Dmitri.

Ryder ignored his name being called as he lengthened his strides. He hurried down the three flights of stairs and bumped into Arian as he made his way to the hidden doorway from the manor that connected to the mountain.

Once Ryder was in the mountain, he kept walking. He didn't know where he was going. Only that he had to put some distance between him and Kinsey so he could get himself under control.

Ryder soon found himself standing in the large cavern staring at the black bars of the massive cage that held the four sleeping Silver dragons.

The cavern had only a few torches scattered around the perimeter. A ball of magic swirled above the cage, casting a faint white light over the dragons.

Ryder walked to the cage and placed his hand upon the dragon nearest him. These weren't his dragons, but they were dragons. Right now he needed to remember who he was.

Because every moment he couldn't have Kinsey was tearing him apart.

He hadn't realized how much he hungered, craved her until she was within arm's reach. She was closer than she had been in years, but yet she was further away than ever before.

Ryder rested his forehead on the bars and focused on the dragons' breathing. These were the last four dragons on the realm. Every time he came to see them, it made Ryder sad. They should be flying, their wings outstretched and the sun upon their scales.

He closed his eyes and thought back to his Greys. How he loved to rub their single horn that projected above their noses. They had made a sound at the back of their throats that rumbled in their chests, which sounded very much like a purr.

Ryder smiled at the memory. His dragons always brought him comfort, even when it was just a memory of them. There was only one other thing that could do that to him—Kinsey.

His smile vanished. Kinsey. What a fool he'd been to

take for granted the time they shared. How easily she once walked into his arms, lifting her face for a kiss.

How they had laughed and talked, walking arm in arm down the street.

What Ryder wouldn't do to have that time back. He told Dmitri last night he was willing to fight for Kinsey. Sleeping beside her had only solidified his decision.

But the longer she was around him, the more distant she became.

Ryder petted the Silver as he wondered what prompted Kinsey to act as she did. When she first arrived at Dreagan she was shocked and angered to find him there. Now, she appeared as indifferent to him as she was to everything else.

His hand paused and his eyes flew open. Indifferent? Kinsey wasn't indifferent. She was afraid. What she was doing was attempting to erect a wall between them that would keep Ryder out forever.

The only problem with that was that Kinsey had no idea how determined a Dragon King could be.

Ryder made his way to each of the Silvers and petted them while he began to decide how to bust through Kinsey's wall. She had to still feel something for him. Why else would there have been such anger the day before?

Touching the Silvers helped Ryder to sort his way through his thoughts, but he wished he could shift and take to the skies. He needed to fly.

To dive through clouds, turning over and over again, wrapping the clouds around him. There was something beautiful and amazing about looking down at the earth through his dragon eyes.

Hopefully they would find Ulrik soon and put a stop to this nonsense. The one thing Ryder was grateful for was that Kinsey was at Dreagan. Security—really their dragon magic—was heightened to ensure that no Dark could venture onto the land.

Unbeknownst to every human who entered Dreagan, they were being scanned by Ryder. He couldn't tell who was working for Ulrik—yet. But every face, every voice was being logged into a database along with where the person went and how long they were at Dreagan.

The mates were watched by multiple Kings at any given time. So if Kinsey had to be anywhere, Dreagan was the best place to be. No matter who was using her or why, Ryder knew she would be safe.

Which allowed him to think of how he could break down her barriers and get her back in his arms again.

Ulrik stood in the shadows of the cavern until Ryder walked out, his boots making a slight echo on the stones. Ulrik slid his gaze to his Silvers. He counted five Kings who came to see his Silvers in the last two hours.

All this time he'd thought his dragons were the ones trapped, but he was beginning to see that the Kings were as well. They needed his Silvers, whether they knew it or not.

Did the Kings even realize how often they visited his dragons? How many times they touched the scales, caressing them? Some simply stood in the cavern staring at the Silvers.

Ulrik didn't need magic to know those Kings were thinking of their own dragons. Up until he was able to get part of his dragon magic back, Ulrik had gone mad several times over wondering about his dragons.

The first time he snuck onto Dreagan, he spent an entire day with his Silvers without a single King knowing about it. It almost killed Ulrik to leave them, but each day drew him closer to the time he could awaken them and rid the world of the humans.

Ulrik came as often as he dared to Dreagan. It amused him how many times he stood near Con in the shadows of the cavern. The almighty Con hadn't even been aware his enemy could've killed him a hundred times over.

That had tempted Ulrik on several occasions. To end Con and take over as King of Kings. Everything he'd dreamed of and worked toward could come to fruition.

There had even been one instance when Ulrik nearly gave in to that desire and killed Con while he looked upon the Silvers. Being stabbed in the back was just what Con deserved after all he'd done to Ulrik.

But that wasn't who Ulrik was. He wanted Con to know he attacked him. He needed Con to know that he was going to lose—and die.

Only then would Ulrik get his satisfaction and his vengeance. Only then would he be able to face the future without the cloud of anger and resentment weighing him down.

When he was King of Kings, Ulrik would remove every last human from the realm and then he would return the dragons. He smiled as he thought of the Fae. With the mortals gone, the Fae would have no reason to remain.

The earth could return to what it was always meant to be—a dragon realm.

It was a dream Ulrik had held onto for thousands of years. He couldn't believe how close he was to fulfilling it. All that had gone wrong so long ago would be set right.

Ulrik searched for a twinge of remorse at the thought of killing Con, but there was nothing there. Whatever had bonded him and Con together millions of years ago had been severed with Con's betrayal.

Con had been part of his family at one time. Ulrik

would've died for Con. How had he not seen the true Constantine?

That was because Con was a great actor. He pushed all his emotions aside. He shut down and refused to let anyone in. Con was a master at it.

All too soon the peace that Con built around himself would be shattered. Ulrik had refused to fight him when Con became King of Kings. It was a mistake Ulrik had made because of love. He'd loved Con as a brother then.

That ridiculous emotion changed Ulrik's life forever. It made him an outcast, banished from his home and his brethren.

Con used to tell him not to allow emotions to rule his life. It took the treachery of his most trusted friend for Ulrik to see how true Con's words were.

All emotion but one was erased within Ulrik. He lived, breathed, and cultivated the resentment housed inside him. It pulled him past the brink of madness.

It focused him.

For tens of thousands of years Ulrik had been setting a plan in motion. And it was going beautifully.

Ulrik walked from the shadows to his Silvers. "Hear me," he whispered.

He didn't need to speak to them. Their link was mental, but they liked the sound of his voice. In response, the one closest to him moved his front limb.

"A wee bit longer," he soothed. "Then you'll be free of this cage and the sleep. We'll bring our own brand of justice down upon the mortals. And this time nothing will stop us."

Ulrik walked to each of the dragons, whispering their names as he touched them. Being near them gave him strength, reminded him of how important it was that he win.

He would win. Of that he had no doubt. Ulrik had known from the beginning he could beat Con. He hadn't wanted to before. Now was a different story.

Ulrik returned to the shadows. Just as he was about to teleport away, he heard voices. His enhanced hearing picked up Dmitri's and Thorn's voices.

"He wants her," Dmitri said.

Thorn chuckled. "Of course Ryder does. It's obvious in the way he looks at her."

"She's verra beautiful."

"I'm just thankful she's on Dreagan."

"I'd feel better if we could locate Ulrik," Dmitri said.

They walked into the cavern and stood beside the cage looking at the Silvers. Thorn crossed his arms over his chest. "After the last run-in we had with Ulrik, I think it's imperative we know where he is at all times."

"He must've been watching all of us for years. How much did we give away without knowing?"

Thorn exchanged a look with Dmitri. "Probably too much. I believe Ryder is the only one being targeted right now."

"Can we assume that? With the network Ulrik has, he could be aiming his malicious intent at any number of us at once."

"With MI5 crawling over Dreagan, there isna much Ulrik can do without exposing himself as well."

Dmitri squatted down and rubbed the forehead of one of the Silvers. "Do you really think that will stop him? He wants the humans gone. This is the perfect time for him to strike, because he knows we willna do anything."

Ulrik smiled knowingly. Everything was lining up. There were just a few more critical things that needed to happen before he could challenge Con.

"You sided with Ulrik before," Thorn said. "Will you again?"

Dmitri blew out a breath. "The truth is, I'm tired of hiding who I am. We've done it for so long that we've accepted the invisible chains around us. This was our realm, Thorn."

"Then we agreed to share it."

Dmitri gave a shake of his head. "Did we? Or were the mortals put here for us to annihilate? Did any of us ever consider that?"

"I'm mated to one of those humans," Thorn said in a low voice.

Dmitri held his gaze. "You'll no' find me taking one into my bed. It's why I've always chosen the Light Fae. I'm glad you and the others have found love, but can you really trust your women? Look what Ulrik's woman did. It'll happen again, Thorn. Mark my words."

Ulrik's smile grew. This discord within the Dragon Kings was growing, just as he knew it would.

CHAPTER EIGHTEEN

Ryder picked up a jelly donut and bit into it. Out of the corner of his eye he saw Kinsey glance his way. Since his return from visiting the Silvers, Ryder had ignored her.

And she didn't like it.

He found her looking his way every so often with a side glance. She hadn't said a word, but her constant shifting in her chair was giving her away.

Ryder clicked a tab on the computer and music filled the air. Seether's "Words as Weapons" began to play. Ryder set the playlist to shuffle and repeat before he checked on the scans of Ireland.

Still no sign of Ulrik. Where was he? Ryder couldn't help but think they were missing something that was right in front of their faces.

There were still sections of Ireland to be scanned. While that worked, he checked on the mortals on Dreagan. The software program he'd written that captured all the information about the humans was collecting data at a rapid rate, cataloging it perfectly.

Ryder scanned the list. Over fifty agents on Dreagan. Surely MI5 wouldn't continue to keep such numbers on Dreagan when there were other threats across Britain.

Something kept nagging at Ryder. He began to read over the data on the agents more closely.

There was a tap on his shoulder. He blinked and looked up to find Kinsey standing beside him. The annoyed look on her face had him asking, "What is it?"

"You did it again."

"Did what?" he asked, glancing around before he paused the music.

She pointed to the three monitors he had taken over. "You got engrossed. You've been staring at those screens for three hours. I've left twice without you even hearing me."

Ryder slid a hand down his face. Damn. He was supposed to be keeping an eye on her. If he was going to take responsibility for Kinsey, he couldn't allow himself to become so absorbed in his work.

"Don't worry," she said as she rolled her head from side to side, stretching out her neck. "I went to the kitchen and the bathroom only. What are you looking for?"

"I'm no' sure. Just a feeling that something isna right."

Kinsey put her legs together and bent forward, placing her hands on the floor to stretch. "You said MI5 was used against you before. Perhaps that's what you're thinking about."

He watched as she remained in that position for a moment before she straightened, flipping her long hair over. "Possibly. My feelings are no' usually off."

"All right." She came to stand beside him. "Since I'm still searching through tens of thousands of e-mails of crapola, give me something else to think about for a bit."

She read over the data on one screen. "Wow. That's a lot of information."

"I wanted to make sure we had everything."

"What about pictures of these people?"

Ryder cut her a dry look. "It's the first thing taken."

"Show me."

With a few punches of the keys, he pointed a monitor toward her. The faces of the MI5 agents began to play through one by one every three seconds.

"Stop," Kinsey said.

Ryder quickly halted the rotation. His mouth dropped open in surprise.

"Your instincts weren't wrong," Kinsey with a sad look. "What are you going to do?"

Ryder looked into the face of Esther North. She wore colored contacts, making her eyes brown, and dyed her hair black. Not even the fake nose and chin could hide who she was.

"Whoever taught her is good," Kinsey said.

"MI5 trained her."

Kinsey looked down at him. "Is she with MI5 then after what we saw in her file?"

"That's a good question. I'm going to need to show Con and Henry this."

"Henry has already been up here twice. He tried to get your attention to see if you found anything about his sister."

For once, Ryder was glad he'd been too preoccupied to know someone was there. "You didna tell him?"

Kinsey shrugged one shoulder. "I don't know him. I figured it'd be better if it came from a friend. But he suspects we found something."

"You can no' lie to a spy, especially one as good as Henry."

"Thanks for the reminder." She began to walk around the rows of monitors when her mobile rang. Kinsey halted, her gaze going to Ryder.

His head followed Kinsey as she rushed to her phone. Her face lost color when she read who the caller was.

"It's my boss," she said.

Ryder stood, drawing her gaze. "Put it on speaker and answer it. Stay calm. Doona let them know you know anything."

She gave a nod and hit speaker as she answered, "Hello?"

"Kinsey. It's Cecil. How is everything going at Dreagan?" came a nasally British male voice over the line.

Kinsey licked her lips and sat in her chair. "It's going good."

"Are you finished yet?"

Ryder gave a nod when she looked at him.

"Almost," Kinsey answered.

Cecil chuckled over the line. "That's my girl. Have you upsold them on anything?"

"Not yet. I'm almost at that point."

"They're powerful and the company is loaded," Cecil said. "I don't care what you have to do, but get something sold."

Kinsey held Ryder's gaze. Her violet eyes held worry and anxiety. "Their system is pretty good, and they know it."

Ryder gave her a smile of encouragement. They needed her to stay, but it couldn't appear easy. She needed to have a reason.

"No system is bulletproof. You're the best we have, Kinsey. Find their flaw and use it against them. Make them see how vulnerable they are."

Ryder wanted to roll his eyes. Vulnerable, his ass.

Dreagan was the most secure system on the planet. It was more secure than any intelligence agency in the world.

"Yeah. Okay," Kinsey answered. "They don't leave me alone for a second, Cecil. I'm actually in the bathroom talking to you so I could have a moment alone."

Her boss made a sound over the link. "That means they've something to hide. Have you seen anything about dragons?"

Kinsey continued to hold Ryder's gaze as she said, "Dreagan is Gaelic for dragon. Of course there is dragon stuff all around the estate."

"Have you seen a *real* dragon?"

She hesitated. Ryder didn't move as he waited to see what she would do. Kinsey was smart. She knew she was being used by her company, though she wasn't sure who was pulling the strings. She might fear him, but she comprehended she was safer at Dreagan.

"No. There is no such thing as dragons," Kinsey said with a chuckle. "Nice joke though."

Cecil released a long-suffering sigh. "I was hoping you'd have better news. I fully expect you to e-mail me later with an order from Dreagan."

"And if they don't take my recommendations?"

"Break something," Cecil stated in an irritated tone. "You need the sales. Brian has already outsold you for the month. And quite frankly, I'd rather not have Clarice bring me into her office again. Save us both, Kinsey. Get another order."

He disconnected the call. Kinsey sat back in her chair with her eyes closed and her hands on her head.

"Do you believe him?" Ryder asked.

She cracked open one eye. "It's very competitive at Kyvor. We get paid a nice salary, but we have goals in place. We meet those goals, we get a nice bonus."

"And those goals are up-selling clients on things they might no' need."

Kinsey closed her eyes and shrugged. "It's the way of businesses. Brian wasn't close to outselling me last week. He must've gotten a huge order recently. Cecil is a bit slimy, but I don't think he's part of this plot."

"Perhaps no', but someone could be pulling his strings."

At that she dropped her hands and looked at him. "Meaning, they want to make sure I stay at Dreagan."

"Has Brian ever beaten you before?"

"Never."

Ryder twisted his lips. "There's a reason they want you to remain here."

"And I don't like it. It means they want me to do something for them."

"Or they're going to frame you for something." Either way, Ryder didn't like it.

Kinsey turned her chair to face him. "I don't know what to do."

"I'm no' going to let anything or anyone hurt you. Trust me, Kins, and we'll get you through this."

She stood and walked to the window. "You're asking a lot of me."

"I know." Ryder quietly rose and walked to stand behind her. "We need to know this enemy. Same as you."

"The enemy of my enemy is my friend?" she asked with a wry smile.

He was so close he could smell the lavender from her shampoo. "Yes."

"These people have been watching me. I don't like that at all. I don't owe them anything, and to know they put me in this situation willingly infuriates me." Her voice broke, as the full impact of her situation fell upon her.

Without thinking, Ryder took her by the shoulders and turned her to face him. He wrapped his arms around her, closing his eyes with delight when she rested her head on his chest. "We've been through rough situations before with the females that are here. We'll get you through this one as well."

"Thank you," she said with a sniff and lifted her face.

Ryder gazed into her violet eyes as her dark hair brushed the back of his hand. He'd wanted her in his arms for so long. Now she was there, and he yearned for her kisses.

His head began to lower. Kinsey pulled out of his arms the same time the door opened and Con and Henry walked in. Ryder had no choice but to release her.

Her rebuttal stung, but for just a heartbeat, he'd witnessed the hunger in her eyes. She wanted his kiss. That's all he needed to see.

"Tell me," Henry demanded from the other side of the monitors.

Ryder sat in his chair and cleared the monitors that had Esther's pictures from Ulrik's store, MI5, and Dreagan. Then he motioned both him and Con around the monitors. "It'll be easier to show you."

"Don't hold anything back," Henry stated.

Ryder shared a look with Kinsey before he showed the recording of Esther at Ulrik's. "After finding this, Kinsey got into MI5."

"Show me her file." Henry stood still as a statue, his face set in hard lines.

Ryder pulled it up on one screen with her picture taken at MI5 on another. "She wasna with MI5 long, apparently."

"I was with her that day," Henry said in a hoarse voice. "I took her to lunch, then dropped her off for an interview. She lied to me."

Con put a hand on Henry's shoulder. "She probably knew you would've talked her out of it."

"Damned straight I would've," Henry said with a frown. He then checked the date on her file and that on the recording at Ulrik's. "Why did they relieve her of duty? Just two weeks later she was at Ulrik's."

This was the part Ryder was regretting having to show Henry. "There's more, unfortunately."

"More?" Henry asked with raised brows. "How much bloody more can there be?"

Ryder pointed to the screen that was collecting the data on MI5 agents on Dreagan. "As soon as MI5 arrived, I began gathering every bit of information from the humans possible. It's recorded and filed away to be sorted out as needed."

"Smart," Henry admitted.

Con gave a nod. "Always thinking ahead."

"My instincts told me I was missing something." Ryder motioned to Kinsey. "She wanted to see the pictures of all the agents. That's when we came across a woman with an MI5 ID stating she was Phillipa Carlisle," he said and put up the picture of Esther.

For long minutes Henry didn't say anything as he stared at his sister's picture. Finally, he said, "I'd recognize her anywhere under any disguise, but this is very good."

"I think it's time we talk to her," Con said.

Henry faced Con. "No. It's time I talk to her."

CHAPTER NINETEEN

Kinsey watched Henry's face become as stoic as she'd seen Con's. It was eerie how they could appear so indifferent with a flip of a switch.

Where the hell was her switch? Because she was still heated from Ryder's touch earlier. Damn her traitorous body.

"Where is Esther?" Con asked Ryder.

While Ryder looked over the data that logged in every visitor, Kinsey studied the four monitors that had six camera feeds on each screen.

Ryder let out a sound as he typed something. "She didna log in under the same name as before, but I picked up her fingerprints."

Kinsey was impressed. Fingerprint scan as well? When had Ryder done that? And how?

Her need to continue to learn and grow her skills made her itch to have him teach her. In their year together, Ryder had taught her so much, which helped to make her one of the best in the business.

At one time Kinsey actually thought she was catching

up with him. She nearly snorted aloud at the thought. Ryder far surpassed everyone. If she were an immortal dragon, then she would probably be just as good.

Henry said, "Is she alone?"

It took but a moment for Ryder to answer, "Aye. She's walking around the store inspecting the outside."

"I'll go to her."

Con put out a hand to halt Henry. "She's your sister, so I agree you should talk to her. However, if you want her brought—quietly—then you better let one of us do it."

"Agreed," Henry responded immediately.

Con's black gaze swung to Ryder. "Let's go."

Kinsey released a breath when Con and Henry walked from the computer room. She needed some time alone to compose herself after she'd nearly given in to the urge to kiss Ryder.

What was wrong with her? What happened to that talk she gave herself earlier where she would stand like an oak against Ryder's pull?

"I was a freaking twig," she murmured.

"I'm sorry?"

Kinsey wondered what she had to do for karma to side with her instead of against her. She turned her head to Ryder and said, "Just talking to myself."

Ryder pushed his chair back and got to his feet. "You coming?"

"Uh . . ." What did she say? She was curious, but this had nothing to do with her. "I think the less people standing around Esther the better."

"Kins. Come on."

It was pointless to argue with Ryder when he had that stern look in his eye. She jumped up and hurried to catch him. They were several steps behind Henry and Con.

"Why?" Kinsey asked. "Is it because you think I'll find something on your computers?"

"No."

Well. That stung. She was certainly good enough to hack through any firewall or protection Ryder put in place.

"The only one who can allow you access is me," he said.

He didn't trust her then. Not that she blamed him after how she came to be at Dreagan. She wouldn't trust her either. "Then you want to see if Esther recognizes me."

"No."

Now Kinsey was out of ideas.

"Ulrik is smart enough to make sure that none of his people know each other so they can no' compromise him or his objective," Ryder explained.

Kinsey gave him a quick look out of the corner of her eyes. "You sound like you admire him."

"I appreciate the time it took to put this plan in place. I also value his thinking in setting it all up. I respect his skills in battle."

"Battle?" she repeated. "We're not in battle yet."

Ryder looked at her as they reached the bottom of the stairs and turned right. "We've been in battle with Ulrik since the moment he was banished from Dreagan. It's taken some of the other Kings longer to realize that."

"Did you no' tell them?" she asked, her curiosity growing in spite of her inner voice warning her not to dig too deep. She was in a perilous situation with only an ex-boyfriend who promised to keep her safe.

Ryder shot her a half-smile. "I did."

In other words, no one believed him. Or rather, Con hadn't believed him. Kinsey stared at the back of Con's blond head. He might be almost as gorgeous as Ryder, but there was a coldheartedness about him that made her want to keep her distance.

At all times.

As if he knew she was thinking about him, Con paused at the door and looked directly at her. Kinsey raised a brow. With someone like Con, she couldn't show a hint of fear. Otherwise, he would pounce.

While she shuddered a bit inside, outwardly, she exuded calm and arrogance. Something a man like Con would recognize and most likely respect.

One side of his mouth lifted in a quick if-you-blink-you-miss-it smile. But those chilling black eyes of his said something altogether different. There was a warning there.

When Ryder put his hand on her lower back, Kinsey didn't step away. Whether Ryder knew it or not, he gave her the courage to continue following Con and Henry when all she wanted to do was run back to the computers where she felt safe.

"Ignore him," Ryder whispered near her ear. "Con likes to make people uncomfortable."

Kinsey turned her head slightly to Ryder and lowered her voice. "He does a bloody brilliant job."

That's when she made the mistake of looking in Ryder's hazel eyes. Gold, blue, and green mixed together so it looked like one color bled into the other and then another. They were mesmerizing, compelling.

Hypnotic.

Kinsey should've known better than to be that close to Ryder after their near-kiss. She shivered when their fingers grazed, and she wished their fingers were entwined.

"Watch," Ryder began as his gaze darted over her shoulder.

Kinsey realized what happened a heartbeat too late. Because she was so engrossed in Ryder, she didn't pay attention to where she was walking and tripped over the raised threshold of the door.

She felt herself falling as everything slowed to a crawl. Henry turned and started back toward her while Con simply stood and watched her.

But it was powerful, familiar arms that wrapped around her, yanking her up before she could hit the ground.

Kinsey's heart was beating double time. She lifted her face to thank Ryder, but words deserted her. His mouth was mere breaths from hers.

Her hands were splayed on his chest where she could feel his heart beneath her right palm. Without meaning to, she swayed against him.

One large hand was pressed against her back, right above her butt. The other held the back of her head. His wide lips were parted, and his gaze refused to release her.

She knew what it felt like to be kissed by Ryder. How with just a touch he could make the world fade away, how he could fill her mind with just one thought—him.

No one had kissed her like him since he'd left. And she had looked for such a man.

Just one more kiss. What could that hurt?

"Are you all right?" Henry asked as he reached them.

Kinsey hastily stepped out of Ryder's arms. She felt him hesitate, as if he wanted to keep her there, but he released her.

Damn that was close. She was really going to have to watch herself, because to give in just a little to Ryder's magnetism was to give him all of her again.

"Yes, thank you," she told Henry before she turned and walked out the door.

Behind her, she heard Henry ask Ryder, "Did I interrupt something?"

She wasn't able to hear Ryder's response. A pity. She would've liked to know what he was thinking. Not that it mattered. She was over him.

Keep telling yourself that, honey. It might be true when you're dead.

Kinsey felt like screaming. That hole in her chest that threatened to swallow her was back, as if she hadn't spent the last three years doing her damnedest to fill it in.

The tragic and appalling part was that she really thought she had.

It only took being next to him again to remind Kinsey that she'd allowed herself to believe she was moving on when she hadn't been.

Suddenly she was engulfed by depression and misery. She wasn't the strong individual she'd thought. She was weak and exposed. And so tired of pretending.

Why did it take coming face-to-face with the man who'd torn her world apart to reveal the truth? She'd told the lie of being fine so many times that even she believed it.

But she wasn't okay. She was torn, bloodied, and still bleeding. The wound was a trickle now, but it had yet to heal. Kinsey feared it never would.

Then to be tempted by what she couldn't have was the worst sort of anguish. What had she done to deserve such torment?

The biting wind cut through her sweater, but Kinsey barely felt it. She was too caught up in her own misery and the bleak outlook for her future to care.

Something heavy and warm was placed over her shoulders. She instinctively reached up and felt the flannel inside the coat. Henry gave her a nod after he settled the coat on her shoulders and walked beside her.

"You look like the rug just got yanked from underneath you."

She didn't want to talk, but she couldn't be rude either. "It did."

"I'm an arse, Kinsey. I apologize for interrupting what was clearly something intimate," he said.

With a shake of her head she said, "I'm glad you did. What we had is over."

"Are you sure? Because it didn't look that way to me. In fact, it looked quite the opposite."

Kinsey followed Ryder with her eyes as he joined Con ahead of her. "It is. He made sure of it when he left."

"Perhaps he left for a reason."

"He already explained his side," she said. "It still doesn't make up for the three years he let pass. At any time he could've returned or called. Hell, even a text would've been nice."

Henry looked at her with a sad smile. "Did you ever stop to think that perhaps Ryder assumed you'd moved on and wanted to give you a nice life?"

"No. With how easily he finds and tracks people, he knows I didn't have anyone serious in my life."

"Right," Henry said, searching for something else to say.

Kinsey stopped and touched his arm. "I know about Rhi."

"Don't," he stated in a voice laced with anger. "I don't want to hear you tell me to walk away like the others have."

"I won't. I know how it feels to love someone I can't have."

Henry's face relaxed as he blew out a breath. "I think you could have Ryder. If you wanted him."

"That look you wear? The one that says you're on the brink of shattering, the one that tries to hide the agony within you? I know it all too well. I've lived it for years. Time doesn't heal all wounds. It serves only to keep the wound festering. A constant reminder of what we'll never have. It doesn't allow us to move on or forget.

"It teases us with the hope that we might get past such suffering, but in an ironic twist of fate, we're reminded by inconsequential, mundane things that the pain is as much a part of us as the organs that keep us alive."

Kinsey turned her head to look at Ryder. His short blond hair was ruffled in the wind as snow flurries hung seemingly in midair. He stood as unaffected by the weather as he did the passage of time.

She huddled deeper into the coat. "Ryder and I are worlds apart, and it's never been more clear than at this moment. That bitterness that takes up more and more space where our hearts used to be is going to smother everything else. I'm living proof of that."

CHAPTER TWENTY

Austin, Texas

Rhi cruised the hills of Austin. The sun was shining bright and the temperature was only in the mid-forties. She adjusted her sunglasses before she glanced at the seat beside her.

Her watcher was there. It made her smile when she teleported to the storage unit where she kept the Lamborghini parked.

She almost asked if he wanted to go for a ride with her, then decided against it at the last minute. If he wasn't going to respond to her, then she wouldn't talk to him.

It wasn't until after she got into the sports car and started it up, the engine rumbling deeply, that she felt his presence beside her. How else was he supposed to keep up with her unless he rode beside her?

Rhi bit back a laugh when she tried to imagine what he would do if someone else had been with her. Would her watcher cling to the top of the car? Or run alongside her?

Driving was one of the few human experiences that

she truly enjoyed—besides shopping and getting her nails done. Though she could teleport anywhere she wanted, as well as use the Fae doorways to go to other realms, there was something calming about driving around.

But her awesome car definitely had something to do with it.

She pressed the accelerator, revving the engine as she zoomed through the traffic, weaving in and out of the cars. The Lamborghini responded lightning quick. It was the epitome of a sports car, and she truly loved being behind the wheel of such a machine.

Rhi laughed out loud when she zoomed around a bright red Ferrari. The man in his late fifties watched her as she hauled ass past him.

"Tell me that wasn't fun, sweet cheeks?" she asked her watcher. Then she rolled her eyes as she recalled she wasn't supposed to talk to him.

But she could almost feel his smile. Whoever he was, he was having fun.

"Doesn't it get old not talking? I know it does for me," Rhi said. "I told myself I wasn't going to talk to you, because I hate that I get silence in return."

She looked his way, trying to imagine his face. He would have black hair for sure, but was there silver in it? She didn't get the vibe that he was a Dark Fae. So no silver, but was his hair long or short?

Long. Definitely long.

"And more silence," she stated grumpily. "One day I'm going to discover who you are and why you've been following me. For your sake, I really hope it isn't on Usaeil's orders."

The Queen of the Light wasn't thrilled about Rhi walking out on her duties as Queen's Guard, but it was something Rhi had had to do.

"Usaeil has forgotten what it means to lead our people. And with the rumors of the arrival of the Reapers, she's needed more than ever."

Rhi could feel her watcher's gaze on her.

"Why are the Reapers back now?" she asked. "It might have something to do with that missing bit of text that Balladyn couldn't find. The Reapers have the entire race of Fae on pins and needles."

She slowed the car as she exited the highway and drove under a bridge to make her way back. Rhi was silent for a long time as she thought over all Balladyn had shared with her about the Reapers.

Wasn't it those in charge who should take the arrival of the Reapers seriously? Usaeil would rather talk about her next movie or magazine cover than a valid threat.

The more Rhi thought about Usaeil's dismissal of the Reapers, the angrier she became. It didn't matter that no one—not the lowest Fae or a king or queen—could stand against the Reapers. Usaeil should at least be comforting the Light, assuring them with knowledge.

By the time she returned to the storage unit, Rhi knew she had to see the text that Balladyn found with her own eyes. She parked the Lamborghini and shut off the engine, but she didn't exit the car.

Then something occurred to her that left her cold inside. The Reapers were judge, jury, and executioner for the Fae. No one knew how the Reapers were chosen or where they went, but without a doubt, every Fae knew the Reapers put balance back into the world.

Her watcher had shown up near the same time as whispers of the Reapers reached her. She also hadn't made such great decisions lately. Could she be targeted by them?

Rhi turned her head to look at the empty space her watcher occupied. Her blood was chilled at the thought of dying, but there was also a small voice that said she might actually find peace. "Are you a Reaper? If so and you've come to kill me, then get on with it. Drawing this out is just wrong."

Silence. Always silence.

She closed her eyes and faced forward. There was one time she'd wished for death—when her Dragon King lover left her. Rhi had even ventured into an area that guaranteed her death. And yet she'd somehow lived.

Her grief had been so profound that she wondered if she'd dreamed it all, because when she woke she was back at her cottage in Italy.

A hand covered hers.

Rhi looked down at her right hand. She couldn't see her watcher, but she could feel him. He was comforting her in the only way he could. And she had a feeling he wasn't supposed to be doing even that.

It wasn't the touch of someone about to end her life. She breathed a little easier, even as she contemplated some of her latest decisions.

"Thank you," she whispered.

His fingers tightened around hers for a moment, and then his touch was gone.

She opened the car door and climbed out. As she straightened, movement out of the corner of her eye caught her attention. "Ulrik," she said when she found him leaning a shoulder against the side of the entrance with his arms crossed over his chest.

He wore dark denim and a long-sleeved goldish taupe Henley with the sleeves pushed up to his elbows. His long black hair was pulled back in a queue showing off his chiseled features.

"Hello, beautiful."

The fact he was there caused her to be leery. She shut the car door and faced him. "How did you find me?"

"The same way I knew of your cottage in Italy. I pity you deserted it, by the way. The place suited you."

"I need privacy. The fact you knew about it made it pointless," she retorted.

He smiled, but it didn't reach his gold eyes. "There's no need to get upset. You've paid me plenty of visits lately."

"True. So what do you want?"

"To talk."

She leaned her hip against the black Lamborghini. "Try again. You blasted me with dragon and Dark magic the last time we met."

"Did I? My apologies. You know I'd never intentionally harm you."

Oddly enough, Rhi believed him. "You look . . . different."

Rhi blinked, shocked to her very core when she saw a true smile from Ulrik. It filled his eyes, and that's when she saw a contentment about him she hadn't seen before.

But as quick as it came, it vanished.

"You look different as well." He tilted his head to the side as he studied her. "If I didn't know better, I'd say you've been well and truly bedded."

Rhi held his gaze, determined not to look away. Her love life—as well as who she took as a lover—was no one's business. Especially anyone, even remotely, connected to Dreagan.

"I'll be damned," Ulrik murmured with a grin. "Did you give in to Balladyn?"

She looked down at her Christian Louboutin black booties as if bored. "This is where you tell me why you're here."

"All right. You doona want to talk about Balladyn, then we willna. Let's talk about Dreagan."

"We won't be discussing that place either, because I know why you want to talk about it."

His black brows rose. "Do you?"

"Stop," she said harshly. "I'm tired of the games. All games. I'm tired of everyone wanting something from me, and more than anything I'm beyond exhausted with everyone wanting to talk about that asshole. I'm done with him, with whatever it was we had. It's been over for thousands of years, and I've finally accepted that. So do me a favor and never mention him again. Or I won't be responsible for what I do to you."

For the second time in minutes, Ulrik gave her a rare—and brief—smile. "That's what I wanted to know."

"What?"

"I wanted to see if you've let him go. You have."

Rhi pushed away from her car and hooked her thumb in the front pocket of her jeans. "Why do you care?"

"Oh, you know exactly why."

She swallowed hard. "Keep your revenge to the one who deserves it."

"Con will get his. Of that you doona need to fear."

Fear? No, that's not what she felt at all. She wasn't sure she could name the emotion within her. "I still have friends there, Ulrik."

"Meaning you'll come to their defense if they ask."

"They won't have to ask. I'll be there for them. Always."

He nodded and dropped his arms before he stood straight. "I hear Henry is looking for you."

"How do you know all of this? Henry wouldn't talk to you, nor would any of the Kings."

"True. Verra, verra true," he replied with a wink.

Rhi was fast losing patience. "You're not going to tell me?"

"What would be the fun in that? So you could run back to Dreagan and tell them?"

"Of course not." Not unless he endangered the others, which was a very real possibility. "You already attacked Con."

Ulrik laughed, but it was hollow and fake. "My dear, Rhi, that wasna a battle. You'll know when I challenge Con."

"Is it going to be soon?"

Ulrik shrugged and walked to the passenger side of the Lamborghini. He stopped and leaned his arms on the roof, his hands clasped together. "Stay safe."

Then he was gone. Rhi turned in a circle looking for him, but the King of the Silvers had apparently teleported away.

"Since when do the Dragon Kings have that ability?" she asked herself.

Ulrik's power was to bring people back from the dead. Teleportation was something only the Fae and Fallon, one of the Warriors, was able to do.

If Ulrik had the ability to go anywhere he wanted at any time, then that was a distinct advantage over Con. She started to go to Dreagan and tell Con, but she hesitated. If the positions were reversed, she knew for a fact Con wouldn't tell her.

It wasn't as if she would never tell one of the Kings what she'd learned, but she wasn't in a hurry to do it.

"Later," she said and looked to her watcher. She hit the button that would close the storage unit and lock it. "Time to leave."

CHAPTER TWENTY-ONE

Kinsey shifted uncomfortably from both the cold and the situation as she stood behind a row of thick hedges that separated the manor from the distillery.

Beside her was Henry, who looked as if he were about to be sick. Con was on her other side, his gaze focused through the hedges. Ryder was strolling the grounds, whistling, as if he were on his way to one of the other buildings.

"I don't want to believe this about Esther," Henry said.

Kinsey glanced at the Brit, hurting for him. But there was nothing to say to make it any better. The facts were all laid out, and though Henry didn't want to accept it, he already had.

She turned back to peering through the leaves of the evergreen to watch Ryder as he approached Henry's sister.

Esther glanced up when she heard Ryder and tried to duck out of the way, but there was nowhere for her to go. That's when Ryder pretended to just see her.

"Hello," he said with a smile. "Can I help you with something?"

Esther shook her head of dark hair. "I'm fine, thanks," she responded in a perfect Welsh accent.

"It's freezing," Ryder said and glanced at the sky. "We're supposed to have a nasty snowstorm later. Come inside for some tea with the other agents."

"Thank you, but I'm fine."

Ryder walked closer to her and lowered his voice as he glanced around. "You're trying to prove you can do as much as the men. I get it. But you can no' do that if you're frozen solid. Your lips are turning blue, lass."

She hesitated, absently rubbing her gloved hands together. As if on cue, the flurries turned into flakes that began to fall harder. Kinsey wondered if it was something one of the Dragons Kings had done since it was timed so perfectly. Now that she knew what Ryder's secrets were, she looked at everything—and everyone—at Dreagan as magical.

Whereas just a few moments before Esther had looked hale and hearty, she appeared to weaken right before their eyes. Kinsey frowned. Was it more magic she was witnessing?

"He's got her," Con whispered when Esther followed Ryder into one of the buildings.

Kinsey didn't know one red-roofed building from the other, but wherever Ryder was taking Henry's sister, it was someplace that was secluded.

She, Con, and Henry walked in through a second door, pausing when they heard Ryder's voice over the huge copper stills.

A moment later they walked through another glass door. It wasn't until Kinsey neared it that she realized it was a small room next to an office. Inside the room was an old iron fireplace that Ryder was feeding wood.

Esther sat on a chair huddled in front of the growing fire as if she were frozen from the inside out. She was so intent on the fire that she never heard the door open or the three of them walk inside.

Con pulled Kinsey with him as they moved behind Esther. Henry remained by the door. Then he slammed it shut. Esther's head jerked up, her gaze meeting her brother's.

"Hello, Esther," Henry said. "Fancy seeing you here, sis."

Kinsey had to give Esther credit, she remained in character while putting her hands near the fire. "I don't know an Esther."

"Give it up," Henry said, his voice dripping with anger and agitation. "I know it's you. You're good. I'll give you that, but you forgot to make sure to cover the small scar near your temple. The one I gave you years ago when we played cricket."

There was a drawn-out pause before Esther sighed and gave a shake of her head. "What the bloody hell are you doing here, Henry?" she asked in the same refined British accent as her brother.

"I asked first. When were you going to tell me you joined MI5?"

She lifted her chin. "Eventually. How did you find out?"

"Me," Ryder said. "I check everyone who walks onto Dreagan."

Esther shrugged, as if she didn't care that her cover was blown. "I like MI5. It suits me as it always suited you."

"Do our parents know?"

She looked at him as if he'd just asked her to strip naked. "Of course not. What kind of daughter do you think I am?"

"I'm wondering what kind of sister you are," Henry said as he clasped his hands behind his back. "You lied to me. Repeatedly."

"And how many times have you lied to me and our parents?" she retorted. "Too many to count, that's for sure."

Henry scrubbed a hand down his face. "So MI5 is working out great for you, aye?"

"Yes."

"Is that why they decommissioned you?"

She got to her feet and glared. "How do you know that?"

"That doesn't concern you."

"It does if you're looking into me," she said and moved a step closer to him.

Henry looked down his nose at her. "Which side are you on, Esther? Are you on the side of MI5 that I've been working to eliminate? The ones who focus on people like those here at Dreagan, concocting all kinds of lies to keep them under surveillance?"

"No. Never," she said, appalled.

Henry gazed at her a long time before he said, "Prove it."

"Stuart, your boss and friend, took a liking to me. He didn't approve of the group training me and took me under his wing. He said if I was going to be an agent, he was going to make sure I was trained right. That's how I learned what the two of you were doing. I offered to help out."

"And?" Henry urged when she stopped.

She threw up her hands in aggravation. "What do you think? I was relieved of duty."

Kinsey saw the subtle way Henry shifted his feet. Ryder also positioned himself closer to the door. Whatever answers Esther was giving, they weren't the ones they were looking for.

Henry bowed his head. He stood with his hands on his hips as the silence of the room was broken only by the pop of the fire.

"It's time to stop with the lies," Henry said without lifting his head. "It's easy to become so engrossed in them that even when we need to tell the truth, we can't. I've been there many times. You have to force yourself to let go of the shroud of lies."

"I'm not lying."

At this, Henry's head lifted. His eyes were now as hard as iron. His entire demeanor changed. Gone was the concerned brother. In his place was a man intent on getting answers—no matter who stood across from him.

"Stuart never mentioned you. He would've, Esther. He, more than most, knows how important family is since his brother was an MI5 agent killed in the line of duty. He would've alerted me the moment he discovered you."

Esther shrugged, as if she didn't care that he'd caught that lie.

"As for the rest, I was there when most of the bad seeds were terminated. You weren't one of them. You have one more chance to tell me the truth."

She resumed her seat and looked back into the flames of the fire. "Not going to happen."

Kinsey didn't so much as move a muscle. She couldn't believe a brother and sister who seemed as close as Henry and Esther could grow apart so drastically. The idea that it could happen to her and her sister made Kinsey's stomach roll with dread.

Kinsey spotted Henry give a nod to Ryder. The next moment, Esther bent over at the waist. She struggled to breathe while doing her best to remain seated.

"What . . . are you . . . doing?" Esther asked in a voice that was more whimper than shout.

"Getting answers," Henry stated.

Kinsey couldn't actually see Ryder doing anything to Esther, but it was obvious that he was.

"He's no' hurting her," Con said in a low voice.

Kinsey glanced at him. "It sure looks like it."

"Every King has their own special power. I can heal anything. Ryder's is weakness. Esther isna feeling any pain. She is experiencing fragility."

Kinsey felt a little better knowing that, but that didn't make it any easier to watch. She'd learned about Ryder and the other Dragon Kings in stages and was barely holding it all together. Without a doubt, she knew she'd be at a complete loss if she found out all at once.

Now that Kinsey realized what Ryder was doing, she could see the feebleness of Esther's movements. It was like all the energy had departed her body, leaving Esther as weak as a newborn.

"I'll not tell you anything," Esther rasped.

Henry crossed his arms over his chest. "Yes, you will."

Con stepped around Kinsey and walked to stand beside Henry. "Perhaps she'd prefer to speak to me."

As soon as Con appeared, Esther's gaze widened, a gleam of surprise and glee filling them. Kinsey knew firsthand how laid back Con appeared—when he was anything but. And right now, even Kinsey could tell that Con was angry.

But more than anything, the recognition in Esther's eyes gave her away.

"Constantine," Esther said.

Henry pivoted to stand between his sister and Con. He faced the King of Kings. "No. This is what she wants."

"Then let's give her what she wants," Con said with a shrug.

Kinsey slid her gaze to Ryder to find him watching her. She wished she knew what he was thinking, and she still wasn't entirely happy with the fact that she was in the room. If nothing else, she was getting a taste of what the Dragon Kings were capable of.

And it made her wonder why any human would dare intervene in their war.

It wasn't as if humans were any different when they interrogated others. In fact, there was usually pain involved. Esther wasn't feeling any of that. Kinsey wondered if the spy had any idea how lucky she was to be getting off so easy.

Ryder's hazel eyes held her, refusing to allow Kinsey to look away. Not that she wanted to. How she wished she didn't continue to gravitate toward him when she became uncomfortable or fearful, and yet that's exactly what happened.

Twice now she'd nearly kissed him. There was no way she could withstand much more of his seduction. And Ryder wasn't even trying to seduce her.

Yet.

Kinsey knew how sexy and charming Ryder was when he wanted. He'd not turned that on her, but if the look he was giving her now was any indication, it was coming. Soon.

Why the hell did that give her a jolt of exhilaration?

She took a step toward him before she even realized it. Kinsey drew up short instantly. This same irresistible attraction she felt was how she and Ryder first came together across a crowded street.

A hundred years from now she would still recall that moment of looking up from the streets of Glasgow and finding Ryder standing still in the middle of people moving all around him. His gaze had been locked on her, much as it was at that moment.

Kinsey had attempted to turn away then, but she didn't bother this time. He'd walked across the busy intersection without ever looking away from her, not stopping until he stood before her.

His smile had been amazing, his face swoon-worthy.

At that precise moment, Kinsey had become Ryder's. Now, four years later, much to her horror, she realized she was still his.

Would always be his.

"I'm sure you have questions," Con said to Esther, splintering into Kinsey's thoughts.

Kinsey silently thanked Con and focused her attention back onto Esther before she gave in to the urge to go to Ryder. But she could still feel Ryder's gaze, still sense the desire that filled the air.

"Yes," Esther said.

Kinsey's mind echoed that word as her blood heated, thinking of being held within Ryder's strong arms.

Henry returned to his position, his narrowed gaze on his sister who stared at Con as if he'd been delivered to her upon a silver platter.

"Ask away," Con urged her.

Esther's smile was slow. "Show me who you are."

Con's laugh was loud and hollow. "What you see is

what you get. I'm nothing more than a man running a verra large, verra profitable company."

"You're dragons," Esther said, her hand upon her chest as she drew in a large breath. It was everything she could do to hold her head up.

Kinsey looked at each man in the room to see their reactions. They all observed Esther intently.

Henry gave a shake of his head and snorted. "You can't tell me you really believe that dribble all over the news."

"We . . . have proof," Esther said breathlessly and added a smile despite her growing weakness.

Con cocked his head to the side. "What proof?"

"Eyewitness," she whispered as if it took her great effort.

"A bloody lie," Henry stated.

Con squatted down so he could look Esther in the eye as she began to lean to the side, her body unable to keep her upright. "Have you wondered where Henry's been?"

Esther shook her head, unable to voice any more words she was so weak.

"Perhaps you should've," Con said. "He's worked tirelessly to protect innocents all over the world. He's been a friend to us here on Dreagan. Henry has a knack for judging people, does he no'? Perhaps you should consider that."

When Con stood, he shot a look to Ryder.

Kinsey watched as Esther fell unconscious. Henry was there to catch her in his arms. He stood, holding her carefully despite the anger on his face.

"We need to discover how much she knows as well as who she's working with," Henry said.

Ryder considered Henry. "She's your sister. Do you have any idea what you're wanting us to do?"

"What needs to be done. This is my home now too. I'll protect it," Henry stated. "Besides, I want her to learn the truth of everyone. She's chosen the wrong side."

"And if her mind can no' be changed?" Con asked.

Henry turned his face away. "I'll deal with that if the time comes."

CHAPTER TWENTY-TWO

It was nearly midnight when Ryder quietly walked into his room. The afternoon and evening had been filled with more work at the computer. As difficult as it'd been, he didn't talk to Kinsey about anything other than work—which had been torture when all he wanted was her in his arms.

And with them digging into Ulrik, Kyvor, and now Esther, there was a lot to do.

Dinner was eaten at their desks. At ten, Ryder had called an end to the day for Kinsey. She didn't argue. She simply rose and walked away, covering a yawn with her hand.

He'd debated whether to venture into his room again. Ryder had gotten away with sleeping with her the night before, but he was taking a chance two nights in a row.

But he couldn't stay away.

He closed the door softly behind him. Tonight, Kinsey was buried under the covers with her dark hair spread out around her. Ryder walked to the other side of the bed and removed his shoes.

Just as the night before, he gingerly sat and slowly lay back. His thoughts wandered through the day and all that had happened. Time and again, he returned to the memories of their near kisses.

She wanted the kiss, wanted him. Of that Ryder was certain. He could see it in her eyes, hear it in the way her breathing changed. Why did she keep pulling away when she wanted it as much as he?

He knew he'd hurt her, but it wasn't in a mortal's nature to keep turning away from something they craved. That's where he'd underestimated her. It was going to take much more than her desire to make her give in to him.

For the first time, Ryder began to worry that he might not win Kinsey back. It made it all the harder, because she was at Dreagan. She knew their secrets and was part of their lives. He was getting to see firsthand how it would be if he took her as his mate.

He wanted it so badly he could taste it.

His eyes closed, promptly shutting out dismal thoughts of Kinsey refusing him. Instead, he returned to thinking about the second time she nearly allowed their kiss.

The way her fingers had pressed into his chest and how she'd leaned against him were all signs she wanted their kiss. Ryder slowed the recollection, committing every second to memory from the way her lips parted and her chest heaved to her eyes dilating.

There was a sigh before Kinsey turned over in her sleep toward him. Ryder moved his head to look at her. Her face was mere inches from him.

He carefully lifted his arm up to drape over his pillow. There was a desperate need to touch her, hold her. But somehow Ryder kept his hands to himself. He didn't want her waking.

If all he could have was lying beside her as she slept, then that's what he'd take.

Ryder didn't know how long he lay there listening to her breathe while wondering what she dreamed of. To his surprise, Kinsey scooted closer to him.

He moved his arm to lightly rest around her. A smile formed when she shifted once more until her head was on his chest. Only then was Ryder able to close his eyes.

Kinsey was where she was always meant to be—in his arms.

Kinsey snapped open her eyes. She'd had the weirdest dream that Ryder had been in bed with her. She sat up and looked at the pillow, but once more there was no evidence of anyone having laid their head there.

She rose and showered, thinking about the dream the entire time. Even while she dried her hair, she recalled how vivid her dream had been. It was so clear she would've bet money Ryder was in bed with her.

Did she want it so badly that even her subconscious mind was turning against her?

After she dressed, Kinsey made her way to the kitchen. This morning there was no sign of Lexi, Thorn, or anyone else. There was a plate of bacon next to a toaster and a loaf of bread.

Kinsey poured some coffee while the bread was in the toaster. When it was done, she lightly buttered it and stood by the counter eating toast while looking out the window.

The snow still fell heavily, thickly covering the ground. It was going to make things difficult for the MI5 agents, which worked in Dreagan's favor.

That made her smile. Then she stilled. Was she on Dreagan's side? After the talk Con, Henry, and Ryder had had with Esther, it was all Kinsey had been able to think about.

The dragons still frightened her, but not as much as the day before or the day before that. The longer she was around Ryder and the others, the more comfortable she became with the idea of who they were.

That wasn't something she'd seen coming. But it made sense. Just as it was easy for her to acknowledge that she was on Dreagan's side. If she could be neutral, she would, but someone at Kyvor had made sure to put her smack in the middle.

So Kinsey chose a side. Dreagan's.

After what she saw the night before with Ryder weakening Esther with his power, she wondered if there was someone at the estate who could control the weather.

She finished eating before she made her way up to the computer room. Ryder was there finishing off a jelly donut, a deep frown on his face as he looked at something on one of the screens.

"Good morning," Kinsey said.

He gave her a nod without looking in her direction. "Morning."

"Did you stay here all night?"

"No."

That's all she was going to get. Kinsey shrugged and took her seat. She pulled her chair forward and rested her hands on the virtual keyboard that immediately lit up. She could really get used to this kind of technology at her fingertips all the time.

No sooner had she touched a key than one of the screens flashed red before listing pages of information.

"How long has this been ready?" she asked.

There was a pause from Ryder as he glanced at her screen. "A few hours."

"Why didn't you look?"

"Other business," he said before turning back to his monitor.

Whatever Ryder was looking at must be important. Kinsey scrolled through the pages of documents listing Esther's assignments and the reports filed by her and her handler.

After reading a dozen reports that were putting her to sleep, Kinsey switched to another monitor and checked more Kyvor e-mails. She opened each and every one, scanning the words.

This is the part of her job she hated. Ryder could probably write some software to do this for her, but Kinsey wanted to be the one to find the needle in the haystack.

Clarice Steinhold had been used as a patsy, and so had Kinsey. But people made mistakes. It was just a matter of Kinsey looking in every nook and cranny, every e-mail and memo that went out. There was something, somewhere.

Ryder believed she was innocent, and right now that sufficed for everyone. How much longer would Con and the others leave her be before they questioned her as they were most likely doing with Esther?

Kinsey didn't want to think about Henry's sister right now. Her attention needed to be directed at the information before her. It was bad enough that the words began to blur. She was so tired of reading stupid e-mails talking about meetings and how some person or other wasn't doing their job that she could puke.

She stopped and rubbed her eyes. A glance at the time

showed she'd been at it for hours. Kinsey then rose and stretched to give her poor muscles something to do. When she looked over at Ryder, he was still intent on whatever he was working on.

With a yawn, she sat back down and spotted the note Ryder left her. It was a code to another piece of software he'd designed that would look for encoded e-mails.

Kinsey didn't waste another moment opening the software and putting it into action. While it worked, she decided to read more of the reports from Esther when an e-mail to Harriet Smythe caught her eye. It was from someone named Brewster.

She opened it, her stomach dropping to her feet as she read.

It's all set. If KB has knowledge of the truth, it's hidden well. A search of the house and computer came up empty. We'll try for the mobile phone within the next day or so.

Kinsey could barely pull in a breath. KB. That was her. It had to be her.

She scrolled down to read the previous message from Harriet.

Is everything ready? We've put a lot into this plan. Nothing can go wrong. I need to know everything she knows.

Kinsey's hand was shaking as she moved the cursor with the trackpad to the attachments sent in a previous e-mail. As soon as they loaded and she saw pictures of her and Ryder, Kinsey leapt from her chair.

"Kins?" Ryder asked in concern as he turned to her.

She could only point to the monitor and their pictures. Ryder rolled his chair over. He was silent as he scanned all ten pictures of them strolling through the streets of Glasgow during the day, eating dinner, exiting a movie theater, and lounging on her sofa. He said nothing as he read through the e-mails.

It wasn't until he sat back and she saw his troubled expression that she asked, "Does this clear me?"

"I never believed you were guilty to begin with, you know that. However, this is definitely on the way to absolving you."

What? Surely she didn't hear him right. "What do you mean 'on the way'? This proves I wasn't involved."

Ryder turned his chair to face her. "Look at this from Con's point of view. What this proves is that you found an e-mail where someone is talking about KB."

"KB is me," she insisted.

"How many other employees at Kyvor have those initials?"

She raised a brow. "Need I remind you about the pictures?"

"It's better to gather all the information. It'll be relevant at some point."

Kinsey was usually much better at collecting material, but she'd never had her name slung through the mud before. This was her life, and it hit her harder than she'd imagined.

"I want to find out who is responsible."

Ryder gave a nod. "We know who's responsible. Ulrik. We need to ascertain the ones doing his dirty work in order to prove you've been used by him."

"Con still thinks I'm part of it, doesn't he?"

Ryder rocked back in his chair and closed the lid to the box of donuts. "Con wants definitive evidence before he'll clear you."

"All right. Then I'll find it. I know I'm not a part of this."

"I do, too."

She met his gaze, losing herself in his eyes. They were more green than blue at the moment, but the gold bled everywhere. Such gorgeous eyes. They made her think of forever. "Why do you believe me?"

"Because I know you."

"That was three years ago."

He lifted one shoulder. "I still know you."

Was he trying to tell her that she should know him as well? How could she when he hadn't shared his secrets? Despite that, she knew he was the one person who would stand with her. That kind of assurance went a long way in giving her the courage to dig ever deeper into his world.

"What are the odds that we'll find what we need?" she asked.

At this Ryder dropped his gaze. "I doona know. In the past, Ulrik has covered his tracks so well that I've no' been able to find the links connecting everything."

That wasn't good news at all. If even Ryder was stumped then Ulrik had to be really, really good. Or lucky. Or . . .

"What is it?" Ryder asked.

Kinsey lowered herself back into her chair. "In all my years doing this, I've never seen anyone with half as much skill as you have. Not even the expert hackers who were convicted and then got hired by corporations to ensure they didn't get hacked."

"Your point?" Ryder asked, a slight smile on his lips.

"If you can't find what's missing to connect everything to Ulrik that means that he's really good or lucky."

Ryder blinked, a look of alarm covering his face. "Or he's no' working alone."

Kinsey nodded. "Have you not thought of that before?"

"Briefly. But Ulrik wouldn't share his revenge with anyone, so that couldna be what's happening."

"Is he that good with computers?"

Ryder's lips twisted. "I doona think so."

"Is he that lucky?"

"He's been damned lucky lately. Too lucky."

They shared a smile, because no one was that lucky.

CHAPTER TWENTY-THREE

Ryder was at once both happy at what Kinsey had found and anxious at her musings.

"Are you going to tell Con?" Kinsey asked.

Ryder gazed into her violet eyes. From the moment he spotted her four years ago on the streets of Glasgow, he'd had the compelling urge to protect her.

Well, that wasn't his first thought. His first thought had been that he wanted her. On the heels of their gazes clashing, Ryder knew he'd have her. That's when the need to protect her began.

From then on, that emotion only intensified and expanded until it occupied his thoughts constantly. After he left her, Ryder made sure he kept watch over her since he knew better than most just what monsters were out in the world.

Now that Kinsey was once more by his side, he hadn't been able to cap the need to safeguard her. The longer she was on Dreagan and the more information they uncovered, the more he knew she was in serious danger.

"Ryder?" she asked with a furrow of her brow.

He swallowed and began to reach for a donut. Just before his fingers grabbed a pastry, he hesitated. It wasn't the donut he wanted.

It was Kinsey.

He'd been hard since the first night he slept beside her. Leaving her that morning had been nearly impossible.

"Aye," he finally answered. "I'll tell Con."

"We'll tell him," she corrected.

There was movement at the doorway and then a blond head emerged. "Tell me what?"

Before Ryder could speak, Kinsey was talking.

"I found an e-mail with pictures of me and Ryder."

Con briefly looked at Ryder. "What else?"

Ryder knew how important it was to Kinsey that Con believe she was innocent, so he sat back and allowed her to answer all the questions.

Kinsey's wide violet eyes were trained on Con as she pointed to the monitor. "The e-mail was exchanged between Harriet and another individual."

"Harriet is the person above your boss, correct?"

Kinsey gave a firm nod, a slight lift to her lips. "Correct. The individual mentions KB."

To help, Ryder swiped the thread of e-mails from Kinsey's computer to the wall behind Con. Constantine turned to read them.

Kinsey's quick smile she shot toward Ryder made his gut clench. She thought it was enough to absolve her in Con's eyes, but he knew Con would think differently.

The information was certainly going to help, but it wasn't going to clear her altogether.

"Interesting," Con said as he turned back to face Kinsey. "The pictures confirm it's you they speak of. Otherwise, KB could be anyone."

Kinsey's lips flattened for a heartbeat. "I know. Ryder

and I already spoke about that. The fact is, that e-mail is about me."

"They got into your flat and computer."

Ryder leaned back in his chair, his hands laced behind his head. "I already thoroughly checked and cleaned her computer and mobile when she arrived. There was nothing on it."

"That you found," Con said.

Ryder held his gaze for a long stretch of silence. Ulrik had gotten something past Ryder once. That wasn't going to happen again. "There was nothing."

"I'm happy to hear it." Con then shifted his attention to Kinsey. "This is certainly important. It proves they were watching you for some time. It also shows that these people knew our true natures, and they fully expected you did as well."

Ryder closed his eyes in frustration. He then sat up, his gaze snapping open. "In all of this, we've assumed that Kinsey was working with those at Kyvor."

"I'm not," she stated.

He ignored her and continued. "What if they were hoping she did know something to force her to talk about it?"

"When they learned she knew nothing, then they changed tactics," Con said with a nod.

Kinsey sat back down and rested an elbow on the table. "To do what?"

"If you didna have information to share, then they were going to put you in the nest with us," Ryder told her.

Her lips parted as the truth hit her. "So that I would turn to them scared out of my mind and give them what they want. That's why Cecil was so adamant that I remain this morning."

Con pointed to the e-mails behind him on the wall. "There is more. This isna the first e-mail."

"Or the last," Ryder added.

Kinsey puffed out her cheeks before she blew out a breath. She turned her chair to face the table and began typing. "All right, you little buggers," she said to the screen of e-mails. "Just try and hide from me."

Ryder rose and followed Con from the room. Con waited in the corridor. "She's innocent."

"So both of you keep saying."

"You just saw proof."

Con merely looked at him. "Did we? How long have you been looking through those e-mails?"

"I've been focused on other things. Kinsey has been sorting through them for the better part of yesterday and today."

"In all those e-mails, she manages to find one that would clear her? You doona think that's odd?"

"I think she's good at what she does. I think she's been looking through every e-mail. She didna stumble upon this one."

Con twisted his lips. "Fair enough. So she found the e-mail. With her initials and pictures of the two of you?"

"We'll find the data needed to clear her name for good."

"And if you doona? Have you thought about that, Ryder?"

It'd crossed his mind a time or two. "I doona need to."

"Perhaps you should."

Ryder looked to the doorway. The rows of monitors hid Kinsey from view, but he could hear her talking to herself. "She's no' a part of this."

"I hope you're right. If you're wrong, then you've given Ulrik everything he needs to tear us apart."

Ryder watched Con walk away. He was sure of Kinsey. And yet, he couldn't help but worry. The implications

Con mentioned were staggering. Ryder wasn't just putting his own honor on the line. He was putting the entire way of life for everyone at Dreagan in jeopardy.

He strode back into the computer room, walked around the monitors, and grabbed Kinsey's chair. He jerked it back, turning it so she faced him. Then he put his hands on either side of her face and gazed into her violet eyes.

"Ry—" she began.

He kissed her, claiming her lips in a kiss that he'd been dying to give. Her mouth softened beneath his, parting so their tongues met, dancing against each other.

It was heaven. Pure, utter bliss.

Ryder knew he stepped over the boundaries Kinsey had set upon her arrival, but in all honesty, he didn't care. Not at that moment.

Now he needed to feel her, taste her. To remember what it was to have her as his. To know the curve of her cheek, the touch of her hand, the smell of her skin.

He ended the kiss the moment he sensed she was about to pull back. But he didn't release her. Instead, he continued to hold her head between his hands.

"I know you may hate me, and you've every right. But look around, Kins. This is home to us. Dragons and their mates. If you want to hurt me, then hurt me. Doona take the others down as well."

Her hands came up and grasped his wrists. Then she tugged his hands away firmly and forcibly. "I thought you believed me."

"I do." Ryder straightened, his gut twisting with all the doubt and worry. "I staked my word on it just now."

"Not from what you just said."

"We've been betrayed before. If you've come to get your revenge, all I ask is that you leave the others out."

She rolled her eyes and swiveled her chair back to the

computers. "You're a real piece of work. Telling me in one breath that you've got my back and believe me, and in the very next spouting drivel about revenge." She gave a loud, angry snort. "Oh, I wanted to get back at you, but I'm past that."

"All right."

"No!" she shouted and turned her head to glare at him. "It's not all right."

Ryder felt something tighten around his chest, making it difficult to breathe. What had he said wrong? Why was she reacting so? All he wanted her to know was that if she was working with those at Kyvor to leave the others out of it.

He gave a shake of his head, unable to find the logic to connect what he'd done to her emotional outburst.

"Either you believe me or not." Her eyes shot flames of annoyance and hurt.

"I believe you."

"Right," she stated sarcastically. "And don't kiss me again." She faced the computer, and this time she turned on her music, blaring it loudly.

His smile began slowly. So that's what had gotten her so riled. The kiss.

She hadn't just responded willingly, she'd wanted it as much as he. That must irritate her when she was trying so hard to pretend as if she had no feelings toward him anymore.

Now he knew differently.

Now Ryder was going after her with all he had. The fine line between love and hate had just been crossed with their kiss. It might not have been the words and caresses he'd been dreaming about giving her, but it was a kiss.

He tasted the hunger, the passion. The eagerness.

Ryder resumed his seat, where the smile quickly

evaporated as he stared at the screen. Whatever wee bit of elation he'd felt vanished as he looked at the pictures of them together.

He easily piggybacked on Kinsey's hack into Kyvor and went to the e-mail string about Kinsey. He pulled every picture they had of them onto a secure server.

Every moment of his time with Kinsey hadn't just been recorded, it had been shared with a group. It took Ryder longer than he wanted trying to determine who the group receiving the e-mails were, but whoever set it up had gone to great pains to bounce the signal all over the world, creating an e-mail address within an e-mail address within an e-mail address.

It was taking him forever to break through one of the addresses, and every step that brought him closer to discovering the truth left a bad taste in his mouth.

"Why didn't you tell Con that Ulrik might have someone working with him?"

Ryder paused in his typing at the sound of Kinsey's voice. "Because it's a theory."

"Theories are what break open cases sometimes."

"I've a million speculations about Ulrik. We doona have the time to chase all of them. He's already ahead of us."

"Then it's time for you to gain an advantage," she insisted. "There's no way Ulrik can be running things on his own."

Ryder ran a hand down his face. "It's no' so simple, Kins. We can no' trust anyone."

"Especially not humans."

"I didna say that."

"You didn't have to. I understand," she said, her voice laced with ire.

He sighed. "So many want to expose us."

"And why do you care?" she asked as she threw up her hands. She spun the chair to face him. "You're a bloody Dragon King. You can't be killed by anything other than another Dragon King. Why not show the world who you really are?"

"We did that once. It didna work verra well, if you remember from my story."

She looked down at her hands, picking at her thumbnail. "You've magic and powers. You can shift. You can fly and breathe fire. Why do you hide from us?"

"Because the alternative is to go to war with your race, and a second war means that one of us will be annihilated."

CHAPTER TWENTY-FOUR

Henry called upon every ounce of his training in order to keep his cool, but nothing worked. He wanted to yell and hit something. Hard.

He stared at a face he knew, but his sister was no longer the same person. MI5 and Ulrik had done their job to perfection. The girl he remembered who always had a dirty joke to tell and who was known for her infectious laughter was gone.

The woman in front of him had been reprogrammed, thoroughly erasing everything that made her special.

"Stop looking at me like that," Esther said from the chair in the middle of the cavern.

Con used his magic to make the room impossible for Esther to leave without Con beside her. So there was no need to tie her. But Con took it one step further and altered the cavern so it looked like an interrogation room instead of a cave.

Henry raised a brow. "Like what?"

"Like you don't know who I am."

"I don't."

She gave him a scathing look. "Do you think it was any different when you went to work for MI5?"

"I know it." He motioned to her. "You've erased all that you were. I didn't."

"Ah, dear brother, that's the rub. Because you did. You think you didn't change, but you're wrong."

Henry wasn't going to get into a debate with her about his life. This was about her. "I did a little digging through my contacts at the agency. You're no longer working for MI5, and haven't been for quite some time."

In response, she merely looked at him, her expression closed.

It's what he would expect from an agent. Henry clasped his hands behind his back. He wanted to ask specifically about Ulrik, but something held him back.

Henry didn't question his instinct. Though there was no doubt Ulrik was her new commander, Henry wasn't going to give her a name to latch onto. With all Henry knew about Ulrik, the Dragon King had most likely given her another name.

And another name was exactly what they needed. Despite Ryder's skill with computers, Ulrik managed to somehow keep anything from being connected to him.

"Who are you working for?" Henry asked.

Esther crossed one leg over the other. Her coat had been removed. She wore a thick taupe sweater and navy pants. If anyone saw her on the street, they wouldn't look twice at her. Just as Henry was able to blend in, Esther worked that trait as well.

"Do you even know who you work for?"

She smiled slightly. "Of course."

"Then why not tell me a name?"

"You're here with these . . . things . . . and you don't know?"

It was Henry's turn to stare noncommittally. If Esther thought she was good, she was in for a rude awakening. So far Henry had taken it easy on her because she was his sister.

And he began to suspect she expected just such a reaction.

Esther gave him a meaningful look. "You do know who these people are?"

"I do. They're honest and loyal. They're my friends."

"Then you'll go down with them."

The more Esther talked, the more Henry could see she wasn't his sister anymore. Blood was the only thing that bound them now. "You're so sure you'll win."

"I know it."

"Very confident of you. You can say that knowing who my friends are? Unless you don't really know."

Esther made a face. "They're dragons."

"Well, she got one thing right," said a voice Henry had been yearning to hear for weeks.

He whirled around to find Rhi standing behind him. She briefly met his gaze as she walked into the cavern. His heart was pounding, his palms sweating. Rhi was within reach. All he had to do was lift his arm and he could touch her.

He stopped himself before he gave anything away to either Rhi or Esther. It was bad enough he was head over heels in love with Rhi and that every King on Dreagan knew it. Later, he would tell Rhi of his feelings. Once they were alone.

Esther regarded Rhi with a mixture of curiosity and wariness that she hid well, but Henry knew what to look for.

"Your sister. Interesting." Rhi walked around Esther slowly, her gaze never leaving his sister.

Esther waited until Rhi stood in front of her before she asked, "Who are you?"

"You seem to know so much. I thought you'd know."

"I wouldn't be asking if I knew," Esther retorted.

Henry stood to the side so he could see both Rhi and Esther. Rhi appeared as if she'd interrogated others before, and as a Queen's Guard, perhaps she had.

Everything about Rhi made Henry love her more.

Rhi chuckled softly. "I don't think you've quite comprehended just how in over your head you are, darlin'."

"Beautiful, with an Irish accent. A seductress by the way she holds herself," Esther said as if talking to herself. Then she looked Rhi up and down. "And dresses. I'm guessing you use your body to gain information for those here at Dreagan."

At this, Rhi's smile grew. "That's a fair enough assessment. Except for one fact. I don't work for Con or anyone here. I'm a friend."

"So many friends," Esther said with a bite to her words. "Where were those friends earlier?"

Henry made himself focus on his sister. It was difficult since all he wanted to do was gaze at Rhi. She looked amazing in tall stilettos that had a black heel and a zipper at the back. The shoes had ultra-thin stripes of various colors from her toes to her ankles.

Skinny black pants that skimmed her lithe legs and stopped at her ankles were paired with an orange sweater. It didn't matter what she wore, she was gorgeous.

Rhi glanced at Henry. Then to Esther she said, "You proclaim to know those here on Dreagan. If you truly did, you'd know they don't need friends."

"Then why are you and Henry here?" Esther asked with a cocky smile.

Henry moved to stand beside Rhi. "Because that's

what friends do. They don't need me, but I'm here for them. Just as they'd be there for me if I needed them."

Esther shot him a contemptuous glare. "I thought you were smarter than that, big brother."

"I could say the same of you. It seems lying comes easily."

"You should know. You did enough of it through the years."

"I only lied about my assignments and where I was," he argued. "Other than that, I told you the truth."

His sister's smile was mocking. "Another lie."

"It's pointless to tell her anything," Rhi said to Henry. "She's not going to listen."

Henry was in agreement. "What do you suggest?"

"The truth. All of it," she said and waved her hand around the room.

Henry hesitated. "I've only begun to question her."

"Fear is a powerful motivator," Rhi stated and turned her back to Esther. She leaned close to Henry and whispered, "She doesn't fear you."

He knew that all too well, but it was his sister. Henry didn't want to turn her over to Con. He'd seen what Con could do to a person. They were never in any physical pain, but he used everything he could against them to get what he wanted.

A prime example was Grace, who was terrified of thunderstorms, and what did Con have Arian do but use his power to create a vicious storm?

But all of that was better than what humans did to their prisoners when an interrogation took place. Waterboarding, mutilation, drugs, and anything pain-filled they could think of was used.

"No. She doesn't fear me," Henry said blandly.

"Then let's give her someone she will fear."

Henry jerked his head to look at Rhi. "You can't be serious. You really want Con in here?"

Rhi flicked her long black hair over her shoulder and glanced at a corner. "I'm talking about me."

"You?"

"Don't act so surprised. I'm very good at this," she said with a lift of a black brow.

"No doubt." They needed answers, and Henry obviously wasn't going to be the one getting them. "Are you sure you want to do this?"

A serious light filled Rhi's silver gaze. "Yes. I owe you this."

"Owe me?" There was something in her tone that sent warning bells tolling in Henry's mind.

Rhi took his arm and walked him through the doorway into the tunnel. There she stopped and faced him. "I'd like to talk later. Right now, let me do this."

Talk. That wasn't what he wanted to do at all. Kissing. Now that's what he'd been dreaming about—when he actually slept.

"Henry, you look like hell. Get some rest and eat. You'll feel better," Rhi said, giving him a little push.

He took one step before he halted, a conversation with Con filling his mind. "I don't think it'd be wise for you to interrogate her alone."

"Because Con doesn't trust me?" she asked with a smile. "Way ahead of you, sweet cheeks."

No sooner were the words out of her mouth than Rhys turned the corner and walked toward them.

"Rhi," Rhys said and held out his arms.

The Light Fae threw her arms around his neck. Henry watched the embrace, hating the jealousy that soured him to the point he wanted to physically harm Rhys.

Rhi stepped out of Rhys's arms and turned to Henry. "See? It's all good."

"Henry," Rhys said in a tight voice.

He nodded to the King of the Yellows, noting that the smile was gone from Rhys's face.

"All right then," Rhi said as she widened her eyes and rubbed her hands together. "It's time we got some good intel."

Rhys waited until Rhi was in the cavern with Esther before he took a step closer to Henry. "Your sister willna be harmed."

"I know. I wanted to be the one that she spoke with. I thought she might share with me."

Rhys looked inside the cavern. "You're a good man, Henry. You've done amazing things to help us."

"Why do I get the feeling there's a 'but' coming?"

"Because there is. You're going to find a woman to love you."

Henry felt the fury rumble through him. "I already have."

"She's Fae. There can no' be a relationship. With only one kiss you can no' see anyone but her. If you take her to your bed, you'll never be able to have sex with anyone else."

"I don't want anyone else."

"Dammit man," Rhys said as he moved closer, his voice no more than a whisper. "If she has sex with you more than once, it'll begin to kill you. Can you no' understand that?"

Henry had never wanted anything like he wanted Rhi. "I'd gladly die to be in her arms once."

Rhys raked a hand through his long, wavy, dark hair. "You willna see reason."

"There's nothing to see." Soon they would understand that. He and Rhi belonged together. They were perfect.

And she wanted him. She'd declared that when she kissed him. The Kings were just envious because she was finally getting over the jackass King who'd allowed her to get away.

Now that Rhi had him, she didn't need a Dragon King. That made Henry smile. He would be all she ever needed, just as she was all he'd ever wanted.

Henry turned on his heel. It didn't even faze him that Guy was standing behind him. Henry rammed his shoulder into Guy's as he passed.

Yes, very soon Rhi was going to be his.

CHAPTER TWENTY-FIVE

"We've got a problem," Rhys whispered in her ear.

Rhi blew out a long breath as she felt her watcher move from her side to the corner. She'd hoped the Kings would be able to talk some sense into Henry, but the human was in love with her.

Except it wasn't real love. It was an imitation of the real thing, something a Fae forged within a mortal because the humans had no defense.

"I know. I'm going to talk to him," she said.

Rhys gave her a look that said it was going to take much more than talk with Henry.

Esther chose that moment to clear her throat. Rhi faced the human and studied the straight back, impassive face, and confidence of Esther North. If the mortal thought she knew what was going on, Rhi was about to blow her mind.

"Oh. Are you ready?" Rhi asked in a sickly sweet voice, a smile on her face.

Esther's smug expression intensified. "Henry is one of

the best at what he does. If he couldn't get anything out of me, neither can you."

Rhi looked at her nails, admiring the black polish that covered her entire nail. From nail tip and fading toward her cuticles was an orange glitter polish called Orange You Fantastic. It went wonderfully with her sweater and shoes.

There was nothing like matching all over. Including the orange and black lace bra and panties she wore. Rhi never felt sexier—or more put together—than when she matched.

"I'm definitely what you mortals call a girly-girl," Rhi said as she lowered her hand to her side and smiled once more at Esther.

She could feel her watcher's grin as well. If only she knew what he actually looked like.

Rhi's smile grew when Esther allowed a momentary lapse of uncertainty to creep into her hazel eyes.

"I do like my clothes and getting my nails done. I go often," Rhi said matter-of-factly.

Rhys grunted and crossed his arms over his chest. "Nearly every day."

Rhi threw him a wink. Then she focused on Esther. "The thing is, Henry *is* very good at what he does. So good that he was able to stop some very bad people within MI5. I helped as well. But that doesn't change the fact you're his little sister. It's part of who is he that he wants to protect you. He can't do that and interrogate you. Which is why we're here."

Esther lifted her chin. "I'm not going to tell you anything."

With a snap of his fingers, Rhys removed the magic Con had used to mask the cavern.

Esther blinked and took in the stone floor and walls, the torches lighting the area, and the dragons etched into the granite.

"Dreagan," Rhi said with a nod. "From the moment I first saw this place thousands of years ago, I felt the magic of it. It's a special place, and not just because the Dragon Kings call it home. It's unique because of the magic that flows through the ground and water and air. All the world used to feel like this, but now only Dreagan and a few distinct places manage to hold such magic."

"What did you give me?" Esther demanded.

Rhi held out a hand and another chair appeared. She dragged it to Esther and set it directly in front of her. Then Rhi sat. She looked Esther in the eye and said, "You've been given no drug or herbs. The room was cloaked in magic so you wouldn't know where you were. You've not been restrained because you can't leave this cavern unless Con is with you."

Esther jumped up and made a dash for the doorway. Rhi sat back and crossed one leg over the other, exchanging a look with Rhys. A heartbeat later, Esther let out a strangled cry as she was thrown backward at the doorway.

"Come resume your seat," Rhi said. "It's time we began our questioning."

It took a moment for Esther to get to her feet and make her way back to the chair. She sat and pulled off the wig. Then she ran her fingers through her brown hair.

Rhi then said, "You've chosen your side in this war, and sadly, you've chosen poorly."

"Anyone on the opposing side would say that."

"True," Rhi said with a shrug. "However, I'm speaking the truth. It's a certainty because I choose to be a part of this. I've seen both sides, Esther. You've only gotten a portion of the reality."

Some of Esther's confidence returned. "And what is the truth?"

"I prefer that we discuss who you're working for first. Once I get all the information we need, then I'll tell you all that you want to know."

"No."

Rhi raised her brows and blinked before cocking her head to the side. "No? I thought that was fair."

"I'm not going to tell you anything, but I do want to know what you are."

"What," Rhi repeated with a smile. She turned her head to look at Rhys. "Methinks she's catching on quick."

Rhys chuckled and said, "Doona get out of hand."

Rhi stood and walked around the back of her chair to lean her forearms on it. "What am I? That's something I seem to be answering quite a lot recently. It's a fair enough question, I suppose."

She stopped herself from looking to the corner at her watcher. It was becoming more and more difficult for her not to look his way. If she wasn't careful, others would begin to suspect.

"Answer me this, Esther," Rhi said. "Do you really believe the men here are dragons?"

"Yes," she replied immediately.

"Do you believe they are the only other beings on this earth?"

Again Esther said, "Yes."

"That's . . . very naïve. And you're very wrong actually. Though to be fair, most humans are as mistaken. I've shown you who I was from the moment I walked in. I did magic, spoke of mortals, and even mentioned immortality. Is your brain unable to comprehend what's right before you?"

Esther's face lost a little color. "I thought the dragons were only male."

Rhi squeezed her eyes shut briefly, trying for patience. "They are. I'm not a Dragon King. I'm a Light Fae."

"Wh . . . what?"

Rhi turned to Rhys. "By that reaction, I'm inclined to believe she's not had any encounters with Fae, much less Dark."

When Rhi faced Esther once more, the mortal's face was white and her eyes dilated. "That's right. Fae. And if there's Light, there is also Dark. The Dark are the ones who've been setting the cities on fire and doing all the killings. The Dark are also on the same side as you."

"No," Esther said with a small shake of her head.

"That's a definite yes," Rhi stated. "Henry has been working hard to track the Dark and keep other humans free from them, because you mortals are drawn to all Fae. But it's the Dark who kill. You won't even know it's happening. You'll be too attracted to them, too desperate to have them fill you to know that while they're having sex with you, they're draining your soul."

"No," Esther said again.

Rhi quickly took her seat again. "Tell me who you work for."

"I can't."

"Perhaps I should call in a friend," Rhi said. She used her magic and had an image of Balladyn fill the doorway.

Both her watcher and Rhys jerked, believing it was really Balladyn at first.

Rhi stood and moved the chair out of the way so Esther could get a full view of Balladyn. Rhi then used her magic to ramp up the desire within Esther.

Her eyes were wide with fear while at the same time she moaned with need.

It was beyond cruel for Rhi to do this, but the Kings needed answers. She walked to stand behind Esther, and then bent so her mouth was near the mortal's ear.

"Isn't he gorgeous?" Rhi whispered. "He wants you. And you want him."

Esther tried to shake her head, but her legs spread instead.

"If he takes you, you'll die. You'll experience pleasure like you've never had before, but all the while, your soul will be sucked out without you even being aware. Until it's too late. Shall I let him have you?"

Esther attempted to get to her feet, but Rhi put her hands on her shoulders to keep her seated. "No!"

"Then tell me who you work for."

"No."

Rhi moved the vision farther into the cavern, right toward Esther. "I'm going to let him have you."

"Please no," the human said, tears falling freely from her eyes.

"Then tell me who you work for. Now!"

"Sam MacDonald," Esther yelled as he turned her face away from the approaching Balladyn.

Rhi waved her hand, and the image of Balladyn disappeared. She looked to Rhys. "Let Ryder know we have a name."

"Balladyn?" Rhys asked with a frown.

Rhi shrugged and patted Esther's shoulder. Henry's sister had her face buried in her hands as she sobbed. "I needed a Dark Fae."

"But Balladyn?" Rhys asked again.

Rhi would tell him of her relationship with Balladyn. But not yet. "He's the first one who popped into my head."

"Mmm-hmm," Rhys mumbled. "Why do I get the feeling you're keeping something from me?"

"I'm always keeping something from you," she joked.

But there was no answering smile in return. Rhys took her hands in his. "Rhi, I want happiness for you, but it isna with Balladyn. He tortured you. He tried to turn you Dark."

"I'm not Dark."

"I know, but that's no' my point. You've been rejected for thousands of years by the one man who is meant to be yours. You want to have someone in your life again, but doona turn to Balladyn. I beg you."

Rhi inhaled deeply. "Who should I turn to, Rhys? Another King? Or Henry, perhaps? How about Ulrik?"

"Rhi," he began.

She pulled her hands from his grasp. "I love you like a brother, and I know you mean well, but you don't understand any of this. You fell in love once, and you got the girl. You and Lily will live happily ever after. I'm thrilled for you."

"There's someone out there for you."

At this she smiled wryly. "That's what someone in a relationship says to a single person. And it's a load of shit. I've been alone for countless centuries. What does it matter who I take to my bed?"

"Because I know you," Rhys said softly. "I know only the love you felt for your King will ever fulfill you as you need."

Rhi raised a brow. "Not so sure, stud. I'm feeling pretty fulfilled now."

"What the . . . ?" He trailed off in surprise. "Who is he?"

"None of your business."

"It is my business. You're my business. You're family."

That made her eyes sting with tears. Damn Rhys. "Don't let Con hear you say that."

"Fuck Con," Rhys all but roared. "I'm no' talking about him. We're talking about you."

Rhi put her hand on his arm. "I know what I'm doing, Rhys. I'm lonely, yes, but not stupid."

"Loneliness can hit people hard. It can also mix up their feelings so they do things they normally never would."

"Trust me," she said with a smile. Then she winked. "And tell Con I said he's welcome for getting his information."

Rhi teleported out before she gave in and told Rhys everything about Balladyn.

CHAPTER TWENTY-SIX

Kinsey was having a difficult time keeping her eyes open. It wasn't just the long hours staring at the screen, frustration mounting with every search coming up empty. No, it was the dreams that plagued her sleep.

Dreams of Ryder.

Her stomach quivered with delight as she recalled one particular dream where she'd been sleeping on Ryder's chest, his arm wrapped around her and caressing her back.

Then he began to talk, his words just above a whisper as he told her how much he missed her and how he wished he'd never left. He went on to say how many times he'd wished she were in his arms.

If only all of that were true. Kinsey tried to focus on the monitor as it scrolled through the e-mails, putting aside all those that were encoded—and there were dozens of them.

All of which were being deciphered by the software.

But it wasn't the e-mails Kinsey kept thinking about. It was her dreams. They'd begun her first night at Dreagan. In the beginning, she wasn't thrilled to have Ryder invade her mind again.

Perhaps it was because she was with him all day, but now she found herself eager for night so she could drift away to dreams of happiness with Ryder.

Though it was dangerous. Her fantasies were creating a life that could never be between them. Kinsey needed to keep herself grounded in reality.

She glanced at Ryder to find his short blond hair in disarray from him running his hands through it. He'd gone through two boxes of donuts already, with a third waiting.

Finally she understood how he could eat so much and stay looking so . . . spectacular. He linked his hands behind his head and leaned back in his chair as he gazed at the screen. Every once in a while he'd glance over at the monitors to his left and check the cameras around the property.

His intelligence, honor, and compassion were what had hooked her. None of that had changed in the last three years. If anything, Ryder appeared as if he were the only one who was keeping Dreagan going with the computers, software designs, and hacks. At least one of the other Kings should know how to do everything Ryder was.

But every King had their own job. Since they lived forever, she supposed there wasn't a need to have someone else know computers.

Kinsey always thought of herself as very good at what she did, but Ryder ran rings around her without even trying. He had four or five programs going at once while doing multiple searches. The two dozen screens weren't nearly enough.

She wasn't sure why he performed searches on certain people, but once he had the information, the screen vanished and he moved on. Kinsey wanted to know what he did with the data as well as why he looked into those people.

More and more, she found herself thinking about him. And not just about him being a dragon. Several times she actually caught herself thinking about living at Dreagan and being his.

Lexi did it without a problem. And there were other women there as well. They didn't have an issue with the men being dragons.

Kinsey could finally admit to herself that it wasn't so much that Ryder was a Dragon King—although, seeing him shift had terrified her.

She'd held onto that fear for months, because it was easy. Being with him, talking to him again made her realize he was still the same man she knew. He was just an immortal dragon.

Then she could concede that it wasn't him shifting that made her so angry. It was the fact that he hadn't shared his secret with her.

Three years ago, their relationship had progressed to the point of them talking about spending their lives together. Then to have him up and leave without an explanation only to discover his secrets now?

It broke her heart all over again.

The reasons behind him not sharing didn't matter. The other Dragon Kings managed to do it without an issue. But not Ryder.

Because she wasn't meant to be his mate.

Her pieced-together heart shattered all over again.

Kinsey's vision blurred as tears filled her eyes. She hastily blinked, but a tear managed to escape. How unfair life was to give her something that meant everything, only to take it away.

On top of that was an even crueler situation as Ryder was brought back into her life—but only as a reminder of what she'd never have.

She discreetly wiped away the tear and sniffed. Her gaze jerked back to her screens when Ryder looked her way.

"It's late."

Kinsey nodded, unable to speak.

His chair squeaked when he shifted. "You didna touch much of your food, Kins. Did you no' like it? Tell me what you'd like next time, and I'll make sure it's here."

"It was fine," she mumbled.

Ryder blew out a breath. "Let's call it a night. My eyes are crossing."

She knew that was a lie. Ryder could look at these screens for months without it bothering him. He was giving her an excuse to go to her room.

And she took it.

"I'll see you in the morning then." Kinsey got to her feet and walked from the room without looking his way.

She met Dmitri on the stairs and gave him a small wave. It wasn't until she was in the room that she leaned back against the door and closed her eyes.

After a moment, she flipped on the lights and began to take off her clothes. Everything was piled in the chair. Mostly because she wasn't obsessed with folding every piece of clothing. But also because she didn't have the time or inclination.

Kinsey removed her bra and grabbed the olive green tank top and put it on. Then she washed her face and brushed her teeth before climbing into bed.

Except, unlike the last two nights, she didn't fall right to sleep. She was wide awake, staring at the ceiling.

And thinking about Ryder.

Foremost in her mind was their kiss. Her lips still tingled from it. His taste . . . chills raced along her skin. She could still taste him.

The power, the desire.

The hunger.

If he hadn't pulled back, she wouldn't have been able to. For three years she'd yearned to have his lips on hers again. When it happened, she'd been too shocked to move at first.

But her body remembered what to do. Her arms went around his neck and she eagerly opened for him.

Her body pulsed with need. A need that only Ryder had ever been able to call up—or quench. She squeezed her legs together and rolled onto her side, but it didn't do any good. Her sex ached to feel Ryder slide within her, filling her as only he could.

Kinsey had no idea how long she laid there thinking of Ryder and replaying all the times they'd made love in her mind when the door opened.

She remained on her side. The light from the hallway lit the room in an expanding triangle as the door opened. A large form filled the crack before the door was quickly—and quietly—shut.

Kinsey didn't move a muscle. Who was in her room and why? She was getting ready to scream Ryder's name when the form stepped away from the door and the shadows there. The glow from the moon shed little light, but it was enough for her to see wide shoulders and a profile she recognized all too well.

Ryder.

With her fear gone and replaced with curiosity, Kinsey slowly released the breath she'd been holding. Ryder was in her room.

Ryder was in her room!

What the hell? She was furious.

Wasn't she?

Unfortunately, fury wasn't anywhere close to what she was feeling. That was reserved for exhilaration. And anticipation.

Her heart rate increased, and it became difficult to breathe. All because Ryder was in the room. She wished now she was on her back so she could watch him. He'd moved out of view, walking behind her to the opposite side of the bed.

When the bed shifted with his weight, Kinsey could barely contain herself.

What about your pledge to ignore him? Weren't you done with him?

She was just a woman, a woman with desires. She'd have to be dead not to want him. And she was anything but dead.

He'll break your heart again.

It was already broken. What did it matter if she gave in and took some pleasure? After the past three years, didn't she deserve that much?

At this, her subconscious was quiet.

There was a sigh from Ryder as he lay back upon the bed. For several minutes, he didn't move. Then he turned toward her, stroking her hair.

Just like in her dreams!

Had they been dreams? Was this the only time he'd come into her room? She'd been dead on her feet the past two nights, so a nuclear blast could've gone off and she wouldn't have known about it.

Her heart beat double when his hand came to rest on her waist. Then, slowly, he scooted close until their bodies were molded together, her back to his front.

The covers stopped her from knowing if he had his

pants on, but there was no denying he was bare-chested. She used to run her hands all over his chest and the dragon tattoo every chance she got.

And she wanted to do it now.

"I'm so glad you're here," he whispered.

Kinsey squeezed her eyes closed. Those words hit her squarely in the chest. She wanted to believe him, to take those words and hold them against her heart forever.

But Ryder used to say sweet things like that all the time before he'd left her.

"Doona ever leave, Kins."

If he kept this up, she was going to cry. To have the man she was in love with leave unexpectedly, and three years pass with no contact only to have him say everything she'd dreamt he would say was brutal.

And glorious.

This time she knew what was going to happen. This time she understood her place in his world perfectly.

This time, she'd be the one to leave.

She played a dangerous game. She was the lamb and Ryder the lion. He'd shredded her heart and her life effortlessly before. He could do it again.

Warm lips met her shoulder where he placed a light kiss. "Doona be afraid of me. I'll always protect you."

Kinsey moved back against him, allowing her shoulder to rub against his bare chest. Heat radiated from him, cocooning her in everything Ryder.

Another kiss was placed on her ear before he tenderly nuzzled her neck. She felt his cock thicken and grow against her back. Her nipples hardened and moisture gathered between her legs.

She knew Ryder well enough to know he'd never take advantage of her when she'd made it clear she didn't want him. If she was going to have her night in his arms, she was going to have to make the move.

Kinsey covered his hand draped over her waist with hers. Then she turned her head to look at him over her shoulder.

He froze, waiting to hear what she would say or do. Kinsey took his hand and placed it on her breast. They gazed at each other for long seconds.

Then he squeezed her aching nipple through her tank top.

CHAPTER TWENTY-SEVEN

Ryder stared into striking violet eyes, unable to believe that Kinsey wasn't just awake, but wanting him to touch her.

He ran his thumb over the hard nub of her nipple. Her lips parted and her eyes rolled shut. His cock jumped with yearning. He wanted inside her right that minute, but he pulled himself under control.

Three years had passed since he'd last held Kinsey. He wasn't going to rush anything. They had the entire night without interruptions. Hours of nothing but them, the night, and desire.

Ryder rolled the nipple between his fingers, hating the shirt in his way. She rocked back her hips, rubbing against his arousal and causing him to moan.

"I missed that sound," Kinsey whispered.

He moved so he could roll her onto her back. Her lids opened, meeting his gaze. Desire was there, thick and evident. No longer was she trying to hide it or pretending that she didn't want him.

"What else did you miss?" he asked.

She touched his hand and then his face. "This and this." Then she placed her hand on his chest, right over the dragon head. "This." She reached down and cupped his rod through his pants. "And this."

If it was possible, he wanted her even more. His cock was impossibly hard, aching to slide into her wet heat and claim what was once his.

Ryder massaged her breast, continuing to tease her nipple as he did. She pressed her head back into the pillow while pushing her breast into his hand.

He loved her breasts. They were full, heavy. And extremely sensitive. He'd loved to drive her wild just by playing with them.

"Please," she begged.

Ryder knew she wanted his mouth on her nipple, but he wasn't finished teasing her yet. When he didn't move to do as she asked, Kinsey kicked her legs out of the covers.

As soon as he saw the black lace panties, he nearly lost control. As sexy as they were, he'd much prefer her out of them—and the shirt.

Ryder glided his hand down her side until he found the hem of her shirt. He slipped his hand beneath and pushed up the shirt as he reached for her breast once more.

The moment his hand clasped around her breast, she moaned loudly. The sound was music to his ears. Entirely too much time had passed since he'd heard that beautiful sound.

With her lovely breasts now exposed and her shirt bunched around her neck, Ryder situated himself atop her. Immediately her legs parted so she wrapped them around him, bringing him close.

If only his pants were gone.

Her hands roamed around his shoulders, arms, and

back. Every time he pinched her nipples, her back arched. Ryder wanted to pause time and savor every millisecond.

From her breathing, to her moans, to the feel of her warm skin against his palms. He was in paradise, and he couldn't get enough.

Ryder wrapped his lips around a nipple. He flicked his tongue over the rigid bud before sucking. Then he moved to the other one.

Kinsey's fingers dug into his shoulders, her breathing becoming more irregular. "Ryder," she moaned.

Unable to help himself, he rocked his arousal against her. The pleasure was intense, but not nearly enough. He wanted more.

He wanted all of her.

For eternity.

Ryder lifted his head and placed his lips on hers. This time he didn't hold back. He poured every ounce of his hunger, his yearning into the kiss. He released his desire and let it flow between them.

In seconds the kiss turned fiery, each trying desperately to get closer to the other. It was a frantic, sizzling kiss. One that scorched from the inside as well as the out.

Kinsey pushed him onto his back, straddling him. She held his gaze and jerked off the tank top. He grasped her wonderful breasts, kneading them.

Her head fell back as she began to roll her hips. But Ryder wasn't yet ready to hand over the reins. He flipped her over and stood.

He unbuttoned his pants while she smiled, watching. Ryder pushed them down his hips and stepped out of them. Then he grasped her ankles. She let out a gasp while smiling. Ryder yanked her, stopping when her butt reached the edge.

Holding her gaze, he dropped down onto his knees.

Her smile faded, replaced by desire. It filled the room, palpable and intense.

He lifted one ankle to his mouth and kissed it. Caressing up her long legs, he touched and kissed every part of her until he reached her hip. Then he gently placed her leg down. He repeated the process on her other leg, opening them so he could see her sex.

Ryder gazed at the dark curls that hid her most sensitive area. He'd waited a long time to taste her.

Kinsey was breathless waiting for Ryder to lower his head. When he did, his tongue tenderly licking her clit, she fisted her hands in the covers and moaned. He laved her sex as if he were a starved man.

Pleasure erupted within her, swarming her with warmth and need. Every care and worry soon evaporated into nothing as her entire being was centered upon Ryder.

It was as if they hadn't been separated by three years. He knew exactly what to do to bring her to climax quickly, effortlessly.

It rolled over her like a wave. The pleasure so profound that she was unable to do anything but experience it. No thought, no sound came from her.

As the climax faded, Ryder rose over her. She opened her eyes and touched his cheek. How she'd missed him and the way he could make her feel.

"No dark thoughts," he said.

No dark thoughts. An excellent idea. Kinsey didn't want the past, the present—or the lack of a future—to intrude on her special night.

He bent and gathered her in his arms before he straightened. Kinsey was smiling as she tightened her legs around his waist. With her arms wrapped about his neck, she looked into his hazel eyes.

There was so much she wanted to say, but she couldn't

get any of it out. Not only wasn't it the right time, but there wasn't any point in it. It would only cause more friction between her and Ryder.

"Stop thinking," he ordered with a half-smile.

"Make me."

Always up for a challenge, Ryder lifted her before slowly lowering her atop his rigid arousal. Kinsey gasped at the feel of him stretching her.

The deeper he went, the more she felt as if she were whole again.

"So damn tight," he murmured while winding her hair around his hand. "I doona think I can be gentle."

She tightened her thighs, allowing her to move against him. "I don't want gentle."

The next instant she was against a wall. Ryder pulled out of her and began to thrust. Hard, fast, deep. He kept a tight hold of her hair as he filled her time and again.

Kinsey closed her eyes and took him, savoring every moment. She erased many of her memories with Ryder, but she hadn't forgotten how it felt to have him sliding within her.

He held her without effort, his powerful muscles shifting and moving. This was the alpha side of Ryder, the part of him that had to be in control, dominating everything around him. It made her stomach flip with excitement.

She sank her fingers into his thick, blond locks. His lips found hers again, their tongues dancing in time with their bodies.

It was erotic and stimulating.

Then he was walking. The feel of his cock moving just slightly as he strode from the wall to the bed, left her gasping for more.

"I need you," she begged.

He nuzzled her neck below her ear then asked, "How?"

"Any way you'll take me."

He growled, the sound reminding her of him in dragon form. It thrilled her, causing chills to race along her skin.

"That's my girl."

She found herself back on the bed with Ryder still buried deep within her. Then he took her legs and lifted them so they were next to his head. Only then did he begin to plunge within her again.

This angle brought him even deeper so that he touched her womb with every thrust. Her eyes were focused on his face, on the set of his jaw and the hunger in his gaze.

He was allowing her to see the yearning in his soul—for her. It took her breath away. But did she dare believe it?

Ryder couldn't get enough of her. The more he was in her, the more he had to have. He knew he wouldn't be able to let her go again. He'd been an utter fool to do it the first time. It was a mistake he wouldn't repeat.

She felt amazing, her tight walls wrapped around him, tightening as she built to another climax. He watched her, the ecstasy and happiness on her face was a reminder of what they'd had.

He gripped her ankles tighter, his own orgasm coming quickly.

"Yes," she said.

Ryder thrust faster. Her breathing quickened as her moans grew louder. He wanted her limp with pleasure, at least that had been his initial goal. Now he knew he'd be the one limp and content alongside her.

A strangled cry tore from her lips as she peaked for the second time. The feel of her walls tightening around him was too much. Ryder drove into her twice more before he plunged deep and fell over her, catching himself with his hands as he climaxed.

For three years he'd shunned women as he pined for Kinsey, but she was back in his arms. For the time being, at least.

When he opened his eyes, she was gazing up at him with a grin.

"Wow," she whispered.

Ryder smiled and gave her a quick kiss. "Ditto."

"Don't leave."

Just what he wanted to hear. They climbed beneath the covers. This time when she curled against his chest, she was awake.

"You've been here both nights, haven't you?" Kinsey asked.

He thought about lying, because he wasn't sure how she would react. But he quickly decided against it. "Aye."

"Why?"

"I had to be near you. The first night after I got your shoes and jacket off I was going to leave, but I couldna. So I thought I'd lay beside you for a wee bit. The next thing I knew, you were lying just like this."

She drew in a deep breath and released it. "And last night?"

"I told myself I'd stay away, but I wasna strong enough. That one night with you reminded me of what we had. I wanted more. You slept deeply those nights. Did I wake you tonight?"

"I couldn't sleep."

"Why?"

There was a brief hesitation. "Several things. Mainly trying to clear my name, sorting through all the data we've collected that led us to even more data."

"What else?"

"You."

He wasn't sure whether to be excited or worried that he was on her mind. "What about me?"

"Being with you again is a reminder of what we had."

"And how I hurt you." No amount of apologizing would ever make up for what he did. No excuse was forgivable for hurting someone as special and giving as Kinsey.

She gave a little nod. "Yes."

"Do you think you'll ever forgive me?"

"I don't know."

CHAPTER TWENTY-EIGHT

"I don't know."

Those words haunted Ryder the rest of the night, even as they made love again and again. Passion and need blended with the desires of the past that still held them both in its thrall, refusing to let go.

But he could sense Kinsey continued to hold a small portion of herself back, and that hurt Ryder more than he expected.

He was used to the Kinsey who gave all of herself to him, but that woman was gone.

In her place was one more reserved and a little cold. A woman who didn't trust as easily and assumed everyone was always lying.

That's what he'd done to her.

No amount of lovemaking was going to redeem him or erase the hurt he'd caused. It didn't matter that their bodies moved in a rhythm all its own, a tempo that was just for the two of them. Nor did it matter how much pleasure he wrung from her.

None of it mended her heart that he'd so carelessly broken.

That wasn't true. It had torn Ryder apart to leave her, but he'd done it to protect Dreagan and the other Kings.

Why hadn't he gone back to her when he'd discovered the spell was broken and they could love again?

He slowly pulled his arm from beneath Kinsey's head and sat up on the side of the bed. He sighed, not wanting to answer that question—even to himself.

Ryder stood and pulled on his jeans, not bothering to buckle them. He walked to the window, but he wasn't looking out. His gaze was focused on his reflection.

He hadn't gone back to Glasgow for Kinsey because there hadn't been time.

Lie. Or a half-lie.

There were occasions he could've gone. Why hadn't he? What held him back? It wasn't Con's reaction, because Ryder didn't give a shite about that.

He ran a hand down his face, his reflection in the glass troubled—just as his heart was. Because the truth was he was scared he'd lost Kinsey.

By not going to her, he didn't have to face a truth he feared more than anything.

And yet what did fate have in store for him? None other than dropping Kinsey right in his lap.

Ryder closed his eyes. What an utter fool he'd been. All those times telling others that nothing scared him, when he'd known deep down in the pit of his soul that the mere thought of not having Kinsey's love terrified him.

He opened his eyes, his chin to his chest. His mistakes were in the past. Ryder was getting a second chance, and he wasn't going to blow it again. Nothing—and no one—was going to get in his way of reminding Kinsey how good they were together.

His image in the glass faded as he shifted his focus to beyond the window. The entire landscape was drenched in white. It was normally a time of year he loved, but that wasn't possible this time. Not when everything he wanted was just out of reach.

He braced his hands on either side of the window and glanced over at the bed where Kinsey slept. He should be rejoicing because she'd welcomed him, not worrying. But that was exactly what he was doing. Worrying.

Worrying because something kept nagging at him. He couldn't put his finger on it, but there was something he was missing. Something he should've seen—and he felt like it was important.

Ryder grabbed his shirt and boots and quietly left the room. It was doing him no good to stay and contemplate what Kinsey was thinking when there was work to be done. Despite his millions of years on the planet, he had no clue what went on in the mind of a female.

Something rammed into his shoulder. Ryder blinked and spun around to find Rhys wearing a deep frown.

"Where the hell have you been?"

Ryder ran a hand down his face. Fuck. He just now remembered hearing someone call his name through their mind link. Not once had he taken a night to himself, and that's all he'd wanted. Ryder should've known something important would come up. It always did.

"Tell me what you need," he said to Rhys.

Rhys lowered his gaze to Ryder's hands that held his boots and shirt. "Get dressed. I'll meet you in the computer room in a bit."

He watched Rhys walk away. A glance down showed his hands were shaking, he was shaking. With his inner turmoil about Kinsey, the danger of Ulrik and the Dark, MI5 on the grounds, and everyone constantly shouting his name, he needed a moment to himself.

Ryder made his way downstairs through the secret doorway to the mountain. It had been days since he'd been in his true form, and it was playing havoc with his mind. He dropped his boots and shirt inside the mountain.

His strides were long as he walked the tunnel, but soon he was running. He'd prefer to be in his mountain where he was completely alone. The fact it was too far away kept him there, close to Kinsey should she need him.

Ryder found the first cavern large enough to hold him, but he spotted white scales. Dmitri.

The next cavern appeared to be empty until he heard a rumble and peered into the darkness to see mocha-colored scales. Anson.

He skipped the next five and continued down until he was sure he was alone. There Ryder shifted, uncaring that he still wore his jeans.

A calmness stole over him, easing the onslaught of emotions that battered him like a storm. No matter how much they looked like humans, they were and always would be dragons. He shook his great head and spread his wings before snapping them shut.

He closed his eyes, imagining that he was soaring through the air, sweeping in and out of the clouds. The band of tightness that had constricted his chest since the moment Kinsey said she didn't know if she could forgive him began to ease.

If only he could be flying. Then he could remember who he really was—or rather who he'd once been. He'd be able to work out all the problems facing the Dragon Kings and Kinsey. Because in the air, everything came into focus with a clarity that always astounded him.

"Of all the Kings, you're one I never worried about."

Ryder snapped open his dragon eyes to find Con sitting on a boulder with one leg braced on the rock and the other on the ground. He twirled the gold dragon-head cuff link at his left wrist and glanced up at Ryder.

"You look like hell, my friend."

Ryder briefly looked away. He felt like it too. Unwilling to return to human form, he opened his mental link to Con and said, "*I'll be fine.*"

"Hmm," Con said after a moment. "I'm no' so sure. Kinsey is messing with your head."

"*There's a lot going on between Ulrik, the Dark, and now trying to clear her name.*"

Con released the cuff link and leaned his forearm on his bent leg. "I trust your judgment, Ryder. You've never let me or any of the Kings down. It's why I didna allow Rhys to interrupt you and Kinsey last night. Everyone deserves a night off here and there."

"*But?*" Ryder urged.

"There was a breakthrough with Esther. She gave us a name."

This shocked Ryder so much he shifted into his human form. They should've told him immediately. When he thought of all the answers he could've learned from a single name, he wanted to shout his fury at losing those hours.

Then he remembered who he'd been with.

"You should've let me know," he told Constantine.

"I did a search of the name."

The thought of someone else messing with his equipment irritated and infuriated Ryder.

"Ah," Con said with a slight smile. "You doona like the idea that I was in your space?"

"Nay." No use beating around the bush. It was always best to be honest with Con, no matter the outcome.

Con gave a little tilt of his head in acknowledgement. "I can understand that. We've all had our jobs for the last several hundred years."

"What did you find?"

"Nothing."

Ryder walked to the corner where a notch was carved into rock where clothes were stashed for just such occurrences. He took a pair of jeans and a flannel plaid button-down and put them on. "How deep did you search?"

"No' as deep as you will. I wanted to see if anything would come up. There was nothing."

"Which means there's definitely something."

Con nodded his blond head. "I agree. I've got a meeting in Paris tomorrow. I'll be leaving later this afternoon."

"Since when do you tell me what you're doing?"

"Since all of you have been snooping into my life."

Ryder grinned. "We just want to know who the lucky lady is."

"No' going to happen." Con dropped his arms and stood. "I'm sending Asher to a distributer meeting in Prague tomorrow."

"Do we expect a surprise visit?"

"I always expect the Dark now. Doona factor out Ulrik either."

Ryder crossed his arms over his chest. "I'm good, Con, but I'm already stretched to the limits with all the searches I'm doing."

"Then make use of Kinsey. While she's here," he added as he walked from the cavern.

So much for Ryder wanting to get away. He had no choice but to get to his computers immediately. The fact

Con left him alone last night was surprising, but also concerning. It was out of character for Con in a very big way.

Ryder hurried from the mountain. It wasn't until he was halfway up the stairs that he remembered his boots. He'd get them later. There was too much to do for him to waste time turning around.

He got to the room and took his seat, pulling his chair forward. The computers recognized his presence instantly and the virtual keyboard lit up.

On one screen was a name typed into a search: Sam MacDonald. A common enough name. So common that over eleven thousand pulled up.

Ryder narrowed the search to look for men around the same age that Ulrik appeared—mid-thirties. It reduced the number to right at four thousand.

Still too many names. Next, he tightened his search to any of the Sams who owned their own business. That significantly lessened the hits to fifteen hundred. Ryder couldn't focus the search on hair or eye color, because Ulrik would be able to change those if needed. Nor could he search by area.

He was going to have to go through each and every picture to see if any of them matched Ulrik. That was going to take an enormous amount of time.

Ryder looked up at his monitors. The eight closest to him were all either running searches or showed live feeds from the cameras throughout Dreagan.

With no other choice, he moved what Kinsey had been working on to the last four screens farthest from him and took over another four.

He continued searching for Ulrik in Ireland and Scotland, going through every Sam MacDonald who owned a business to see if they were Ulrik, checking on MI5 who were still on Dreagan, trying to tie Ulrik to sending

Kinsey to Dreagan, not to mention clearing Kinsey's name.

Kinsey. She was never far from his thoughts. Even when he was as swamped with work as he was right now, she was still there in his mind.

Their night together only reminded him of everything wonderful she brought to his life. Immortality was monotonous when spent alone.

Ryder didn't go looking for love. He'd had his share of women, but none of them caught his attention—and his heart—like Kinsey.

Her infectious smile, her genuineness and sincerity, and her empathy were what hooked him. Her beauty and amazing violet eyes might have first caught his attention, but it was just a benefit to everything else she was.

And he'd ruined her.

How many times had he seen humans move on from such loss and find happiness again? Millions of times. Ryder had honestly thought she would do the same. He should've known Kinsey was different from the rest.

Ryder didn't want to spend the day with his computers as he normally did. He wanted to be with Kinsey. It wasn't enough to have her in the same room working with him.

He wanted to see her smile, to hear her voice as they talked about anything and everything.

He wanted to eat a meal with her across the table from him instead of stuffing bites of food in their mouths as they worked.

He wanted to walk the grounds of Dreagan with her, to take her into his mountain and show her his home. It was a place no human had ever been, but he wanted her to see it.

Ryder's shoulders fell. As much as he yearned to do

all those things, he wasn't sure Kinsey would be willing. Perhaps after they discovered her innocence. He'd had a night in her arms. That was all he could spare right now.

All those at Dreagan were counting on him. What he wanted and needed would once more be put on hold for the good of Dreagan and his brethren, as well as their mates.

Ryder rolled his head from side to side. It was time to get down to business.

CHAPTER TWENTY-NINE

Kinsey opened her eyes. She blinked at the sun shining through the window and smiled as she recalled her night in Ryder's arms.

A night like that could change a woman's life. Kinsey should know. He'd done it to her before. And he almost repeated it last night. The only thing that kept her safe was that she didn't give herself completely.

She turned her head, hoping to find him. Her smile died a little when she found Ryder gone. But this time there was an indent in the pillow. Proof that he'd been with her.

Kinsey threw off the covers and rose from the bed. She quickly showered once she saw the time. Today she threw her hair up in a messy bun at the back of her head and didn't use any makeup. She threw on a pair of leggings, a waffle-knit red shirt that went under her favorite flannel shirt that was a blue, white, and red plaid, and her boots.

It wasn't until she was walking into the kitchen that she realized the plaid shirt once belonged to Ryder. He'd left it behind.

Kinsey turned around to change when she found four women in the kitchen doorway. She recognized Lexi and smiled.

Lexi moved away from the women to her. "Hope we didn't startle you," she said in her American accent. "We saw you coming down the stairs, and the others wanted to meet you."

"All right." What else was Kinsey supposed to say? That she was more comfortable with computers than people? Strangers were no problem, but people that were friends of Ryder's? Well, that could be tricky.

Lexi's smile grew. "I promise we don't bite."

"That we leave up to our men," said a tall woman with short blond hair. "I'm Grace."

Her accent sounded American mixed with something else. French, perhaps? "Hello."

A woman with wavy blond hair and kind brown eyes smiled as she said, "Hi, Kinsey. I'm Iona. I hear you're giving Ryder hell. Good for you."

Another Scot, though her accent was barely there, as if she'd spent a lot of time away from Scotland. Kinsey chuckled. "He can run circles around me on the computers, but don't tell him I said that."

"Never," Iona said with a wink.

Kinsey turned to the last woman who had sandy blond hair pulled back in a ponytail and beautiful powder blue eyes. She shot Kinsey a half-smile.

"That's Samantha, though we call her Sammi," Lexi explained.

"Sammi," Kinsey said with a nod, unsure of how to approach her.

Sammi glanced at the others, then spoke in a thick Scots accent. "They don't want me to ask, but I need to."

"Ask what?"

"We've heard you're afraid of Ryder."

Kinsey should've known something like that wouldn't stay private. She'd hoped it would remain between her, Tristan, Con, and Dmitri.

Though she didn't know how many Dragon Kings were on Dreagan, she knew it had to be several. Add in the women, and it was a lot of people. Almost like a small village.

Nothing stayed quiet or private in a village.

Lexi touched Kinsey's shoulder. "You don't have to answer."

"No, it's okay." Kinsey swallowed. "Yes, I said that."

Sammi took a deep breath, a small frown forming. "You spent a year with him. You knew him."

"I didn't, actually. He kept secrets from me."

"But he saved your life," Iona added.

Kinsey nodded, agreeing. "That he did. However, seeing a dragon drop from the sky breathing fire, only to shift right in front of me to the man I knew was terrifying."

"Not once in a year did he allude to being a dragon?" Lexi asked.

Kinsey turned and grabbed a mug to fill it with coffee. It was too early in the morning to be answering such personal questions without at least two cups of caffeine in her. "No."

"But you saw the tattoo, right?" Grace asked.

She turned back around with the coffee between her hands to face the women. "Each of you are mated to a Dragon King, correct?"

"Yes," they answered in unison.

Just as she'd figured. "Tell me how long you were with them before they told you who they really were."

All four looked at each other, suddenly very uncomfortable. Whatever hurt Kinsey thought she was getting past reared its head again. She knew the answer. Why did she have to ask it? Did she like being hurt again and again?

Sammi was the first to say, "Tristan was sent to help me since I was being targeted by the Mob, which of course is run by Ulrik. I saw him in dragon form when I fell from a mountain and he caught me. I'll admit, I was scared for a bit."

"My father was murdered," Iona said. "That's why I returned to Scotland. Since Campbell land borders Dreagan, I became the custodian. I fell for Laith the first time I saw him, and loved him before I knew he was a dragon. I learned about Dreagan and the Dragon Kings slowly, so when Laith shifted, I was in awe, but never afraid."

Kinsey wanted to curl up into a ball. She started to tell the others never mind, that she didn't need to hear any more, but Grace was already talking.

"I had writer's block and found Arian's mountain. I saw him battle a Dark Fae, and I'll tell you, I was horrified and scared out of my mind. I'd only known Arian for a few hours, but he was injured from the Dark magic. I couldn't leave him. Helping him back to the mountain prompted him to tell me everything. Mostly because he thought I was working for Ulrik, which I kept telling him was wrong," she ended with a laugh.

Kinsey stared into the black liquid of her coffee. Her blood pounded in her ears as each story was confirmation of what she'd suspected from the beginning.

Long minutes passed before she realized there was silence in the kitchen. Kinsey looked to Lexi who was staring at her. "And you?"

"I don't think it matters," Lexi said.

Kinsey appreciated her kindness. "It does. Please tell me."

Lexi swallowed, sadness in her slate gray eyes. "I already told you how I saw a Dark kill my friend and I began hunting them. I knew there was something different about Thorn, so I followed him one time when he left me at the flat. I saw him shift in the warehouse in Edinburgh to burn the bodies of the Dark he'd killed."

"Don't forget how Guy wiped your memories of Thorn, and yet they returned to you," Grace said.

They could wipe memories? Now that was something Kinsey hadn't known. Interesting. And freakishly chilling.

Lexi shrugged at Grace's words. "The point we're all trying to make, Kinsey, is that the first time we see them we're all a little scared. They're huge and powerful and immortal."

"The point, Lexi," Kinsey said with as much of a smile as she could muster past the hurt in her chest, "is that each of your men showed you who they were. They chose to make that decision. Ryder kept it from me. He left me. For three years I had no contact with him or a way to talk to him. Then, out of nowhere he's there. One minute as a dragon, and the next as a man."

Sammi's gaze was full of misery and sorrow. "You're in love with him."

"No," Kinsey stated firmly. At one time she was, but not anymore. "That time is long gone."

"Perhaps not," Grace said.

Kinsey walked past them as she said, "It was nice meeting you."

She hurried up the stairs to the third floor. The walk down the corridor to the computer room seemed exceptionally long that morning. She couldn't help but feel as if everyone at Dreagan was watching her.

Or it could be the dragons in the pictures lining the hall.

Either way, it was eerie.

"Did you sleep well?"

She halted at the voice coming from inside a darkened room she'd just passed. Kinsey backed up and leaned to peer inside the room. A form moved from the darkness and walked into the hallway. Constantine.

"I did," she replied. So she had been watched.

Con walked slowly toward Ryder's office, motioning her to follow him. "I'm glad to hear it," he said with a bit of an edge to the words.

"Why don't I believe that? You say the right words, but your tone says something completely different."

He cut his black eyes to her. "I appreciate your frankness, Kinsey."

"Because you don't get it from humans often?"

"Nay, I doona. They're intimidated by me."

She snorted. "Just the way you like it."

A small smile lifted one corner of his lips. "Perhaps."

That's when it hit her that Con knew about her night with Ryder. "You don't approve of me and Ryder, do you?"

He halted and turned to face her. "If I say yes?"

"I'd tell you that you don't need to worry. Whatever was between us is gone. I enjoy being with him. He's an amazing lover."

"You wouldna continue the relationship?"

"No." She was really getting good at lying. Soon she'd be able to convince herself.

Con's look was doubtful. "What of Ryder?"

"What about him? He's a Dragon King and immortal. Not to mention he left me."

"I believe he regrets that."

Kinsey shot him a dubious look. "Why tell me that? You don't approve of us, but imparting that kind of information could change things if I was of a mind to try."

"Are you? Of a mind to try?"

There was no emotion on his face or in his gaze. Kinsey wasn't sure if he was teasing her or testing her. "No."

"You said that a wee bit fast."

"Truth comes quickly."

Con gave a nod before he pivoted and walked away. She shook her head, wondering why every encounter with Con left her more confused than before.

Despite her wanting to ignore Con's words, she couldn't. Did Ryder really regret what he'd done? He'd said as much when he thought her asleep, but she hadn't believed him. She wasn't even sure she believed Con.

They could be attempting to get her to fall for Ryder again so they could use her as a mole in Kyvor.

She started toward the computer room when she heard her mobile phone ringing. Kinsey walked faster, but it stopped long before she reached her chair.

When she checked the phone she saw that Cecil had called her three times last night and twice that morning. She set her coffee down with a groan.

"Bad news?" Ryder asked without looking in her direction.

Kinsey turned her head to answer him when she saw he was now working on fourteen of the monitors. "It's Cecil. I forgot to turn in a work order yesterday to give me a reason to remain on Dreagan."

"They didna put a tracking device on your phone, but they could hack in and locate your GPS. However, on Dreagan, they wouldna be able to find you."

That was a small comfort. "If that's true and my tracking isn't showing up, then they know I'm still here."

"Aye," he said, typing.

She leaned back in her chair. "Will you sign whatever work order I draw up?"

"Of course. We need you here."

She almost asked if they would allow her to leave, but then she realized it didn't matter. If she wanted to prove her innocence, she needed Ryder. The only way to do that was to stay on Dreagan for however long it took.

Kinsey pulled out her tablet and typed up three different work orders. They weren't anything that would look suspicious. In fact, they were add-ons to what she originally was sent to Dreagan for.

When she finished, she handed the tablet to Ryder, who signed without looking at what she wrote.

"Aren't you even curious about what they say?"

"Nay," he replied before returning to his monitors and scrolling through picture after picture of men.

Kinsey sent the orders to Cecil. Then she picked up her phone to return his calls when she hesitated. "I thought you'd still be in bed when I woke."

Ryder gradually turned his head to her. "You were sleeping soundly, and I was needed here."

"We didn't talk much last night."

"You were clear in your thoughts."

Was he upset? Had she hurt his feelings? That thought unsettled her. For a while she used to want to wound him as he'd hurt her, but those thoughts had faded quickly.

Now the idea that she caused him to suffer distressed her. He'd wanted honesty last night, but she hadn't been able to give him the answers he wanted to hear.

But how easy it would've been to give in and see if she could have a future with Ryder.

CHAPTER THIRTY

Kinsey saw Ryder tense slightly when her mobile rang again. She didn't glance at him as she answered it, putting it on speaker as she continued to run encryption software on the e-mails.

"Hello, Cecil," Kinsey said. "I was just about to call you." It was a lie, but Cecil would never know. The man was too concerned about gaining another title to consider anyone might be lying to him.

"Good, good," his voice came over the mobile. "I was getting worried."

Kinsey paused in her typing and looked at her phone. There was strain in his voice. Her gaze shifted to Ryder to find him looking at her as well. She shrugged, letting Ryder know she didn't have a clue what was going on.

"Because I was late with the work orders?" she asked.

Cecil laughed nervously. "I told you it was important."

"And I said I'd get it done. I did."

"Well, girl, you've never let me down before. This would be a bad time to start."

That took Kinsey aback. "What's that supposed to mean? I've always done my job."

"Of course you have," he said quickly, then laughed to try and divert her questioning. "There's just a lot going on around the office."

But Kinsey wasn't going to let it go. "Why would you think I'd let you down?"

"Well," Cecil said with a slight hesitation. "They put a lot of emphasis on how well my people do."

"They always have. Yet I've got the distinct impression that you're making it sound much more serious. What's going on?" she asked.

Ryder gave a nod of approval at her approach, which made her want to smile.

Cecil stuttered over himself before he said, "Nothing you need to worry about."

"We're way above quota. Right?" she urged when he was silent.

"Right."

But his answer was much too hasty. Kinsey lifted her hands helplessly to Ryder. He motioned for her to continue where she was going with her questions.

"Is your job in jeopardy, Cecil?"

His nervous laughter was answer enough. "In this era of hacking, encryptions, spying, and protection of everything electronic, my job is never completely secure."

"Then perhaps I should talk to Harriet. She needs to know that you're doing a good job managing us out in the field."

"That's not necessary. I wanted to let you know I got your work orders. Good job."

The line disconnected. Kinsey frowned at the mobile phone and sat back in her chair. "That was odd."

"He's being pressured," Ryder said.

"Obviously. But by who?"

"Whoever made sure you were sent to Dreagan."

She bit her lip and slid her gaze to him. "I really hate not knowing who this asshole is."

"Then what's stopping you?" he asked with a wink.

Kinsey returned his smile. Ryder was the best there was at hacking. "I'm waiting on you."

He gave a push with his feet that sent his chair rolling toward her. Ryder stopped it right before they crashed into each other. "Let's go over what we know."

"All right. We know that someone at Kyvor used the desk of Clarice Steinhold to put in the fake work order with my name sending me here."

Ryder tapped his finger on the table. "We also know that they were smart enough to block the camera on the computer as well as have those in the office recording their movements in and out of the building erased."

"Right. Then there's the fact of the e-mail where they mention me and looking through my house and things for information on you and Dreagan."

"Let's no' forget they want you to remain at Dreagan."

Kinsey made a face. "They're so obvious. Oh, and we can't forget the picture they have of us and how they followed us, taking pictures while we were together."

There was something in Ryder's gaze that warned her there was more coming right before he said, "They've continued to follow you, Kins."

"That's not funny." She really wasn't in the mood for jokes, but she prayed that's exactly what this was. It was bad enough to discover her every move while she was with Ryder had been observed. If they continued to follow her after he left, she just might lose what little restraint she had.

"No, it's no'," Ryder said and blew out a breath. "I went

in behind you yesterday onto Kyvor's servers and I found a file labeled KEY. It was buried under dozens of useless files. I probably wouldn't have even found it except for the layers of firewalls and viruses surrounding it. That's what I was working on when I sent you to bed last night."

"But you got through?" That was a stupid question. Of course he'd gotten through.

He rubbed his jaw and gave a slight nod. "After hacking through another five-step process, I did. These people wanted whatever was in that file to stay hidden and protected."

At this Kinsey laughed wryly. "I hope that whatever was locked away so securely was something we could use—like a list of names associated with Ulrik."

"If only that were the case."

Kinsey couldn't take much more. She cocked her head to the side. "Just tell me."

"It was a week-to-week account of your movements for the past three years. Who you saw, what you ate, where you went. They even mentioned what you wore."

She couldn't draw breath into her lungs as the room began to swim around the edges of her vision. My God. How could these people be there every day and she not have seen them? Was she that oblivious?

No. It wasn't her. She'd had no reason to think she was the object of some study. Perhaps if she'd known Ryder's secret she might've paid more attention.

"There are pictures to go along with every report turned in," Ryder added.

Kinsey turned her chair clear of the table and got to her feet. It felt as if the room were closing in around her. She was shaking and she was chilled to the very marrow of her bones.

Her mind was stuck on the fact that someone knew

every detail of her life. She grabbed her stomach as it rolled viciously.

"Take a deep breath," Ryder said, his voice right by her ear, soothing and deep. His arms came around her, gentle and secure. "Close your eyes and concentrate on my voice."

That she could do. It was much better than thinking of the other. Kinsey let her eyes close and focused on his voice and the warmth of his body.

"I've got you, Kins. It's going to be all right. Just breathe. That's it. Breathe."

She stopped hearing his words and laid her head back on his chest. His strong arms supported her body and her worry. And it felt so bloody good. She couldn't imagine facing this alone, but as long as Ryder was near, she wouldn't have to.

Little by little, the overwhelming emotions began to subside.

Ryder tightened his hold around Kinsey. He closed his eyes in relief when he felt her relax against him. She'd gone white, her body tense as she'd begun to hyperventilate.

He hadn't wanted to tell her what he'd discovered, but Kinsey had a right to know just how much those at Kyvor had violated her privacy.

All because he'd been with her.

After all Ulrik had done to the mates, Ryder had actually assumed he'd escaped what the other Kings had been put through because he'd left Kinsey years before.

Ryder couldn't have been more wrong had he tried.

A sound behind him had him turning his head. He saw Dmitri just inside the doorway. Dmitri raised his brows in question.

Ryder gave a small nod of his head to let him know

that everything was all right. But was it really? He kept telling Kinsey it would be, and yet he was beginning to wonder if those words were false.

He gently turned her so that she faced him. Ryder rested his chin atop her head when he heard her soft sigh. At least she was calm once more.

Before, Ryder had been fixated on uncovering who was behind all of this. Now he was going to take it a step further. He was going to kill every last one of them.

"Thank you," Kinsey whispered.

Ryder stroked a hand down her hair. "Better?"

"Yes." She stepped out of his arms. Then her gaze moved past him.

Ryder missed her instantly. He turned to face Dmitri only to find Thorn had joined him. "Lads. What can I do for you?"

"Actually, we've come to see if you could use some help," Thorn said.

This was a first. The only time a King ever came to Ryder's sanctuary was when they needed something. That's also really the only time they ever contacted him.

Dmitri slapped Thorn on the back as he walked around the monitors. "Ryder, you need to be focused on the important things. I can watch the cameras around Dreagan. I know these MI5 wankers, so doona mind spying on them."

Thorn followed Dmitri around the computers. "Tell me what you need, Ryder."

Ryder glanced at Kinsey to find the corners of her lips tilting up in a grin. He gave a nod and kicked his chair to Thorn while Dmitri pulled up one of the spares.

Thorn sat and looked at the monitors as if they might jump out and bite him. "Sooooo. What do I do?"

Leaning over to use the keyboard, Ryder moved things

around on the monitors. He pointed to the two top ones in front of Thorn. "These are running facial recognition software looking for Ulrik in Ireland."

"You think that's where he's at?" Thorn asked.

"I doona have a clue. He's no' in Scotland, I know that. These will run on their own. If the program finds something, it'll flash red and pinpoint the location."

Thorn smiled widely. "Easy enough."

"Now, this bottom one on the left," Ryder continued. "It's decrypting e-mails from Kyvor. The first one should be finished soon. Read through them as they come up. If it's encrypted, my guess is that it's important. If it has to do with Ulrik, Kinsey, or us, let me know. Otherwise, put it in a folder for me to go back over a second time."

Thorn's smile wasn't as big. "Aye. I can do that."

"On this bottom right screen is—"

"I think I'd like to switch with Dmitri," Thorn interrupted.

Dmitri laughed and shook his head. "No' going to happen."

Ryder straightened, chuckling. "I'm running a search on Sam MacDonald business owners. Go through each photo and see if it's Ulrik."

"Easy enough," Thorn said.

Dmitri chuckled as they watched Thorn take a deep breath and lean his arms on the table as he began to look through the pictures of the Sam MacDonalds.

Ryder pulled up another chair next to Kinsey. Now he would be able to concentrate on uncovering exactly who'd sent Kinsey to Dreagan. He knew it was Ulrik, but this time he was going to get proof.

"You look surprised," Kinsey whispered.

He glanced at Dmitri and Thorn. "I am. No one comes to help."

"Now they do."

Yes, now they did. Ryder wondered if Con had sent them, then he realized it didn't matter. They were there helping. That's what was important.

"Where were we?" Kinsey asked. "Ah, yes. You told me that they documented every move of my life for the past three years."

Dmitri made a sound at the back of his throat. "That's messed up."

"Four if you include when I was in Glasgow," Ryder added.

Kinsey made a face. "What were they looking for?"

"I'm wanting to know that myself."

CHAPTER THIRTY-ONE

Ireland

Rhi was cautious as she walked through the Dark palace. Even though she was veiled, she didn't leave anything to chance. She'd been held with the Dark once. That wasn't going to ever happen again.

Behind her a few steps was her watcher. If only she could see him when she was veiled, but Fae magic didn't work that way. Which sucked, if she were being honest.

She'd been in the palace for a few hours with no sign of Balladyn. Though that wasn't why she was there. She was in the Dark palace because she wanted to see what they knew about the attacks on the Dragon Kings as well as pick up any other information she could.

Unfortunately, she'd gotten nothing on the Reapers. All she'd managed to gather was what she'd heard in the bars and the Light castle—everyone was terrified.

Although, she did overhear several conversations about the Dark moving around Ireland. That made her wonder, because it wasn't something they did. But the Dark were being cryptic about it—even in their own palace.

Interesting.

Rhi was beginning to itch from being in the Dark palace for so long. She longed to bask in sunlight and chase away the darkness that was creeping upon her once more.

But she hesitated. She wanted to help the Kings, but there was a driving need within her, pushing her to learn the truth about the Reapers. She didn't know how, but she couldn't dispel the feeling that the knowledge about the Reapers was going to be important.

The Reapers wouldn't just show up for no apparent reason now after thousands of years. Someone sent them. Who and why? That's what Rhi needed to know.

She was getting ready to leave and call to Balladyn so that he might take her to his library to see the texts about the Reapers when she turned the corner.

Rhi came to a halt when she found Balladyn standing next to Taraeth. They were talking to someone, but he was hidden by a column.

Balladyn was in all black, his silk shirt molding to every contour of his body. His look was understated, yet powerful. A direct contrast with Taraeth, who wore black leather pants, a silver shirt, and what looked like a black satin robe left unbelted so that the red inside could be seen.

Crass and showy. Just like Taraeth.

She moved forward. Balladyn's gaze jerked her way. He couldn't see her, but just as the first time she'd veiled herself in the Dark palace, he sensed her. Balladyn didn't say anything. His expression told her just how annoyed he was that she was there.

Rhi caught sight of a gray suit. There was something about the way the man moved that had her shifting to the side to see who it was. That's when she caught a glimpse of black hair pulled back in a queue.

Ulrik!

Rhi should've known. It was no secret that Ulrik was working with the Dark, but seeing it was a reminder of how bad things were for the Dragon Kings. And the Light Fae, if Rhi were honest.

Ulrik traveled fast to have been in Austin with her, and then in the Dark palace—changing into his suit. Rhi wasn't sure why Ulrik did anything, but it infuriated her that he'd found her in Austin and spoken so ambiguously.

There was no way the Light would be able to stay out of the war between the Dark and the Kings for much longer. The Fae Wars would happen all over again.

Unless Ulrik could be stopped.

Yet Rhi didn't teleport to Dreagan and notify them of where Ulrik was. Why should she? The Kings wouldn't venture onto Dark property to find him.

Ulrik was a friend. Or was he? Rhi wasn't sure. She didn't want him to die, which was what had to happen for the war to stop before it really began. Because the only other option of Ulrik forgetting his revenge wasn't going to happen.

Though Con was a complete dick, Rhi didn't want him to die either. Unfortunately, one of them would have to. It was the only way.

She pressed herself against the wall as Balladyn and Taraeth came her way. Rhi tried to look around them to catch another glimpse of Ulrik, but he was walking the opposite way. There was a woman beside him, a Dark Fae who he had his arm around.

So Ulrik had found a woman. Rhi wasn't surprised it was a Dark. There was too much hate and bitterness for Ulrik to be with a Light. And with his abhorrence of humans, he'd spend eternity alone before he took a mortal to his bed again.

Rhi followed Taraeth and Balladyn. After fifteen

minutes of listening to Taraeth ramble on about how great he was, Rhi rolled her eyes, wanting to remove his ability to speak.

She turned her thoughts to the new set of OPI polishes for the Venice collection. The alert had come over her mobile, and she was itching to get to the store and pick up a bottle of each shade to see what Jesse could do with them.

With names like A Great Opera-tunity, Tiramisu for Two, and Gelato on My Mind, how could she resist?

"Do you see my point?" Taraeth asked Balladyn.

Balladyn bowed his head. "Of course, sire."

Rhi frowned. Damn. She should've been paying attention instead of thinking about the new polishes. What if she'd missed something important?

Taraeth gazed at Balladyn for a long moment in silence. "I've been through a lot of men in your position, Balladyn. You've remained the longest."

"Because I'm good at what I do."

"Yes," Taraeth said with a nod. "Too good at times. I'm not above . . . removing you . . . should I begin to question your loyalty."

Balladyn's impassive face changed. A muscle ticked along his jaw, and anger radiated from his red eyes. "Question my loyalty? I'm one of the few you should never mistrust."

"You've been preoccupied of late."

"My job is to protect you and carry out your orders. I'm making sure that any decisions you make won't come back to cause damage."

"You actually think it would?" Taraeth asked with a laugh. He held up his only hand and looked around. "In my palace?"

"You've allowed Dark to be recruited by them. Him," Balladyn quickly corrected himself.

Them? That hadn't been a slip of the tongue. Balladyn knew something he hadn't bothered to share with her. Because she hadn't asked the right questions.

Now she would.

Taraeth walked in a circle around Balladyn, the robe flowing behind him dramatically. Rhi rolled her eyes. "The Dark would never follow him. They know who their true master is. I could call them back any time."

"The longer they're with him, the more he feels as if he's in control."

"I'll set him straight soon enough."

Balladyn clenched his jaw. "And if he wins? He'll wipe the world of the mortals, thereby driving us out of this realm."

"We won't be leaving this realm."

"It's a possibility. Regardless of what he's promised."

Taraeth took a deep breath and stopped before Balladyn. "This is your reasoning for acting so different these past few months?"

"Of course. You may believe the word of a Dragon King, but I don't. I'm going to make sure that regardless of the outcome that this place is protected."

Rhi nearly laughed. Taraeth was so full of himself he'd missed Balladyn's choice of words. No doubt Balladyn was going to protect the palace—for himself. He wasn't doing anything to protect Taraeth.

Without a word, Taraeth walked away, leaving Balladyn in the corridor. Balladyn looked to where she was standing and gave her a curt look.

Rhi gave him a flat look. If he only knew how long she'd been in the palace, then he might have a reason to be angry.

She followed him down the hallway to a Fae doorway. As soon as she stepped through, she recognized his compound. It was no longer in ruins. Rhi waited until her watcher was with her before she continued after Balladyn.

Once she was in Balladyn's chamber, she pushed the door closed and unveiled herself. Balladyn had her pressed against the wall a second later.

"Have you lost your damn mind?" he demanded, anger and worry filling his gaze. "Do you know what Taraeth would do to you if he ever got his hands on you? I can't believe you were so reckless."

Rhi tried repeatedly to get a word in edgewise, but Balladyn was having none of it.

"It was beyond stupid for you to go there. You shouldn't even be here with me," Balladyn said and whirled around. He ran a hand through his long hair and paced the width of his chamber.

"I was veiled."

That stopped him in his tracks. His head jerked to her as he gave her a fierce glare. "I can sense you, Rhi. If I can, others could as well."

But he didn't sense her watcher. Ever. It was more that he was attuned to her, which was why he was able to sense her. Yet Rhi decided to keep that tidbit to herself. With the mood Balladyn was in, he wouldn't want to hear any of it.

"Taraeth still believes I'm searching for you to turn you Dark," he said with a snort.

She crossed her arms over her chest and glared at him. "And whose fault is that? You're the one who kidnapped me in the first place."

"Don't remind me." He put his hands on his hips and hung his head. "I can't take that back, but I can keep you away from him. If you'd only cooperate."

Rhi dropped her arms and walked to him. She stopped before him and put her hands on his face, bending her knees so she could tilt her head to the side and see his face. With a smile, she lifted his head so she could stand straight. "I know what I'm doing."

"You're good and lucky. Don't get cocky."

"Yes, sir."

That made him grin. His red eyes softened as he gazed down at her. "Now that I like coming from your lips."

"Don't get used to it," she warned with a wink.

Balladyn wrapped his arms around her, bringing her against him. "You'd never let me."

Rhi rested her head on his chest for just a moment. It felt good to have someone again. She closed her eyes and savored the moment—because it couldn't last long.

"Why were you at the palace?"

Rhi lifted her head and stepped out of his arms. "I wanted to see what the Dark were saying about the Reapers."

"And you couldn't ask me?"

"Yes, but I wanted to hear it from them."

Balladyn shook his head "Rhi."

"I was hoping to run into you though."

"To see my library and what I found on the Reapers, right?"

She flashed him a smile. "You're so smart."

"This way," he said and turned on his heel.

Rhi could feel her watcher's displeasure increase the moment they left the Dark palace and arrived at Balladyn's compound. Well, in truth, he hadn't been pleased to be at the Dark palace to begin with.

"I could've brought these to you," Balladyn said. "It would've been better than you coming here and chance being seen."

Rhi lifted a shoulder nonchalantly. "Nothing ventured, nothing gained."

"The Fae have said that around the humans so often that it's become one of the mortals' favorite phrases."

They walked through a large arched doorway from his chamber. Rhi smiled when she saw the sheer number of bookshelves and books lining the walls.

A massive light hung from the ceiling with what appeared to be candles, but Balladyn was obsessive about his books. He'd never let fire anywhere near them.

There were standing candelabras all around the room. They brightened as Balladyn walked past, alighting the chamber in a warm glow.

Balladyn strode to a large table where books were stacked and others lay open. There was a tablet of paper with his writing on it.

"This is everything I found," he said. "And I looked through every book I have."

Rhi took another look around the room and the mind-boggling number of books. It must have taken him days to go through each one while continuing his duties as Taraeth's right hand.

She came to stand beside him. "Take me through what you found."

CHAPTER THIRTY-TWO

Kinsey was never happier to see the sun setting behind the mountains than she was then. Another day passed without any answers. She and Ryder weren't the only ones frustrated.

Even Thorn and Dmitri were agitated since they were in the room and learned whenever they got close—then found nothing.

Although Ryder never discarded anything. Whatever they found—however inconsequential—he kept, tucked away in case they needed it later.

There were dozens of those kinds of finds. Anything that caught Ryder's eye was put into a file. Kinsey tried to discern what he was seeing that she wasn't, but she had yet to figure it out.

Ryder was gifted with all things electrical and even mechanical. She was still awed by the fact he'd built every camera used on Dreagan. They were so small and obscure, hidden so that no one ever saw them, and yet showed the most amazingly detailed pictures on the screens.

Kinsey looked around the computer room. Everything

in there Ryder had built. Did any of the other Kings even realize how astonishingly gifted he was? Did they have a clue how fortunate they were that he was able to do all he did?

Ryder kept Dreagan ahead of even the prototypes coming out of big corporations without stealing from or spying on them. This was all in his head.

How the hell had Kinsey not seen this when they were together?

The answer to that was easy—she'd been in love. She'd been too engrossed in her feelings and being with him. She hadn't looked for secrets or anything.

As if realizing she was staring at him, Ryder shifted his head toward her. "We've done enough for the day."

Which meant he was sending her off while he kept working. Not this time. "I'm fine. I just need a little break."

"As do I," Dmitri said. "Dinner is nearly ready."

Kinsey glanced at Dmitri as both he and Thorn stood and walked from the room. They were leaving as if everyone was gathering together. For the past few nights, she and Ryder had taken their meals in the computer room.

"It's fine," Ryder said. "I keep a recording of the cameras and will go back over it later."

She nodded, listening with half an ear.

"You ready to go down?"

Her eyes jerked to him. Go down? That's what he'd just asked, right? Surely he didn't mean that they were going to sit around a table like one big happy family.

Right?

Ryder chuckled as he leaned an elbow on the arm of his chair and scratched his chin. "It's no' as bad as it sounds."

"Which part? I'm assuming everyone will be there."

"No' all of us. Some are still patrolling, just no longer from the air. Concessions needed to be made with MI5 here."

"You have the cameras though."

He shrugged and motioned to the monitors Dmitri had been staring at. "Cameras and our magic only do so much. Our barrier of magic keeps out nearly all humans as well as causing the Dark considerable pain if they pass through it. Anyone or anything that ventures onto our land through the magic and we're alerted."

"I gather you don't chase after every rabbit?" she asked with a smile.

Ryder laughed as he pushed back his chair and got to his feet. "Our magic lets us know when it's an animal or not."

"Are the Dark able to shift into animal form?"

"Thankfully, no," he said as he held out his hand for her.

Kinsey took it and let him pull her to her feet. They walked slowly around the monitors to the door. "That's a plus. Now, you said *nearly* all humans."

"There are rare instances, like with Grace. She saw right through our magic and entered Arian's mountain unaware of where she was. Though we have no' found anything, I suspect she has enough magic from an ancestor that gave her the ability to look past ours."

"Was she interrogated?" Kinsey asked with a side look.

Ryder's face lost his smile. "At length."

Wow. Well, she had asked. Perhaps Kinsey was lucky in getting to search for those responsible for putting her at Dreagan. Or maybe she should really be thanking her stars that she knew Ryder, otherwise she might be questioned like Grace or Esther. Which reminded her . . .

"Where's Esther?"

Ryder put his hand on her back as they descended the stairs. "Still being kept isolated for the time being. She gave up a name, and though I think it's relevant, we need proof."

Kinsey heard the sound of voices before they reached the bottom. She slowed, her heart beating fast. Then she halted altogether.

"It's going to be okay," Ryder assured her. "You've already met several of us."

"Why now?"

Ryder waved to a man with long black hair and the most amazing pale blue eyes she'd ever seen. The man gave her a nod and kept walking.

"This occurs most nights. I didna want to force everyone on you your first or second night."

"But my third sounded good?" she asked with a knowing grin.

Ryder lifted one shoulder. "I couldna put it off any longer. Several of the mates have already talked to you. Everyone else wants to meet you."

"And how is Con with this?"

Ryder laughed before he gave her a slight push to get her moving again. "Con is Con."

As if that explained everything. And in a way, perhaps it did. Kinsey decided to go with the flow, even as her stomach felt as if a flock of birds had taken up residence.

Each time she walked through the manor, Kinsey took in as much as she could. It had an understated elegance. You knew whoever lived there had money, but it wasn't the gaudy extravagant décor some people decorated with.

Dreagan felt homey—despite its size, location, wealth, and the fact it was home to Dragon Kings.

She gawked at the glimpse of a library as they walked down a wide hallway. From what she saw with one peek, wealth lined every bookshelf. But it was the kind of wealth she could appreciate.

The paintings, some well over seven feet in height and ten feet wide, were placed periodically throughout the manor. They passed one such piece with a gold dragon that had a row of quills running down its back and tail. The dragon had two horns extending forward from its forehead. Royal purple eyes seemed to pierce her as it flew from the sky right toward her.

The sight of the dragon nearly made her miss the backdrop of the mountains and the sun breaking through the clouds. It was obvious that whoever painted this wanted the viewer to see the dragon first and foremost.

"What do you think?" Con asked as he came to stand beside her.

Kinsey hadn't realized she'd stopped until that moment. Ryder was silent beside her, letting her take it all in. She returned her attention to the gold dragon. "He looks aggressive."

"Most would believe all dragons look that way," Con said.

She tilted her head to the side. "I'm not an art enthusiast, so I don't know the correct words."

"Just say how the painting makes you feel," Ryder urged.

That she could do. Kinsey took a deep breath and released it. "I get the sense the artist wanted me to feel the dragon's power, his might. The intensity of the dragon's gaze is undeniable. It's as if he's homed in on a target. His supremacy is unquestionable."

"Does this frighten you?" Con asked.

"Yes, but not as before."

Out of the corner of her eye she saw Con turn his head toward her. "Meaning?"

"I no longer fear that a dragon is coming for me."

"But," Con urged.

She licked her lips and moved closer to the painting. "What scares me is that all of you are like caged animals. You have sixty thousand acres, but it's still a cage. Now MI5 has closed you in even more."

Kinsey started to touch the dragon, but stopped herself before she did. She turned to face Ryder and Con. "When cornered, animals lash out. It's simply a matter of time before the Dark, Ulrik, MI5, or even humans force such a situation."

"And you doona think we can control ourselves?" Ryder questioned her.

She shook her head, trying to think of a way to reword her thoughts. "Not at all. You could've wiped us out thousands of years ago. You didn't."

"You worry we'll have no choice, leaving us only one option—showing ourselves to the world," Con stated.

Kinsey swallowed before she nodded. "How long do you think the Kings will remain on Dreagan unable to shift or fly? I see Ryder looking out the window to the sky all the time. Same with Thorn and Dmitri. They don't even know they do it. There is a longing within them, a yearning they're having to control."

"They've no' had to control that yearning in a very long time." Con blew out a breath. "Aye, Kinsey, I've seen what you've seen. Your worry is one of my own."

A slight frown lined Ryder's brow. "We're all doing fine. We've been in this situation before. We'll get through this one."

"This isna like before," Con said. "And I know none of you are fine. The episode this morning proved that."

Episode? Kinsey saw the look pass between Con and Ryder. Something had happened involving Ryder. She wanted—no, she *needed*—to know what it was.

"This isna the time for this conversation," Ryder said, his voice pitching low in warning to Con.

If Kinsey waited, chances are Ryder wouldn't tell her what had happened. Now, with Con, she might have an ally. "Since you and Con know what occurred, it's me who you don't want to find out."

"Kins," Ryder began before he blew out a breath. "It's nothing."

"Then tell me," she pleaded. She wasn't sure how she knew that it was important. Maybe it was the way Con spoke about it or how Ryder wanted to quickly discard any mention of it.

It might have been three years since she and Ryder were together, but she realized he was still very much the same man she remembered. Whenever he didn't want to talk about something, he pretended it didn't matter.

"You used to do this," she said. "Whenever I'd ask about your family or your past, you would pretend that it was no big deal and change the subject. Remember the times I caught you staring at the night sky? I'd ask what was wrong. You would tell me you were just fine. But you weren't. Just as you aren't now."

Ryder briefly closed his eyes. "All of us go to the mountain to shift from time to time. We need to feel our true forms."

"Do you go every morning?"

He shook his head.

But this morning, after a night in her bed when she

said she wasn't sure if she could forgive him? Did she send him to the mountain? Did her words cut him that deep?

She could barely draw in a breath at the thought. Kinsey didn't want to hurt him. One night in his arms and everything changed.

No, that wasn't true. She'd always been in love with him. Her anger had carried her through the last three years, but as soon as she saw him, she was his once more. She just hadn't been able to admit it.

Until now.

"Things aren't all right, Ryder," she said and walked to him. She put her hand on his chest, over his heart. "You and the other Kings have been in control for a long time, but Ulrik has changed the game. It's okay to admit it."

Ryder's gold, green, and blue eyes held hers. "Nay, it's no' all right to admit."

"You can't tackle a problem properly without at first admitting there is a problem."

"We all know who the problem is. Ulrik. The Dark," Ryder stated angrily.

"And your problem? What's bothering you?"

He made a face. "I doona have a problem."

"We all have problems. You're a Dragon King. You can admit your problem."

Ryder started to turn away, then stopped. "You! You, Kinsey Burns, are my problem. Because I can no' have you."

CHAPTER THIRTY-THREE

Kinsey had feared she was what bothered Ryder, but to hear it from his lips. And the way he said it—as if admitting it was the last thing he wanted to do.

The longing in his voice nearly broke her. She stared into his hazel eyes and melted. With thirteen simple words, he blasted his way through the walls around her heart.

And it scared her as nothing else could.

Her heart and soul were fully exposed, as if she were standing naked in the hallway. Ryder watched her with expectation and hope. Everything she wanted was right before her. She just had to have the strength—and guts—to take the chance again.

She knew Ryder's secrets now. For three days she'd lived in his world.

Because I can no' have you.

Kinsey wanted to rest her head on his chest and wrap her arms around him. She wanted to lean on him once more and let him shoulder her troubles. She wanted to know that he would be with her each morning when she woke.

She wanted the dream she'd once had with Ryder. She wanted it all.

He moved closer to her until their bodies were nearly touching. "Tell me you doona want me. Say the words, Kins, and I'll never bother you again."

Was he serious? As if she could say them. She couldn't have said them the day she arrived at Dreagan, and she certainly couldn't now.

"I can't," she whispered.

He dropped his chin to his chest and sighed, a pleased look passing over his face.

"Perhaps the two of you could continue this after dinner," Con said.

Kinsey had completely forgotten Con was there. She'd been so absorbed with Ryder that everyone vanished.

Ryder smiled as he lifted his head. "I agree. We've already kept the others waiting too long."

Kinsey found herself walking between two very handsome Dragon Kings. A few days ago, it would've been disconcerting. Now, it just seemed like an everyday occurrence.

They got a few steps from the painting before Con said, "I'm pleased you didna think I looked too aggressive."

Her feet halted as she stared after Con entering the arched entryway to the dining room. Con. The gold dragon was Con? Why hadn't she thought to ask who it was?

"I was going to tell you it was Con when he walked up and shook his head to stop me," Ryder said.

Kinsey looked at him and laughed. "At least I didn't say something stupid."

"You said everything right. Con is warming to you."

"Right," she said with a snort. "I don't think Con warms to anyone."

Their conversation ended when they walked into the dining room. The room had an even more inviting and warm look than the rest of the house, if that were possible.

The table was a rich dark brown with years of use evident in the markings. It only made the table more beautiful, in her opinion.

The legs of the table were carved into dragons and it appeared as if the table rested upon the shoulders of the dragons.

"Dragons holding up the world," Kinsey mused. Art mimicked real life. She wondered if the Kings even knew it.

Ryder leaned close. "What?"

"Nothing," she told him as he guided her past chairs already filled to two empty seats across from each other.

Kinsey was seated beside Lexi on one side and a handsome man with impossibly long black hair and eyes the color of champagne on the other.

Grace sat across from him and winked at Kinsey before grinning like a fool at the man. "This is Arian," Grace said.

Kinsey nodded at him, and was greeted with a smile.

"I've heard a great deal about you," Arian said. "I'm glad you could finally join us."

"Me, too." What else was Kinsey supposed to say? Her parents' entire house could easily fit inside the dining room it was so large. And she didn't even try to introduce herself to everyone. There were too many people, and she'd never remember their names.

But they were all looking her way. It was like being under a microscope. She understood their curiousness, because she felt the same about them. Thankfully, everyone was pleasant, offering smiles and waves when she looked their way.

Once Con took his seat, there was a moment of silence. As if on cue, everyone reached for a dish and then passed it to the right.

It wasn't long before each dish had passed before Kinsey—and there were many. She chose her food and set about eating, listening to the many conversations around her.

"We're getting close," Ryder said to a man on the other side of Arian.

"Can you work faster?" the man said.

Thorn grunted next to Ryder. "You're welcome to join us anytime, Laith."

Laith laughed. "I've got a pub to run, remember?"

A pub? That shouldn't surprise Kinsey. They did sell the finest Scotch in all the world. Why not own a pub? She was beginning to think there wasn't anything Dreagan didn't have its fingers into in some way.

Lexi leaned over and asked, "You overwhelmed yet?"

"Does it show?" she asked, praying she appeared as calm as she wanted to.

Lexi grinned and took a drink of wine. "Not at all. You're doing a good job. I think the first time I sat at this table I'd been at Dreagan a month."

A month?! And Ryder had only given her a few days?! Kinsey was going to have a serious talk with Ryder when they were alone.

"Even during that time I'd met over half of everyone," Lexi continued. "Still. It was a tremendous amount. You're doing terrific for only a few days."

Kinsey smiled tightly at Ryder. "I think I'm going to kill him."

Lexi laughed so hard she had to cover her mouth with her napkin. "I'd like to see that."

"Be at my room at midnight."

Lexi elbowed her with a wink. "You do know that's Ryder's room?"

Oh my God! What else was she going to learn? Maybe she shouldn't ask that. It was tempting the universe to throw something else at her.

Lexi turned to the woman on her other side and began talking, leaving Kinsey to once more eavesdrop on other conversations.

A few minutes passed before Arian looked at her and said, "How are you finding things at Dreagan?"

"Beautiful, intriguing, magical, and welcoming."

"You sound surprised at the last part."

She looked into his champagne eyes and nodded as she swallowed her bite of food. "I am. I'm not sure what I expected when I arrived and realized this was where Ryder lived." She glanced at Ryder to find him deep in conversation. "When I understood I was surrounded by Dragon Kings, I imagined . . ." She stopped, unable to find the words.

"The worst," Arian supplied for her.

Kinsey set down her fork and wiped her mouth with her napkin. "Yes. I do believe I did. Though, until I prove my innocence, I'll keep expecting the worst."

"Ryder willna allow anything to happen to you."

Arian said it with such conviction, as if everyone could see it but her. Kinsey put her hands in her lap and looked at her plate. "Why do you say that?"

"Open your eyes, Kinsey. It's right there for you to see, if you'll allow yourself."

She turned her head to him. "I assume you know my past with Ryder."

"I do," he said with a bow of his head. "Doona consider us gossiping about you, but rather a group worried about one of our brothers."

She raised her hand to stop him. "Of course. There's no need to explain. You're a family, and families protect their own. The thing is, I thought he was The One."

"And now he's no'?" Arian asked with a frown.

Kinsey glanced around the table at all the faces talking, laughing, and enjoying life. "He left me."

Arian blew out a breath. "Can you no' forgive him?"

She didn't know why she felt the need to confide in Arian. Having only just met him, she shouldn't be telling him anything, and yet she opened up to him. "I'm afraid to."

"You're afraid he'll hurt you again, aye?"

She nodded.

Arian shifted so that he was turned toward her. "Ryder is a good man. We all make mistakes. Immortality doesna mean we're perfect. In many cases, we make more mistakes than mortals."

"I couldn't handle another heartbreak like that."

"I was never in love before my Grace, so I can no' pretend to know what you're feeling. Although, I can tell you that you're no' the only one sitting at this table who's been hurt in the past. There's Sophie, who was hurt terribly by the man she loved."

Kinsey looked down the table to the left to see who Arian was looking at. There was a redhead with a vibrant smile who gave a nod to them. Kinsey looked at Arian. "So she forgave him?"

Arian made a face. "In order to move on with her life she did. It also gave her the power to love again with Darius."

In other words, there wasn't a soul at Dreagan who was in her same predicament. No one could begin to understand her worry about trusting someone who had ripped her heart out before.

"Everyone deserves a chance," Arian said. "Con's giving you one because Ryder asked. Consider giving Ryder another chance. You just might be surprised."

By the time dessert arrived, Kinsey was more confused than ever. Her emotions were all tangled and mixed so she didn't know where one ended and another began.

She wanted to be with Ryder, but the fear stopped her cold. The past three years had been the worst of her life. Lonely nights, lonesome holidays, and empty relationships that went nowhere.

They—whoever the hell "they" were—said that whatever didn't kill you made you stronger.

Kinsey wasn't so sure of that. She felt trampled, crushed by all she'd endured. Yes, she'd survived because a new day dawned and she had to work to pay her bills. So she got up, showered, dressed, and went to work.

At least there her mind was mostly occupied. It was after work when she had to think about dinner that got her. All her friends were in relationships, and she hated being the third wheel, so she never went with them.

Grocery shopping for one was miserable, but worse was when she went to the movies by herself. She hadn't thought it would be a big deal. It's not like she ever talked during a movie.

But it was sitting alone, no one to elbow at the funny parts, or cry with after a sad movie that struck her the most.

So very many lonely nights spent at her cottage. The

few times she'd allowed her friends to set her up with blind dates had been disastrous—as they always are. And the dates she found online weren't much better.

It wasn't as if she got through a month and shouted for joy that she'd survived. She kept her head down and plowed through one day after the other, only belatedly realizing every New Year's that another year had passed.

It wasn't until she reached Dreagan that she felt like she was alive again.

All because of Ryder.

Their gazes clashed, locked. Held.

She knew what he wanted. It was there in his hazel depths. Kinsey gave him a smile. That's all it took for Ryder to stand and walk around the table to her.

He held out his hand for her. Kinsey didn't hesitate to give it to him. Neither looked around as they left the dining room and headed to his bedroom.

Whether she could open her heart to him or not, her body wasn't going to be denied.

CHAPTER THIRTY-FOUR

Ryder shoved open the door to his room and pulled Kinsey in after him, not bothering to turn on any lights. She yanked at his shirt as he pushed her against the wall for a kiss.

They frantically removed each other's clothes, losing their balance and laughing through their kisses. The laughter died the moment they were finally skin to skin.

With his chest heaving and desire coiling tightly within him, he ran his hands down her back and over her shapely bum to her thighs. He gripped her legs and lifted her so that she straddled him.

He pressed her against the wall, kissing her deeply. Her nails gently scoured his scalp as she moaned and shifted her hips.

Ryder tightened his grip to keep her still. But she was having none of that. She reached between them and grasped his engorged rod, her fingers stroking and teasing.

He moaned, belatedly realizing Kinsey had broken the

kiss and somehow managed to slip from his hands. Ryder looked down to find her kneeling in front of him.

His cock jumped eagerly when she lifted her face to him and smiled seductively. A breath left him in a whoosh when her lips slid over his head, taking him deep in her mouth.

The pleasure of her warm mouth over him was exquisite. He closed his eyes and dropped his head back as he fisted his hand in her hair.

The strings that bound him to Kinsey strengthened, tightened as they shared their bodies. The future crystalized before him, and he knew Kinsey had to be a part of it.

She'd softened toward him already, but Ryder knew it still wasn't enough. He was going to have to prove himself in a big way. Then spend the rest of eternity making up for being the fool who'd walked away from her and the love they shared.

Ryder groaned aloud when she cupped his sac, rolling his balls in her hand. He pulled out of her mouth and tugged her to her feet.

Then he had her against the wall, one hand hooked beneath a knee as he slid inside her. Kinsey's eyes went wide as he filled her.

There was no need for words. Their hands and lips—their bodies—said everything. The beauty of their lovemaking, the deep connection it wrought, couldn't be denied by either of them.

And as he looked into Kinsey's violet eyes, she knew it as well. Whatever walls she'd kept erected around her heart the previous night were coming down, one by one.

Ryder could feel it, sense it. He didn't bust through

them, but instead opted to let them fall when she wanted. Three years ago she began to love him not knowing the real him. Now she knew—everything.

This time her decision would be based on all the facts.

Their gazes were locked as he began to move his hips in long, hard thrusts. Ryder felt his love for her growing, encompassing every inch of him.

He'd left Glasgow without ever telling her. He wasn't going to make that mistake again.

"I love you."

Her lips parted, her gaze searching his to see if he spoke the truth. Ryder was done hiding anything from Kinsey. He wanted her to know every part of him—the good, the bad, and the ugly. She was the only one for him, the only one he could ever see himself standing with.

Ryder didn't expect her to respond, nor did he let her. He increased his rhythm, pushing her toward her climax. He needed to hear her scream of pleasure, to know that he gave her fulfillment.

He held her close, heart to heart. She was his life, his very breath.

Her fingers dug into his scalp and her breath hitched a moment before he felt her clench around him. She moaned, her eyes falling shut as the climax swept over her.

Ryder watched the pleasure cross her face, the ecstasy and delight that pulled her lips into a small smile that made his gut clench.

His arms held her as she sagged against him. He bent and grasped her other leg, keeping himself deep inside her as he walked to the chair.

He then sat, his hands moving to her hips. Kinsey dropped her head back, her lips open in a soft sigh. With her hands on his shoulders, she began to move her hips.

His balls tightened when she rolled her head from one shoulder to the other before straightening. Then her eyes slowly opened, the seductive glint in her violet depths making his heart beat faster.

Only Kinsey made him feel this way. Millions of years, and a single woman moved him as no one else ever had—or even came close.

The moonlight streamed through the window over her. Ryder caressed a hand up her back as she rotated her hips. As if she knew she held him in thrall, she pushed him back when he attempted to rise up for a kiss.

She then reached up and pulled her hair free of the ponytail that was half-fallen. He groaned as she shook out her long dark locks.

All the while she continued to move her hips, keeping him at the edge of a climax.

To his delight she ran her hands down her chest, pausing to cup her breasts and pinch her nipples. Ryder sucked in a breath when the tiny buds hardened.

Did she have any idea how sexy she was? How she kept him teetering on a climax with little effort?

Ryder followed her hands as they continued down her front to where their bodies met. She caressed her swollen clit and moaned.

And it was more than he could take.

In a split second he had her on her back on the floor as he pounded into her body, the need to claim her body and heart burning fiercely within him.

She met his thrusts, urging him onward. And when he

drove so deep inside her that he touched her womb, she held him tight as he climaxed.

Rhi stared in silence at the piece of paper on the table in front of her. Just as Balladyn had said, it took them going through over sixty books, gathering the clues and pieces together.

The only hiccup came with some of the older texts that were faded too badly to make out. Not even magic fixed them. Those were the parts Balladyn had guessed at, and she agreed with his assumptions.

Then there were the books in an ancient Fae language that hadn't been used in eons. Rhi understood only a word or two out of an entire paragraph. Balladyn, at least, knew a little more than she, enough to put things together.

It hadn't taken much to place the words in the correct order. Even as she read them a fourth time, it still sent a shiver over her.

Fae be warned. A group with immense power and magic are judge, jury, and executioners for Death— Reapers. They enforce the law and right balance. Be advised, if a Fae discovers a Reaper . . .

That's all they had. It infuriated Rhi that they couldn't finish the message. She wanted to know what would happen if a Fae discovered a Reaper. Rhi was also curious to know if there was more to the message they hadn't found yet.

Sixty books to find thirty-three words.

"Do you still have someone following you?" Balladyn asked.

Rhi stopped herself from glancing to the side to her watcher just in time. She regretted telling Balladyn about him now. Maybe Rhi was wrong, but she didn't think her watcher meant her any harm.

"No. I think I was being paranoid."

Balladyn's red eyes narrowed as he closed the tome in his hand and gently set it down as he stared at her. "You've never been paranoid."

"True," she said with a shrug. "Then again, I've never left the Queen's Guard and told Usaeil off either."

For a long moment Balladyn watched her before he gave a nod. "Perhaps you're right. As long as you don't have that same feeling anymore."

"I don't."

"There's that, at least." He closed more books and gathered a few in his arms before he walked to the cases and began to shelve them away. "Do you feel better about seeing the passage?"

Rhi sank into the high-backed chair that looked as if it had come right out of the Renaissance period and sighed. "I wish I could say yes."

"I tried to warn you."

"How do we find the rest?"

Balladyn glanced at her over his shoulder as he put away the last book in his hand. He turned and walked back to the table and gathered more books. "Did you not hear me when I said my library was more extensive than any Fae's?"

"I did actually."

"Then you'll understand when I say I've been through each of my books. Twice. There's nothing else. Perhaps whoever was leaving the messages was stopped by the Reapers."

Rhi looked to where her watcher stood. "That's definitely a possibility."

"But you don't think so." Balladyn gave a little shake

of his head and grinned as he returned to putting away the books.

Rhi observed him for a moment. "You do have a nice collection. But is it every book?"

"No one even knows how many books there are. Most of what I acquired was pillaged from the Fae realm after the Light left. Many I couldn't get to because some Dark destroyed them."

"I need to find the rest of the message."

Balladyn paused while shelving a book. He slid it into place and laid the remaining books in his hands on a shelf as he turned to her. "Why? Why is this so important to you?"

"I wish I could explain, but I don't understand it myself. It's something I have to do."

He strode to her, pulling her to her feet. "Don't. It doesn't matter what the rest of the message says. It's enough of the warning at the beginning. Don't meddle with these Reapers, Rhi."

"So you admit they're here."

He sighed and dropped his arms. "I never said they weren't."

"Have you seen one?"

Balladyn looked away, refusing to meet her gaze. That was a cue that he knew something.

Rhi moved into his line of sight and forced him to meet her gaze. "You know something. Spill."

"Rhi," he began.

She held up a hand and said, "Eh. Don't even try. Just tell me what you know."

"Dammit," Balladyn muttered and ran a hand over his jaw. He stared at Rhi for a long stretch of silence. Then he said, "There's been mention of a Fae seen in Edinburgh with white hair."

"Fae?" she asked. "Are you sure?"

"He has red-rimmed eyes."

"Ah. That's definitely a Fae. I've never heard of a Dark having such coloring."

Balladyn crossed his arms over his chest. "Neither have we. It's bothering Taraeth as well, though he's trying to hide it. I believe the white-haired Fae could be a Reaper."

"Maybe we should try and find him."

"No!" Balladyn shouted.

Rhi jumped, because at the same time she felt her watcher come up behind her. "Okay," she said, drawing out the word, waiting for both men to calm down.

It took Balladyn longer than her watcher.

"Rhi, I gave you this information because I thought it would stop whatever you were thinking of doing. Don't use it to do something reckless."

She smiled at that. "Come with me, then."

Balladyn's arms dropped to his sides as he blew out a breath. "I wish I could."

"You can. Leave all this behind."

"I can't. I'm going to rule the Dark."

Rhi smiled tightly. It hurt that he chose the Dark over her.

"I can do much for the Dark," Balladyn explained.

Rhi touched his face. "They're Dark. They're evil. What is there to do?"

"I'm Dark."

"You don't have to be."

He gave her a confused look. "This is who I am, Rhi. I thought you understood that."

She certainly did now. "Yeah."

"Stay," he urged her when she turned around.

Rhi turned and blew him a kiss. "I'll see you soon, lover."

She veiled herself and exited his room, hurrying to the Fae doorway that would take her out of the compound. Rhi didn't breathe easily until she'd stepped through. As soon as she saw she was in Cork, she teleported out—to Edinburgh.

CHAPTER THIRTY-FIVE

Ryder wanted to stay just where he was. It didn't matter that the floor was hard, because Kinsey was in his arms. Something had happened when they made love. He felt certain that she would open her heart to him again.

But there was so much hanging over their heads. Until he could show absolute proof of her innocence, everyone at Dreagan would be wondering about her. Ryder didn't want Kinsey subjected to that in any form.

He kissed Kinsey's forehead as she slept. Then he gathered her in his arms and got to his feet. Ryder used his foot to pull back the covers before he lay her down.

Once she was covered, he gave her a light kiss on the lips. "I'll be back soon," he whispered.

Ryder gathered his clothes. He yanked on his jeans and slid his arms into his shirt, but didn't fasten either. He grabbed his boots and slipped from the room.

In the corridor he put on his boots and buckled his pants. It wasn't until he went to button his shirt that he found himself laughing as he recalled Kinsey yanking it open, popping off the buttons.

Ryder ran a hand through his hair and left the shirt open as he walked to the computer room. He was at the door when Dmitri walked out and stared at him in surprise.

"I expected you to take another night off," Dmitri said.

Ryder shook his head. "There's too much going on."

"You can say that again. I'm glad you're here. Most of the e-mails have been decoded."

It was the concern in Dmitri's gaze that alerted Ryder. "How bad is it?"

"No' good, my friend."

Ryder pushed past him and entered the room. He hurried around the monitors to see Thorn rubbing his eyes before looking back at the screen.

As soon as Thorn spotted him he said, "Am I ever happy to see you."

Ryder sat in his chair and took a few seconds to look at each monitor. MI5 hadn't done anything out of the ordinary the entire day, which was expected with the weather.

The facial recognition software had finished scanning Ireland with no sign of Ulrik.

In more bad news, there were so many shell corporations within shell corporations from Kyvor that Ryder would never be able to find them all—or those involved.

A smile began to form when he saw an alert on one of the monitors showing a capture from a CCTV of Ulrik outside The Silver Dragon in Perth. At least they knew where Ulrik was now.

Ryder's gaze landed on the screen before Thorn with the pictures of every Sam MacDonald who owned a business. He then turned his eyes to Thorn.

"None of them were Ulrik," Thorn said, regret and anger filling his voice.

Damn. That's not what Ryder wanted to hear. "Esther seems too smart to be fooled by a name. She's MI5. She'd check the name and the business."

"We're going to show her a picture of Ulrik and see if he's Sam MacDonald," Ryder said. "I doona know how Ulrik is keeping himself so well hidden, but he's doing a great job of it."

Thorn cleared his throat. "You need to read the e-mails your software decrypted from Kyvor."

With a touch of a few keys, the folder was open on Ryder's monitor. He read them from the oldest to the newest. The first, dated five years prior, merely referred to Dreagan without actually naming it. But with each e-mail sent at the middle of each month, it became clear that those at Kyvor were looking into Dreagan and the Dragon Kings.

What froze Ryder's blood was when he spotted an e-mail dated the exact month and year he first met Kinsey. He clicked open the e-mail and read in shock.

"DK #12 has shown interest in a human female. You'll be delighted to know she works for us—Kinsey Burns. For now I suggest we don't interfere and see how far the connection goes."

Ryder wanted to hit something. No. He wanted to kill whoever this was. It proved that these people had been watching the Kings for far longer than anyone knew.

All his cameras, all his software and gadgets couldn't alert him that they were being watched. Not even their dragon magic could do that.

"Ryder?"

He blinked and found Thorn looking at him with concern. A glass of whisky was set in front of him. Ryder swung his head around to see Dmitri take Kinsey's chair.

"I brought a couple of bottles," Dmitri said. "I think we're all going to need it."

Thorn took his glass and drained it. "Con already left for Paris. We've got until tomorrow evening to sort this out."

Ryder's gut clenched. Thorn was right. If Con were here, Ryder knew he'd want Kinsey interrogated immediately.

He ignored the glass of whisky and read the next few e-mails. They didn't say anything of importance, just listed how often he'd been seen with Kinsey.

It wasn't until six e-mails later that he felt as if he'd been blasted with Dark magic. He reached for the whisky and tossed it back. No sooner had he set the glass down than Dmitri refilled it.

Ryder drank that one as well before he could face the screen again and take in what he'd read.

"*We've made contact with KB. She's receptive to our offer. Will proceed with the plan.*"

"You doona know what the offer was," Thorn said.

Dmitri grunted. "It's obvious they're using her to get to Ryder."

Ryder didn't know what to believe. He knew what his heart told him, but his mind was telling him something else entirely. Was he so in love that he hadn't seen he was being betrayed?

Just like Ulrik.

Thorn refilled all three glasses. "Keep reading," he urged.

Ryder wanted to destroy the entire room with a round of dragon fire, but he found himself clicking on the next e-mail instead.

For the next several, the focus was on him and his movements. His watcher seemed irritated that he'd not seen Ryder doing anything magical nor had he witnessed Ryder shifting.

Ryder noted the date of the next e-mail he was to open. It was a month after he'd left Glasgow. In all his life he'd never felt nervous about anything, but the emotion was filling his gut now to the point he felt ill.

Dmitri shoved the glass of whisky into his hand. It must be that bad for them to prepare him ahead of time. Ryder took a deep breath and opened the e-mail.

"We've a perfect opportunity with KB. She's distraught and easily convinced right now. I'm pushing things ahead of schedule."

From then, his watcher focused entirely on Kinsey. He was the one taking pictures of her and filing daily reports of her comings and goings. But these second reports were going to the group Ryder had yet to discern.

Thorn pointed to the screen. "You can skip the next ten. The e-mails don't say much other than he miscalculated the depth of her hurt. Whatever his plan was got pushed back."

Ryder still went through each e-mail. He didn't want to miss anything. It could be a single word usage that gave him a clue to something later.

When he came to the e-mail Thorn had told him to skip to, Ryder didn't hesitate. He opened it immediately.

"KB has taken the bait."

That's all the e-mail said, but it left Ryder cold. It was dated nearly fourteen months after he'd left. He'd been watching over her all that time, but only checking in to make sure she was all right. He hadn't watched her every move.

Ryder stared at that single sentence for several minutes. He'd truly believed Kinsey was innocent. Even Dmitri had said her reactions were those of someone not hiding anything.

Could they've been so wrong?

"Ryder, you may no' want to hear this, but I think we should have someone watching Kinsey," Dmitri said.

He nodded, knowing Dmitri was right. "She's in my room," Ryder said.

A moment later Dmitri said, "Anson is standing outside the door. If she wakes, he'll bring her straight here."

Ryder looked at his two friends, neither of who would hold his gaze for long. Ryder had staked his life on Kinsey's innocence.

The only thing that kept him seated was knowing that none of the Kings or their mates could be killed. But there was much he'd shown Kinsey. All of which she could easily take back to Kyvor and hand over.

Ryder clicked on the next e-mail. One by one he read until he came to the latest one, sent just a few weeks earlier. All of them discussing KB's progress and how she'd taken to their program with ease.

He was numb. Utterly and totally numb.

The woman he loved had come to betray him.

Was this hollow feeling what Ulrik once experienced? Had Ulrik felt as if he didn't know which way was up? Did Ulrik have the desire to hurt, to maim—to kill?

It was no wonder Ulrik had begun slaughtering the humans. It's the same thing Ryder wanted to do. Because it was mortals who couldn't leave the Kings alone, who kept meddling in their affairs as if it were their right.

Ryder slowly pushed away from the computers. The mixture of sorrow, distress, pain, and rage were about to erupt.

"I doona need to remind you MI5 is still here," Dmitri said.

But his voice came as if from a great distance. Ryder stood, the need to shift so great he had to fight the urge to remain in human form.

"Ryder!"

Someone was shouting his name. He heard them, but there was no need to answer. Ryder knew what he had to do. Because he wasn't going to let Con or any of the others take what was his right—bringing Kinsey to justice.

He'd offered her safety, shelter. His love.

And this was how she repaid him?

She'd ripped his heart out with nary a thought. He'd wondered if she wanted revenge for his leaving, and now he knew. But it was going to end that night.

Ulrik, the Dark, and MI5 had all tried to get to Dreagan and the Kings in some way. And Kinsey had slipped in under the radar. Ryder felt like the biggest fool.

But he was going to protect his home and his family in the only way he knew how.

CHAPTER THIRTY-SIX

Kinsey woke feeling sick to her stomach. She rolled to her side to stop the nausea, but nothing helped. When she broke out in a sweat, she threw off the covers and made a dash for the bathroom to kneel before the toilet. As her stomach rolled viciously, her head began to pound.

She grabbed her head and fell to the floor. The pain was unimaginable, as if someone were inside her head. She cried out, squeezing her eyes closed, praying it stopped.

Ryder! Where was he? Kinsey needed him.

Ryder heard the screams when he was halfway to his bedroom. He started running with Thorn and Dmitri on his heels. As he approached the bedroom he saw the door open and panic set in.

He rushed into his room to find Anson kneeling over Kinsey in the bathroom. The light was on but Kinsey had her eyes closed with her hands on either side of her head as she curled up on her side. Her cries tore at Ryder as he saw the pain she was in.

Ryder grabbed a blanket off the bed as he strode into the bathroom. He covered Kinsey's naked body then touched her arm.

Anson looked up at him, his black eyes troubled. "I heard the screams and found her like this."

"Careful," Dmitri cautioned Ryder when he tried to roll Kinsey onto her back.

Ryder needed to get her to Con. Con could heal anything. That's when Ryder remembered Con was in Paris. He didn't know what to do. As angry as he was with Kinsey, she was in pain. If he was going to get a confession from her, she needed to be lucid enough to answer his questions.

"Kinsey," Ryder called. "Can you hear me?"

Tears streamed freely down her face, telling him the agony she was in. Ryder began to gather her into his arms to take her back to the bed. He was about to stand when she grew quiet.

He watched as her arms fell to her sides and the lines of hurt eased from her face as her body relaxed.

"What the bloody hell," Dmitri murmured.

Thorn gave a shake of his head. "I doona like this, Ryder."

He didn't either, but he wasn't sure what to do. At least Kinsey was no longer in pain. That was a plus. But there was no denying something was going on. He just needed to determine what.

If she were an electronic of some kind, Ryder would know exactly what to do. As it was, the human body was as foreign to him as designing an engine was to others.

"What are you going to do?" Anson asked.

Ryder looked at each of the Kings and shrugged. "I can no' leave her on the floor."

Just as he began to stand, Kinsey sat up, her eyes opening. The blanket fell away, but she either didn't realize it or care. And the Kinsey Ryder knew would've cared.

All four of them froze as they waited to see what she would do or say. Seconds ticked by without a sound from her.

"Kinsey," Anson said.

Ryder frowned as she ignored him. Then she rose to her feet and started for the door. Ryder pointed to Thorn who quickly shut the door before Kinsey could reach it.

Ryder then rose and moved to stand before her. He didn't like the others seeing her without clothes, but he was more concerned with her attitude. "Kins, you're naked. Don't you want to put on some clothes?"

She turned her head and looked right through him. Ryder exchanged a look with Dmitri and Anson. No matter what, Kinsey wasn't leaving the room.

Ryder put a hand out to stop her when she attempted to walk past him. With just a small shove from her slim hand, he found himself on his back.

"What the hell?" Thorn asked.

Ryder was thinking the same thing. He jumped to his feet and put himself in front of Kinsey once more. This time he was prepared when she went to push him.

This time he didn't budge an inch.

She cocked her head his way. Then she used both hands to ram him. Ryder found himself sliding back on the hardwood until he met the rug, which scrunched beneath his feet.

Anson came up behind Kinsey and tried to get his arms around her, but she somehow managed to dislodge him.

"Her strength has more than tripled," Ryder said, grabbing hold of her shoulders and stopping himself. "We can't be gentle with her anymore."

Thorn frowned. "But Ryder. You love her."

"Right now she's a threat to Dreagan. We need to stop her."

Dmitri nodded vigorously. "I wholeheartedly agree."

Before they could take her down, she sent an upper-cut to Ryder's jaw, nearly knocking him out. He stumbled backward trying to get his bearings as he heard his friends shouting.

Something hit the back of his legs. Unable to right himself, he fell backward, right into the chair. He shook his head, trying to clear it. When he blinked and the room stopped spinning he found Anson and Thorn rising from the floor and Dmitri bent over holding his cock as he braced a hand on the wall.

It took half a second for Ryder to see that Kinsey was no longer in the room. He jumped up and rushed to the open door to catch a glimpse of Kinsey—still naked—going down the stairs.

Ryder sent out an alert to all the Dragon Kings on Dreagan through their mental link. Then he rushed after Kinsey with Thorn, Dmitri, and Anson right behind him.

Guy grabbed Elena and pulled her out of Kinsey's way at the base of the stairs. The Kings knew what to do. The mates were taken deep within the mountain while two or three Kings stood guard.

The rest of the Dragon Kings would take up posts throughout Dreagan, the mountain, and the entire estate.

Ryder met Guy's eyes and gave him a nod to let Guy know that he was going to take care of the problem—in whatever way was needed.

"Are you up for this?" Thorn asked as they hurried after Kinsey through the house to the hidden doorway into the mountain.

Ryder didn't pretend not to know what he asked. "Kinsey betrayed me, betrayed Dreagan."

"That doesna mean you have to kill her."

Anson grunted. "In case you missed it, Kinsey has strength I've never witnessed in a mortal without magic."

"Maybe she's a Druid," Dmitri offered.

Ryder shook his head. "She's no' a Druid."

"I hate to say it," Thorn said. "But maybe you didna know her as you thought you did."

Ryder didn't say anything as they entered the mountain. He paused, trying to determine what she could be after. It wasn't the Silvers, because she couldn't wake them even if she managed to open the magical lock.

It couldn't be the weapon the Dark sought that Con hid, because it wasn't kept there. Not to mention there was no way she could get to Con's mountain.

That left one possibility—Esther.

Ryder turned to his friends. "She's going after Esther."

"We'll come at her the other way," Dmitri said as he nudged Anson.

The two each took a tunnel, one to the right, and one to the left. Ryder looked at Thorn and kept following Kinsey.

"You're no' Ulrik," Thorn said.

Ryder kept Kinsey within his sights. "Perhaps. But I think I know exactly how he felt."

"Why Esther?"

"Because she gave up a name," Ryder said. "Kinsey hadn't wanted to be there when we interrogated Esther."

Thorn came even with him as the tunnel widened. "Why did you bring her?"

"Con wanted it, and I thought if Kinsey was allowed to see how we questioned others she might lose some of her fear."

"No' to mention we let her be a part of clearing her name," Thorn added.

The more Ryder thought about it, the more of a fool he felt. It was the worst feeling—nearly as bad as when he watched his dragons fly across the dragon bridge to another realm.

"We're going to stop her and figure this out."

Ryder glanced at Thorn. "Doona bother trying to make the situation better. Nothing can do that."

By the time they reached where Esther was being held, Ryder was prepared to knock Kinsey out. When they turned the corner, Kinsey and Esther were already in hand-to-hand combat.

Thorn rushed to Henry who was laid out on the floor. "He's alive," Thorn said.

At least there was that.

The sound of footsteps approached as Dmitri and Anson finally reached them. Anson gave a shake of his head while Dmitri circled around the women to get behind them.

Ryder watched the fight for a moment. He expected Esther to be a strong fighter because of her training, but Ryder was shocked to discover that at times Kinsey was better than the MI5 agent.

Esther was fighting for her life while Kinsey acted like a robot. No hit Esther landed seemed to cause Kinsey any pain, while Esther winced and groaned when Kinsey landed her hits.

Kinsey landed a particularly bad hit in Esther's stomach that caused her to bend over gasping for air. Ryder was about to send his power into Kinsey to weaken her and take her down when Esther let out a scream and clutched at her head.

The same thing Kinsey had done.

Thorn was by Ryder's side in a moment. "That's no' a coincidence."

"Never is," Ryder said.

Esther grew quiet. A moment later she straightened and looked at Kinsey with the same flat stare that Kinsey had.

"What did they do to them?" Anson asked.

That was something they had to know. As well as everyone involved, because it was obvious Ulrik hadn't done this alone.

"If we let them continue fighting they're going to kill each other," Dmitri said.

As soon as Kinsey rushed Esther, Ryder focused his power on her, weakening her. But it wasn't enough.

Dmitri used his power of thought cancellation on Kinsey. It stopped her immediately. Ryder then weakened Kinsey even more, causing her legs to give out. She crumpled to the floor, but her gaze was still locked on Esther.

"Kinsey willna stop," Thorn said.

Anson jerked his chin to Esther. "We doona know when she'll be triggered again."

"We need Hal." Though any of the Kings could use their dragon magic to make them sleep, Ryder wanted to make sure they remained that way for a long period.

He sent Hal a quick message. Luckily, Hal was one of the Kings guarding the mates so it didn't take him long to reach them. He rushed into the cavern and glanced at Ryder.

"Make them sleep," Ryder told them.

Dmitri was staring at Kinsey, who was still attempting to get to Esther. "Deeply."

Hal walked to each of the girls and touched them, sleep gas forming around them. When he gently laid Esther on the ground, he turned to Ryder and stood. "What happened?"

"We're trying to figure that out," Thorn said.

Ryder waited for Thorn or Dmitri to tell Hal and Anson of Kinsey's betrayal, but neither spoke of it. Ryder wasn't sure whether to be grateful or not.

Because he was going to have to tell all the Kings.

There was a sound behind them as Henry began to wake. He pushed himself to his hands and knees and sat on his haunches. He looked around him. "I'm guessing I missed something."

It was Dmitri who said, "You could say that."

"How bad?" Henry asked.

Ryder blew out a breath. "Bad enough."

CHAPTER THIRTY-SEVEN

Paris, France

Con poured another glass of cabernet sauvignon, watching the red wine fill his glass. Before him sat a meal fit for a king with actual gold plates, crystal glasses, and half a dozen silver candlesticks on the table alone.

He looked past the flicker of the candles to the woman across from him. Usaeil. Queen of the Light. She raised her glass to him, her silver eyes alight with happiness.

"I've a benefit to attend in Los Angeles next week," she said, dropping the American accent and allowing the Irish to come through. "I want you to go with me. I'm tired of attending these things alone."

"You know I willna," he said and took a drink of wine.

"They're going to find out soon enough." She rose and walked around the suite.

He looked over her beautiful form and the gold lamé minidress with her thick black waves falling down her back. It wasn't an accident that she wore gold. Con knew it was all for him.

Usaeil paused at the sofa and sat on the arm, crossing

one long, lean leg over the other. "Why not let them discover the truth with the rest of the world?"

"I told you I'd tell my Kings when the time was right."

The smile dropped from her face. "I'm tired of hiding, Con. You're a king. I'm a queen. We shouldn't have to hide. We make the rules."

He leaned an elbow on the arm of his chair and slowly took another drink. Usaeil had become more and more volatile of late, and Con was pretty sure he knew why—Rhi.

As he regarded Usaeil, he crossed an ankle over his knee. "I doona lead my men that way."

"Perhaps you should. It's working for me."

"Is it?"

One black brow rose, her silver eyes glaring daggers. "You dare to question my rule. Have you been talking to Rhi?"

Damn. Con should've known Rhi would say something to Usaeil. "You know I've no' spoken to Rhi lately."

"When was the last time?"

He didn't like jealousy in any form, but especially when there was no cause for it. "I'm no' going to have you dig into my life."

"Why? Do you have something to hide?" She stood and stalked toward him. "If you won't tell me what I need to know, then that makes you guilty."

Con set down his glass and got to his feet. He looked down at Usaeil. "And you're paranoid. Rhi has gotten under your skin, and you're allowing her to stay there."

"When was the last time you saw her?"

He didn't say another word as he walked around her and headed toward the door.

"If you walk out, I'm going straight to Dreagan and telling everyone about us."

Con never did well with threats or ultimatums. He halted and slowly turned back to Usaeil. She smiled widely, triumphant. If she only knew how furious he was, but Usaeil was only interested in herself—just as all Fae were.

He'd learned that the hard way before. He was learning that lesson a second time. And he should've known better.

"I knew you could never leave me," she purred as she walked to him. She placed her hand on his chest, moving aside his suit jacket to cover his heart. "What we have is special. Everyone will enjoy what we have."

"And what exactly do we have?"

Usaeil laughed as she looked up at him and rubbed her breasts against him. "Why, love."

Con's blood ran cold. It was so much worse than he'd feared. Why hadn't he seen the signs? But he knew the answer. He'd been too preoccupied with keeping Dreagan safe and bringing down Ulrik. Usaeil had been there to relieve his body when he had a need.

That's all it was to him.

That's all he assumed she'd thought as well, because that's how it began between them.

"What do you see for us?" he asked her.

Her eyes closed as she rested her head on his chest. "Eternity. We'll be mated, and I'll have the tattoo on my arm of the dragon eye. We'll unite the Light and the Dragon Kings into one faction. Your Kings can take Light as their mates as Kiril has and solidify the union."

"And the war with the Dark?"

"That's your war, my love." She lifted her face and gave him a wink. "You can easily take the Dark. You've done it before."

Con took a deep breath and slowly released it. "And you'll do what? Stand by and watch?"

"Of course. I've got a movie to make starting tomorrow. I can't take the time to lead my army."

"Then give it to someone who can. We could use an ally."

She burst out laughing and patted his chest before walking toward the bedroom. "You're a Dragon King. You don't need anything."

Con couldn't remember ever fighting so hard to remain calm and cool as he was in that moment. He needed to say something to get her attention. Rhi was definitely a trigger, but there had to be something else.

Reapers!

He followed her, but stopped at the bedroom door, leaning against the doorjamb. "And what of the Reapers?"

Usaeil was in the process of shimmying out of her slinky dress when he spoke. In a blink the gold dress was back in place. "You've been talking to Rhi!"

"No' about you. When I do speak to Rhi it's about the Dark and the war."

"Liar. Rhi asked me the same things. She thinks I should be gathering the army to help you and calming the Light about the Reapers."

Rhi was right. Though Con would never tell her that. "I'd no idea the two of you had such a conversation."

"No one tells me how to rule!" Anger billowed around Usaeil like wind. "I've reigned over the Light for thousands of years and never led them wrong."

"Why no' calm them about the Reapers then?" Con shouted over the wind.

She rolled her eyes. "The Reapers are just stories told to frighten the Light away from turning Dark."

"What if they're more than that?"

She scowled at him, looking at him as if he were mud

on the bottom of her shoe. "I no longer require you tonight."

And with that she was gone.

The silence was deafening after the noise of the wind. But Con wasn't fooled. Usaeil could be veiled, though he wasn't sure for how long. He knew it was longer than most Fae.

Except for Rhi.

Con noticed that Rhi was able to remain veiled for even longer than Usaeil. He pulled out his phone and sent a message to his pilot and driver to be ready to leave Paris immediately. Then he pivoted and returned to the table. He took another bite of steak and a long drink of wine before he walked from the room.

It was a good thing Usaeil couldn't read minds, because Con was thinking about Rhi. It was disturbing that Rhi had left the Queen's Guard, and now that she and Usaeil seemed to be on the outs, the Queen was acting strange.

Rhi also questioned Usaeil. And urged sound advice. Con wished he was surprised, but the fact was—as reckless and irritating as Rhi could be—she was a skilled warrior with a strong mind that saw so much.

The only reason Usaeil didn't take Rhi's advice was because Rhi was the one giving it, and Usaeil's feelings had been hurt by her leaving the Queen's Guard.

But Con knew why Rhi left. The Light Fae suspected Usaeil was having an affair with a King. How long before Rhi pieced it together and confronted him? Con suspected it was going to happen sooner rather than later.

He exited the hotel and got into the waiting car. As he was driven to the airport, it angered Con that he couldn't just shift and fly back to Dreagan as he would've before the video leaked of them.

But times changed—and not for the better. He feared it was a permanent change. It wasn't one he was prepared to defend against his men.

In truth, there were times he regretted keeping his vow to protect the humans. If he'd joined Ulrik, none of this would be happening.

He and Ulrik wouldn't have argued.

Ulrik wouldn't have been banished and his magic bound.

The dragons would never have had to leave.

The Kings would never have had to hide in their mountains for thousands of years.

The Fae would never have had reason to come to the realm.

Not to mention there wouldn't have been Fae Wars or the constant fighting with the Dark.

Con wouldn't be preparing to kill a dragon who had once been his best friend.

All so the Dragon Kings could continue to hide on Dreagan, shifting only in the mountains—but never flying.

It wasn't fair to any of the Kings. Or to himself.

Con looked around the plush Jaguar sedan and wanted to bellow his fury. He felt confined, restricted. Restrained.

Because he was. He was a Dragon King. One who not only ruled the entire realm, but other Kings as well. And where was he? Grounded with the possibility of his wings being permanently clipped.

He thought of the Kings. It had taken him longer than he wanted to admit to turn them away from Ulrik the first time. As fractured as they all were now, he wasn't sure how many would side with him.

The Kings wanted to be in the air in their true forms. They hadn't been happy about only being able to fly at night, but at least there had been that.

Con fisted his hands. He was backed into a corner, just as Kinsey had said. And the urge to lash out was strong—very strong.

Even if he turned on the mortals and killed them, he would have to face the mates. All but one was a mortal, and he suspected they wouldn't be pleased with their entire race annihilated.

It didn't matter which side Con chose, he was damned either way.

From the moment he was a young dragon and he understood what it meant to be King of Kings, he'd set his sights on obtaining the title.

And he had—though it hadn't been pretty.

Was his time coming to an end? It didn't matter how strong he was physically or magically, if his men sided with Ulrik, he would have no one to lead.

Con wondered—and not for the first time—if his decisions that altered their course and sent the dragons away had been the right ones.

The more he saw what the humans were doing to the planet, the more he believed he'd made the wrong decisions.

As soon as he saw the lights of the airport, his hand was on the door handle. The car had barely come to a stop before he had the door open and stood on the tarmac.

He strode to the helicopter. The blades were already spinning and it was waiting on him. Con paused when he caught sight of Lily in the pilot's seat. He then quickly got into the chopper and put on the headset.

"Ready?" Lily asked.

Con nodded and they took off. He watched the lights of the city grow smaller as they lifted off. "What are you doing here, Lily?"

"Flying you."

"Without Rhys beside you?"

She chuckled, but her white knuckles gripping the stick told another story. "I'm immortal."

"Are you going to tell me what's happening at Dreagan?"

Lily glanced at him with her dark eyes. "It's Esther and Kinsey. It's like someone took control of them and they fought each other."

Con didn't know how much more bad news he could take. "Who was injured?"

"No one. Ryder got control quickly. The women are unconscious for the moment."

His fingers reached for the dragon-head cuff link and turned it. "Get us home quickly."

With every mile eaten up, dread filled Con. Because he suspected what he'd long-feared had come to pass—another mortal had betrayed a King.

CHAPTER THIRTY-EIGHT

Ryder stared down at Kinsey who lay unmoving upon the slab of granite in the small cave. Esther was in another cave next to them.

"Con is on his way back," Thorn said as he walked up.

Ryder expected as much. "Who called him back?"

"No one. Lily was in Paris picking up a gift for Rhys when she learned what happened here. She went to the airfield and took over as pilot."

Ryder didn't blame Lily for telling Con. No, the blame for everything rested squarely on his shoulders. Because love had blinded him to the truth.

How had he missed it? There had to have been clues. Was he so intent on winning Kinsey back that he'd missed something important? How did he tell anyone that? Everyone at Dreagan had counted on him, and he'd failed them.

"What's your plan?" Thorn asked.

Plan? Ryder wanted to laugh. He couldn't process anything past the point of Kinsey betraying him. There was an emptiness in his chest where his heart had once been.

He didn't know what the next step was or even what to say. How could he plan anything?

Dmitri came to stand on the other side of Kinsey, but his gaze was on Ryder. Ryder didn't want to listen to anything they said. He just wanted to be alone with his grief so he could try and sort out when everything had gone wrong.

If he could just find that out, then he would have his answer. He'd be able to know how Kinsey betrayed him and exactly when. Closure. That's what it was called.

Not that it would help dull any of the pain.

What had they once told Ulrik? That time would help to heal him? That was the biggest load of shite. They had eternity. Something like this never healed.

It sat in their minds and hearts, festering like a wound until everything around it was rotted and black. Dead.

Ryder could hear people talking around him, but none of it penetrated the haze of fury and treachery that surrounded him. He stopped hearing them.

All he saw was Kinsey, the woman he'd loved with his entire soul. Now he was going to have to kill her for her deceit.

Yet when he looked at her, he tried to mesh the woman who'd fought Esther with that of the one in his arms just a few hours earlier. The woman who'd laughed and joked with everyone at dinner. The woman who had looked at the painting of Con with such wonder.

Con had been right. Kinsey was a very good actress to have fooled all of them. All but Con, that is. He'd suspected her from the beginning. And Ryder had only seen a chance to gain Kinsey's love again.

"Are you going to kill her?"

The words came from behind him as well as in his head. Con. Ryder wanted to ignore him. Instead he looked to the ceiling. "I'll no' have you and the others do it."

"We saved Ulrik a lot of pain by doing it ourselves. He cared for his woman. No matter how angry he was, he'd never have been able to look her in the eye and kill her. And neither will you."

"I've already thought of that. I doona plan to have her facing me."

Con walked around the chamber and leaned against a wall across from Ryder and Kinsey's prone form covered with a blanket. "That's a good plan. You'd still carry the stain of her death upon your soul."

"She betrayed us. Me."

"I know," Con said softly.

So Thorn and Dmitri had told him. Ryder should've expected that. "I gave you my word she was innocent."

"Aye, you did."

Ryder lifted his gaze from Kinsey to Con's face. "But you didna trust me."

"It wasna about trusting you. I trust every King here. However, I saw the love you held for Kinsey."

"And you knew it blinded me," Ryder finished with a nod.

Con raised a blond brow and removed his cuff links. He put them in his pants pockets and began to roll up the sleeves of his dress shirt. "Doona presume to know what I'm thinking, Ryder. What I was going to say was that I knew you were hoping for the best, but preparing for the worst."

Ryder blinked. Con was right. He had prepared for the worst. Every stroke of the keys by Kinsey had been recorded and logged.

"Love blinds," Con said. "But so does anger and betrayal."

Ryder ran a hand down his face, suddenly wanting to sleep for a millennia he was so tired. "She could've—"

"Doona allow your thoughts to go down that road," Con interrupted him. "It willna do anyone any good. Let's concentrate on piecing all this together."

"I tracked everything Kinsey did at the computers. I'll begin there." Ryder pivoted and started walking away when Con's voice halted him.

"I'll remain with her."

Ryder turned his head to the side, but didn't look back at either Con or Kinsey. With a nod, he strode into the tunnel heading back to the manor.

It wasn't until he once more sat in his chair staring at the monitors that he realized everything was different now. He saw the world differently. All because of a single treachery.

Ryder pushed thoughts of Kinsey aside and tapped the table. The virtual keyboard appeared instantly. He moved evidence of Kinsey's duplicity to other monitors. Then he typed in a few commands and everything Kinsey had done over the past several days filled the screen in front of him.

He began to go through them one by one.

Dmitri waited until Ryder disappeared around a corner before he walked into the cave. He glanced at Kinsey, but his attention was on Con. "He's a wreck."

"Aye," Con agreed. "Any of us would be in that situation."

"He has that same look Ulrik wore."

Con didn't so much as blink as he returned Dmitri's

stare. "Ryder has informed me we willna be repeating the past."

"You mean he's going to kill her?" Dmitri asked in surprise.

"He says he is."

Dmitri shook his head in shock. He knew he'd never be able to do such a feat. "He'll never be able to do it."

"I doona believe so either. It'll crush Ryder in ways he doesna understand."

"But you do now. Just as you did so long ago. Does Ulrik no' understand you were trying to help him?"

"When someone is hurt that deeply, they doona see truth."

Dmitri leaned back against the wall and crossed his arms over his chest. "There's Esther as well."

"I know."

The only evidence that Con felt anything was a sigh that escaped him. Dmitri was surprised the King of Kings showed even that wee bit of emotion.

Everyone worried about how Henry was going to react. And they had a right to worry. Henry was an ally. The Kings didn't need another enemy.

"We could have Guy wipe their memories," Dmitri suggested.

Con put his hands in his pockets and looked at Kinsey. "I contemplated that on the flight over. It was my plan until you, Thorn, and Anson told me what had occurred."

"Meaning you think they were programmed?"

"Meaning magic was used."

Dmitri shrugged. "Our magic is stronger."

"A mortal's mind is a delicate place," Con said as he slowly walked around the slab of granite. "We could force our way in and brutalize their minds."

"We need Tristan," Dmitri said.

Con added, "And Roman."

Dmitri sent a mental call to both Kings as he observed Con. "What are you thinking?"

"I'll tell you when Kellan confirms my suspicions."

There was only one reason to call Roman. Since he could control metal, Con must assume there was something within Kinsey and Esther.

Dmitri dropped his arms and walked to Con. "What if whatever made Kinsey do this was done against her will?"

"I've thought of that as well. For Ryder's sake, I hope that's the case."

"I watched her with him," Dmitri said. "She has feelings for Ryder, deep feelings. And it didna look fake."

Con's black eyes glanced at Kinsey. "Sometimes our eyes deceive us. Sometimes even instincts we've relied upon for centuries get it wrong. The only thing that's going to help is to get proof and answers."

"You were no' there when Ryder discovered her betrayal. I might no' want a mate of my own, but now I understand why you've worked so hard to prevent us from having those entanglements."

Con looked at him for a long time. "You think so?"

That was an odd thing to say. Dmitri had just given him a compliment and that's how Con reacted. Then again, Con had been different of late. Perhaps it was the lover he'd taken.

"Aye," Dmitri said.

Con was silent for a long while. Then he said, "Do you think we should live alone? To never have someone to share our beds and our futures?"

Dmitri stopped the frown that formed before it became visible. Con didn't ask such questions. Ever. Was it some kind of trick? No. Con wouldn't do that.

"We're dragons, but we have needs, no matter what form we're in. There are no dragons here, so we've no choice but to turn to the mortals. Or the Fae."

"Hmm," Con replied.

But Dmitri wasn't finished. "I think we should remain alone. It's no' like we can have children. History has proven that no human can birth a baby by us that lives. We put our way of life on the line with every mortal we allow to know our secret."

"What do you suggest?"

"I think if we need to ease our bodies we do so with the Light Fae."

Con raised his brows. "Why the Light?"

"The answer is obvious. They're no' mortals. They already know of us, so we doona need to hide our true nature."

"What if a King finds his mate with a Fae?"

Dmitri shrugged, confused by the question. "Kiril already has. The human mates might be immortal, thanks to the ceremony, but at least Shara can defend herself and Dreagan with her magic. What can the other mates do? Nothing."

"You'd have us mix dragon and Fae?"

"Doona twist my words," Dmitri said. "I merely suggested that if we had to mix with a race, the Fae are better than mortals."

Con nodded as he continued walking around Kinsey back to his original spot. "That's interesting to hear."

"You can no' tell me you have no' thought of it."

"I didna say that."

Dmitri smiled. "So that's who you have as a lover, a Light."

"I didna say that either."

"You didna have to," Dmitri replied with a chuckle.

"We've long thought it might be a Fae." Then his smile died as he thought of Rhi. "You might want to keep it a secret from Rhi."

"I've no' admitted anything," Con said. "About anything. You've come to conclusions I'd like verra much for you to keep to yourself."

Dmitri heard the anger tingeing Con's words. These weren't speculations on Dmitri's part. Whether Con wanted to admit it or not, he'd just revealed the truth.

Though Dmitri declined from asking if Con's lover was in fact the Queen of the Light—Usaeil. Because if it was and Rhi discovered it—all hell would likely break loose.

And it was just a matter of time before Rhi found out.

Dmitri wanted to make sure he wasn't anywhere near when Rhi did. Because the Fae was likely to go nuclear on everyone, leaving destruction much worse than what had happened at Balladyn's fortress.

He eyed Con, wondering if Con knew how close to the fire he was playing.

CHAPTER THIRTY-NINE

Mikkel drummed his fingers on his desk. His office lights were kept dimmed, allowing for many shadows about the large room to hide all sorts of things.

He stared at Harriet Smythe for a long minute. The tall blonde had done wonders for his plans from the moment he'd begun tutoring her twenty years earlier. She wasn't just a beauty that knew how to use it to her advantage, she was a quick learner and had a sharp mind.

However, right now, he was furious with her.

"It's going to work out." Harriet's clear blue gaze held his, her conviction there for him to see.

But it wasn't enough. "How can you be so sure? Both Esther and Kinsey are still alive."

"We need Kinsey alive," Harriet said. "That's the only way you'll get what you need from Dreagan."

Mikkel sat forward in his chair and placed his forearms on his desk. Never far from reach were his six mobile phones placed in a neat row. "If you honestly think the Kings haven't realized what's been done to Kinsey, then I've given you more credit than you ever deserved."

"Kinsey won't fail us," Harriet stated firmly.

There was a snort from the shadows behind him. Mikkel didn't turn around to look at Ulrik, though he wanted to. Harriet for her part suddenly realized they weren't alone in the office.

Mikkel smiled. He loved when those who worked for him were reminded of how lethal and dangerous he truly was. He enjoyed their fear. But it only partially made up for him no longer being a Dragon King.

That made him think of Ulrik attempting to gain his magic again by going behind Mikkel's back. He hadn't disciplined Ulrik yet for that—but it was coming.

Just as he would betray Ulrik, killing him right after Ulrik put an end to Con. Mikkel would be King of Kings and the planet could be returned to what it was always meant to be—a dragon realm.

But that was for later. Right now he had to take care of this mess. Mikkel didn't want to kill Harriet. She was loyal and bright, but she'd let him down.

"You've failed me epically," Mikkel told her. "The whole point was for Kinsey to get in, gather all the information, get it to us, and then let her betrayal become known to Ryder so he'd kill her for us."

Harriet swallowed and opened her mouth to talk.

Mikkel spoke over her. "I'm not finished. Then there's Esther. I thought I told you not to send her in yet."

"Did none of your probing into Esther's mind reveal that she had a brother who worked for MI5 and who was helping the Kings?" Ulrik asked from the shadows.

Mikkel wanted to demand why Ulrik had waited to tell him that bit of information, but he held himself in check. Barely. Instead, he focused his growing ire on Harriet, whose eyes had gone wide.

"What?" she asked. "That's not possible. We did every background check there was. She's an orphan."

Ulrik tsked. "She was trained by MI5. I'm fairly certain they could make you believe whatever was needed."

Mikkel had had enough. He stood, his chair flying back to hit the shelves behind him. "What?" he bellowed. He stalked around his desk to Harriet. "Are you telling me Esther was sent to spy on us?"

Harriet backed up, the stiletto of her shoe getting caught in the rug and causing her ankle to twist. She caught herself by grabbing the back of a chair set before the desk. "I'm thorough in my work. You know that."

"No' thorough enough!" Damn, he hated when his Scots accent came through with his anger. He was getting better at controlling it, but sometimes it slipped through.

"Kinsey should've killed her for giving up a name anyway," Harriet hurried to say.

He looked over her pale face and the fear in her gaze. "The only reason you're alive right now is because you've done what no other has been able to do. You got a human onto Dreagan. This is your last chance, Harriet. If you can't finish what you started, then I'll claim your life."

"I'll finish it," she vowed with a firm nod. "I've never let you down before. I'll fix this and prove I'm worthy of continuing to work for you."

He gave her a nod. Without another word, she hurried from his office.

"Do you believe her?" Ulrik asked.

Mikkel turned to face his nephew. "I hope she comes through because she's been a great asset. In the end, however, I'm sure she'll have to die."

"Even if she corrects the problem and gets you all you need and want from Dreagan?"

Mikkel narrowed his gaze on Ulrik who stood still as a statue against the wall. "She failed me. I can't believe you asked such a question. You were King of the Silvers. You above all else knows what it means to keep those below you in line."

"Without a doubt."

"Then why ask me that?"

Ulrik stepped from the shadows and leaned his hands on the desk. "Because of what she's done for you."

"Others can take her place," Mikkel said with a wave of his hand. "All her work has been saved so anyone can step in at any time."

"You believe it's that easy?"

"I do."

Ulrik slowly straightened. "Just as you believe anyone can be a Dragon King."

At this Mikkel smiled. "Not at all. It takes a special kind of dragon. You took what was meant to be mine."

"Stronger. Braver. Smarter. More powerful. With more magic." Ulrik paused. "Aye. A special dragon."

Mikkel didn't like this attitude Ulrik was showing. It was time Mikkel reminded him who was in charge of who. "You've been spending a lot of time with Muriel of late. You favor her."

"She's good in bed."

"Kill her."

Ulrik showed no emotion as he stared silently at Mikkel. "I'll no' kill one of Taraeth's favorite slaves on your whim."

"I'm telling you to do it," Mikkel said. "You will do everything I say."

Ulrik tugged the cuff of his dress shirt at his wrist and buttoned the suit jacket. "You can no' start killing off the Dark."

"I'm not. You are."

"So you want Taraeth's anger directed at me."

"What I want, *nephew*, is for you to remember your place."

Ulrik's silver gaze hardened for a split second. "How can I not? You remind me of it constantly."

"Then you should know I'll no' stand for any back talk, nor will I allow you to grow a spine."

Ulrik could kill him. Right then. It wouldn't take much. He had Mikkel at a disadvantage, though Mikkel didn't realize it yet. The thought of seeing Mikkel's surprise as the life drained from him was exhilarating.

But he had a plan for his uncle. Ulrik needed to remember that before he lost what little control he had over his anger and showed Mikkel exactly who was King of the Silvers.

He was tired of hearing what Mikkel was going to do when he took over. His uncle would never get close to ruling. The fact Mikkel didn't even realize that Ulrik had all of his magic back and was once more the King of the Silvers proved how unprepared Mikkel truly was.

Ulrik was going to enjoy bringing Mikkel low. Though it wasn't time. Right now he got pleasure watching as Mikkel upset the order of things at Dreagan.

Though it didn't go unnoticed by Ulrik of just how they were using Kinsey against Ryder. A betrayal. And not just any betrayal. Ulrik had seen Ryder with Kinsey. They were mates, regardless of whether Kinsey had accepted it or not.

Ulrik knew how it felt to have a woman he thought to be his deceive him in such a way. That didn't sit well with Ulrik in the least.

It was time he went to Dreagan and took a look at the

situation. Obviously Con wasn't there or Kinsey would already be dead.

Ulrik cut his hand through the air at whatever Mikkel was saying that he didn't care about. "I'm no' killing Muriel. You want to take your anger out on me, then take it out on me."

"What better way to hurt you than taking something you care about?"

Ulrik chuckled wryly. "Oh, uncle. If you really knew me, you'd know I doona care about anyone. Now, I need to return to the store."

"I'm no' finished with you yet."

A third slip in less than half an hour. Mikkel wasn't nearly as in control of himself as he led others to believe. Ulrik would have to remember that. It could be used against his uncle.

"Then what do you need of me?" Ulrik waited impatiently as Mikkel tried to think of something for him to do. "Exactly. When you need me, you know where to find me."

Ulrik walked from the office and down the hallway to the front door. Fast moving clouds hid the moon, making the night seem darker.

It was a night for wreaking havoc.

Ulrik got into his McLaren Spider and drove away from the manor on the west coast of Scotland. It would take him a few hours to drive back to the store, but that was time he didn't have.

He waited until he was forty minutes from Mikkel's before he pulled over at a small village. He went inside a restaurant and used his new skill of teleporting to take him to Dreagan.

As always, he arrived in his mountain. It was the one

place he knew he could go that no one at Dreagan would ever think to look for him.

From there he used the tunnels below the mountains to take him toward the mountain connected to Dreagan Manor. Dreagan was on high alert, which made Ulrik waste more time avoiding Kings who patrolled the tunnels.

He paused to look in on his Silvers for a moment. Later he would go and spend more time with them. For now, he had to find Kinsey and Esther.

Ulrik located Esther first. She was lying on a chunk of rock, unmoving. The mortal Henry North paced the cavern as Banan attempted to talk to him.

Next to Ester in the adjoining cavern was none other than Kinsey, who was also unconscious. Except Ulrik didn't find Ryder with her. It was Con and Dmitri.

Ulrik wondered why neither of the mortals had been killed yet. Unless Con sent Ryder away as he'd done to Ulrik so long ago. But the Kings didn't look as though they were getting ready to slay a human.

They were in their locations for battle.

Just what was going on? This wasn't what he'd expected to see when he arrived. No wonder Harriet was so sure she could get Kinsey to do what she wanted.

Ulrik wished he'd learned exactly what it was Harriet and her team had done to Kinsey and Esther, because it was enough that they knew the women weren't dead.

Some kind of tracking device perhaps? That was the most plausible answer.

Ulrik ducked into the cavern across the narrow corridor as he heard voices. He saw Tristan and Roman walk into the chamber where Kinsey was.

"Tristan, I need to see if you can get into her mind," Con ordered.

Ulrik moved to the other side of the cave opening so he could see across the way into Kinsey's cavern. He watched as Tristan moved to stand at her head. Then he placed his hands on either side of her head and closed his eyes.

"I can no' find her," Tristan said with a frown.

Ulrik knew then that Kinsey hadn't truly betrayed Ryder by her own choice. Mikkel and Harriet were controlling her. And that changed everything.

CHAPTER FORTY

Ryder finished going through the log of Kinsey's every key stroke since she'd arrived at Dreagan. He'd expected to find instances where she saved information about Dreagan and forwarded it or even downloaded it to a PIN drive.

Yet there was nothing.

Kinsey was good, but she wasn't good enough to get through his firewalls because there hadn't been enough time when she was alone to get through them.

Even if she had broken through his firewalls, that would've immediately sent him an alert. But there hadn't been any sort of alert.

It was as if Kinsey had done nothing more than try and clear her name. Yet Ryder knew that couldn't be the truth. He had damning evidence of her agreeing to spy on Dreagan for Kyvor.

He checked a second and third time, but there was still no evidence that proved Kinsey did anything other than what he'd asked her to do.

Ryder hid the virtual keyboard and pushed back from

the table. With a sigh, he got to his feet and walked from the computer room.

The manor was strangely quiet as he made his way downstairs. It seemed so odd after the cornucopia of laughter and conversation around the dinner table just a few hours earlier.

The silence and stillness reminded him what Dreagan had been like after they sent their dragons away and took to their mountains.

Ryder stopped when he descended the last stair. His mind ran through everything that could happen to Dreagan and those who called it home because he'd allowed his feelings to get in the way of precautions, and it made him ill.

Kellan hesitated on his way toward the foyer. He eyed Ryder for a moment before he said, "Delaying the inevitable only makes things worse."

"I should've seen it."

Kellan put his hands on his hips and released a long breath. "Ryder, I'm going to tell you something that Con never will. All of us could've seen it in her, but none of us did. No' even Con. Doona allow the blame to rest so heavily upon your shoulders. As soon as you discovered the evidence, you acted. No one was hurt, and nothing was done to Dreagan. It's going to be all right."

Ryder nodded, appreciating Kellan's words. He didn't bother to tell Kellan that nothing would ever be fine again, because there was no point. Kellan had his mate, he'd found love. He didn't understand what it felt like to have the woman he wanted only to lose her to treachery and deceit.

There was only one other King who did—Ulrik.

Not that Ryder would be calling him up anytime soon to commiserate.

Kellan patted him on the arm as he continued toward the foyer and walked out the front door. Ryder's feet felt like lead as he made his way to the entrance of the mountain.

He didn't encounter another soul until he reached the cavern where Kinsey was being held. When he saw Tristan standing at Kinsey's head with his hands on her, Ryder halted.

"He says he can no' find Kinsey," Dmitri whispered.

Ryder frowned. What was that supposed to mean? Even unconscious, Tristan should be able to see her thoughts.

On the other side of Dmitri, Roman shifted his feet. Ryder looked from Roman to Con who was staring back at him. Tristan could read someone's thoughts, and Roman could control metal. It made sense to bring Tristan to Kinsey, but why Roman?

Ryder started to walk to Con to ask him what was going on when Tristan winced, his face contorting. Ryder froze, instantly on alert.

"Magic was used," Tristan said. "Druid magic."

Druids? The last time a Druid used magic was when Darcy unbound some of Ulrik's magic. Darcy had family on the Isle of Skye, and the Druids there weren't enemies of the Dragon Kings.

The next largest sect of Druids were those at MacLeod Castle married to Warriors. There were other Druids around the world, but most kept to themselves.

"It seems we've yet another problem," Con said.

As if they didn't already have enough.

Tristan opened his eyes and looked at Ryder. "The magic used is a spell blocking me from getting to Kinsey."

"I doona understand," Ryder said.

Dmitri grunted behind him. "Ditto."

"Add me to that list," Roman said.

Tristan looked from Ryder to Con. "Imagine the brain is like a house with thousands of rooms. Kinsey is locked inside one of the rooms, and I'm going to have to bust through the door to get to her."

"Will it destroy her mind?" Con asked.

Tristan hesitated as his dark brown gaze moved to Ryder. "There's a possibility, depending on how much of my magic I'll have to use to get in."

"Do it," Ryder said. All the while praying that Kinsey would be whole when it was over.

If they wanted to know the full extent of what happened, they needed her awake and cognizant, not under the control of Druid magic.

Tristan nodded and closed his eyes again.

Kinsey held out her hands in front of her. Was she blind? Why was everything black as pitch? She didn't know where she was or how she had been taken from Ryder's bedroom.

"Ryder!" she shouted for the hundredth time.

Her throat was sore from screaming. With her not being able to see, she moved at a snail's pace, inching her feet forward so she didn't trip on anything.

The last thing she remembered was falling asleep in Ryder's arms after they'd made love. Wait. No. After that there was something . . .

Kinsey stopped walking and concentrated, trying to pull up the memory that teased the fringes of her mind. It felt like forever before a flash of tile flickered in her mind.

The bathroom. Suddenly she recalled being nauseated and rushing to the toilet. There was nothing after that except waking up in the darkness.

"Where are you, Ryder?" she whispered.

Emotion choked her, but Kinsey refused to give in to the tears. She had to keep moving and figure out where she was. Ryder had said he'd protect her. She knew without a doubt he would find her, because that's who he was.

Kinsey began to shuffle her way forward once more with her arms out in front of her. Eventually she'd have to run into a wall or something. Until then, she would keep moving.

"Ryder!"

She gasped and halted as it felt as if the world was spinning around her a million miles a second. Her stomach rolled, and despite the darkness, she closed her eyes.

Nothing helped. She could still feel it turning this way and that, rotating from side to side as if trying to dislodge her.

Kinsey held out her arms to the sides. To her shock her left hand connected with a solid surface. She quickly put her back to it and slid down the wall until her knees were at her chest.

She wrapped her arms around her legs and kept her eyes squeezed tightly shut. Added to the twists and turns was the odd sensation of feeling like someone had paused the world and then quickly pushed play again.

"Kinsey? Can you hear me?"

The male voice came through at a whisper. Disappointment filled her that it wasn't Ryder, but she recognized the voice. Though she couldn't put a name to it.

"Kinsey, this is Tristan."

Yes, that was Tristan's voice. What was he doing in her head, she wondered?

"Listen carefully. It's going to take a lot for you to answer me, but I need you to try."

What was he talking about? Hadn't he heard her screaming for Ryder? The situation was becoming more and more odd. All she wanted to do was be back in Ryder's room with his arms around her.

She opened her mouth to say his name, but the spinning increased so she couldn't even lift her head. Wind howled around her, pushing her back against the wall so she couldn't move.

"You're in danger, Kinsey. I can't help if I can't find you. Say something. Anything," Tristan urged her.

She could barely hear him anymore. Fear took hold then, pushing her to act. Each time she lifted her head, the wind took her breath, preventing her from speaking.

Kinsey had no choice but to keep her head buried against her legs. "Tristan! Hear me," she yelled as loud as she could. "Please help me!"

If Tristan responded, Kinsey didn't hear him over the roaring in her ears.

"Ryder, I need you," she whispered.

Was this how she would die? Huddled and scared? This wasn't the woman she was, nor was it the person she wanted to be.

Kinsey put her hands back against the wall. Slowly, she used her hands to help her get to her feet. Only by turning her head to the side away from the wind was she able to take a breath.

"Ryder! Tristan! I'm here!" she screamed at the top of her lungs.

She jerked when it felt as if someone had touched her. Suddenly there were hands all over her, pushing and pulling her this way and that.

"Ryder! Help me!" she cried.

More hands found her, their fingers biting into her flesh. Kinsey fought against them, kicking and punching.

As unexpectedly as it all began, it abruptly ended. With the wind no longer holding her, Kinsey fell face-first to the ground. The darkness vanished, leaving a room so white it blinded her.

She pushed up on her hands and knees and looked around, wondering what to do now.

"Kinsey?" Tristan called. His voice was louder, clearer now.

"I'm here."

"You've made it through the toughest part. Now you just need to find your way back."

"Back? What are you talking about? Where's Ryder?"

There was a pregnant pause before Tristan said, "I can no' help you because someone has trapped you within your own mind. You're the only one who can get yourself out."

"I want to talk to Ryder."

"It's because of my power of being able to see your thoughts that I'm here."

Now she was really confused. "So you've done this before?"

"Nay."

Well that was reassuring. Kinsey got to her feet. "If you are only supposed to see my thoughts, how are you talking to me?"

"Dragon magic."

As if that explained it all, and she supposed it did. "Is Ryder all right?"

"He's fine. We just need to get you sorted out."

That's when it hit her. "What did I do, Tristan?"

"What do you mean?"

"Stop it," she said and dropped her chin to her chest. "Stop trying to not answer me or stall. Just tell me the truth. What did I do?"

He sighed loudly. "You know what you did."

"Remind me," she demanded. The nasty feeling in the

pit of her stomach multiplied by a hundred. It had to be
something very bad for Tristan to not want to talk about it.

"You came here to spy on Dreagan and Ryder. We all
know how you've betrayed him."

Kinsey's knees threatened to buckle. Betray? She'd
never do that to Ryder or anyone.

It took her a full minute to pull herself together. There
was only one way she was going to get out of this. She had
to put all the emotions aside and tackle this like she would
any work project.

After she found her way back to wherever she was supposed to go and faced Ryder and the rest, then she could
allow the emotions to come through.

Because if Tristan helped her, it was for one reason
only—to get information.

CHAPTER FORTY-ONE

Ryder hated not knowing what was going on. He trusted Tristan, but it was his mistake about Kinsey, so he should be the one helping her.

But his power would only hurt her, not help. His ability to build anything electronic did nothing either. So he stood, helplessly, watching as Tristan tried to reach Kinsey.

"I found her," Tristan said. "She's asking about Ryder."

Ryder was at one moment relieved that Kinsey's mind might come out of this intact, and another furious that they were in this position.

After a moment, Tristan dropped his hands and stepped back. "I've never communicated that way before."

"You spoke with her?" Con asked.

Tristan nodded. "The magic was hard to pierce on my end and hers, but Kinsey managed it. She kept asking what was going on. I told her she was trapped in her mind and must find her way back."

"You couldna lead her out?" Dmitri asked.

Tristan ran a hand through his light brown hair streaked with gold. "I wish it were that easy. Only Kinsey knows the way around her mind. If I attempted to help her, I might get her trapped somewhere."

"How long is it going to take to find her way?" Ryder asked.

"I've no idea."

Roman stepped forward then. "I suppose it's my turn now."

"It is," Con said and motioned him to come closer to Kinsey.

Ryder stepped between Roman and Kinsey. Then he looked at Con. "Why is Roman here?"

"I want to see if there's anything implanted in Kinsey," Con said in an even tone.

Ryder turned and looked at her. Implanted. He hadn't thought about that, but there was a possibility there could be. "Why use magic only then to use technology?"

"To cover both bases," Con said.

Ryder moved back, giving Roman the space he needed. His instincts kept telling him to protect Kinsey, but the proof upstairs warned him to do nothing. He'd never been more confused in his life.

"Kinsey asked for you," Tristan said as he came to stand beside Ryder.

He hated how his heart leapt at the thought. "She's probably worried about how much I knew."

"She sounded genuinely confused about all of it."

"As we've learned, she's a verra good actress."

Tristan crossed his arms over his chest. "Is she? I'm beginning to wonder."

That got Ryder's attention. He swung his head to Tristan. "About?"

"Her mind was laced heavily with layers of magic. Why did they need to do that if she wanted to spy on us?"

Ryder shrugged and turned his attention back to Roman. "She might have had them do that to help her in her acting."

"That's a possibility."

Or they could've used her.

No. Ryder refused to hold onto that small bit of hope. With the evidence they'd discovered and Kinsey's actions, the truth was staring him right in the face.

Roman held his hands palm down over Kinsey's stomach. Within moments he said, "I've found something. It's in her left arm just above her wrist."

"How deep is it?" Con asked.

Roman walked around to Kinsey's left arm. "Just beneath the flesh."

"Remove it."

Ryder clenched his fists as Roman pierced her flesh and an elongated metal tube about half an inch slid from her skin. Con then placed his hand on her and healed the wound.

"It's a tracker," Roman said.

Dmitri muttered a string of curses. "They wanted to keep track of her."

"That's for certain," Tristan said.

"Should I destroy it?" Roman asked as he held the bloody object.

Con shook his head. "No' yet."

Roman handed the tracker to Con who tucked it into his pocket.

"Now what?" Ryder asked.

Con turned to Tristan and Roman. "Repeat these same steps with Esther."

The two gave a nod and walked out of the cavern.

Dmitri cleared his throat and mumbled, "I'm going to . . . go do something else."

Once he'd left, Ryder faced Con. "I've looked through everything Kinsey did three times."

"And?" Con urged.

"Nothing. I can no' find a single thing that would alert me that she did anything."

Con nodded absently as he stared at the floor for a long minute. Then he looked at Ryder. "The evidence you found that she betrayed you, is it in her own words?"

"No. Nothing I found was ever from her or forwarded from her."

"We know you were followed before you met her."

Ryder shrugged nonchalantly. "Right."

"We know that after you left Glasgow, they concentrated on Kinsey. But she was already working for Kyvor before you met her."

"All that's true. What are you getting at?"

"I know you must've looked in on her. How much did you see?"

Ryder glanced away, annoyed at the questions. He scrubbed both hands down his face before he threw them out to his sides. "No' as much as I wanted, but most might think it was bordering on stalking."

"Did you ever see her inside Kyvor?"

Ryder paused, frowning. "No. I was able to hack into their feed, but there was always something wrong with one camera or another. I'd see Kinsey on one floor, but not another."

"Do you think they might have known you were looking?"

He gave Con a flat stare. "Absolutely no'."

"Even if magic was used?"

That drew Ryder up short. He'd never thought about magic. "The Druid would need to be exceptionally powerful to cast a spell like that."

"And trap someone within their own minds after taking control of them."

Ryder looked at Kinsey and wanted to gather her in his arms. "Everything pointed to her."

"Which, I think, was precisely the point," Con stated. "They wanted us to kill her."

He found Kinsey's hand beneath the blanket and held it. "What now?"

"We find out Esther's part in all of this." Con's gaze was narrowed through the door. "I'm wondering why they would send a second spy, and then have them fight each other."

"Kinsey came to kill Esther. It wasn't until the middle of the fight that Esther was triggered."

Con rubbed his hand over his jaw. "Interesting. See what you can do about leading Kinsey back. I'm going to go to Esther."

Ryder watched him leave then looked down at Kinsey. "I can no' believe I doubted you. I promised to protect you, and yet I didna. You could've died. I could've been the one to kill you. Kinsey, please come back to me. Find your way back. I need you."

Ulrik listened to the exchange in Kinsey's cavern with interest. So Mikkel was using a Druid. What had he said to convince the Druid to help him?

He needed to discover who the Druid was and in what way they were helping Mikkel. Because if the Druid was as powerful as Ulrik suspected, it could put a serious cramp in his plans.

Ulrik remained where he was, watching Ryder with Kinsey after Con left. Con didn't seem that upset that another King had found his mate. Some might think Con was becoming accustomed to such things.

But Ulrik knew it was just Con being Con.

Everything would be completely different had a tracker not been implanted and magic used on Kinsey. Ryder wouldn't be whispering affections to Kinsey.

He'd be burning her dead body.

Ulrik drew in a deep breath. It was time for him to leave. He'd learned all he needed. Just as he was about to step from the cavern, Con walked into the tunnel and simply stood there.

He watched his nemesis and onetime friend. Con's gaze searched the shadows as if he were looking for something. Ulrik smiled. Did Con sense him? Why not have the Kings scour the mountain for him?

Ulrik expected that exact reaction, but Con remained silent. He looked first one way and then the other. His attention returned to the area Ulrik was in. Not everything was in place for him to challenge Con, but if his old friend wanted to battle now, then Ulrik would do it.

Except Con didn't come his way. Ulrik was confused by Con's actions. First he didn't outright kill Kinsey, and now he wasn't coming for Ulrik.

Was he getting weak?

Or was Con up to something?

If there was one thing Ulrik knew above all else about Con, it was that Con was one of the most intelligent people he knew. Con never let emotion rule him, and he looked at every situation with multiple possibilities.

It was one reason he'd become King of Kings.

Ulrik stood silently for several minutes as Con stared his way. Then Con turned on his heel and walked into the cavern where Esther slept.

After ten minutes, Ulrik left the cavern and took the long way around to his Silvers. When he reached them, he hurried to the cage and placed his hands on two of the four.

"I'm here," he whispered.

He felt them pushing at the magic keeping them asleep. Ulrik wanted to wake them and see them soar, but he couldn't. Not yet.

"Know that I'm here and will free you verra soon," he promised.

He moved to the next two and repeated his words. Then he spent the next few moments running his hands along their warm silver scales.

Ulrik then thought of his mountain and was instantly teleported there. He removed his suit jacket and shirt and folded them atop a boulder. Next he took off his shoes and socks before he removed his pants.

He stood naked deep in the middle of his mountain, the place he'd passed centuries asleep. It was so long ago. His time as a dragon felt like a distant memory.

But no longer. It was time for him to remember who he truly was. It was time he recalled what ruled his heart.

He drew in a deep breath and slowly released it. Despite having all of his magic returned, he'd not shifted into dragon form. The way Mikkel watched him made it impossible, and there simply wasn't room at his store.

Here, however, was another matter entirely.

Yet Ulrik hesitated. He wasn't sure he even remembered how. Eons had passed since the last time he shifted. Then it had been a mere thought for it to happen. What would it take now?

He looked down at his hands. Human hands. It was all he'd seen for thousands of years. He needed to see and feel himself in his true form, the form he'd been born to.

Ulrik closed his eyes and thought of shifting.

Nothing happened.

But he refused to give up. He focused on his breathing, on feeling his dragon magic move through him as thick as blood and as powerful as its own entity.

He imagined unfurling his wings and snapping his tail against a bolder. He envisioned looking into the water and seeing the long tendrils that ran from the top of his head down his back as well as the shorter ones surrounding his mouth—and obsidian eyes staring back at him.

When Ulrik opened his eyes he stared down at black talons and silver scales. He smiled and spread his wings wide.

CHAPTER FORTY-TWO

How did one find their way in their own mind? That's what Kinsey faced. She wasn't sure what to do or where to go. Tristan made it sound so easy, and yet there was nothing but white all around her.

First nothing but darkness. Now this.

Black and white.

Was that a metaphor? Or was it simpler than that and she just needed to cling to something that sounded real-istic?

Kinsey squared her shoulders. There was no one but herself there, no one she could turn to for help. She'd been on her own for three years. During that time she'd learned how to do all those things her stepfather and then Ryder had done for her like fixing a leaky faucet or hanging a new light.

But this was different.

This wasn't something she could attempt on her own using YouTube or Google before calling in professionals if she screwed things up.

If she messed this up, that was it. There was no do-over or reset button.

Would she even know if she totally botched things? That was a sobering—and alarming—thought. It only added to her stress level, ramping her anxiety up to the point that she thought she might vomit.

It was her mind. Who knew her better than herself?

Kinsey crinkled her nose. Well, other than trying to lie to herself on occasions, ignoring her instincts, and not being true to herself.

Right now her mind looked blank. She didn't know which way to walk or even if she should. But she couldn't stay still. Remaining where she was only ensured one thing—her death.

She turned in a circle, but there was no blinking sign that told her where to go. With no other choice, Kinsey started walking.

"You came here to spy on Dreagan and Ryder. We all know how you've betrayed him."

Tristan's words played over and over in her head. She could shout her innocence all she wanted, but no one was going to listen. She heard the accusations in Tristan's words.

That could only mean that Ryder had found some damning evidence that pointed right to her.

Except she hadn't done anything. Kinsey knew that for a fact.

There might have been times she'd wished he was the mole in a Whac-A-Mole game, but she'd never wished Ryder any real harm. How could she when she'd loved him?

There hadn't been a soul at Kyvor or anywhere else who'd approached her about Ryder or Dreagan. That wasn't something she'd forget. So if no one spoke to her, and she hadn't gone to anyone, what evidence did Ryder have?

Kinsey wouldn't know until she found her way through her mind and was able to wake.

If this wasn't all some kind of trick.

That drew her up short. What if it was a trick? What if it hadn't been Tristan who she'd spoken with? Ryder knew she was innocent of anything. He would never let any harm come to her, and he certainly would've found some way to talk to her with Tristan.

What was real and what wasn't? Somehow Kinsey was going to have to sort it out. She might not be in her mind at all, but in some prison and pumped with drugs.

With the missing time from when she woke in Ryder's room to finding herself here, anything could've happened. It could've been moments or days that she was missing.

She squeezed her eyes closed and halted her thoughts. Her imagination was leading her down all sorts of paths, and only one of them was the right one. If she didn't listen to her feelings and follow her heart, it would all be for naught.

Kinsey drew in a deep breath. As she slowly released it, she opened her eyes. Unfortunately she was still in the all-white room.

"What's real?" she asked herself.

What she knew was that magic existed. So did the Fae, dragons, and Druids. If magic was part of the world at Dreagan, who was to say that it hadn't somehow been used on her by someone? Since dragons, Fae, and Druids were all able to use said magic, any of them could've done this to her.

Kinsey felt some of her anxiety ease as she accepted the truth of that.

If magic had been used, which seemed likely, then she

could be trapped in her mind. What better way to keep her from finding the truth about those setting her up?

More of the tension eased from her shoulders. Yes. She trusted herself and her instincts, and they were leading her to the right answers.

Her mind was clear, focused.

She had to find her way back to herself so she could talk to Ryder and get to the bottom of this fiasco. Kinsey was tired of being fucked with by these people—whoever they were. It was time she exposed them and the depravity within Kyvor. It didn't matter if the entire company was corrupt, she was bringing it all down.

Her steps were long and purposeful now. She might be a simple mortal with no magic, but she had skills and a brain. No longer was she going to stand there and allow this to happen.

There was no excuse for her ignorance of the situation before. Had she really looked, she'd have seen it all. But she'd buried her head in the sand and pretended that nothing mattered. Where had that gotten her?

Back in Ryder's arms.

Well, besides that, it had put her in a situation that could very well claim her life. She knew now what she wanted. It was her broken heart that kept pushing Ryder away, but as soon as she could, she was going to tell him the truth—that she'd always loved him.

And always would.

She wanted Ryder and his life of dragons and magic. Even if that meant she was in the middle of a war. Because if the war involved Ryder, then she was going to stand by his side and help in whatever way she could.

Though if she really was locked in her mind as she assumed was the case, and she believed it was Tristan who'd contacted her, then she also had to acknowledge that Ryder had some proof of guilt directed at her.

"Just another fight ahead," Kinsey mumbled to herself.

She was fighting now, and she'd continue when she got out of this mind-prison she was in. Facts were facts, and she couldn't dispute them. But she could find the evidence and do what was needed to prove it wasn't her.

No matter what questions Con or any of the other Kings put to her, she knew she was innocent. Maybe Tristan could read her mind and know she was telling the truth. She'd demand he use whatever magic was needed to show that she wasn't part of Kyvor's plots.

It was a great plan. She knew exactly what she needed to do, even after she found her way back. There was just one tiny insignificant problem—she didn't know how to get back.

Tristan made it sound easy. Not that she thought getting out of her mind was going to be a piece of cake. But all he'd said was to find her way out.

As Tristan had spoken, she'd envisioned her mind like a maze. But it was nothing like that. There were no rooms, no doorways, no windows. Nothing.

She could be walking for eternity. If she didn't know what to look for, she could pass it by without even knowing it.

Kinsey stopped and put her hand to her stomach. Ryder. She needed to concentrate on him. He was the one thing that mattered above all else.

Her injured heart had led her to say and do things from the moment she'd arrived at Dreagan that made her want to cry. Despite it all, Ryder had stood beside her, touting her innocence to anyone who listened.

That kind of man was one in a million. He hadn't cared

what Con or anyone thought. Ryder formed his own opinions and never wavered from his belief that she was being set up.

He'd been kind, gentle, supportive, and loving all while never putting any pressure on her. He'd held her in bed each night, offering her comfort and shelter without her even knowing it.

When she said she wasn't sure if she could forgive, he hadn't pushed her away. How she wished she could take back those words and tell him the truth—that she had forgiven him.

He was a man—a dragon—who deserved a woman who stood tall beside him. Kinsey very much wanted to be that woman. She knew she could be that woman. She could only hope Ryder gave her a chance to demonstrate it.

Kinsey began walking again. It would be so easy to fall to her knees and give in to the trepidation and terror that gripped her. To release the dam of tears that threatened to spill at any moment.

But she was going to keep going. For Ryder. For herself.

For their love.

She began to hum to fill the silence. To help her, she let an image of Ryder fill her mind. His beautiful eyes of green, blue, and gold stared back at her, urging her to return quickly.

It seemed as if a great weight had settled upon her shoulders, attempting to slow her, to stop her. She attempted to shrug it off, but it settled upon her like a mantle.

Kinsey quickened her pace. Sweat poured off her as she struggled to keep moving. No matter how she tried to start running, the weight held her back—held her down.

It was magic. She knew it. How did one combat magic when she didn't have any?

Attitude.

Kinsey chuckled as she imagined her mother saying that. It was her favorite response to anything Kinsey and her sister had a problem with.

"It's all about attitude, girls," her mother would say.

Kinsey fell to one knee as the magic loomed over her. She felt like a candle flame that was about to be extinguished. It took a great amount of effort to get back to her feet. She was hunched over, unable to stand straight because of the weight.

"I'm not giving up!" she yelled, letting her anger lace her words. "You won't best me!"

Kinsey threw back her head and laughed. "I won't be beaten. I'll endure. I'm going to find my way back to Ryder. The Dragon Kings will know the truth." The laugh died as she raised her fist into the air. "Do you hear me?"

If there was one thing Kinsey had learned during the years after Ryder left it was that she was strong. Stronger than she ever gave herself credit for.

She'd gathered her broken heart and pieced it back together. She'd faced each day instead of hiding. She'd held that minuscule kernel of hope within her that one day she might find love again, that Ryder might come back into her life.

She'd become a hacker who was respected and revered in the computer world. She'd learned to take care of every aspect of her life from the trivial to the important.

All that showed her that she could beat whatever magic was being used now.

Kinsey gritted her teeth and fisted her hands as she began walking. Every step was an effort, but she didn't give up. She hummed louder as she kept moving, always moving.

She didn't know how long she'd been walking before

she realized she was standing straight. The weight was all but gone. Kinsey walked faster and faster until she was running.

The white stretched endlessly before her, but she didn't stop. She couldn't. If she did, she knew she might not begin again.

Kinsey was smiling widely. Somehow, someway she'd beaten the magic. In all her life she'd never felt so strong. Magic was powerful, but it wasn't everything. She'd just proven that fact.

Suddenly she slammed into something. Kinsey intuitively lifted her arms to shield her face as she fell forward in slow motion as some kind of goo tried to hold her.

She landed on something hard and looked around. There were memories playing all around—her memories. Some so old she'd forgotten them.

Some more recent.

She got to her feet and walked to the one where Ryder was kissing her. Kinsey watched it replay over and over, her fingers against her lips as she recalled the feel of his mouth on hers.

Then she recalled how she'd gotten there. She looked over her shoulder, but only saw more memories that stretched on forever. No more white room.

"Ryder!" she bellowed and started running again—to her future.

CHAPTER FORTY-THREE

Ryder held Kinsey's hand. He'd been there several hours waiting for her to wake. But he wasn't the only one. Henry was also waiting on Esther.

Neither woman had so much as stirred since Tristan spoke to them in their minds and the trackers had been extracted. But that was little consolation to Ryder or Henry.

While he waited, Ryder was going over everything in his mind about Kyvor. He began to methodically put it in order of when he and Kinsey unearthed the information and how it fit into the timeline of occurrences.

Of all the things they found, it had all been about them following Kinsey. It was the encrypted e-mails sent by someone Ryder had yet to look into that mentioned Kinsey. And cryptically at that.

Since the e-mails said very little, Ryder gathered there had to have been face-to-face meetings. In order to learn who these people were, it was going to require turning the tables on them.

If they could watch the Kings, then the Kings could watch them. And Ryder was very good at watching people.

Thorn poked his head into the cavern and said in an excited voice, "Esther has woken."

Ryder was happy for Henry, but he was still waiting for Kinsey to open her violet eyes.

Thorn felt bad for Ryder. He quietly slipped back into the chamber with Esther and the others. Con stood off to the side with his arms crossed over his chest. Roman watched the siblings with an almost confused look in his eyes. Dmitri looked as on edge as he usually was. Only Henry was smiling.

"Henry?" Esther asked, a frown upon her brow. She glanced around the room and at the men. "Where am I?"

At this, Henry's MI5 training kicked in. His smile dropped. "What's the last thing you remember?"

Esther's gaze dropped from Henry's as she searched her mind. Then she sat straight up, alarm and a touch of fear clouding her face. "What did they do to me?" Esther asked more to herself than Henry.

"Who?" Henry urged.

Esther gave a quick shake of her head as she rubbed her temple. "I need to get back to London."

"You're no' going anywhere," Con stated in his cool tone that brooked no argument.

Esther jerked her head to him. "You're Constantine."

Con's black gaze slid to Henry who shrugged in response. Thorn exchanged a look with Dmitri. At this rate, they were ready for anything.

"I know you worked for MI5," Henry told his sister.

Esther gaped at him. "What are you talking about?"

"Stop the lies. I saw your file."

"That's not possible. Stuart promised to keep it from you."

Henry's hazel eyes blazed with anger. "He wouldn't dare."

"It was the only way I'd take the assignment."

Dmitri said into the silence of the cavern, "I think it'd be better, lass, if you came clean with the entire story."

Esther pressed her lips together, then she nodded. "If you read my file, you know I was recruited by MI5. I wanted to tell you, but they forbid it. Then the debacle within MI5 happened. Stuart found me cornered by some of the rogue agents attempting to kill me. He and I killed them before helping others within the agency."

She paused and swung her legs over the side of the granite slab. "As I watched so many people who I thought were on my side turn against me, I knew the only way we'd ever learn how deep this went was to get to the core of things. I went to Stuart with a plan to infiltrate the group focusing on Dreagan."

"And what did Stuart tell you?" Henry asked.

"That he was going to call you and get you to do it, but I stopped him. I can be very convincing when I want to be."

"Don't I know it," Henry mumbled. Then he said, "Where did you know to begin?"

Esther shrugged. "I didn't. Everyone we questioned either refused to talk or died while we interrogated them."

"Died?" Roman asked.

Esther's gaze moved to him. "Not because of anything we did to them. Before we tied them to chairs, a few managed to kill themselves. Others just . . . died. Right before our eyes."

Henry didn't need to look at the others to know that everyone in the room except for Esther knew magic was involved. Ulrik had sunk to a new level, but then again, Henry said that every time they learned something new the banished King had done.

"You're different than earlier," Henry pointed out as

he observed his sister. She appeared more relaxed, despite the situation.

Her brows rose. "Earlier? Henry, I've not spoken to you in months. The last time we saw each other was a year ago."

"We had a conversation only a few hours earlier."

She was shaking her head before he finished. "That's not possible."

"Then how did you end up here?" Con asked.

Esther threw up her hands. "I don't even know where here is."

"Dreagan," Con supplied.

That stopped her cold. Henry watched as she withdrew into herself and her memories. "What are you remembering?" he pressed.

"Oh dear Lord," Esther whispered.

A bottle was quickly shoved into her hand by Roman. Henry tried to warn her that it was whisky since she hated the taste, but he didn't have time. Without even looking to see what it was, Esther lifted it to her lips and drank.

She lowered the bottle, coughing as the whisky made its way down her throat. Her eyes became redder the more she glanced at the bottle, and she rolled her eyes when she read the Dreagan label.

"What did you expect?" Roman asked with a smirk.

Esther took another drink, this one no more than a sip. She put the back of her hand to her mouth as she squeezed her eyes shut for a moment. Then she looked at each of them, landing on Henry last.

"Tell me," he urged.

"We didn't know where to start looking. No one would tell us any names," Esther said. "We were losing patience. Then Stuart had the idea for me to begin posting something on forums about how MI5 was ruined and I was looking for payback."

Henry nodded, understanding now. "That's why you were decommissioned."

"Yes. It took just over a month before I was contacted by a man named Sam MacDonald."

"Did you see him?" Thorn asked.

Esther nodded. "I spoke to him several times."

It was Dmitri who held up his mobile phone with a picture of Ulrik on it. "Is that him?"

"It does look like him," Esther said hesitantly. "But a little different. His hair doesn't have the gray in it at the temples. And his eyes are different."

Con dropped his arms and moved a step closer. "Different colors?"

"No. This man has colder eyes."

"But he looks like the man Sam you spoke with?" Henry asked.

Esther said, "Yes. Besides those differences."

"We've finally connected him," Dmitri said with a smile. "I can no' wait to tell Ryder."

Con held up a hand, stopping Dmitri. "No' yet. Please finish, Esther."

"Sam recruited me," Esther continued. "I was brought into a company called Kyvor. I'm not sure what all they did, but the top executives seemed more interested in Dreagan than their business."

Roman snorted. "Surprise, surprise."

"I went there every day for three months answering their questions and helping them track some of you. There was a woman they were interested in. I never knew her name, just her initials. KB."

Henry looked to Con. "Kinsey."

"Aye," Con said, his lips thinning slightly.

Esther let out a deep breath. "I remember going to the building. They said they had one more test for me before they let me out into the field. I walked into a large room. It was empty except for two chairs." She paused and touched her forehead before dropping her arm. "A woman sat in one chair. She had me take the other. And I remember nothing after that until I woke up and saw you."

"Do you recall what you were supposed to do?" Roman pressed.

Esther gave a shake of her head. "I don't."

"Do you recollect anything about the woman?" Con asked.

"She was stunningly beautiful with shoulder-length blond hair and green eyes. She also liked expensive things. She had a Chanel purse and Christian Louboutin shoes," Esther added.

Thorn got Esther's attention. "What did she say to you?"

"She said hello and called me by my name. I asked for hers, but she didn't tell me. She said a word I didn't understand."

Con's lips twisted. "Gaelic, I'm sure."

"Gaelic?" Esther repeated and looked to Henry. "I think it's time you filled me in on things."

Henry looked at Con who gave him a nod. It was apparent with the tracker and the magic that Esther hadn't been there of her own accord, which Henry was grateful for.

Now came the tricky part.

"What do you know of Dreagan?" he asked.

Esther shrugged and crossed her arms over her stomach. "It's a large company that's been around for generations that supplies the world's finest Scotch. I know that

Constantine doesn't like to show his face. That applies to anyone at Dreagan, for that matter."

"But you knew me," Con said.

Esther smiled, but it froze before it fell away. "I don't know how. I've never seen you before. Your name, yes, from the records at MI5."

Henry rubbed his hand on the back of his neck. "Esther, you can't remember anything because magic was used by the woman you spoke with."

His sister blinked at him.

Henry then pointed to the tracker Con held up. "That was pulled out of your wrist. We believe these people took over your mind and sent you here to infiltrate Dreagan and discover their secrets."

"Secrets on whisky?" she asked.

Henry released a deep breath. "No. Secrets on the people here. Things that could cause trouble."

Again Esther just looked at him.

This was harder than Henry had expected. He didn't just want to come out and say who the Kings were, but it was coming to that. He'd thought Esther might ask more questions about the magic, and when she hadn't, it threw him.

"Show her the video," Roman said as he handed Henry his mobile phone.

Henry gratefully took the phone and put it into Esther's hands. Then he pushed play.

The room grew quiet as Esther watched the video of the Dragon Kings shifting and battling the Dark Fae while everyone observed her reactions.

When it finished, she handed the mobile back to Roman and lifted her gaze to Henry. Her eyes were a bit dazed, her face pale. "Are you telling me that's real?"

"I'm telling you those dragons you saw on the video

are the ones here at Dreagan. The men standing in this room."

Esther's lips parted as she released a breath. "Dragons. That's . . . unexpected."

"I had much the same reaction," Henry said, trying not to smile.

"And the others in the video?"

"Dark Fae," Con said. "Our enemies."

Esther suddenly frowned. "There was a woman with a sword in that video. I think I know her, or I've seen her someplace."

"She interrogated you earlier," Henry explained. "Her name is Rhi, and she got you to give up a name—Sam MacDonald. She's a Light Fae."

"Light and Dark Fae, magic, and dragons," Esther said. "Is this why Kyvor is so obsessed with Dreagan?"

Con nodded. "And why they used you."

"I don't like being used." Esther swallowed and lifted her chin. "My goal was to take these people down. Let me finish what I started."

Henry knew his sister was capable, but it wasn't up to him. He looked to Con to find the King of Kings with a question in his black eyes. Henry gave a small nod.

"Well, Esther," Con said. "It looks like you've just joined your brother as our ally."

CHAPTER FORTY-FOUR

The longer Ryder waited for Kinsey to wake, the more impatient he grew. What was taking her so long? Did she not want to return to her life? Had she gotten lost within her mind?

That was out of Tristan's control, but Ryder wasn't above calling in a favor from the Druids at MacLeod Castle. Not when it came to Kinsey.

And to think he'd been ready to kill her.

His stomach twisted at the thought that he'd nearly lost her for good. The evidence against her was condemning, and he'd reacted instantaneously.

Now that he'd had time to calm down and think things through, there wasn't anything specifically from Kinsey. No texts, e-mails, pictures, or documents showing she was part of Kyvor's game.

There had been a knee-jerk reaction because of what had happened with Ulrik and his woman. Was it happenstance? Or was there much more to everything?

Ryder was leaning toward it meaning more. There were too many coincidences for him to overlook. The correlations between Kinsey and Ulrik's woman—damn, why couldn't he remember her name?—was so obvious now that he was looking at it in another way.

With all the times Ulrik went after the Kings' mates and failed, Ulrik changed tactics. He wanted a King to kill his own mate.

No. Ulrik wanted Con to execute a mate.

No amount of time could make any of the Dragon Kings forget that fateful day they'd killed Ulrik's woman and the repercussions that event caused.

Now, with all that was going on and the enemies closing in on them, as well as Con fighting every King who found his mate, it would destroy Dreagan from the inside out if Con slaughtered a mate only to learn she was innocent.

"What is it?" Con asked as he walked into the cavern.

Ryder blinked, focusing his gaze on Con. "If you'd been here when I discovered the evidence against Kinsey, would you've killed her?"

There was a slight pause before Con slid his hands into his pockets. "I doona make hasty decisions with a life— any life. No, Ryder, I wouldna have killed her without talking with her and learning what I could."

"Say you did. Say you talked to Kinsey and couldna find anything that showed she wasna guilty."

Con's black gaze narrowed slightly. "Why the questions?"

"Please. Humor me."

"All right. I'd need damning evidence. I'd need to see or hear her talking about betraying you before I took such drastic action."

Ryder let out a long sigh. That's what he'd wanted and needed to hear. It was the Constantine he'd known for so long. Yet Con had recently made some decisions that Ryder worried about. Not to mention the lover Con had taken. A Fae.

There could only be trouble there.

"I think it's time you indulge me and tell me what that was all about," Con said.

Ryder knew Con deserved no less. He spent the next twenty minutes going through his thoughts and conclusions with Con about Ulrik, Kyvor, and Kinsey's connection.

When he finished, Con was silent. Finally Con took a deep breath and said, "That's a lot you've sorted out. Did you think I'd kill Kinsey so easily?"

"I know the safeguarding of Dreagan and our secret is the main objective."

"So is protecting mortals."

"Who are no' out to expose us."

Con bowed his head in acknowledgment. "Point taken. I've known for a while that Ulrik is attempting to fracture us from the inside out. Every attack on us has been to that point."

"He nearly succeeded this time."

"I know. What was your plan had Kinsey no' attacked Esther?"

Ryder shrugged and looked at Kinsey. "I was going to talk to her, but I realize now I wouldna have believed anything she said. I was too upset."

"Then things worked in our favor."

Ryder wasn't so sure of that. Not yet, at least. He turned his head to Con. "They wanted Kinsey and Esther to kill each other."

"I think they wanted Kinsey to kill Esther. This Druid, whoever she is, is a problem. If Kinsey didna alert anyone to Esther giving us a name, is there a chance someone hacked our computers?"

Ryder gave him a hard look. "You're seriously asking me that?"

"I had to ask. Then that leaves one option. The Druid is powerful enough to be linked so deep inside Kinsey's and Esther's minds that she knew what was going on."

"As soon as Esther gave up the name and Kinsey saw me doing the search, the Druid knew. Then she triggered Kinsey."

Con lifted one shoulder. "Then how did Esther get triggered?"

"Maybe all her training somehow kicked in? We may never know."

"No, I doubt we ever will."

Kinsey was so tired of running. It didn't matter how far she went, she wasn't getting anywhere. Memories rushed by her in a blur, but there was no way out.

She was going to be trapped in her mind. After all her fighting the unknown force, after finding Ryder again, she was going to lose it all.

"No!" she yelled.

She'd come too far to have it slip from her hands so easily. Kinsey wasn't going to give up. She'd run as far and as fast as needed until she reached wherever she was going.

Out of nowhere two doors appeared before her. She skidded to a halt to stop from running into them. One door was white, the other black.

"Not another representation of good and bad," she said with a twist of her lips.

If there were two doors, that meant only one would take her back to Ryder. The other . . . it didn't matter what the other did because she wouldn't be with Ryder.

The darkness earlier had blinded her, keeping her

nearly in one spot. The magic used on her took her hearing and held her down.

The white had allowed her to see, or did it? The magic used pressed her down, making her weary and exhausted.

Neither was better than the other.

Kinsey tried to walk around them, but she couldn't go anywhere. Her only choice was to pick a door and hope it was the right one.

She went to the white door and put her hand on the knob. Right before she turned it, she drew her hand back as something deep inside her shouted, "No!"

Kinsey stepped back and looked at the black door. It reminded her of the three years she'd lived in a kind of obscurity after Ryder left.

It was only when he entered her life once more that she saw the world anew.

"Only light comes out of darkness," she whispered.

Kinsey grasped the knob on the black door and opened it.

CHAPTER FORTY-FIVE

Ryder didn't want to talk anymore. He just wanted Kinsey to wake up.

"If Esther came out of it, so will Kinsey," Con said. "She's a strong one."

That made Ryder look at Con anew. "You've something nice to say about her after all of this?"

"It's the truth. If you also consider it polite, then so be it. Though I'll admit I think she's a good match for you. In every way."

Ryder was so taken aback that he could only stare at Con. He knew how hard Con had tried to dissuade both Kings and mates from being together, and yet he was giving his approval now?

"Doona look at me as if I'm dim-witted," Con grumbled. "I've come to know Kinsey in the time she's been here. I've seen her with you and the others. Despite her initial fear, she's accepted you and this way of life."

Ryder opened his mouth to respond when Kinsey gasped, her back bowing off the granite as her eyes flew open. He held her as she gripped him tightly, her gaze locked with his.

She was panting, her chest heaving as she touched his face. "Is it really you?"

"It's me," he said with a smile. "You found your way out of your mind."

Her eyes slid closed as she buried her head against his chest and cried. "No. I found my way back to you."

Ryder held her as he saw Con slip quietly from the chamber. He smoothed his hand down her hair and rejoiced in having her with him.

"I didn't do anything," Kinsey said, her head snapping up. "I never betrayed you or anyone here."

"I know." Ryder hurried to calm her.

She shook her head. "No, don't just say that. I need you to know that it wasn't me."

He cupped his hands on either side of her face. "I do, Kins. I know it wasn't you. I thought it was when the e-mails were encrypted. It stated that you were on board with what they wanted."

"What?" Her brows furrowed deeply. "The only thing I agreed to—ever—with Kyvor in writing was about developing new strategies."

"Did that involve any meetings?"

"Of course," she said with a nod.

Ryder moved his hands down to her shoulders. "Do you remember who was in the meeting?"

"Sure. It was me, Cecil, Harriet, and Harriet's assistant."

"Describe the assistant."

Kinsey thought back for a moment and said, "She was really beautiful. The kind of beauty you only see in movies."

"Her hair?"

"Blond, almost like a gold color."

"And her eyes?"

Kinsey laughed. "I didn't get that close to see."

It was enough of a description to match what Esther had said. "I suspect Harriet's assistant was the Druid who put the magic in you. We also found a tracker in your wrist."

"A tracker?"

He hated the shock and alarm in her voice, but the worst was over. "We got it out. We found the same magic and tracker in Esther as well."

"I don't really know what to think right now," Kinsey said. Then she looked down and saw the blanket had fallen to reveal her breasts.

"I'll explain everything," Ryder said. "Just know you are officially cleared of everything."

"But we don't know who set all this in motion at Kyvor, do we?"

Ryder shrugged. "It's Ulrik. Esther confirmed she met with him after MI5 sent her to spy on Kyvor."

Kinsey's eyes widened. "Esther is MI5? I thought they decommissioned her?"

"To set up her spying. I believe both of you met the Druid responsible for the magic placed on you."

Kinsey's lips twisted. "Harriett's assistant."

"Aye. We need to find her."

"That I can help with."

"I was hoping you'd say that." Ryder wanted to shout with joy that Kinsey would be staying. He didn't care how long it took. He would show her his love and that he wanted her in his life forever.

Kinsey fiddled with the edge of the tartan blanket. "I still want to know who set me up."

"I suspect that was Ulrik, but we'll find out for sure."

Her smile was slow as it spread over her face. "It looks like I'm in need of a job."

It was Ryder's turn to smile. "I'm fairly certain I can help with that."

"Con would allow that?"

Ryder laughed. "I should've taped his words earlier. He likes you, Kins."

"Now that's a shock," she said with a small laugh. "But I'm glad. I like it here."

"Are you ready to return to the manor?"

She pulled her hand from his and sat up, wrapping the blanket around her. "There's something I need to say first."

Ryder waited for her to continue. From the dread on her face, he feared the worst.

"I'm sorry," Kinsey said.

Now that, he wasn't expecting.

"I'm sorry for everything." She licked her lips and lowered her gaze to the ground. "I should never have feared you, and I certainly should never have told you I wasn't sure I could forgive your leaving me. After being at Dreagan and seeing the enemies, I understand now." Her eyes returned to his. "I'd have done the same thing. This is your family. You protect your family.

"But I was lying to myself when I said I didn't have feelings for you. I lied to others about that as well. I never stopped loving you. Never."

Ryder wanted to pull her against him, but she held out a hand to stop him.

"You were so patient and sweet, and I . . . wasn't. You deserve better than that. I'd like . . . that is, if you're willing . . . I'd very much like to start again. I may have done too much or said the wrong things, but I love you.

I'll go through interrogations or whatever to reassure you and Con and the others that I mean this."

Ryder halted any more words with a kiss. He was so happy he could barely contain himself. Kinsey was going to be his.

"I know you mean every word," he whispered as he caressed a hand down her face. "I love you, Kinsey Burns. It killed me to leave you, and I doona want to ever be apart from you again."

Fresh tears welled and fell down her cheeks. "You've no idea how happy you've made me."

"You've got that wrong, lass," he murmured with a grin. "I'll be the one who's the happiest."

A seductive smile filled her face. "Perhaps we can show each other just how happy we've made the other."

"Ohhh. I like that idea. Shall we commence things here?"

"As long as no one can see or interrupt us," she said and threw off the blanket.

Ryder hastily set up a magic door that would block anyone from entering—or seeing. His laugh bounced off the stones as she tore open his shirt, sending buttons flying once more.

EPILOGUE

Three days later . . .

"Do we really have to?" Kinsey said as she reached down and wrapped her hand around his cock.

"Hmmm. Did you say something?"

She chuckled and kissed his cheek. It had been the best three days of her life. They hadn't left Ryder's room, and it was wonderful.

"I suppose we need to get to work," she said with a sigh.

Ryder lifted the laptop. "I've been keeping up with things."

"With one screen. Admit it, you miss your monitors."

He shrugged and set aside the laptop. "That I do, but I like you in my arms. Perhaps we should set up the monitors here."

"Or we could set up our bedroom in the computer room."

Ryder thought about that for a moment. "Nope. I doona like either idea. Let's keep things the way they are."

She laughed as he rolled her onto her back and kissed her. When he lifted his head, she ran her fingers through his blond locks. "I can't believe everyone believes I'm innocent."

"Because you are. And now we have two more allies," he said with a smile and a wink.

"Two more mortals. That doesn't concern any of you?"

"You're my mate, Kins. You'll only be mortal until the ceremony, which I'd like done soon. I doona like the idea of someone hurting you. Once you're mine, you'll be immortal."

That thought still boggled her mind. She and Ryder had talked at length about how she was going to handle her family. It was going to be a delicate situation, but with her parents in another country and her sister starting her life, they were going to make it work.

"Are you still thinking about the fact you willna be able to have children?" he asked in a soft voice.

Kinsey looked into his hazel depths and smiled. "I was thinking about my family, but I have been contemplating the children issue."

"Do you want children?"

"I don't know. First I was too young, then there was my career. Then you."

"And after me."

"Yes, then after you left. I've not had time to think about it."

"Would you rather hold off the ceremony until you can be sure?"

Kinsey smiled and brought his face down for another kiss. "This is why I love you."

"Because I asked if you wanted to wait?"

"Because you're always thinking about me."

Ryder ran a finger from her forehead down the side of her face, tracing her hairline. "I'll do anything for you,

Kins. If that means waiting years for the ceremony so you can be sure about children, then I understand."

"You're mine, Ryder. I don't want anyone else in my life but you. If we can't have children, then we'll find ways to fill our time. Who knows? We might adopt someday."

"I'd give you as many children as you wanted if I could."

"I know. It's not your fault or mine. It's just the way it's going to be. And I'm okay with that."

He kissed her forehead. "If you doona stop talking like that, I'm going to take you again and forget about going to the computer room and working."

"Now that sounds like a plan," she said as she wrapped her arms around him. "Except we have work to do."

Ryder dropped his head onto the pillow and rolled onto his back. "And a plan to put in place." He turned his head to look at her. "Are you and Esther sure of this?"

"Yeah."

He sat up and swung his legs off the bed to stand. "Then let's get to work."

Rhi meandered the streets of Edinburgh veiled. It was weird walking amidst the mortals unseen. She heard their conversations, listened to their laughter, and shared their smiles—and their tears.

She'd been there days but had yet to see a Fae with white hair. It didn't matter if she walked the graveyards, the tourist sections, the underground, or the back allies, there was nothing to see.

Her watcher, however, didn't seem thrilled to be in Edinburgh. In fact, she got the distinct impression he wanted her to leave soon.

Rhi paused and leaned a shoulder against a building. Was it a quirk of fate that she hadn't seen the white-haired Fae? Or did her watcher have something to do with it?

If the white-haired Fae was thought to be a Reaper, then she could deduce that her watcher was one as well. Her watcher could be telling the others where she was to keep them away.

"This is really getting old," she grumbled to herself.

All she wanted was answers, but she wasn't going to come by them easily. No, Rhi was going to have to be devious and sneaky in order to get what she wanted.

She just hoped it was worth it.

Rhi was passing a store selling magazines when she spotted Usaeil on the cover. Rhi rolled her eyes. Her queen loved how the human population adored her. Pretending to be an American and having a career as an actress had shifted Usaeil's attention from her people.

Then Rhi read the caption above Usaeil's picture. A NEW MAN? it said.

Rhi stared at the fuzzy picture of a scene inside a hotel room with Usaeil and a man in a suit. With blond hair. Rhi couldn't see his face. It could be Con, but then it could be someone else.

She knew Usaeil was having an affair with a Dragon King. And now this picture? Con would never allow himself to be photographed, which meant this was all Usaeil.

Rhi unveiled herself, tossed some money onto the counter, and grabbed the magazine. It was time she showed Con and got his reaction.

Ulrik stared at the list of names. He had narrowed it down to three. One of those was the spy Mikkel was using on Dreagan. Ulrik sent three texts to his best investigators to have them watch all three people.

One of them was the spy—and one of them would soon be his.

Ulrik closed the file and returned it to the secret compartment in his desk drawer. Then he leaned back. He felt calmer than he had in . . . eons. Shifting had done wonders to clear his mind and focus him.

The anger swirling within him had been reined in. Mikkel would be taken care of in due time. Until then, Ulrik would continue with his plans.

He reached over and tapped a key on the keyboard. His computer screen flashed a picture of Harriet with blood draining from her eyes, nose, and ears as she sat unmoving in her desk chair.

Ulrik smiled at Mikkel's failure. Yet there was a Druid in his employ that was powerful enough to pique his interest. He was going to have to meet her soon.

The Dragon Kings had won a small skirmish. Ryder had his mate, and Henry's sister was alive. It was Mikkel's lack of foresight that caused them to fail. But Ulrik had something in mind that was going to set the Kings back.

Somewhere in Sweden . . .

V watched the woman fighting with her lover in the crowded bar. The man was uninterested in reconciling, and the woman was heartbroken. That was something V could help her with.

Loud music began to play as the woman pushed her way through the throng of people trying to get to the door. V reached the door before she did and held it open for her.

"He's no' worth it."

She brushed away her tears. "Excuse me?"

"I saw you with him," V said as they walked outside. "He doesna care. You deserve someone who cares about you. Someone who'll give you the attention your exquisite beauty deserves."

"And you're that man?" she asked, sniffling.

V smiled. "I could be."

She looked through the glass windows inside the bar. Then she faced V. "Prove it."

His arm snaked out and yanked her against him. With his other hand he traced the line of her jaw. "I'll do much more than that."

He kissed her deeply. She moaned into his mouth, her fingers clutching his shoulders as she forgot all about her tears and the man who didn't want her.

V maneuvered them toward an alley, but she broke the kiss. She looked up at him with her pupils dilated and her breathing ragged.

"My roommate is gone for the night. Let's go back to my place."

V took her hand with a smile. "Yes, let's."

Don't miss

THE REAPERS

A New Series in the Dark Kings world!

Dark Alpha's Claim, available 11/17/15

Dark Alpha's Embrace, available 2/16/16

Dark Alpha's Demand, available 5/17/16